DAVID D· HAMMONS

CURIOSITY
QUILLS PRESS

A Division of **Whampa, LLC**
P.O. Box 2160
Reston, VA 20195
Tel/Fax: 800-998-2509
http://curiosityquills.com

Cover Art by Amalia Chitulescu
http://ameliethe.deviantart.com

ISBN 978-1-62007-714-6 (ebook)
ISBN 978-1-62007-715-3 (paperback)
ISBN 978-1-62007-716-0 (hardcover)

For Jessica, who calls me her Prince Charming.

CHAPTER ONE

Did you know that fairy tales are real?" asked the cat.

"Cheshire Cat, help me!" I shouted to the grin floating above my head.

The Queen of Hearts, sitting in front of me behind her gilded judge's pedestal, swung her club and barely missed my head. I turned and fled the courtroom, bursting out the heavy wooden doors and into the grounds of the Palace of Wonderland.

"Off with her head!" the Red Queen shouted at my back.

The Cheshire Cat, or at least his grin, kept pace with me as I ran, screams of soldiers chasing me. At first I thought the cat was frowning. But then his body reappeared, and I realized he was just upside down. He wasn't much bigger than a regular, fat, housecat. His white fur had horizontal black stripes all along his body, and his puffy tail swished with interest as he looked back at our pursuers.

My shoulder throbbed from slamming open the wooden, heart-crested courtroom doors. I tried not to cry, but couldn't help it. They'd said very bad things about me in the courtroom, things that weren't true.

I had to escape.

"Off with her head!" screamed the Queen, her bulbous, mink fur-covered body careening into the courtroom doors as she and fifty card-bodied men with spears and swords crashed into the doorway.

The queen was too fat to fit through the door, and her hips jammed into the sides of the frame. The fifty soldier cards collapsed like bowling pins against the queen's stuck backside.

I laughed, even though I heard the crack of the door about to break.

"This part will probably be told different," the Cheshire Cat noted.

If he found the stuck queen funny, as I did, he didn't show it. With that constant grin, it looked like the Cheshire Cat thought everything was funny.

"What do you mean?" I asked, laughing at the silly danger as I turned to run.

"This part. This fairy tale. I enjoy them all, don't you know? Every one of them. Especially yours, because I'm in it!"

I found a tear in my bright blue summer dress, most likely from when I'd grown fifty feet tall inside the White Rabbit's house and scraped against the chimney. There were grass stains on my stockings from rolling down the hill with Tweedledee and Tweedledum. I'd lost my hair band to a dodo bird, one of my shoes to Bill the Lizard, to say sorry for hurting him during the chaos at the White Rabbit's house, and the other shoe to the Mad Hatter. That skinny, silly man with the tall, silk hat was still inside the courtroom, laughing at the cards and wearing my shoe over his ear.

"Mom's going to be mad about my clothes," I said.

"That will likely be different too," said the Cheshire Cat.

I ran across the green grass of the royal croquet grounds, and stopped when I reached the low wall that surrounded the palace. It wasn't tall, but I was only seven, and my fingers barely touched the top of the moss-covered barrier.

"Where do we go, Cheshire Cat? What do we do?" I asked.

I could hear the distant cracking of the door as the cards pressed against the queen's huge behind, the wooden courthouse shaking with the pressure.

The palace sat on a high plateau overlooking the rest of Wonderland. I stood upon the grassy croquet course, next to the flamingos who'd been used as sticks and left leaning against red-painted-white rose bushes.

"Do? Oh come now, doing is no fun. You should be looking. Look at the fairy tale around you," insisted the Cheshire Cat.

"Mr. Cat, I…" I started.

"Call me Cheshire."

"Okay, Cheshire."

"On second thought, call me Lou! Call me Oxford, or Arkham or Homer!"

"Cheshire Cat, please!" I said.

"Relax. This is Wonderland. What can go wrong?"

"I'll relax when I get back to that garden and away from the Queen of Hearts."

"Did you know that everyone will know who you are? Of course you don't. You don't know that yet."

"You're talking nonsense again, Cheshire Cat."

"I said to call me Virgil, did I not?" asked the Cheshire Cat.

"Can you help me get over this wall? Here, grab my hand."

"But… why do you want to go?"

"Because I'm scared."

"Off with her head!" the stuck Queen shouted, her voice echoing against the walls.

"Why are you scared? You're in a fairy tale," the Cheshire Cat insisted, standing on his hind legs and waving his front paws at the world around me.

"I thought I was in Wonderland?" I asked.

"True, true, they are different. In the fairy tale, Alice is much nicer, for one thing. She doesn't ask silly questions, and she most certainly never comes back," the Cheshire Cat noted.

I stuck my tongue out at the silly, floating cat.

"Things get muddled up in the journey through the rabbit hole, true. Lots of unknowns with all those echoes. In the fairy tale, Alice is from England, and in reality, you're from Misery," said the Cheshire Cat.

"I'm from Missouri," I corrected.

"Same thing. In reality, you're from the twenty-first century United States, but in the fairy tale, Alice is from the jolly nineteenth century UK. You lucked out on that one, though I prefer the twenty-eighth century. It's much cleaner."

"How could I be in a fairy tale?"

"You're not. You're real. The fairy tale is an echo. Let me continue." The Cheshire Cat stood on his hind legs and drew a book out of nowhere. He grinned at the flipping pages, reading like he had all the time in the world. "Oh yes, this is good indeed. In reality, Wonderland is a place of magic. In the fairy tale it is too, but I'm much prettier in real life. It's a subtle difference, but an important one."

I blinked and the book transformed into a mirror, which the Cheshire Cat used to admire his reflection.

"You're not making sense, Cheshire Cat," I said.

"What you read is only an echo of this world, dear Alice. Echoes and tales, myths and legends, and little Alice mixed up with it all. Oh, but you're not little, now, are you?"

My legs felt strange. My arms felt very strange, since they could touch the ground. I braced myself with my hands on the grass as I realized my limbs were stretching like taffy.

"Oh! This will be helpful," I said, my voice suddenly booming as my head grew higher than the wall. I'd been growing at random times all day, most likely the lingering effects of a magic bottle marked "drink me" and a cake marked "eat me" I'd eaten earlier.

There was a sudden crash from the courthouse. I was afraid that the Queen had escaped through the doors, but I saw that it was the courthouse wall that had collapsed. Standing in the rubble was the

Mad Hatter. He bounced up and down like a jackhammer, a piston pumping through the top of his hat.

The Hatter had pounded his way through the courthouse with his piston-tipped hat, and started bouncing my direction.

"Dddddon't worrrrry, Alice, I'lllll help you!" the Mad Hatter said, ricocheting against the walls and buildings like he was in a pinball machine.

By this time the entire palace, and all the creatures near it, had come to see what the noise was about. There were animals laughing at the Mad Hatter, talking vegetables and flowers singing along with the Queen's angry shouts, and decks of cards coming from all around. Diamonds, clubs, and spades in soldier and workers' garbs encircled me on all sides.

I would have been scared had my feet not suddenly grown as big as a house.

"Everyone calm down. There's no need to be mad," I said, my voice booming over the crowd.

"But we're all mad here, Alice, remember?" asked the Cheshire Cat.

"Right. I guess that's okay. But I don't want to be mad."

The Mad Hatter raised his hand to protest, but crashed back into the courthouse. This caused the doorway to cave in and freed the Queen of Hearts.

"Off with her head!" shouted the Queen, just as angry as before. "Off with her incredibly large head!"

"Hatter, are you okay?" I asked, unable to see the ruins of the courthouse through the clouds around my head.

"Peachy!" shouted the Hatter.

"Oh no. Oh no, no, no!" I heard a squeaking voice.

I felt the sensation of a furry spider crawling up my leg. I shrieked with fright and swatted, scaring all of Wonderland into silence. But there wasn't a spider running up my leg. It was the White Rabbit, bouncing quick enough to dodge my hand as he leapt onto my arm.

"I'm sorry, White Rabbit," I said, "I didn't mean to hit you."

"No, no, no, go away! Get gone! You don't belong here!" the White Rabbit insisted, coming to a rest on my shoulder. He wore a silk suit and examined his silver pocket watch with fright.

"That's not the tale I've read," said the Cheshire Cat, floating to my other shoulder.

"She needs to go!" the White Rabbit said. "Back that way, go!"

The White Rabbit pointed down the hill, a long distance away. I didn't see where he was pointing, but I did feel a sharp pain in my foot.

"Ouch!" I said, looking down to see the deck of cards stabbing my toes.

The cards piled on top of one another and bent together. Then they catapulted into the air like they'd been shuffled, stabbing and swatting at me.

I shrieked and stepped over the wall, running. As I ran, I looked back and saw the cards still chasing, still shuffling to stab my eyes. There on the ground, I saw the Queen of Hearts, her fists raised in fury. She stood beside the Mad Hatter, who was bouncing against the walls. The Knave of Hearts was still inside the wrecked courthouse, his hands in cuffs. I'd been charged with terrorizing Wonderland. The Knave had been charged with stealing the Queen's tarts. We had both been sentenced to death.

There was one more playing card standing beside the Queen. The Ace of Spades. He was the only one in all of Wonderland who did not looked shocked at my appearance. In fact, I thought I saw him smiling. But he was far away, and I was under a hail of cards, so there was no way to be sure.

"That way, that way!" shouted the White Rabbit, still on my shoulder.

"She can go any way she likes," countered the Cheshire Cat.

"No, she can't! That way!"

"Where am I going?" I asked, keeping my eyes closed as I ran, stumbling over hills and trees.

I swatted at an avalanche of cards that fell over me, biting and stabbing. I thought I heard the Cheshire Cat say something else, but it was lost in a sudden rush of wind. I must have tripped, because I fell forward.

When I landed, my hands struck muddy water and cold concrete. It was dark.

I hit my lip on the ground and looked up, blinking through the dim light.

I thought I must have stumbled into a forest, that thick limbs were blocking the sun. But the sky wasn't dark because of trees; it was dark because it was night. The orange glow of a streetlight cast shadows over the pavement where I lay.

"Alice!" I heard shouted from a distance.

I rose to my feet, water from a puddle soaking into my stockings. I blinked my eyes clear, not believing what I saw.

In glowing neon letters, shimmering against the night sky, was the word "Lew's."

I was outside Lew's Drive-Thru, a fast food restaurant not far from my home in Strafford, Missouri. I stood on the cracked, puddle-strewn pavement near the drive-through window, and saw my mother exiting her silver SUV to run toward me.

My mother shrieked with relief as she picked me up. I no longer felt a mile high. I didn't even feel my normal seven-year-old height as my mother squeezed me against her shoulder.

"Thank goodness I was here—what were you thinking? Where have you been? What happened to your dress? Say something!" my mother insisted.

Squeezed against my mother's shoulder, I looked back at the drive-through. There was a big, round mirror, the kind that allows the servers at the restaurant to see when cars are coming. There were two cat's eyes and a toothy cat grin in the mirror. I blinked, and they were gone, but I could have sworn I heard a voice say, "Echoes and tales, echoes and tales. But this one isn't finished."

CHAPTER TWO

I **spent Christmas in a mental hospital.**

I spent my birthday talking to a woman in a church office. She had board games and toys and lots of stuffed animals. All she wanted to do was talk, and never let me play with the toys or games.

I spent the school year laughing with my friends about the wonderful things I'd seen in Wonderland.

I spent the next year at a different school. None of the kids knew me, so they all thought my stories were dumb.

No one came to my birthday party that year.

I found a lost bunny in our backyard, just before Christmas when I was ten. It was probably an Easter gift, let loose after it got too big. All I wanted was to keep it as a pet. I named it Beatrix. I told my parents I didn't want anything else for Christmas, no presents, just that I could keep Beatrix.

We had to take Beatrix to a farm. I got a makeup kit for Christmas.

I only asked Beatrix once if she was related to the White Rabbit. I was just curious, and she only nuzzled her pink nose in reply.

The day I turned eleven, my parents gave me my first blue pill.

Attention Deficit Hyperactivity Disorder complicated by a serious case of schizophrenia. That's what caused me to see Wonderland, so the doctors said. If I'd left the real world and journeyed to "Wonderland" it was only because my warped mind invented a fantasy. I told the doctors I didn't believe ADHD was real. They told me they didn't believe Wonderland was real. The blue pills would allow me to tell the difference between reality and fantasy.

I used to think that if I could just find the right rabbit hole I could show my mother that Wonderland was real.

It was all my imagination, the doctors said. It was all a story. A good story, they agreed. So good that I thought it was real, and couldn't cope with the difference between reality and fantasy.

The blue pills, they said, allowed me to focus.

The blue pills let me know what I'm supposed to do: I'm not supposed to talk back; I'm not supposed to question; I'm not supposed to believe in fairy tales; I'm not supposed to throw my makeup away and cry over rabbits.

Echoes and tales. That's what the Cheshire Cat had said.

No.

That's what my imagination had created. The Queen of Hearts, the Cheshire Cat, the Mad Hatter, and the White Rabbit: all dreams.

When I started high school, I tried to stop taking the pills. It'd been almost a year since I'd talked to a rabbit. When my mother found me dumping the pills down the sink, she tugged my arm so hard my elbow popped, and didn't let go till we arrived at the doctor's.

The doctors made me realize I'd just been saying that Wonderland was only a dream, mouthing the words to make people leave me alone. They refilled my prescription.

There was a counselor at school the doctors made me see. Her name was Mrs. Friend. She had a tiny office next to the principal's. The office had wood-paneled walls that were really just plastic with a fake wood coating. The walls sounded nothing like wood when you knocked on them. They sounded like milk jugs.

Mrs. Friend told me I was spoiled. She said she didn't care who I was, who I thought I was, that she wouldn't allow me to act out. She always spoke like she was yelling behind clenched teeth, and would erupt into barely contained rage if I ever said a word that wasn't in complete agreement with what she said.

If I ever tried to not take my medicine, Mrs. Friend would find me.

If I ever tried to question my teachers, Mrs. Friend would find me.

If I ever tried to believe in Wonderland, Mrs. Friend would find me, and then she'd get my mother.

They wouldn't let me out of the house. They wouldn't let me visit friends. Not until my delusion was well and truly cured.

It felt like my entire sophomore year was spent staring out my window, at the little creek in our backyard. At first I wondered if there were still rabbit holes near the trees, just beyond the creek at the edge of the grass.

Then I stopped.

I don't know why. I just realized at some point that there were no rabbit holes. Rabbits can't talk, of course they can't. There was no rabbit hole to another world, of course there wasn't. I believed only in what I saw, and I definitely never saw a fairy tale. My junior year of high school, it all made sense.

I stopped believing in Wonderland.

"Alice, finish your food—don't play with it," my mother scolded me.

My mother, sister, and I sat at the kitchen table. My mother was dressed to perfection even at lunch. The summer sun glinted off her plastic-sequined blouse and her rhinestone-covered hairpin in a way that made me unable to look at her without being blinded by refracted light.

There was a taste of hairspray in my mashed potatoes and meatloaf. I never liked meatloaf. The idea of a loaf of meat was not only awful, but seemed silly. Bread comes in loaves. And you can put honey on bread. When I tried putting honey on my meatloaf my mother slapped my wrist.

"You can only put ketchup on meatloaf, Alice," my mother said.

"Ketchup isn't a sauce, it's ketchup," I replied. "Putting ketchup on a meatloaf that's a loaf but not bread just makes an incomplete hamburger. In fact, the concept of a meatloaf with ketchup is just a hamburger that got broken in the factory. Did we accidentally make meatloaf instead of hamburgers?"

"Alice, what nonsense."

"You could always make a salad," my sister, Lorina, suggested. She was home from college and had chosen to ignore the existence of meat as an option for eating.

Salad was for rabbits, and I wasn't allowed to talk about rabbits.

"Can I put honey on it?" I asked.

"Honey as a salad dressing?"

"Then it could be a salad for bees. Except your salad has strawberries in it, so if you put honey in it…"

"Enough, Alice," my mother insisted. "Eat your meatloaf."

I poked at my meatloaf but didn't eat it. I had to imagine what it would taste like with honey. My imagination tasted better than ketchup.

"What are you reading?" I asked Lorina after mincing my meatloaf.

Lorina looked up from her salad and showed me her e-reader. Digital letters played across a glossy screen, words so small I couldn't make them out from across the table.

Lorina was taller than me, and skinnier. She kept her strawberry-brown hair straight and always wore single-shade colors. Lorina could brush her hair half a dozen times and it would be straight all day, while I never knew what to do with my blonde curls. I brushed aside the few strands that draped over my eyes, jealous of Lorina's proud brown eyes while mine were a dim blue.

I shifted uncomfortably in my seat, aware of how bright my clothes were compared to Lorina's. She wore a button-up red blouse and a pair of black, fitted jeans, while I had on my blue Easter dress, the skirt hanging over my white leggings.

My mother insisted I couldn't wear an Easter dress in the summer, and that I should show more shoulder to get sun on my pale skin. This might also attract the attention of boys, a concern of hers for which I shared no enthusiasm. She also said my purple tennis shoes didn't match anything.

But I liked my purple shoes.

"Lorina is studying for her finance test," my mother answered on Lorina's behalf.

"It's summer," I said.

"She's taking summer courses online. She's double-majoring in finance and pre-law."

"Technically, there's no pre-law major, mother. It's a liberal arts degree," Lorina answered, taking a drink from her bottled water. "And it's actually a Macro-Financial Analysis test. I had my normal finance class first semester."

"My mistake."

"There's nothing but words and numbers in that book," I said.

"That's what books are for, Alice," my mother insisted.

"Does it tell a story?"

"College doesn't tell stories. College teaches how to succeed in life."

"Do you really need that many numbers to succeed in life?" I asked.

"You most certainly do," my mother answered.

"Could I have less numbers? I like numbers, don't get me wrong. They're very useful to add two things together. But after awhile there's just too many numbers. How many numbers do I need in life to succeed?"

"Don't be silly, Alice."

"Ballpark figure, that's all I need. Two hundred? A thousand? You can't need more than ten thousand numbers before…"

"There is no limit to the amount of numbers one needs to succeed in this world," my mother insisted.

I looked down at my lunch. The ketchup had mixed with my untouched, now minced, meatloaf to make an image of gore on my plate. It made the meatloaf even less appetizing.

"Your head would run out of space with all those numbers," I muttered.

"Yes, it would. That's why you should get rid of things in your mind that aren't useful, Alice. No more fairy tales or nonsense. That way you have space for numbers. You're starting college yourself soon. Don't you think it's time to focus on numbers?"

I looked at my plate. I thought maybe if I mixed my mashed potatoes with the ketchup-mauled meatloaf it could make kind of a casserole. But mashed potatoes with ketchup made me realize there was no gravy.

"Ketchup makes bad gravy," was what I said.

My mother sighed. "You need to take your medicine if you're done with lunch, Alice."

"What if the numbers were letters? Or what if the letters could be gravy? Then you could learn all about gravy in college and it would be the same as learning numbers. Can I learn about gravy in college, Lorina?"

Lorina laughed, shaking her head. "There's no such major," she said.

"Alice, medicine," my mother insisted.

"Because it wouldn't have to be just gravy. It could be all sorts of sauces. Or things that cover other things. Like clothes or roofs. You'd need numbers to learn how to cover things with roofs, but I wouldn't mind if it was about covering things with roofs and not just numbers by themselves."

"Alice!"

I thought about other things that could be covered with numbers. "Weather patterns. Satellites. Space travel could be covered."

"Alice," my mother said, resting a hand on my shoulder.

I felt her touch run through my spine. Pain entered my mind, and thoughts of covering things with numbers fled. I felt nothing, thought nothing, was only aware of the disappointment in my mother's eyes.

"I'm sorry," I said.

"It's okay, dear," my mother answered.

My face was red, but I couldn't feel it. Just the sting in my heart as thoughts like cold water cleansed my mind.

"I'm trying." It was a lie. I had no choice but to feel this way.

"I know. Your sister has a lot of studying to do. Why don't you take your medicine? When you do, come back down and we'll talk about what classes you'll be taking this semester."

"Okay."

I got up from the table. My eyes were still on the mashed potatoes and ketchup-bloodied meatloaf. I had a ghost of a thought wondering how to make ketchup out of apples, so I could have gravy-colored ketchup. I aborted this thought when I saw the impatience on my mother's face, and turned away.

I walked down the hall toward my bedroom. I thought about going straight inside and shutting the door so I could read a book with words. But I heard my mother in my head, scolding me for delaying what was necessary. So I turned to the bathroom instead.

I took a little orange plastic bottle out of the medicine cabinet. Twisting off the child-proof cap, I placed two pills in my palm. The pills were a dusty blue in color, perfectly circular, bearing a manufacturer's seal in the center.

I stared at the pills a moment or two. I felt my arm moving to turn on the faucet, like my body was not my own. A ghost hand brought a glass of water to my lips. I closed my eyes and brought the pills toward my mouth.

I heard a small crash, and froze.

The sound came from my parents' bedroom.

"Curious," I found myself saying. "Dad doesn't come home for another hour."

I paused, staring at the bottle. I placed the two pills back inside and sealed it, keeping the bottle in my hand and vowing to take the medication once I'd investigated the noise.

I walked down the hall and opened the door to my parents' room.

"Did someone leave a window open?" I asked as I entered the room, spotting a trail of socks leading from the dresser to the closet.

The plain, black socks ended where they spilled out of a duffle bag. Dad's bird-hunting shotgun was also in the bag, along with folded suits and as many ties as there were socks.

"Curious," I said.

My voice must have startled it.

A White Rabbit leapt from behind the duffle bag. At first I thought this was strange. Rabbits don't usually come near people. They're prey animals, and know humans are predators. But then I realized this was not strange at all. For the really strange thing about this creature was that the rabbit wore a pristine, well-ironed suit.

It was three-button, and black in color, the same as his tie. He wore a shirt whiter than his fur, and a pair of little black pants over his rabbit legs.

He was bigger than a normal rabbit, which was probably stranger than the suit. Someone could dress a normal-sized rabbit in a suit if they really wanted to. But it would be very hard to breed a three foot tall rabbit.

And then I realized that even this was not strange, save that the creature had changed clothes since the last time we'd met.

"You!" I said to the White Rabbit.

The rabbit made a little yelp and turned to face me.

"Where have you been?" the White Rabbit scolded.

"Excuse me?"

The White Rabbit stuffed black belts and pants, dad's work clothes, and a box of shotgun shells into the duffle bag. "I have been looking all over for you," he said.

"Did you try the door?" I asked.

"There was no doorman to invite me inside, so I couldn't," the White Rabbit stated, completely confident in his logic.

"That doesn't make any sense." A sharp pain invaded my mind. "Oh, no. You're not real—you can't be real!" I went to the window and prepared to shut it, pausing as a light breeze touched my face. "I need to take my pills. My imagination is acting up."

"Alice! Who are you talking to?" my mother shouted from the kitchen.

"No one!" I answered, leaning against the window.

"You're not real," I whispered to the rabbit.

"Oh dear, there's no time," the rabbit said. He checked a silver pocket watch and yelped again. He stuffed one last box of shotgun shells and a hunting vest into the duffle bag.

"What are you doing?" I asked.

"The job I'm tasked with. And the job I need to perform."

The rabbit hefted his bundle with surprising strength. He took one ridiculous bounce toward me and grabbed the bottle of pills out of my hand. Then he took another bound and dashed out the open window.

"Hey! Hey that's mine! You're not real!" I called out the window.

The rabbit paused in the backyard. "If I'm not real then how do I have this?" the White Rabbit asked, shaking the bottle of pills in defiance. He checked his watch, leapt into the air, and bounded into the woods.

"Give those back!" I shouted.

"Alice, what's going on?" my mother cried.

I ignored my mother and leapt through the window, running across the lawn.

Grass crunched beneath my feet. The nearby creek trickled over rocks jutting out of the water. The rabbit made a bridge of these stones, and hopped to the other side.

"Oh dear—oh dear, it's closing, oh dear," the rabbit said, running faster and faster.

I leapt across the creek and shouted, "Come back!"

"That's where I'm going!" the rabbit said. He reached the forest of trees beyond my backyard and stopped dead in his tracks to turn and face me.

I nearly fell over, my purple shoes digging trenches in the soft green grass as I slid to a stop.

"We're going back!" the rabbit said.

Two soft legs sprung from the ground and struck the bridge of my nose. The kick hit me hard and I fell backward.

Falling and falling and falling through darkness I went. The rabbit was nowhere to be seen. There was nothing to be seen.

And then in a flood of light, there was everything to be seen. Flowers greeted me as they splashed over my face with an eruption of daisy petals.

"Oomph!" I said, falling through tulips. "Flowers? We don't have these kinds of flowers in our backyard."

"All war is deception," the flowers sang as they splashed around me.

"Flowers don't sing," I said.

"If you know the enemy and know yourself," sang a rosebush as it flew over my head.

"You need not fear the result of a hundred battles," smiling sunflowers sang, completing the harmony.

"Oh no. Oh no, oh no, oh no!" I cried, swirling about in the haze of colors. "This shouldn't be happening! This can't be happening!"

The flowers that didn't hit me continued upward while I fell downward. As they passed, the still-smiling plants exploded against the invisible walls of what I recognized as the rabbit hole, the same dark tunnel from my previous delusion.

"You're not real!" I challenged, looking up to where the flowers disappeared.

When I looked down, I spotted a flood of oysters clattering and tumbling toward me. I had never seen an oyster fall so far. I had also never seen an oyster fall *up* so far. The oysters seemed just as distraught about their predicament as I was of mine.

"I'm mad. I must be," I said.

"That's good," said a passing oyster.

"We're all mad here," said another.

"Bye!" added a third as he and the other oysters sailed out of sight, their echoing clatter fading to nothing.

And still more came from the bottom of the hole. Flamingos walked through the air, books flew like birds, saucers and plates and suddenly a thousand crumbs burst into view. It was as if a hundred cakes had exploded and were now being sucked through a vacuum.

I saw a mouse leaping from one flying plate to the next.

"Hey! It's you!" the mouse said, slipping on a saucer.

"I'm not talking to you," I replied, closing my eyes. "You're not..."

"Shut up and help me!"

"Oh. My."

I wiped the tears forming in my eyes and saw the little mouse leap downward against the flow of plates and utensils. He jumped into a ladle and onto a dinner plate, eyes wide with fear.

"I, I'm falling too," I said to the mouse.

While the mouse was falling upward, I was falling downward. I suddenly wasn't sure which direction either of us was going.

"Take me with you!" the mouse cried, leaping onto a chipped teacup. "Don't let me fall!"

"Here." I reached up to grab the little mouse.

"Don't let me go—don't let me go!"

The mouse jumped from the teacup to a cake pedestal. There was still half a cake on it, and he leapt inside the frosting with a splash, bursting out the other side and throwing more crumbs into the air.

I held my hand out to grab the cake-dirtied mouse, when a silvery bottle struck the creature in the nose. He missed my fingers and tumbled upward, screaming, "Alice!" as he flew out of sight.

"I'm sorry!" I shouted back, though I didn't know what I was sorry for.

And then at the edge of my vision I spotted a little paper card tied to a broken strand of string. It read "Drink me."

Another card flew into sight, this one saying "Eat me." Then another saying "Read me." A card landed on my forehead, and I was able to grab hold of it.

"Trust me," I read. Then another struck my head, saying, "Doubt me." And another and another. Thousands of little cards, all with two word instructions. "Save me, Take me, Find me, Discard me, Want me," so many I was swimming in paper.

"I don't… which one…" I said, trying to read them all.

And then I saw something cut through the cards like a sickle. It sliced a gateway out of the paper river, allowing me to escape the two-word hurricane.

I leapt at the gap, catching only the faintest glimpse of a crescent grin before it ascended with the rest of the two word instructions.

"Welcome back," I heard, echoing through the wind.

When I broke through the cards I realized I wasn't actually falling any longer. I'd landed on a massive pile of paper. The paper was flying upward, billowing like the smoke from a volcano. With no handhold, I tumbled down like I was sliding on snow, landing with an "oomph," on rough cobblestones.

CHAPTER THREE

W as that…? No. It couldn't have been. Cheshire Cat!" I shouted, scrambling to my feet.

There were still cards that read "Buy me," "Own me," "Need," clinging to my dress. I brushed them off and called again, "Cheshire Cat!"

"Don't waste your breath. He's dead," said a man with a shovel.

"Excuse me? Oh, my!"

I was standing in a large building, completely square, with a cobblestone floor and a slatted tin roof. It was the size of a warehouse, with one wall missing. Light entered through this opening; the other walls had no windows or doors.

The man with a shovel wore khaki pants and a collared shirt. The symbol on his shirt was a club, like the club on a deck of cards, with the number two beneath. He seemed perfectly normal, and had a perfectly normal grimace on his face as he went about his job, digging his shovel into a pile of dodo birds.

"This isn't real," I said, hugging my knees on the ground. "This can't be real. I'm imagining—ouch!"

"Sorry," the man marked with the Two of Clubs apologized. He'd accidentally let one of the dodos he was shoveling nip me in the ear.

It hurt.

The pain was real.

The dodos were pretty calm, despite their high-stacked situation. Most eyed one another with curiosity, discovering every five seconds or so that they'd been clustered together.

"Ah, hey, Mike," one said.

"Hey, Phil," another replied.

"What a game eh?"

"What a game."

"No, game."

"Yes, game."

"And in that game there was no-no."

"But yes-yes makes yes!"

"And the no!"

"Yes!"

"No!"

"Yes, game!"

"Ah, hey, Mike."

"Hey, Phil."

"What a game, eh?"

"What a—gah!"

Mike and Phil were silenced when the man bearing the two of clubs scooped them up and dumped them onto the pile of cards. Dodos and cards flew into the air. I watched them disappear, propelled by an invisible force up and into the darkness of the rabbit hole.

Looking at the rabbit hole felt like I was looking up a chimney. The sight of it made me shiver with dread.

"Ah, hey, Dave."

"Hey, Lew," more dodos said before Mr. Two of Clubs shoveled these into the pile of flying cards.

"I really am mad," I groaned.

"Hey! No being mad here," Two of Clubs threatened. He bopped me on the head with his shovel. That also hurt. "Being mad's what did in the Cheshire Cat."

"The Cheshire Cat isn't real," I mumbled, rubbing the sore spot on my scalp.

"Not anymore he isn't. He's dead."

"Dead?" It felt strange to mourn an imaginary person.

"Dead as a dodo."

Two of Clubs was nearing the bottom of the dodo pile, shoveling up the few remaining birds while wiping the sweat from his brow.

"That can't be," I said.

"It is. Get used to it," said the Two of Clubs.

"The Cheshire Cat... how?"

I was struggling to fight the images around me, trying to convince my mind it wasn't real. Two of Clubs must have assumed I was asking how the Cheshire Cat died, not denying he ever existed.

"Same way all of us ended up here," Two of Clubs explained.

"What?" I asked.

I looked at my surroundings. Dozens, maybe close to fifty men in khakis and collared shirts stood before piles in the warehouse. Like engineers loading coal into the fires of a ship's engine, the men shoveled teacups and doors and red-painted roses onto the pile of flying papers.

I let out a groan of rising despair. "I'm imagining Wonderland again," I admitted.

"Don't call it that anymore," Two of Clubs said.

"This isn't Wonderland? What is it?"

"Ask Ace."

"Ace?"

"Ace of Spades. The man who killed the Cheshire Cat." said Two of Clubs.

"But you can't kill the Cheshire Cat—he's not real!" I said.

"Real dead is what he is."

I tugged at my hair, tears welling in my eyes. "I'm mad. I tried so hard not to be mad."

"Didn't you hear me? I said no being mad here!"

"I'm not mad—I'm not! But I'm in Wonderland so I must be mad!"

"Don't call it that!"

Two of Clubs raised his shovel like a bat and swung at my head. I screamed and ducked, backing away.

"Leave me alone!" I cried.

"We can't have mad people here," Two of Clubs said.

Two of Clubs swung again and I ran, leaping over the pile of dodos.

"Come back!" shouted Two of Clubs.

He tripped on the birds who shouted, "Ah, hey! Hi! Hey, hi!," in a continuous, mad greeting.

I ran until my feet left cobblestones and landed on hard pavement. The sun glared in the sky and blinded me a moment. When I blinked my eyes to focus, I found myself standing in the middle of a city street. Tall, square buildings surrounded me, concrete and asphalt, stoic and stable.

I sighed with relief and said, "It was all my imagination."

Then I blinked. "But how did I get to this city? And where are the cars?" I asked the empty street.

Concrete glistened as if freshly laid. The buildings didn't seem that old either. Each had glass windows up and down their many levels. The structures were rectangular, capped with a flat roof. The buildings' only decorations were carved lines running up the sides like the fuller of a sword.

I looked back and there was the warehouse, and Two of Clubs running into the street.

I still didn't believe what was around me. I couldn't. But fear snapped me into action, and I ran farther down the street.

Buildings surrounded the warehouse in a grid pattern. I made a turn, hoping to lose the shovel-wielding man in a side street.

Water splashed my face. It came from a cart's wheel striking a deep puddle.

I wiped my eyes and looked at the insanity before me. Men with clubs and hearts and diamonds and spades of various numbers on their collared shirts worked with heavy-loaded carts. The carts brought more junk to the rabbit hole, cakes and fans and an endless variety of colorful teacups.

While the previous street had been dry, this one was drenched, with thick droplets of rain falling from the sky. I looked up, but couldn't see a single cloud.

"But there's…" I said, trying to will rainclouds into existence.

I thought I just wasn't seeing them. But the rain came down from a bright blue, empty sky, droplets splashing about the warm concrete.

Another cart splashed me, but I barely noticed. The water evaporated almost instantly from my dress, leaving no sign I'd ever been splashed. The rain cooled the sun's warmth, creating the sensation of swimming while dry.

The men with the carts looked at the rain with concern, not because they were getting wet, but because they weren't. They glared with irritation as the carts splashed through puddles in their rush to get to the rabbit hole.

"Is this really Wonderland?" I whispered.

Another cart splashed me and I stared at the water, fascinated by how it melted off my blue Easter dress.

"Hey!" a passing cart driver marked Four of Clubs challenged. "Who are you?"

"I'm Alice. Who are you?" I replied.

"I'm transporting anything that can't have its wonder removed to the hole." Four of Clubs pointed at his cart full of eggs.

The eggs were dressed in rich clothes, long coats with fur necks. They spoke to each other in refined accents, brushing well-groomed facial hair as they wished one another a "Happy unbirthday," in a constant rumble of voices.

"You're not mad are you?" Four of Clubs asked.

"I'm," I began, "I'm sorry, sir, I'm just not sure what's real and what's not."

"The eggs or the rain?"

"Everything."

"We'll sort through the eggs soon enough. Just don't listen to them," said Four of Clubs.

"Thank you. Umm. Can I touch one?" I asked.

"Of the eggs?"

"Yes, please."

"I suppose."

I knelt down and picked up an egg. It was a normal-sized egg, with a warm shell. Despite its long, fur coat and silk cap, it felt fragile.

"Is it your birthday?" the egg asked through its thick mustache.

"No," I replied.

"Happy unbirthday!" cheered the rest of the eggs.

I smiled.

"Enough of that," Four of Clubs said and took the egg out of my hands. "Don't you have some place to be?"

"Yes," I said, smiling down at the cart of eggs. "Wonderland. I'm in Wonderland! Happy unbirthday, eggs!"

"Alright, that's it. If you haven't had the wonder out of you I'll make sure you do…"

"I'm in Wonderland!" I leapt away from the man's grasp and ran down the street. "Happy unbirthday—I'm in Wonderland!"

I heard Four of Clubs' furious shouting, along with the cheers of eggs making an escape, as I splashed through the street.

My heart raced as the rain sprayed my face. Ice had formed around my thoughts, so thick and old I thought it was a part of me. Now with the cloudless rain and fleeing eggs cracking against the sidewalk, refusing to get their immaculate clothes wet even in their hurry, I shouted for the joy that melted my frozen heart.

"How does the little crocodile keep his shining tail," I sang, dancing around a corner, "and pour the waters of the Nile on every golden scale! How cheerfully he seems to grin!" I stretched my face wide as I leapt onto a windowsill, standing on one foot and reciting the musical poem I'd not said in years.

"How neatly he spreads his claws," I sang, leaping to the ground and stumbling only a bit with my ballerina-like spin, "and welcomes the little fishes in with gently smiling…"

"Get back here!" Four of Clubs shouted, running down the street, chasing a dozen rolling eggs.

He hadn't seen me, so I ducked around a corner out of sight. I sat on the ground, knees tucked, and pressed my hands over my still-laughing mouth. The eggs must have been more than Four of Clubs could handle, because no one pursued me as I sat there watching them go by.

Despite the danger, I couldn't stop laughing. I kept my hands pinned to my lips so I could muffle my screams of delight. It took several minutes for me to giggle myself tired, and I shuddered against the building 'til I could barely feel my legs. When my laughing fit ended, curiosity overcame my worry, and I rose on shaking feet to explore this new part of Wonderland.

Learning that the Cheshire Cat was dead had made me wonder if I'd come to a different place than Wonderland. How was it possible the Cheshire Cat could be killed?

The Cheshire Cat always did put himself in dangerous situations. And the world seems a little less silly. Perhaps with buildings like these, more creatures in Wonderland will have a safe place to sleep.

The streets were straight lines. The signs were hammered tin, marking "street 1" and "street 2" in simple font. No signs marked one building from the next.

I skipped down the sidewalk and spotted a glass window with brooms hanging in a white-walled shop. I wondered if the brooms would dance, and stared inside long enough that I drew the attention of the sour-faced shopkeeper.

"Can I help you?" the apron-wearing man asked through the window.

"Do the brooms dance?" I asked.

The shopkeeper looked at the brooms, then back at me with a blank expression. "Why would they do that?"

"Oh, just asking."

The shopkeeper didn't share my disappointment that the brooms didn't move, and returned to his empty counter. I was about to go inside and ask the shopkeeper his name, and the name of this city, when I heard the sound of horseshoes on concrete.

A team of horses was pulling a red wagon. This was the most colorful object I'd seen that wasn't being taken to the rabbit hole. I waved at the galloping horses and stepped onto the street so they could see me.

"Hello! What's your name?" I asked. "I'm Alice. Where are you going so quickly?"

The horses didn't respond, or even seem to notice me. With a sudden terror I leapt out of their galloping path. The wagon struck a deep puddle and splashed me with a wave of water.

"Out of the way!" a man in khakis and a shirt marked with the five of hearts called. He cracked a whip on the horses from his pilot's seat. The wagon held an enormous iron cylinder and pumps, with half a dozen men holding onto its sides.

I couldn't help but laugh. The water was still warm and my dress dried the instant I stood.

"Now here's a curiosity," I said. "I wonder if there's a fire."

The wagon turned a corner at the intersection of "street 1" and "street 4." Apparently the street grid was laid out on odd and even numbers. Very efficient, but lacking the excitement Wonderland deserved.

"Rabbit Hole Street," I renamed street 1, since it ended with the rabbit hole. "And you'll be Broom Street. Street 4 will be Fire Street. If there's a fire. Excuse me, Bill the Lizard? Is that you?"

Bill the Lizard had just exited the broom shop. He was the same Bill the Lizard I'd seen before, save that he wore a dark gray jumpsuit. He'd looked like a dignified assistant when I was seven, but now he looked like a four foot tall, too-skinny janitor with a tail.

The lizard janitor looked at the dry, clean street, his face without expression. "Hello. Sorry. Lots to do," he said and began sweeping the sidewalk.

"I remember you. You worked for the White Rabbit! You were his servant. Are you a street sweeper now, Bill?"

"That's my job."

"The street seems pretty clean."

"It's my job to sweep the streets."

"Well your job is finished," I said. "Come and join me. I need to find where the White Rabbit went. He knocked me down here, and I'm not sure where I am."

"White Rabbit works for Ace," Bill stated.

"Ace?" I recalled the man Two of Clubs had mentioned. "You mean the Ace of Spades?"

"That's the one."

"Really?" I asked, remembering the plain-faced card I'd seen when I was seven. If there was any viciousness to Ace, I must have missed it with my head literally in the clouds. "He seemed pretty tame before. How did he get so powerful?"

"Go look for White Rabbit at Ace's tower and ask him yourself," Bill advised.

"I will. And I'll give this Ace a piece of my mind for hurting a defenseless, well, the Cheshire Cat isn't defenseless. Or innocent. But it certainly wasn't right killing him."

"Go on then."

"I will, soon. But there's so much to see! I saw a fire wagon go by. I want to see what's happening. It should be fun to watch a Wonderland fire department work. I'll bet they use elephants as water hoses!"

"Elephants aren't allowed in the fire department."

"Excuse me?"

"Elephants," he said. "They can't be in the fire department. Not to man the hoses, at least. No creatures with hooves can do things like that, so they're assigned other jobs. The elephants could pull the fire carriage, maybe, but they're too slow so they have horses do that. Me, I got hands of a sort. So I sweep the streets," Bill explained.

Bill turned his back to me, sweeping his broom across the sidewalk. With each pass of the bristles the street went from bright to dark gray. There was no dust, no trash moved when he worked. But wherever he swept, the sidewalk appeared aged with grime.

"I think your broom is backwards," I said, trying to decide if this was funny or not.

"Works just fine," Bill replied.

"I don't think you're helping this at all. Come on, stop that and let's watch the fire department stop a fire. Not much of Wonderland is familiar to me and I'd like to have a familiar face help explain what's happening."

"They're not going to stop a fire."

"What?"

"They're not going to stop a fire," Bill said.

"Well that can't be right. They're the fire department aren't they?" I asked.

"See for yourself. I've got work to do."

Bill walked around me and continued his job, cleaning the newness from the sidewalk.

"Fine then. If you want to find me I'll be on Fire Street. That's what I've renamed this street. Of course, I need to change the street sign. I wish I'd brought a pen!"

As I turned the corner from Rabbit Hole Street to Fire Street, I realized I might have to change the name again. Instead of a fire, small or large, there was a massive complex of mushrooms.

Tall as one of the fuller-lined buildings, the cluster of mushrooms shone a hundred different colors through the sun-filled rain.

"I'll have to re-rename this Mushroom Street," I said with a smile.

The red wagon was parked in front of the mushrooms. Six firemen with hoses stood at attention. Next to this wagon was a blue one, equally as large. More khaki-wearing men surrounded it. Billy clubs and black handcuffs were belted to their trousers. Two of these men were escorting an enormous blue caterpillar toward the blue wagon.

"Mr. Caterpillar. Hey, Mr. Caterpillar!" I said, waving to the old creature I remembered from my last time in Wonderland.

"It is you," the caterpillar replied with a slow smile.

"You remember me!"

"Does the lily remember the bee?"

"I suppose it would."

"But that would depend on the bee, would it not?" the Caterpillar asked with a smile.

"Enough of that," a man bearing the image of the Nine of Diamonds said, pressing the caterpillar inside the blue wagon. "Step away, miss."

"What are you doing to him?" I asked.

"By orders." Nine of Diamonds closed the wagon doors behind the caterpillar. "We've got work to do. Load this up—and be quick about it! You there, more bundles around the right side." Nine of Diamonds snapped orders to the numbered men around him.

"What has he done?"

"Stand back." Nine of Diamonds left the wagon and instructed his men. They stacked bundles of timber in and around the cluster of mushrooms.

The caterpillar stuck his head against the wagon's barred window, "I don't suppose you have a hookah hidden in your dress?" he asked.

"That would be an interesting dress," I laughed.

"That it would."

"What have you done? I can help you."

"Help me with a cigarette?" the caterpillar asked.

"You really shouldn't smoke, caterpillar."

"It's the least I could hope for."

"Caterpillar… I don't understand. What's going on?"

"You sure you don't have that cigarette?"

"I'm sure," I said.

"Too bad. I really could use it."

With the crack of a whip, the blue wagon rumbled away. It turned off what I hoped to call Mushroom Street and onto street 5.

I chased the wagon a step or two, shouting, "Caterpillar!" before a crackle of fire brought my attention back to the mushrooms.

The firemen threw lit torches onto the stacks of wood. Despite the rain, the mushrooms were dry as the kindling itself. They erupted in flames moments after the twigs were lit. By the time I'd walked back to where the blue wagon had been, the whole cluster of mushrooms was a towering inferno.

Thick, black smoke flew into the sky. The smoke was puffy and swelling. Instead of dissipating, the smoke gathered, roiled, and formed a dark thunderhead. Flames continued to feed the thunderhead 'til it concealed the sun.

Thunder rolled. Lightning streaked across the smoke. As it grew, the smoke became lighter, soaking in the rain to a dark gray-green. Soon it was indistinguishable from a normal thunderstorm. Rainclouds hung overhead and set a chill in the air.

The rain, which had evaporated a moment before, now clung to my skin. With a normal raincloud in the air, the rain became normal as well. And soon I was soaked, cold from a sudden wind.

"Keep those clouds going, men," Nine of Diamonds commanded. "Watch the fire. Over there!"

The firemen were not there to put out the fire. They fed it, tossing more doors and tables onto the inferno. They used their hoses only to contain the flames, directing streams of water to where the fire licked the sides of gray buildings. Wherever the spray hit concrete, it transformed the surface from a newly-pressed gray to a muck gray, soot and dust clinging at every storey.

The sidewalk itself now grew dark. Mud in the rain, invisible 'til it struck ground, soiled everything it touched.

"That's... an odd way to make clouds," I said.

"We do what's needed to make this place right," Nine of Diamonds said. "Now step back. We've got a lot of work to do."

I did as Nine of Diamonds commanded, and stepped back to the darkening sidewalk. A chill ran through me and I rubbed my hands against my wet shoulders to capture some warmth.

"I would have preferred they kept the rain like it was," I said, walking away from the fire. "I'm not sure I like how things are being run in Wonderland." A sudden crack of thunder startled me to a run, and I sprinted across the paved streets in search of shelter.

None of the storefronts or homes had unlocked doors. I tried one with a window that revealed tables and square-shaped chairs. Patrons of the supposed restaurant ate sandwiches on pale bread, never looking up from their meal as they drank water with no ice. The door was locked, and no one seemed eager to leave the restaurant, so I moved on.

The next door was plain white wood, and didn't move when I tugged or knocked.

"Hello? Hello!" I called to a store that sold tools, its owner not moving from behind an unstained wooden counter. "I'd like to get out of the rain, please."

Each store or dwelling had people staring at what they were doing. Eating. Cleaning. Sorting goods. I had never seen so many people in Wonderland. They were all human, not a single animal or talking inanimate object. None of them seemed to respond, so I gave up seeking shelter and ran through the streets in search of a place to wait out the rain.

"A park," I said, turning down street 7. "A park may have a gazebo. I could wait there."

Up street 9 I ran. But there was no park to be found. Each street was the same. Each block was another square section of progressively darkening concrete. The only way I could tell the city didn't go on forever was the descending height of the buildings as I reached the city's edge.

At street 11 I heard a shout and turned to street 12. Here I found a pig, a frog and a fish running around a lamppost. With them were a hamster and a pair of colorful gravy boats. They were all about four feet tall, short for people but large for animals. The gravy boats shook off rain droplets even as they filled with clear water. I wondered where the gravy had gone.

"Hurry round, hurry!" said the pig.

"I don't know why I'm doing this," replied the fish.

"Because we're running."

"But why am I doing this?"

"Why are you doing it?" I asked, approaching the group.

The fish stopped. The rest of the animals plowed into the fish's back like a freight train crashing to a halt.

"You were supposed to keep running!" the pig complained.

"Don't stop—don't stop it's cold—don't stop!" the hamster added.

"Is that why you're running round the lamppost?" I asked.

"It's cold—start running!"

"But I'm not cold at all. I find this weather quite comforting," the fish replied.

"Well we're cold—now run!"

The group started running again, racing each other around the lamppost.

"Racing in circles is no way to get dry," I said, laughing. The sight warmed me, however, and I felt the urge to join.

"Is that what we're doing?" the fish asked.

"To get dry, we race. I learned it from the mouse before Ace took him," the pig answered.

"But I don't want to get dry."

"Keep running!"

I couldn't help but laugh at the ridiculous sight, wiping the rain from my eyes. The fish kept trying to get out of the race, digging in his fins or hopping to the side. Each time the others would shove or drag him back into the flow. The fish looked less like he was racing and more like he was running away from the others.

I heard the splashing of puddles, and turned to discover another blue wagon racing toward us. The galloping horses shook rain droplets off their bodies as their driver whipped them to speed.

"Oh, good. Looks like the horses are finding a way to dry themselves too," I said.

But the blue wagon didn't run past. It came to a clattering halt in front of the lamppost. Diamond-marked men with numbers three through eight leapt out of the wagon, wielding Billy clubs, halberds and black irons.

"Stop that!" Eight of Diamonds called as Three of Diamonds tackled the pig. This sent the group once more into a stumbling train wreck of splashes.

"Oh good, are we stopping?" the fish asked as Four of Diamonds clamped a set of iron handcuffs around his front fins. "Hey!"

"Enough of this silliness. You are all in violation of the edict of the Ace of Spades," Eight of Diamonds proclaimed.

"They were only trying to get dry," I said. "It was a very silly thing to do, getting dry by running around a lamppost, but that's no reason to arrest them."

"They were trying to get dry by running around a lamppost?"

"I wasn't!" the fish shouted.

"That is a violation. Are they animal or mineral?" Eight of Diamonds asked his men.

"Four animal, two mineral," said Seven of Diamonds as he held the pair of gravy boats by their blue-painted handles.

"Send the minerals to the hole. Load the animals in the cage."

"Right."

"But I wasn't trying to get dry. I didn't want to!" protested the fish as he and the other animals were loaded onto the wagon, their fins and hooves and paws clamped in irons.

"They weren't doing anything wrong," I said to Eight of Diamonds. "Why are you arresting them?"

"Were you running with them?" Eight replied.

"What if I was?"

Eight Diamonds hopped off the wagon. He towered over me, at least a foot taller, and looked down with judging eyes. "Are you animal or mineral?"

"I'm a vegetable," I said and stuck out my tongue.

I wasn't scared of this man. He was a card. A human card, yes, but I'd gotten away from the cards when I was seven. Now that I was seventeen, I had even more reason to be unafraid of the Wonderland authorities.

"You don't look like a vegetable. Were you running around the post?" Eight of Diamonds asked.

"You know, I am getting awful cold. Since you khaki-pantsed jerks made the rain become real, I think I need to dry off."

Nose held high, I took a step around the lamppost. Then I kicked up my heels and ran, smiling as I leapt into the air. I came to a spinning halt in front of Eight of Diamonds, sticking out my tongue.

"William the Conqueror said to the pope—I'll take all of England," I sang.

"Stop that singing," Eight of Diamonds commanded.

"It's no small scope, but that place is amuck and I can't say nope! So I'll…"

I thought the bright lights were lightning. I thought the sudden deafening a clap of thunder. The rising pain in the back of my head made me realize I'd been struck by a Billy club. A sharp pain accompanied my throbbing head as cold, wet handcuffs were slapped onto my wrists.

"That's enough of you," Eight of Diamonds said as he shoved me toward the wagon.

I couldn't see straight. I tried to run, but my feet didn't work, and I had trouble focusing on which way was up or down. Before I had a chance to do more than mutter a weak "What?" I was tossed into the back of the wagon.

"By edict of the Ace of Spades, you are all under supervision until you've been acclimated to a proper status," Eight of Diamonds announced as he shut the iron-bound door.

"I didn't want to be dry," protested the fish, earning a Billy club to the fins as he leapt away from the bars.

I was lying on the wagon floor, dripping on the wooden planks, as the wagon rumbled to speed. I tried to rise on my hands and knees but a sudden bump sent me face-first back to the floor.

"Here, let me help you," the pig said.

He took me by the shoulders and set me on the wagon's narrow bench. It was more a splintery plank than a bench, with a twin on the opposite side.

"Don't touch her—she's a vegetable," the fish warned.

"I'm... I'm not," I said, stuttering through fading pain.

"Then why did you say you were?"

"I was just being silly."

"Exactly the problem. You shouldn't have been silly!" the fish exclaimed.

"Why not?"

"Quiet down!" Eight of Diamonds called as he whipped the horses.

"Are you hurt?" the pig whispered.

"I don't think so," I said. I'd had worse bumps.

"That was quite the silly thing to do."

"What? Run around a lamppost singing about William the Conqueror?"

"No, I thought that was a very dry song. Quite the clever way to dry yourself off. The silly thing was sticking your tongue out at the cards. They don't like that."

"Oh."

I looked out the barred window and saw the rooftops of low, square buildings. The wagon reached the outskirts of the city, and I saw fields in the distance.

"Where are we going?" I asked, leaning against the window.

"I hope it's someplace dry," the frog answered.

"I don't," added the fish.

"I'm still wet," said the hamster. "Maybe if this girl finished her song about William the Conqueror it could dry us off."

"No!"

"Keep it down back there!" Eight of Diamonds threatened.

"How does the crocodile to you, too," the pig grumbled.

The wagon continued its rumbling journey to the edge of the city and beyond. There was a sudden change in the scenery, jarring to the eyes, as gray concrete city gave way to wide open fields.

In my memory, Wonderland was colorful and vibrant. I expected the fields to be green, or even purple, and covered with singing flowers and dancing ferns. Instead I saw shades of brown. Light brown from waving grass, golden brown from rows of wheat, and dark brown from tilled soil waiting to be cultivated. More brown shapes walked over the brown grass, cattle grazing far as I could see.

"Hello there," I called to the cows. "Where are the singing flowers?"

"They won't say anything," said the pig.

"Why not? Hello! Cows!"

"They've had the wonder taken out of them."

"The what?"

"He's going to make us dry—he's going to make us dry," wept the fish.

"That's where the flowers went," the pig explained.

"I liked the flowers. They sang even when you ate them," the hamster added.

"And the bees would sing too," the frog agreed.

"Singing in your stomach with a belly full of song. That's what I miss most."

"But there weren't just flowers," I said, looking out the window.

As the wagon left the city behind, the clouds also faded. There was more light, but it was hardly a pleasant sunshine. All around I saw what looked like a normal city outskirts. Farmland, grassland, small square houses dotting hillsides with the occasional barn. A concrete grain elevator loomed over the path our wagon traveled.

"There were country houses, woods, palace grounds with croquet," I said, remembering my childhood experience in what used to be a magical land.

"They still have palace grounds. But they don't play croquet anymore," the pig said.

"What do they play?"

"I don't know. But the old palace grounds are where they take the wonder out of you. That's where we're going."

"I don't think I understand. They take the wonder out of you?" I asked.

"They make you wrong," the pig answered.

I looked out the window. I wouldn't say what I saw was wrong. In fact I would say it was the opposite.

"It looks pretty normal to me," I said.

"Normal? It's normal to dry oneself by running round a lamppost without worrying about being arrested," said the pig.

"It's normal to have a song in your belly," the hamster added.

"I'm normal—I'm normal!" cried the fish.

"I don't think I know what's normal in Wonderland," I said.

"She said it! She said Wonderland! I didn't say it—I'm normal! I don't want to have the wonder taken out of me—I don't need to. Just give me a nice pond to be ignored in." The fish banged on the front of the wagon.

"I won't tell you again—quiet!" Eight of Diamonds commanded.

"What do you think is normal?" the pig asked.

"Well, flowers that don't sing. Cows that eat grass and don't answer back when you say hello. And fish that stay in water and don't whine," I answered. "That's reality. The opposite is a fairy tale."

"Well then a fairy tale is normal to me."

"My reality does sound pretty dull, doesn't it?"

"It's scary," the fish added.

"I'm sure Won…" I caught myself, staring at the slats between the bars. "I'm sure someone here is keeping things… different."

"You mean the Hatter," the frog said.

"The Hatter will save us won't he?" the hamster asked.

"I don't need the Hatter—I just need out. I just need to get out in the rain!" the fish pleaded.

"Do you mean the Mad Hatter?" I asked.

"He's mad! You shouldn't trust him!"

"Yes. He led a resistance," the pig answered. "He told us we were all going to get our wonder taken. Most of us didn't listen, thought that Ace was only taking the wonder out of criminals and leaving law-abiding creatures alone. But I'm not so sure now."

"What does Ace want?" I asked.

The pig shrugged. "Maybe he wants the wonder out of everyone? And now that he's taken it out of rebels, he's moving on to normal creatures too. Just like the Hatter said he would."

"That's not true!" the fish insisted. "He's gone now. The Hatter's gone, gone with the lot of them—and I don't need them! I don't need the Hatter because I'm normal I tell you!"

"That's it," said Eight of Diamonds. He turned in his seat and plunged a halberd through the bars, striking the fish in the gills.

"I warned you," Eight of Diamonds said as he withdrew his weapon. "Quiet down! Not another word!"

The fish fell against the bars in a heap, wet with blood. I did my best to suppress a shriek and leapt to the back of the wagon, as did the other prisoners.

"Is the Hatter going to rescue us?" I asked.

"I don't think so," answered the pig.

CHAPTER FOUR

I decided to try and escape. Once those doors opened I would flee. They couldn't hold me. They couldn't keep me—I wasn't wonderful. I wasn't part of Wonderland, so how could they take the wonder out of me? What did that even mean?

The wagon rolled through brown fields and a forest full of elms and oaks. I saw faces in the oaks, but they weren't real faces. They were swirls of bark making a trick of the eye, illusions of faces where there was nothing but silent shapes in the wood.

The wood gave way to a country cottage. The cottage gave way to a row of duplexes. I found the transition jarring, and thought this must be why a team of men in khaki pants and collared shirts were repairing the cottage. At least I thought they were repairing it. It's possible they were tearing it down, making way for more duplexes.

Broad stretches of low, condensed housing dotted a shallow hill. Smoke from a hundred chimneys cast shadows over the lower buildings. Each chimney was square, brick, and billowing black smoke.

"I don't think they're making rainclouds," I observed.

The shallow hill led to a steep edifice. Smoke from the chimneys hid whatever structure occupied this plateau, but I spotted a round tower rising through the cinders.

I felt the wagon wheels bumping over cobblestones as we approached the smokestacks.

Men and women walked down the hill. They didn't seem in any hurry. And they didn't seem to be looking one way or the other, not at the smokestacks, not at the tower beyond. They seemed to not even be walking, only letting gravity guide their footfalls.

Our wagon came to a sudden halt in front of a smokestack and I got a good look at the building at its base. It was square, brick, and had an arched doorway on one side, with a twin doorway on the other. The structure was enormous, an unmarked brick box five stories tall and completely square.

"Out, the lot of you," Eight of Diamonds ordered.

He opened the door and I prepared to run. But I came face to face with the guard's halberd. Fish scales were still stuck to its tip.

"Slow and steady, one at a time," Eight of Diamonds commanded, gesturing with his weapon.

The pig led the way, tapping my hand as he passed. I hopped out behind him, along with the hamster and the frog. I took a moment to look back at the fish, before Eight of Diamonds shoved me forward with the butt of his halberd.

"Go on then," he said.

"I don't suppose you'll tell me what's going on here," I said as I was shoved into line.

Other creatures stood in front of me. There was a walrus with a bowler hat, an old bulldog wearing suspenders, a hawk with ribbons in its feathers.

"You're going through that door," Eight of Diamonds ordered.

The animals waited, other guards with red diamond numbers on their uniforms keeping them in line. One by one the animals were shuffled through the doorway.

"I'm not from here. I'm not wonderful," I insisted.

"Keep moving," said Eight of Diamonds.

"Do I look wonderful to you?"

"He doesn't look wonderful either," Eight of Diamonds said, pointing at the pig.

"I resent that," the pig declared.

"Shut up you two. Move!"

A man exited the second doorway. There was something oddly familiar about him. I didn't know what it was. He wore a brown jacket with pockets running up and down its sides. One hand rested in a pocket, and the other held a bulbous insect. I had to look several times before I realized the insect was a blue caterpillar.

A guard with the ten of diamonds on his chest approached the man with the coat and undid the irons still chaining his hands together. The man with the coat examined his hands, curious more than anything now that he was free to walk as he pleased.

"Excuse me," the man in the coat said to Ten of Diamonds. "But do you have a cigarette?"

"You shouldn't smoke," answered Ten of Diamonds.

"I shouldn't smoke?"

"Don't smoke."

"Don't smoke." The man with the caterpillar in his hand stared blankly. He blinked a moment, then started walking down the hill.

Another man exited the second doorway. He wore a bowler hat and a very old-fashioned suit. A walrus slumped beside him, flopping along in confusion.

I saw my chance. I grabbed the man with the caterpillar and tore off his coat. Then I gave a swift kick to Eight of Diamonds and ran.

"Hey!" Eight of Diamonds cursed.

"She's running!" the pig shouted and tripped the guard.

"The Hatter's here!" the hamster shouted.

"The Hatter's here!" the frog chimed in.

"Settle down all of you!" Four of Diamonds said, waving his halberd at those chained.

I took advantage of the commotion and hid. I didn't try and escape—there was nowhere to go. Instead I ran to the doorway where the walrus stood, faking that I was going to run inside. At the last moment I dove behind the walrus, the edge of the building concealing my sudden disappearance.

"Come back here!" Eight of Diamonds called, chasing. He must have thought I'd entered the doorway, because he ran straight through it.

I crept along beside the walrus, praying the other guards didn't notice me, and put on the coat I'd stolen from the man with the caterpillar. The brown jacket was a trench coat on my frame, and completely concealed the colors of my dress. I buttoned it together as best I could, my handcuffed wrists preventing me from sticking my arms through the sleeves. I held out my hands, adopted an expressionless stance, and got in line behind the walrus.

"Did you see her come out this way?" Eight asked Four of Diamonds.

Four of Diamonds shook his head and the two of them went to the wagon to see if I was hiding there.

"Alright, let's get back to it," Ten of Diamonds commanded, reforming the lines.

The commotion had already died down as the animals realized the Mad Hatter was not coming to rescue them. Order was quickly restored, with nothing more than the hamster's weeping remaining of the previous noise. Ten of Diamonds resumed examining and unchaining the captives leaving the second doorway. He took the irons off the man with the bowler hat and motioned to the walrus.

"To the zoo with this one," Ten of Diamonds said, calling other guards to escort. He gestured for me to walk forward.

I don't know why, but I remembered how the pills made me feel. I thought of what it was like to not believe, what it was like to imagine nothing but plastic walls and fake wood paneling. I pretended Ten of Diamonds was Mrs. Friend, and kept my mouth shut. Ten of Diamonds didn't say anything. He simply saw my face, my clothes, and unlocked my chains.

"Next one, step forward," Ten of Diamonds said as I left the guarded area.

Walking down the hill, I kept my eyes away from the guards and doomed creatures. I held on to the chill in my heart, gripping it 'til I felt no more eyes upon me. Then I turned a corner and pressed my back against a wall.

I expected my heart to be pounding, but it wasn't. I had to release the chill, and only then did I have any sense of the danger I was in. Still, I had escaped.

"They may have taken the wonder out of themselves," I said, with a grin, "but this is still Wonderland. And I'm still smarter than them."

I took a peek around the corner. The hamster was being shoved inside the chimney-smoking building's first doorway. The pig waited his turn while the frog struggled in vain against his chains.

There's nothing I can do. Too many guards.

The frog tried to leap away but was shoved through the doorway.

"It's better to go through that door than end up like the fish. Maybe they'll be better off. The caterpillar didn't seem very upset."

I looked down the hill and found the caterpillar. He had reached the end of the descent. He looked left. He looked right. He didn't seem to have any idea where he should go.

I bit my lip.

As I watched the man who used to be the caterpillar trying to decide where to go, or where his coat had gone, the White Rabbit rounded a corner too quickly and bounced against his belly.

A handful of black socks spilled out of the White Rabbit's duffle bag, my father's duffle bag. The rabbit looked like he was apologizing to the fat, former caterpillar as he scooped up the socks. The man who used to be the caterpillar didn't seem to mind, and started off in the direction the rabbit had accidentally shoved him.

The rabbit raced up the hill toward the guards. I held my breath, suppressing the urge to warn the rabbit. I exhaled with relief when the rabbit bolted right past Ten of Diamonds. The guard shook his head at the sight of the creature, turning his attention back to his task.

"Curiouser and curiouser," I said, watching the White Rabbit.

The rabbit bounced his way up the hill, heading toward the fog-hidden tower.

"I've already outsmarted them once," I said. "Let's see if I can face down the Ace of Spades like I did the Queen of Hearts."

I ran up the street and called, "White Rabbit!" making sure we were out of sight.

The creature nearly tumbled to a halt as he turned toward me. "You made it!" the White Rabbit said with a smile.

I caught up to the rabbit and the two of us stayed hidden beside a low building. "No thanks to you. What were you thinking kicking me like that?" I asked.

"There was no time." The White Rabbit checked his silver pocket watch. "And there still isn't! Come. You must come with me!"

The rabbit tried to bounce away and I grabbed him by the collar, holding him still. "Hold on. I'm still not sure that this is real."

The rabbit tugged himself free, fixing his ruffled collar. "It's real. And it's in danger."

"I can see that. What have you done with my pills?"

"How can you think of pills when my home looks like this?" asked the White Rabbit.

"Those pills make you disappear," I said.

"They do?" The White Rabbit took the bottle of pills out of his jacket pocket and threw them to the ground.

I picked up the bottle and popped the cap open. "They don't work like that. I swallow them and you go away," I said, placing two pills in my palm.

"Don't swallow them then!"

I looked at the blue pills in my hand. For a moment I paused, not sure if what was around me was real, and if it wasn't, if I wanted the dream to end. The White Rabbit cowered below me, bracing himself for some unknown terror.

I heard the voice of Mrs. Friend, the voice of my mother in my head. They all told me I was delusional, that I couldn't be seeing what I was seeing. But here it was, right before me. I was in Wonderland. Wasn't I?

"I don't want you to go away," I admitted.

"That's good," the White Rabbit whimpered.

"But I have to know for sure."

I tossed the pills into my mouth and swallowed, feeling them catch temporarily in my throat before passing through. I held my eyes closed. After what seemed a long time, I opened them, and there lay the rabbit. He was on the ground, his little paws covering his long ears as if something was going to fall on him.

"You're still here," I said.

The White Rabbit perked up. He looked around. Then he hopped to his feet, hastily brushing his jacket clean.

"You'll scare a rabbit to death like that!" the rabbit accused.

"Sorry."

"Then stop smiling!"

I couldn't. Nothing could stop me from smiling. I looked at the world around me, breathing deep, as if I'd been holding my breath for years. Then I saw the smoke, and the distant, mist-obscured tower at the center of the fortress town, and my smile faded.

"It's not a fairy tale. Is it?" I asked.

"No it's not," said the White Rabbit. "And I didn't bring you here to gawk like an idiot. I need your help. We must get to Ace quickly. There's no time."

"Late again?" I asked, placing the bottle of pills in my little dress pocket.

"Unforgivably! Now, you must come with me."

The rabbit hopped to my side and tugged my arm. He pulled me in jerking bounds toward the high walls at the center of the jumbled fortress town.

"Where are we going?" I asked, trying to pull my hand away. The rabbit wouldn't let go, and held me just as firm as he held the duffle bag full of my father's clothes. "And why did you rob us?"

"Ace sends me to collect things," the rabbit explained.

"What kind of things?" I asked.

"Things to change Won—" The White Rabbit caught himself, shaking his furry head clear. "Things to change this place."

"Change it into what?"

The White Rabbit reached a crossroad. He looked left, then right in twitching motions, repeating the action three times before moving on.

"Into your world," the White Rabbit continued.

"Why would he want to do that?"

"Don't ask me. Ask Ace. Perhaps you can stop him. He wants to make this place like where you're from. But he's never been where you're from."

"I thought Wonderland was a dream."

The White Rabbit paused. He pulled me down by the arm and looked me straight in the eye. "My home is not a dream."

He bounced away, continuing up the street, never letting me slow as I followed. The stone streets grew narrower as we approached the fortress walls, the roofs of the buildings lower. Thick wooden doors were shut, along with shutters at every level of every building. When we reached the edge of the walls, none of the buildings had windows.

"I'm sorry if I hurt your feelings," I apologized to the White Rabbit. "It's been so long since we last met. I thought this was all something I imagined."

"Most people who see us think we're imaginary," The White Rabbit said, leaning against the wall. His eyes went here and there as he spotted guards walking the towers.

"Have others been here?"

"The fairy brought some boys from your world to another part of this one. But you're the only one who's visited Wonderland," he winced as he said it. "That's why I need to bring you to Ace. I need to show him what you are so he'll change his mind. But we're late, so hurry."

"Show him what I am?" I asked.

"Wrecked. Spoiled. Broken inside and out. If Ace sees you, he must let this be Wonderland again," he said, this time ignoring the word in his haste.

"That's not nice."

"I'm not concerned with being nice to you, Alice, I'm concerned with saving my tail."

The White Rabbit yanked my arm hard enough I felt my elbow pop. I tried to pull free, but we were in sight of a set of spade-marked guards standing in front of a medieval gatehouse. They flanked either side of the closed entrance, unmoving and dangerous-looking as the spiked iron gate they guarded. I thought they were statues at first. But their eyes turned toward us, and I suddenly became very aware of the way they held their halberds, stiff and ready to strike at any moment.

"Hail, Two and Three of Spades!" the White Rabbit announced.

The guards didn't move, or show any sign they'd heard the White Rabbit.

"I must see Ace of Spades at once," the White Rabbit said, bounding to a stop before the emotionless pair of guards.

The guards, once more, didn't respond.

"Two and Three of Spades!" the White Rabbit said, jumping in front of the guards and waving his white-furred paws. "I have an appointment with Ace!"

"You're late," Three of Spades said in a flat tone.

"I know I'm late!"

The guards responded with nothing but cold indifference.

"I must see Ace," the White Rabbit insisted. "He has insisted he be given items that I collected."

The guards didn't move.

"Can't you just let us in? He can't be that late," I said to the stone-faced guards.

"Silence, girl! Look, I'll just speak with Ace. I'm sure he'll understand," the rabbit said and tried to hop around the guards.

Two of Spades stamped the butt of his halberd on the rabbit's foot like he was crushing a bug.

"You are late," Two of Spades stated, shoving the rabbit away.

The rabbit hopped in a circle, clasping his hurt foot in his paws. He lost control of the duffle bag, spilling socks and ties onto the cobblestones.

I was upset that the guard hurt my friend, but the White Rabbit had been acting rude, so he should have seen that coming. Still, we needed to get past these guards.

Were they the same fools they'd been when they were playing cards? They seemed to lack the foolishness they used to have. But as I looked into their unblinking eyes, I realized they lacked something else as well. What gave them cold indifference, gave them a lack of discernment. At least I hoped that was the case, because the ties gave me an idea.

"Now hold on just a minute!" I announced, grabbing the White Rabbit by the tail.

The rabbit yelped loud as he'd ever yelped before as I pinned him down. Using one of my father's ties, I created a leash around the rabbit's neck and pulled it tight. The rabbit was still hopping in pain and protesting his loss of an appointment when he felt my hands make a knot around his throat.

"Gotcha," I said.

"Help… help!" the rabbit gasped.

The guards didn't even turn their heads to see what I was doing.

"You won't get out of your appointment that easily," I said.

"I'm not trying to get out of anything!" the White Rabbit said, still trying to escape.

"Traitor!"

At that word, Two of Spades turned his head.

"That's right," I continued. "Traitor! And these guards were just going to let you escape!"

Two of Spades narrowed his eyes.

"How could you have let him run free for so long?" I challenged Two of Spades, holding the gagging rabbit to the ground.

"He's not to have the wonder taken out of him. Yet," Three of Spades warned.

I tugged the rabbit as he reached to undo the knot. "You don't know, do you?" I asked.

The guards glared at me.

"This rabbit is a traitor of the highest order," I said.

The guards blinked, almost at the same time.

"Yes," I continued, sensing an opening, "yes, a traitor. He aided and abetted a wanted criminal who threatened the life of the Queen of Hearts."

The two former cards stiffened at the name of the old ruler of Wonderland.

"No. That's not what I'm doing. Tell them you need to…" the White Rabbit said before I covered his mouth.

"I was waiting for the right moment to tie up this criminal. If you had just opened the gate we could have gone in peacefully, but now I have to use force in front of everyone," I said, gesturing to the town around me.

No one was watching save indifferent people who'd recently had the wonder taken out of them.

"What criminal did he aid?" Two of Spades asked.

"The worst kind. He's the one who first brought Alice to Wonderland," I said, praying my name might mean something.

"Alice?" Three of Spades asked, squinting as he fought to recall a distant memory.

"What are you… doing?" the rabbit pleaded.

"He's a dangerous creature. Look at the things he's brought with him," I said. I picked up the duffle bag and showed it to the guards.

"And you almost let him leave."

Two of Spades examined the duffle bag and drew my father's shotgun. "Not much of a danger," he said.

"Do you remember Alice?" Three of Spades asked.

"Tall child. Queen tried to execute her," Two of Spades said, frowning at the memory.

"Now I remember."

"I don't remember much. But she was a threat."

"Yes. I remember Alice was dangerous."

"She most certainly is," I answered.

"What does she look like? I don't remember that," Two of Spades asked.

"She's a fifty foot tall seven-year-old. Remember how she nearly crushed the courtroom where the Queen of Hearts put her and the Knave of Hearts on trial?"

"I remember that," Three of Spades nodded.

Looking at the wall made me recall that memory, that wonderful day. Sure, the cards had been trying to stab my eyes, but compared to what I'd been through in the last few hours, my previous experience in Wonderland was a dream. If only I could find some of that cake that made me grow so tall. It would have been helpful back in the wagon.

I felt a pit in my stomach, wishing I'd been able to help the pig, the hamster, the fish… I wish I'd been fifty feet tall. I shook away the regret and did my best to focus on what I needed to do in the moment.

"I don't remember that," Two of Spades said. "How could a seven-year-old be fifty feet tall? Doesn't make any sense."

"Of course it doesn't. It's mad," I said. "And this rabbit was trying to bring her back. He needs to be questioned and tried."

"And who are you?" Three of Spades asked.

"I'm an agent of Ace of Spades. I was sent to capture the rabbit and bring him to this appointment. It was supposed to be a trick, until you tried to let him go."

"What happened to Jack of Spades?"

"He's chasing Alice herself."

"Really?"

I was building a shaky stack of lies. I could see the shadows of doubt in the two guards' faces, the indecision of what to do next. I needed to end this conversation and get away from the guards quick as possible.

"I'll prove it," I said. "What's the next appointment on the schedule?"

Three of Spades opened a scroll tucked into his armored cloak. "Private meeting with the queen," he answered.

"Exactly. A private meeting so I could bring Ace of Spades the rabbit without being interrupted and the queen could get her justice."

"His private meetings are usually private."

"Why do you think he scheduled the rabbit before the private meeting?"

"Hmm," Two of Spades said, trying to think.

"Yes," I said, coming up with an ace of a lie, "like I said, this was all a trap to capture a traitor."

"What!" the rabbit said. "No-no-no, I would never…"

"I remember you with Alice," Three of Spades said, glaring down at the rabbit. "You were on her shoulder that day. You were with her when she went back up the rabbit hole."

"But just listen to me!"

"I remember too," agreed Two of Spades.

Two of Spades looked at me, at the rabbit, and then completely turned around to look at the gate. It was the most he'd moved since I saw him. I could see the thoughts swirling in his mind as his eyes searched for something to lock onto.

"I will ensure that Ace's will is done. I will bring this traitor to justice," I insisted.

The guards blinked.

"I will bring Alice to justice," I added.

The guards nodded, and Two of Spades pounded on the gate. Unseen guards behind the walls must have operated the gate, as the iron spikes slowly rose out of the ground.

"Go straight to Ace," Two of Spades insisted. "Bring justice for what Alice did."

"I shall do that," I said.

The two guards nodded at me and stepped aside. Two of Spades returned my father's shotgun and I slipped the duffle bag over my shoulder. The rabbit gagged and I dragged him like a dog.

The compound inside the gatehouse was a patchwork fortress of colors and structures. Soldiers marched along crenellated walls in time with the taps of their halberds upon the stone. Farther inward was a fountain and a narrow tower with a clay-tiled roof and a bell at its top. Adjacent this was a pyramid of sorts, stepped like the ones I'd seen in explorer's pictures of South American jungles. This pyramid was new, however, polished gray stone leading up a square edifice.

All around the fortress were low towers of a dozen shapes and styles. One was stone, its neighbor wooden, another made of round bamboo shafts. Two were metal, one a primitive, gridiron Eiffel Tower, and another looking like it'd been shaped from a single piece of iron. The edges of this last one were jagged and misshapen, as if its mold had countless imperfections.

I couldn't understand anything about the small town inside the fortress. Most baffling of all, there were no people. No creatures. No guards—those were all on the inner and outer walls. It felt quiet and cold, empty.

Fog lay thick over the streets and buildings. While I could make out most of the fortress itself, I couldn't see the round tower at its end. I could only make out a massive, blurry shape through the mist. This was the single, tall tower I'd seen from far away, no clearer close up than it had been at a distance.

I could only hope that the tower was where I was supposed to be headed.

"Where's Ace? Is he in that tower?" I asked the rabbit, still struggling against his makeshift leash.

"Stop, stop—let me go!" the rabbit insisted.

"Oh hush."

The rabbit was more fluff than fight, and I tugged him across the fortress grounds without much effort.

The rabbit soon realized he was only hurting his windpipe by struggling, and hopped along beside me. He dragged his feet, though, only keeping pace with me enough to stop the tie from chocking him.

"That was clever," the White Rabbit finally admitted.

"I've never had any trouble outsmarting Wonderland creatures," I said, my nose in the air.

"Don't count on Ace being so easy to fool."

"And what was your plan? Show me off like an ugly model? 'Here, don't turn Wonderland into this.'"

"Yes! You're a horrible person and Ace needs to see that!"

"That's comforting," I said.

"Ace wants to turn this world into your world. I won't compromise or apologize for taking drastic measures to stop him," said the White Rabbit.

"How does Ace even know about my world?"

The White Rabbit slowed. I stopped in the shadow of a leaning tower.

"I told him," the White Rabbit admitted.

"How did you know?" I asked.

The White Rabbit looked around. The tower-adorned grounds were empty, silent save for a chill wind, but the rabbit insisted we duck beneath the building that resembled the Eifel Tower.

"The rabbit hole," the rabbit said.

"The one you kicked me down?" I asked.

"That one. It's what connects your world and mine."

"But it was at my old house. And I came out through a mirror at Lew's Drive-Thru!"

"The hole moves. It appears in places and times all over your world," the rabbit explained.

"So why has no one gone through yet?"

"Because it closes so quickly. Why do you think I rushed through your things and kicked you down the hole? I had no time. I told Ace I'd get a more proper suit he could model his workers with, and weapons. That's the only reason he let me pass through the rabbit hole. If I showed up with nothing, he'd take my wonder away."

"You should have found me sooner, rabbit," I said.

"I tried. I had no idea where you were."

"And you didn't want to find someone else?"

"Someone else? No! Too dangerous," the White Rabbit blurted out.

"Why? I'm sure you could find someone who would believe you."

"Too dangerous for me! I can control where the rabbit hole opens, but not for long, and it's very possible I can be stranded. In the brief time it stays open, echoes of our world enter yours. I prefer to remain an echo rather than something that can be captured."

"An echo?"

"An image. A thought. Some see it better than others. When you imagine creatures from Wonderland in your world, you're just seeing our echoes."

"Echoes and tales. That's what the Cheshire Cat said," I said, remembering the grinning cat's words. "Fairy tales are real. That's… that's crazy!"

"That's my world. Don't call it crazy," said the White Rabbit.

"I'm sorry."

"The echoes your world hears usually become stories and tales. That's what the Cheshire Cat used to say, at least," the White Rabbit explained.

"He said fairy tales are real. Is that true?"

"Call them fairy tales, myths, legends, I don't care. This is my world. All you know of it are its echoes. I'm trying to protect its reality."

"I'm sorry. It is weird though, right?" I asked.

"It is not weird to hear a story about creatures on this world. You're weird because you actually came here."

"Can I see more? If fairy tales are real here…"

"They're not fairy tales!"

"I'm sorry. If the echoes I heard are real, can I meet some?"

"No time, Alice. We must convince Ace to stop what he's doing to my world."

There was a part of me that wanted to deny everything the White Rabbit said, despite what I saw in front of me. How could what he said be true? How could I be standing in a world whose mere echoes inspired people's imaginations? This was no vision or dream, though. It was reality, so there had to be a science behind what the rabbit was saying.

"It sounds more like a wormhole to me," I said.

"It's a rabbit hole," the White Rabbit insisted.

"A wormhole. It's a break in the fabric of space-time. I've read about them. They pop up and close, and let you travel from one end of the universe to the next instantly. That sounds like what's going on here."

"I've never seen any worms in the rabbit hole. And I'm the only one besides the fairy who goes through it, so I get to name it." The White Rabbit crossed his arms and gave a determined nod.

"How do you control it?" I asked.

"I can't. I can only control where it opens. The Mad Hatter made this for me." The White Rabbit showed me his pocket watch. "The watch has a strange magic. I have no idea how it works. But Ace knows I have it, and if I don't use it for him he'll find someone more dreadful to enter your world."

"My world isn't so bad."

"Your world is terrible. And I want to stop it from infecting mine. Now come with me. I don't want to see these buildings a moment longer than I have to."

The White Rabbit hopped out from beneath the iron tower and continued toward the mist-covered center of the fortress.

High walls separated the misty tower from the rest of the buildings. I looked around for a gate, but couldn't find one. It didn't matter, however, because the rabbit turned another direction.

"Isn't Ace in that tall tower?" I asked.

"He holds court on the croquet field," the White Rabbit explained.

"So not everything has changed in Wonderland."

It turned out the croquet field wasn't a croquet field at all. If this was the same rosebush-lined courtyard where I'd once played the Queen of Hearts in a very silly sport, it had completely changed.

The fog gave way at the edge of the walls and I saw a long plateau surrounded by steep drop-offs and rocky edges. Green grass rolled upon shallow hills with manicured trees. The sun shone on this place of smooth edges and flat fields.

"It's a golf course," I said. "I thought you said it was a croquet field."

"Don't you recognize it, Alice?" the rabbit asked, putting a smug paw on his hip.

I shifted the duffle bag on my shoulder and tugged the rabbit's leash.

It was a normal golf course, as normal as a golf course built on top of a steep plateau could be. The narrow fairways and assortment of cliff-edge hazards made it look difficult to play.

I'd played golf once. I'd gotten bored and drove the cart off the course to get drive-thru ice cream, much to my parents' horror.

No one was playing that I could see. There was a noticeable lack of activity in the cultivated land. Golf courses usually had squirrels darting up and down trees, tweeting birds fluttering here and there, some sort of peaceful wildlife to enhance the experience. All I saw were empty trees and grass that looked freshly cut.

But the smell of that grass was missing. There was nothing. It might as well have been a picture of a golf course.

As we passed the first few holes, I spotted clusters of halberd-wielding men standing at every tee. They didn't stop us from progressing, but their eyes were always on us.

At the fifth tee I spotted players. The first thing I saw was the guards, six of them. Two were dressed the same as all the others I'd seen, with their khakis and black halberds. The four others wore black pants instead of khakis, with swords strapped to black belts. Each wore padded, black leather armor crafted into jackets. They bore a black symbol of 10, J, Q or K on a spade-shaped badge on their collars. The Ten, Jack, Queen and King of Spades.

Two more individuals approached the tee. One was all in red. She wore a tennis skirt with a tight-fitting, red sleeveless top. I could tell even from a distance she was beautiful. The wind blew her blonde hair around a heart-tipped tiara, which she adjusted to sit more stately atop her head.

The other was a man all in black. His black suit somehow glistened in the sun, like an onyx stone made cloth. His black hair was slicked into a perfect part, which the wind passed over without altering. He held a driver in one hand, and placed his tee and ball into the grass with the other.

"You're late," the man in black said as he held his driver against the ball.

"There were briars around the hole and…" the White Rabbit began.

The man in black held out a hand to silence the rabbit. He formed up his stance. He looked to his feet, shifted his position. He looked down the fairway, and shifted once more. Then he pulled the driver back and struck the ball like he'd pulled the trigger on a catapult. The ball flew into the air with a sharp *crack*. He watched the ball sail over the fairway as I approached the tee.

The guards glared, but didn't stop me.

"Are you Ace of Spades?" I asked.

The man in black didn't acknowledge me. He watched his ball fly over the trees. It landed flat in the middle of the fairway. The ball didn't bounce or roll an inch, and sat in perfect alignment with the hole's distant flag.

"Speak," the man said as he turned.

I could see his black tie, darker than every other piece of clothing. It didn't glimmer as his suit did; it trapped the light. This wasn't the color black, it was a pure absence of color, and it hurt my eyes to look at too long.

"You're Ace of Spades, aren't you?" I asked.

"And you're not very intelligent," he replied.

"Excuse me?"

A khaki-wearing guard marked as Nine of Spades held out a golf bag. A large 'A' with a spade beneath it was stitched into its side. The black-tied man dropped his driver into the bag and progressed onto the fairway. Only then did he look at me.

Ace of Spades, it could be no one else, glared at me with dusty blue eyes. His eyes were the only speck of color on him, his clothes black and his flesh pale, almost white. He didn't blink, not once. Those dusty blue eyes looked at me like I wasn't worth wasting time acknowledging.

"Explain your being late, White Rabbit," said Ace of Spades.

"Thorns. I got caught. They were more hidden than I thought they'd be. And this creature followed me back. She insisted she must talk to you," the rabbit lied, looking to me for help.

"This is not an adequate explanation," Ace replied.

"Can we punish him?" the woman with the tiara asked.

"Yes, I believe we must."

"Can we off with his…"

"No, Queen." Ace turned to face the woman in red. He held her chin in his fingertips and looked her in the eye. "We will punish him in an appropriate manner."

"Yes, Ace."

Ace let her go, and continued walking. The woman in red adjusted her tiara and followed.

I couldn't believe what I saw. Ace called her Queen. Her crown had a heart in it. But could this swimsuit model in front of me be the bulbous Queen of Hearts I'd met as a child?

"Are you the Queen of Hearts?" I asked, quickening my pace to stay with the group.

"Punishment for being stupid is just as likely as punishment for being late," Ace answered. "We'll have to see to that."

The Queen of Hearts perked up. Without looking back, Ace silenced her and said, "In an appropriate manner, of course."

The queen adjusted her tiara, biting her tongue.

"How can you be the Queen of Hearts? She's... different than you. Are you a new Queen?" I asked.

"Rabbit, when you face your punishment, educate this girl on how the removal of Wonder works," Ace said in a flat tone.

The Queen didn't acknowledge me. She kept her eyes fixed on Ace.

"But don't you see, Ace. I've brought what you've asked for," the White Rabbit insisted.

"You are relieved of it then." Ace didn't slow his walk. He waved at two guards standing in the rough. "Seven and Six will take you back to the lower town. There you will be punished, appropriately."

"But Ace, look at her!"

"He's done nothing wrong," I said.

"True stupidity must be stamped out. Your punishment may have to be modified," said Ace.

"Do you know who I am?" I remembered the fear my name had struck in the gate guards.

"It makes no difference who you are if what you are is useless."

"I'm Alice."

"Useless. You will be altered to be useful."

"I'm not useless. I'm Alice," I insisted.

"Alice?" the Queen of Hearts said. She stopped and turned to me, her eyes widening. "Alice! Off with her head! Quick, off with her head!"

This actually encouraged me, and I smiled at the familiar threat.

The guards didn't respond, and Ace calmed the queen with a wave of his hand. "Enough of that, Queen." Ace turned to face me, truly focusing his attention on me for the first time. "Is this the Alice you once held on trial?"

"Yes!" the Queen said in barely contained rage, "she devastated my kingdom and…"

"Is the only one to oppose you and keep their head." Ace of Spades grinned at me, as if he was sharing a secret only I could understand. "Even the Knave of Hearts didn't escape judgment. But she did."

"She's from the other world. Look at her—look at her!" the White Rabbit insisted.

"Silence, rabbit. Alice. A pleasure to meet you."

"I thought someone who's trying to civilize Wonderland would be more civilized," I said.

"I thought you were taller."

I blushed, hating myself for it. "Mister of Spades, I don't think it's right that you're taking the wonder out of creatures."

"How did you get here?" Ace asked.

"She followed me," the rabbit lied, struggling to free himself from the guards. "I warned you how dangerous that world is—how horrible they are. Just look at her!"

"Yes, I'm terrifying," I said, rolling my eyes, "so be nicer to people or everything will end up like me."

"Despite being the Alice this queen once feared," Ace said. "I find you in person to be quite stupid."

"I'm not stupid!"

"Prove it then. Why can't I take the wonder from those in this realm?"

"Because you can't."

"You truly are stupid."

The Queen of Hearts bounced from foot to foot, biting her lip and glaring at me with twitching eyes.

"Oh calm yourself, Red, she's just a little girl," Ace of Spades said and resumed walking to his golf ball. "And a stupid one at that. So disappointing."

I ran after Ace, my fists clenched. "You're the stupid one if you think…" I said, when the King and Queen of Spades stepped between me and Ace, swords drawn.

Six and Seven of Spades had reached us and grabbed the White Rabbit by the paws. The rabbit kept his head down in submission, not saying a word in protest as he was taken into custody. The guards held him dangling between each other and walked away.

Ace reached his golf ball and stopped, turning to face me. "You have one opportunity to prove yourself not useless, Alice," Ace said, completely calm.

"Bring the White Rabbit back. Leave my friends alone," I said, though my threats didn't resonate with Ace or his guards. Apparently they had no fear for the legend that was Alice.

"There are no cakes to make you fifty feet tall anymore, Alice. There are no tricks. I am making this world more civilized, yes? You should be proud of the inspiration your world is making."

"Please. Don't hurt the rabbit. I liked Wonderland."

"That's exactly what you could be useful toward. You see, that word no longer applies here."

"Wonderland?"

"The name is gone. It died with the Cheshire Cat."

"I like the name Wonderland. It fits," I said.

"But it no longer does," said Ace. "It's useless to want for something dead, Alice, and that name, truthfully, no longer applies. The wonder has been removed."

Ace snapped his fingers and Nine of Spades approached with his golf bag. Ace examined the distance between himself and the hole, dusty blue eyes calculating.

"But it still needs a name," Ace said and drew a five iron.

"Then give it one yourself," I said, crossing my arms. I tried to stand with defiance, but unconsciously stepped back from the drawn swords.

"That is the one thing I cannot do in this realm. I close my eyes, and think, but no word comes to mind. This new realm that used to be Wonderland needs a name. And you, being from another world, can name it for me."

I heard a creak of leather as Ace squeezed the five iron's grip. He turned away from me, taking his stance a few steps from the ball. He raised the club and took a practice swing, decapitating blades of grass.

Ace turned back to me and said, "Forgive me, Alice. I treat all creatures with contempt if they are not useful. Perhaps my perception of you as the fabled terrorist clouded my judgment of your true person. Still, you are at this moment the greatest ally I could enlist."

Ace turned back to his golf ball, forming up his stance, and continued, "This land is becoming something. Where once it was foolish, useless, now it has purpose, stability."

"It wasn't all that bad before. Was it?" I asked.

Ace chuckled and took another practice swing. "A true name. Give this land a true name, and you will be returned to your world. I'll see to it."

"How about this. Let the White Rabbit go. I'll give you a name if you stop taking the wonder from the creatures of Wonderland."

"And why would you want me to do that? What love do you have for these creatures as they were?" Ace asked.

"It's not right, what you're doing."

"Quite the opposite actually. I'm making them right. You yourself were nearly killed many times, and it's only my hand that's restraining the former ruler from making another attempt." Ace pointed his five-iron at the foot-stomping Queen of Hearts.

I didn't know what to say to that. The Queen of Hearts I remembered would pull her hair out with rage at the slightest provocation. Her thin-framed body and near-obscene amounts of revealed skin now stood in quivering obedience to Ace's restraint.

"She may not be perfect, yet, but neither is this realm," Ace said. "Think to what you saw before, and what you see now. I have brought sense where there was none, justice where there was none, law and order where neither were known."

"You want order and law? Great. So do I. But you don't have to do it like this," I said.

"Yes I do. And you can help improve the process."

"Help you? You killed the Cheshire Cat!"

"Exactly."

"You're a monster."

"Monsters are what formerly resided in this realm. I have destroyed them. And you can help finalize the destruction of evil in the preservation of sense. One last chance, Alice," Ace said, forming his stance before the golf ball. "Provide a true name."

"I can't think of a name," I answered.

"Then you truly are useless." Ace pulled the club back and swung. While his ball sailed toward the green, he said, "Kill her."

King and Queen of Spades marched closer as Jack and Ten drew their blades.

"Wait, wait," I said, backing away. "You can't do this!"

Ace didn't remove his attention from his golf ball as it landed on the green. "A name will come. With time. The process could have been quickened, but your loss will not slow progress."

I looked for help, but the White Rabbit was gone. I backed away, turning to run, but Eight and Nine of Spades were there, halberds at the ready.

"You have to listen to me—you have to!" I pleaded.

The moment Ace's golf ball landed, striking the green inches from the cup, a green top hat with a red ribbon and white tag landed at my feet. The tag read "Duck."

I ducked.

A dozen wooden fists on metal springs burst out of the hat. The fists struck the guards and knocked them backward. The fists that didn't connect flung about in all directions, and I stayed ducked and screaming as the springs flailed above me.

"It's not a duck, it's a hat," said Eight of Spades as he ducked beneath the fists, grabbing me by the shoulder. He took hold of the hat with the other hand and used it to fend off the guards, pulling me as he ran.

The springs recoiled into the top hat, and Eight of Spades put it on. "Run, Alice, run!" he said as we fled across the golf course.

"What are you doing?" I said, though I didn't slow down. I glanced back and saw the guards racing to catch us.

"Don't you remember me, Alice?" the man with the uniform marked Eight of Spades asked.

I saw his face, then, saw past the disguise. He was taller than I remembered, even though I had been very small. His hair was grayer and his skin more pale and wrinkled. But he still had those smiling eyes and permanent grin.

"Hatter!" I proclaimed.

"Welcome back, Alice. How does the crocodile?" the Mad Hatter said. He stopped a moment and took his hat off in greeting. The spring-loaded fists burst from his hat and recoiled when he put it back on.

"You idiot, run!"

It was my turn to grab the Hatter by the arm.

Manicured grass crunched beneath my feet as we ran for our lives.

"Were you one of those guards the whole time?" I asked.

"Part of leading a resistance. Always stay close to the enemy," the Hatter said.

"Why didn't you just kill Ace?"

The Hatter stopped. "Never thought of that."

"Think of it later!" I said, grabbing him and running through the fairway.

I looked back and saw the guards chasing. They carried swords and bulky armor, but they were closing the distance.

"Where are you going—the town's this way!" I shouted as the Hatter turned from the fairway to the rough.

A row of trees and an outcropping of rock formed a border between two fairways. The Hatter leapt through the trees without slowing.

"Won't make it to the town, Alice. Got another plan," he said.

Knowing there were more guards at the gate, I took my chances and followed the Hatter. I felt the slap of branches across my face as I ran through the thin cluster of trees, dashing out the other side and sprinting across another fairway.

"Hatter, where are you going?" I asked.

The madman was running full speed toward the far side of the golf course. I thought there might be a way down from the plateau, another cluster of trees—somewhere to hide or escape. There was one tree, just one, growing over an abrupt cliff edge.

I could hear the shudder of leaves that signaled the guards cutting their way closer.

The Hatter didn't slow as he ran toward the rocky fall.

"Hatter, what are you doing? Stop!" I cried just as the Hatter was about to leap off the cliff.

"What?" he asked, stopping beside the tree.

"You're going to fall!"

"Well that wouldn't be good. Suppose we should look for another place to..." The Hatter made to rest against the tree, but misjudged the distance. He leaned back, and fell over the side of the cliff with a little yelp.

"Hatter!" I ran to the cliff's edge just as I heard the guards shout. "There she is—stop!"

"Hatter!" I shouted to the mists below. "Hatter! You stupid—gah!"

Callused fingers pulled me off the edge. I screamed, but fell only a short distance, and found myself standing on solid ground.

"It's a good thing this platform was here," the Hatter said. "We could have been hurt. Smart man whoever thought up this place. Ooh—a tunnel!"

The Mad Hatter approached a tiny hole set in the outcropping. He got on his hands and knees and motioned for me to follow.

"Well this is a fine kettle of fish," the Hatter said as we crawled through the tunnel. It was dim and damp, and I scraped my knees crawling over rough stone. "Though why anyone would put fish in a kettle is beyond me."

"It's an expression," I said. "It means we're in a bad situation. Are we in a bad situation?"

"Not so bad I'd consider drinking tea from a kettle of fish. That would be mad!" The Hatter's laughter echoed in the tiny tunnel.

"Hatter this is—ah!"

"Gotcha!" declared Nine of Spades. He had followed us over the edge and into the tunnel. His halberd clattered against the slippery tunnel walls as he thrust at me. His weapon struck short, though, penetrating only the duffle bag.

I screamed.

"Hold still you delinquent!" Nine of Spades threatened. His halberd tore the duffle bag, spilling my father's shirts and socks and a box of shotgun shells.

I kicked. "Let me go!"

"No time to dawdle, Alice!" the Hatter shouted. The tunnel was too narrow for him to see my attacker, nor get by to help.

The halberd was so twisted inside the duffle bag that Nine of Spades gave up using it. He groped at my legs to pull me closer.

"Come here!" Nine of Spades said, reaching for a knife at his belt. He pulled and tugged to gain a stronger hold, sending the bottle of pills tumbling out of my dress's little pocket as he grabbed at my side.

"No! No!"

I kicked and crawled. The man had me by the ankle and wouldn't let go. Tugging on the duffle bag still strapped to my shoulder further ripped its canvas sides, and the barrel of my father's shotgun tumbled out.

With a swift thrust, I landed a kick to my attacker's face that freed my foot. Stumbling backward, I tried to get away.

"Go away! Leave me alone!" I shouted, picking up the shotgun and swinging it like a club.

"I'm gonna make you pay for that."

I crawled backward, my hand reaching for a spilled shotgun shell. I let out little grunts of frustration as I slid the round into the chamber and shouted, "Get back!"

The knife came for me, and I pulled the trigger.

The sound of the gunshot in that narrow tunnel was like being inside a thunderbolt. I held my eyes closed, my fingers still clinging to the barrel.

"Ow!" the Mad Hatter shouted a distance ahead. "That thing is loud!"

I opened my eyes. Nine of Spades lay in front of me. He didn't move.

"Heh. You've got quite a roar, little lion. I've never seen a lion's roar do that, but I've never seen an elephant fit in a tin can either. Come, Alice, come," the Hatter said, pulling me.

I couldn't move, could only stare.

"Come!" the Hatter insisted.

The Hatter had to practically drag me to the end of the tunnel. After a few steps, I began to hear music. I thought that my ears were still ringing from the gunshot. But the sing-song rhythm was very real.

The tunnel gave way to a large, round chamber. Tables and chairs, beds and cots, and a long table took up the majority of the space, while in another part of the chamber a workshop had been set up with piles and piles of tools and lumber. A stack of hats rested against a wall, along with shelving filled with even more hats.

The last wall took away what breath I had left. Glowing rock, white as ivory and black as charcoal, made mounds and clusters on the floor. Stalactites dripped from the top of the cavern. Whenever a drop of water hit the smooth rock below, it glowed and sang with a musical note. With all the dripping going on, I could distinctly make out the rhythm of the song.

"Is that... is that 'Chopsticks?'" I asked.

"Would you prefer they play Beethoven? They've been practicing. Least I think they have. The stones rarely talk," the Hatter said. "I ask them to play Beethoven but they don't."

"Hatter, did you see what I just did?" I yelled, not understanding why the Hatter wouldn't even acknowledge that I'd shot a man.

"No time for sentiments!" a fat man said as he bounded down a ladder cut through a stalactite. An instant later a twin of the fat man landed beside him.

"Unless we stop time," the twin replied.

"To do that we'd need more than hats and wooden machines," said the first twin.

"Or butter."

"Anti-time butter?"

"They say time is slippery."

"And anti-slip anti-butter..."

"Would keep it from slipping through your fingers."

"Tweedledee!" I said, smiling. Seeing these two welcome memories stopped the tears forming in my eyes.

"I'm Tweedledee—he's Tweedledum," said Tweedledee.

"I'm Tweedledum," the man's twin replied. "Do you have any butter?"

"It's me, Alice," I said.

"Do you have any butter, Alice?"

"I don't."

"Too bad."

"We could use it," Tweedledee added.

"To stop time," said Tweedledum.

"You remember me though, right?" I asked, almost hysterical. I needed someone to recognize me. I needed someone to recognize the insanity of what I'd just done.

"Of course. It's only been twenty years since we've met."

"Twenty years, twelve days, four hours, five minutes and twenty two seconds. Twenty three. Twenty four," Tweedledee added, counting up the seconds.

"That can't be right. It's only been ten years," I said.

"Time is relative," said Tweedledee.

"Maybe we saw you in the past," added Tweedledum.

"Maybe this is the past."

"Or a future that won't happen."

"The rabbit hole crosses years of light."

"You mix up time quite a bit with that."

"The hole stretches and stirs distance and time like a churn through cream."

"Then smoothes it out 'til it's solid."

"Makes time butter!"

"Slippery is that time butter."

"We could use some of that."

"To go back in time and stop the soldiers banging down our doors."

"Or at least trip them."

"You sure you don't have any butter, Alice?"

"She has what she has and we have what we have," the Mad Hatter said. He'd gone back to the tunnel to make a quick wall of hats. He'd also recovered my shotgun shells and duffle bag, which he held out to me. "Take these. Quickly."

"No, I don't want them," I said and threw the shotgun to the ground. The Hatter used a spring-loaded hand from his hat to grab the gun and place it back in the duffle bag.

"Take them. There's no time."

"No butter either," added the Tweedle twins.

I heard a muffled voice shout through the stalactites, "In the name of the Ace of Spades, surrender immediately!"

The stalactites' dripping tune suddenly sounded like Wagner.

"Are you going to fight them?" I asked.

"What kind of fool do you take me for?" the Hatter asked, recoiling his spring-loaded hand into his hat.

"Is it escape then?" Tweedledee asked, running to the chamber's workshop.

"Escape it is," Tweedledum answered.

"Just watch out for the crow."

"Not the crow!"

"What are you talking about?" I asked.

"This," the Hatter said.

He joined the Tweedles at the workshop, where he kicked aside piles of hats and pulled back a massive tablecloth. Instead of a table underneath, the Hatter revealed a wooden contraption that looked straight out of Leonardo da Vinci's sketchbook.

It was all tanned wood and white canvas, with a blown-glass bubble for a cockpit. It had a corkscrew for a propeller sticking out its front, with a tail like a dolphin's at its back.

"You're going to fight Ace with that?" I asked.

"No, we're quite doomed at the moment," the Mad Hatter noted.

Sounds of brute force shoving against doors signaled the Hatter's makeshift barriers were about to break.

Tweedledee busied himself with extending the machine's bat-like wings while Tweedledum took up a large hammer and struck the cavern wall. I thought this was a very dumb thing to do, until the wall crumbled. It wasn't a wall at all, but a hangar door, with the flying machine set on a launch pad.

"I don't think this is very aerodynamic," I said.

A hat flew in from the tunnel, bouncing on springs. "I'm through!" I heard a guard shout.

"Time to go," the Hatter said and tugged me toward the cockpit.

"Wait! Are you really going to fly this thing?" I asked.

"Of course not, that would be mad! You are." With that the Mad Hatter shoved me into the glass bubble and prepared to shut it.

"There's only room for one!"

"Precisely."

"But what about Tweedledee and Tweedledum?" I asked.

"Hate crows," Tweedledee answered as he cranked the corkscrew.

"Crows fly," Tweedledum added.

"So we don't fly."

"Avoid the crows."

"Unless there are butter crows!"

"Crows make a good pie."

"But you have to add butter to the pie."

"So there's no butter in crows."

"Too bad."

The Tweedles jumped up and down in turns to crank the corkscrew. With each turn I felt the ropes and canvas grow tighter, energy building in the flying machine's wooden frame.

"But those are stupid reasons!" I said.

"We're too fat!" the Tweedles shouted.

"Oh. That's a good reason."

"There you are!" shouted a guard bearing the mark of Six of Spades.

The Mad Hatter saw him coming and picked up a tea kettle from an overturned end table. He threw the kettle and it shattered against the guard's head, knocking him to the ground.

"Ha-ha! How is a raven like a writing desk!" the Mad Hatter hooted.

"Hatter, get in!" I pleaded.

"I can't do that, Alice."

"Then send me home! Send me home like the White Rabbit did when I was seven. He said you made a watch that can control the rabbit hole."

"I won't do that either," said the Mad Hatter.

"Why not?"

"Because I'm terrified of your world. And I won't have Ace turn mine into yours."

Tears welled in my eyes. "Please. Just send me home."

"No. We need you, Alice. You've bungled what resistance we had left, so do us this one favor. Get out of Wonderland. Tell others what's happening here. Tell them of Ace and the Cheshire Cat and the wonder being taken."

There was a clatter as an entire tea set, cups and saucers and cookies, tumbled from the stalactite-covered ladder. "That's the last of the traps!" I heard a guard shout.

"No mercy this time, Hatter," another warned.

"No tricks or tools or rabbit holes can save Wonderland," said the Hatter. "We need to awaken the Sleeping Beauty."

"The Sleeping Beauty? The fairy tale?" I asked.

"I don't know what a fairy tale is."

"It's a story."

The clatter of swords being drawn echoed through the room.

"I'm just a Mad Hatter, Alice," the Hatter continued. "You're the one who traveled through the rabbit hole. Talk to those out there the way you talk to people here. Unite them. Take back Wonderland." He leaned inside the cockpit and placed the duffle bag with the shotgun beside my seat.

"How do I do that?" I asked.

"How should I know?" the Mad Hatter replied.

My eyes searched the cockpit for a way out. My mind swam with incoherent thoughts. My vision blurred as I tried to wake up from this dream.

When I opened my eyes, I was looking at a set of wooden dials and a leather-gripped handle. I exhaled and said, "How do I control it?"

"Your course is locked in," the Hatter said. He tapped a little water-filled sphere on the control panel that resembled a nautical compass. It held a golden arrow pointing forward. "Second star to the right and straight on 'til morning."

"Are you serious?" I asked.

"No, I'm mad."

"All set!" Tweedledee said, stepping away from the flying machine.

"Set and tight," Tweedledum added.

"Not slippery at all."

"No slip. Stiff and true."

"Then it's time to depart Wonderland," the Hatter said and shut the cockpit bubble.

He kicked away a pile of hats, revealing an enormous lever. The hats bounced on springs and landed at the feet of Ten, Jack, Queen and King of Spades, who'd just broken through the last of the traps. The spade-marked soldiers marched in formation toward the Hatter.

"Wait! Wait!" I pleaded, a thousand questions raging in my mind.

"Toodles," said the Mad Hatter with a smile.

He pulled the lever.

CHAPTER FIVE

The flying machine shot out of the Hatter's workshop like a bolt from a crossbow.

For a moment I was certain death would come as the machine dipped toward the ground. Then with a grinding snap of rope and leather, the corkscrew began to spin. The tail began to wave. The wings began to flap.

If there was wonder left in Wonderland, it must have been contained in that impossible machine, because it started to fly.

It took ages for me to catch my breath, to open my eyes. I still couldn't believe I was alive, even as the flapping machine gained altitude. By the time my panting stopped, I was above the clouds, with a billion stars above me.

"That was... what..." I mumbled.

The little sphere of a direction-finder pointed to the second star to my right. I looked at the machine's controls like they were made of glass, not daring to touch them out of fear I might jinx whatever was keeping it flying.

"Straight on 'til morning," I repeated, staring at the night sky.

My adrenaline soon lowered. My heart stopped pounding.

"Straight on 'til morning. But that's from a fairy tale. That's how to get to…" My mouth couldn't form the word. Refusing to believe what was happening, I reached for the bottle of pills in my pocket. "Where are they? Where is—oh, right. I dropped them."

I sat back hard in the cockpit, staring at the stars through thick glass. I was in an impossible machine in an impossible world on an impossible heading. And now, the only people who could explain the meaning of this impossible reality had just sent me away. I curled up in a ball and felt more alone than I'd ever felt before.

I don't know how long I cried. I don't know what I cried for more. Was it the caterpillar and his jacket I stole? Was it the fish or the pig or the hamster? Was it the White Rabbit? I couldn't cry for Tweedledee and Tweedledum. I only laughed, even though I knew I should cry for them, and the Hatter most of all. And I cried just a little for the Cheshire Cat.

The clouds passed in a glorious mirage of color. Though night had cloaked the land in darkness, twilight hues erupted across the clouds. I thought I saw rumbling flashes of lightning, but heard no sound.

I distracted myself from what I'd seen, what I'd done, with imagining shapes in the clouds. I saw a mermaid with a pink tail, a silvery looking glass, a woman dressed for a gala, and a million black specks that formed incomprehensible patterns. I thought, perhaps, this was rain, but couldn't be sure.

I recognized none of the constellations. There didn't seem to be any constellations, just an infinite canvas of twinkling stars. No moon lit the sky, but there was enough light from the stars and lightning flashing in the clouds to see.

Soon the combination of beauty below and serenity above made me sleepy. I tried to fight sleep at first. But what danger could there be in this gloriously colorful sky? I abandoned my attempts to fight sleep, and curled up in that glass bubble of a cockpit, trying to think of the colorful clouds, and not the Wonderland I had fled.

CHAPTER SIX

It was the gunfire that awoke me.

At first I thought it was the sound of cracking twigs and stretching canvas. But as more holes ripped through the flying machine, reverberating blasts caught up with the supersonic bullets.

"Ace!" I shouted, sitting awake in sudden fear, "Ace of Spades—he's here!" Then I screamed and shielded my face as bullets ripped through the flying machine's corkscrew.

I harnessed what little books had taught me about planes and shoved the control stick forward. The flying machine dove through a thin layer of clouds and I saw the ocean below.

Sunlight glistened off a sea blue as I always dreamed the ocean should be. Shimmering waves crested in little whitecaps upon the shore of a crescent-shaped island. Despite my terror, I took a moment to gape at the island's beauty.

Green as the water was blue, with fields and trees and such a variety of hills and valleys I imagined all that was good in nature must have been compressed in this island. What I thought was a mountain occupied its center. But it wasn't a mountain—it was a tree. A massive tree, greater than the tallest sequoia, reaching to a cloud-capping precipice. From its distant lagoon to the crescent shore, the island was breathtaking.

Bullets chased my descent and I could hear them closing like persistent bees. Flashes of light from the shore led me to their source. It was an ironclad ship, rivets and edges in brass casting a gilded reflection upon the water. At its high stern was a turret-mounted Gatling gun flashing and smoking as it fired.

Bullets streaked over my aircraft's wings and shattered the cockpit. Glass fragments grazed my cheek as I struggled to maintain control.

"I hope this counts as morning," I said and turned the stick to the left.

I looked at the spherical direction device to try and see if I was in the right location. Wind from my descent knocked the sphere loose and it fell out of the sky.

I turned right, left, zigzagging through the air and trying to pick up speed to escape when a stream of bullets cut through the right wing. It shattered to tinder, and the wounded flying machine turned into a spinning dive.

My screams weren't as loud as the wind rushing past my face. The stick stopped resisting my pulls as the flying machine disintegrated. I looked around and could only hope there was a soft place to crash.

Visions of a field of mattresses or a massive bale of hay crossed my mind, but I could only see trees and rocks. And then I spotted something else that was green. It was a camouflage green shirt, and the boy who wore it standing on the fuselage of my doomed flying machine.

He looked at me.

I looked at him.

He grabbed me by the arm and pulled me out of the cockpit.

"Wait, wait!" I screamed in terror, reaching for something to hold onto. But my hands found only my father's duffle bag, and I went screaming into the morning sky.

My first thought was of relief. At least I wasn't going to die alone. I wasn't happy about smashing against the rocks, but at least I'd have someone at my side while it happened. My mind didn't have time to wonder how this boy had ended up in the sky.

I held the boy tight and chanced a look at the rocks rising to meet me. Just as I looked, however, the rocks began to drop away. I felt the surge of gravity washing off my shoulders as we sailed over the treetops.

"You can fly!" I shouted.

"And you can't," the boy in green replied.

"Where are you taking me?"

"Away from the pirates."

"You can let me down now."

"We're not far enough away yet."

The smell of surf and tropical forest flowers rose to my senses. My senses then grew to the distinct awareness of being held so close, and I couldn't help myself from thrashing in the boy's arms.

"Hold still—stop that!" the boy commanded.

"Put me down," I said.

"You little bunny, stop!"

Now I really wanted out of his arms. "Let me go!" I kicked and landed a punch on his elbow.

The boy lost altitude and we fell through the forest canopy. Branches cracked around us as he grabbed me at the last moment so that when we hit the ground it was just a painful tumble. I rolled to a stop in a clearing. My father's socks and ties had exploded out of the duffle bag upon impact.

The fall didn't kill me, but it hurt.

The boy popped out of the grass where he'd landed, a sock on his head, and shot to a hover above me. "What the blazes were you doing?" he asked.

"Who are you?" I replied.

"I should ask who you are!"

The boy put his fists against his hips. His clothing was camouflage green everywhere except his brown boots. His copper-brown hair waved in the wind, and brushed against his stubble-laden cheeks. The beginning of a beard, or a haphazard shave, added a wild red color to his face.

The boy stared down at me with eyes green as the forest. I looked at him and saw a deep scar over his right eyebrow that cut across his eye. I would have stared at those eyes much longer had I not also seen the brass-lined, black gun at his side.

I leaped for my father's shotgun and picked it up from where it had landed. "Don't make me use this," I threatened. "I've already used this once so don't make me do it again."

"What? Shoot me with an unloaded gun?" the boy asked.

"It's loaded."

"Unless it shoots compressed air, I doubt that."

"It does. See this wooden thing here? That's the compressed air."

"Yeah, sure."

"Tell me who you are!" I demanded.

"The name's Peter Pan. Now you go."

I dropped the shotgun.

"Not very threatening with your unloaded gun on the ground," Peter noted.

"You're Peter Pan?" I asked.

"Of course I am. And who are you?"

"Do you work for Ace?"

"What?"

"Ace of Spades, do you work for him?"

"There's a guy named after a playing card?"

"Do you work for him!"

"No, of course I don't—I don't work for anyone. I'm Peter Pan of Neverland—and I don't obey any adult. No Aces, Jacks or Queens. No captains neither," said Peter Pan.

"What part of Wonderland is Neverland in?" I asked.

"Wonderland?"

"Over here! They crashed over here!" I heard a distant shout.

"Get down!" Peter Pan said and dove toward me.

I screamed as the boy landed on top of me. He put his back against a fallen log and pulled me beside him, holding his hand over my mouth.

"Shut up," Peter said as he froze against the log.

When I heard the gunfire, I froze too.

"Come out, Pan! We know you're in there," a raspy man's voice shouted through the trees. A burst of rifle fire echoed his challenge.

Peter Pan held his pistol at the ready with his free hand.

Peter whistled through the sides of his teeth, throwing the sound to the opposite edge of the clearing, "Hey, Hook, I'm over here!"

Gunfire tore through the trees where Peter threw his voice. Peter then leapt up and opened fire. His pistol made a clanging sound like an exploding gong as it threw up misty smoke. Whoever he was shooting at quickly discovered the ruse and Peter ducked down just as bullets burst against the log.

"Hook. Peter Pan. What have I got myself into?" I said.

"We're outnumbered," Peter said, exploding bark raining onto our heads. He grabbed a handful of shotgun shells that had fallen near the log and threw my father's shotgun at me.

"Hey!"

"Hold them off just a bit."

"What?"

In seconds, Peter placed five rounds into the shotgun's semi-automatic chamber and turned me and the shotgun toward the gunfire. Then he reached into a pocket and pulled out a brass clock.

"Hold them off!" Peter instructed.

"What are you doing?" I asked.

"Shut up and shoot." Peter turned a dial at the back of the clock, the gunfire deafening its cranking gears.

Bullets continued to erupt from the log as I leaned against the shotgun. My hands gripped the weapon, frozen. I couldn't lift the gun. I saw nothing but the bright flash and the look in Nine of Spades' eyes.

"Useless girl," Peter said as the clock began to tick. He set the clock on top of the log and hit the dirt.

I thought the clock was going to explode, so I dropped my gun and lay flat on the ground.

Tick-tock, tick-tock the sound echoed between gunshots.

Tick-tock, tick-tock.

"Cease fire, cease fire!" the raspy voice shouted. "He's here!" The gunshots stopped and I heard the mumble of fearful men. "He's here! Back to the ship back away now!"

The man with the raspy voice ran into the forest. I heard the sounds of at least a dozen men joining him as they fled through the trees.

Tick-tock, tick-tock.

Peter chanced a look over the log and smiled.

"They're gone," he said. He patted his clock with grinning thanks.

"Of course!" I said, smiling at the silliness of what was happening. "The clock! They're scared of the crocodile. That was Captain Hook wasn't it?"

"And fools the lot of 'em."

"They're fools to think the crocodile's coming just because they hear a ticking clock."

"I'd be scared of it. It tore Hook's hand off—that's why Hook's got a hook for a hand in the first place."

"That sounds like a nasty crocodile."

"It is. But they'll be back once they see it's not here. You sure you can't fly?" Peter asked.

"I had a flying machine, but they shot it down."

"We need to get out of here. Can you make a net?"

"A net?" I asked.

"So I can carry you."

"I don't want to be carried like a fish."

"Well think of something else."

"I can run."

"Run?"

"Yeah. With my feet."

Peter Pan rolled his eyes. "Fine."

"Give me a second to grab my things."

"No time."

Peter collected the scattered shotgun shells and put them in my jacket pockets.

"But these are my father's things," I said.

I picked up a box of shotgun shells by my father's duffle bag and showed it to Peter. He grabbed the remaining ammunition and stuffed it in my pockets.

"Leave the clothes. Take the bullets—let's go!" he said.

Peter tugged me by the arm and I had no choice but to run at his side.

Ferns and wide-leafed plants brushed against my legs as we ran through the forest. Trees stood in tall formation so thick that if I tried to look back at the clearing I'd probably crash into a trunk or limb.

Foxes ran through the undergrowth while birds played in the forest. A family of hedgehogs scurried away as Peter and I disturbed their den.

The possibility of gunfire, I discovered, was a wonderful motivation to run through a lush forest. It was also a great distraction from the fact that I'd wandered into a fairy tale. We seemed to be heading toward the center of the island. But the adrenaline of the firefight soon wore off and I realized I hadn't eaten since I'd first entered Wonderland.

I chanced a look back. There was nothing through the trees save a cluster of butterflies.

When I looked ahead I found we'd left the overgrown forest and entered a more spaced group of wild apple trees. The trees had massive trunks with branches covered in dark green leaves and deep red apples big as my head. After passing three of these beauties, I turned away from Peter's path and stopped, leaning against a trunk.

I held the shotgun against my panting chest and stayed silent a moment.

"What are you doing?" Peter asked, stopping to hover a distance ahead.

"Are they close?" I asked.

"They can't have caught up with us yet."

"Good." I lowered the shotgun.

"But that doesn't mean we should stop." Peter rose a little above the canopy, pistol in hand. His eyes darted hawk-like through the trees, searching for movement.

"I thought Captain Hook was a fool."

"Don't count on that, girl."

"It's how he was in the fairy tale," I noted.

"What fairy tales have you heard?"

"Peter Pan."

"That's me," Peter said.

"And there's fairy tales about you. All about you fighting Hook in Neverland. You feed him to the crocodile in the end, by the way."

"Hah! Yeah, right. Let's get going, silly girl. I don't want you to find out exactly how wrong about Hook you are."

"Not before breakfast."

"Breakfast?"

"Yup," I said and put the shotgun on the ground. I looked at the apples, wondering how best to reach the high-branched fruit.

"You're worried about breakfast when we're being chased by pirates?" Peter asked.

"Just give me a minute."

"We don't have minutes. Not with Hook around. Here, if you want an apple I'll just..."

"I've got it."

The lowest branch not only had no apples, but was too high for me to reach. I looked at the tree, rubbing my hands together.

"Will you hurry up?" Peter asked, putting his fists on his waist and rising quickly into the tree.

"Are they really going to chase us?" I asked.

"Yes. Now get your apple. Here." Peter picked an apple from the highest branch and held it out to me.

"Why did they shoot at me? Are they Ace's men?"

"They're Hook's men."

"But they shot at me."

"They shot at you because you're in Neverland. He'll shoot anything that's not a pirate or the crock'odial."

"Sounds simple enough."

I ran at the tree fast as I could run. With a leap I ran up the side of the trunk then bounded toward a branch. My hands caught, slipped, and I was able to hook an elbow around the smooth branch.

"It is simple. Now hurry up, ya hopping bunny," Peter said and shook his head, still scanning the forest for movement.

"The only question is," I grunted, plucking a stick within arm's reach.

I reached up with the stick and knocked an apple loose. Then I let go of the stick and branch and held out my hand, catching the apple as my feet touched ground.

"Where are we going?" I asked, pointing the apple with warning as I picked up my father's shotgun. "To the Lost Boys? I have to say, it's exciting meeting you, Peter Pan. You're supposed to be just a story."

"And you can stay here and get shot by pirates for all I care."

"Now come on." I lowered the shotgun. "You're Peter Pan. You're supposed to be honorable and courageous."

"And you're supposed to listen to me. This isn't a fairy tale. Those are Hook's men. They'll shoot dead anything that's not a pirate or that monster. That's all you need to know, and if you want my help, take it. Or don't."

Peter's nose curled up. I could spot a poker face when I saw one. But I let it slide.

I took a bite of the apple. "I'm Alice, by the way."

"Alice?" Peter asked.

"Yes."

"Didn't you say you came from Wonderland?"

"Yes. Why?"

"As in, Alice of Wonderland?"

"Yes, what's the big deal?" I asked.

"I've heard fairy tales about you, too. A long time ago."

"You have?"

"Yeah. You were a lot younger though."

"I didn't know people knew about my time in Wonderland."

"It was a very popular book back in England," Peter said.

"Book?"

Peter Pan's ears perked and he looked out over the treetops. "We've got to get going."

"Now hold on, what book am I in?" I asked.

"Like I said, it's been a long time and it was read to me when I was barely able to walk. Suffice it to say, you're in a book, and you say I'm in a book too, so let's both book it and focus on the fact that there are pirates on our tail."

I examined Peter Pan a moment, then examined myself. The way he looked at me, I realized, held the same disbelief I had for him. Neither of us could believe the other existed.

It frightened me.

The sensation made me toss aside all thoughts on the impossibility of my surroundings.

We ran up the shallow rise toward the island's center. I'd seen rocky hills and clefts in my brief flight over the island, but it seemed we were ascending to a more wooded part of the landmass.

I finished the apple in less than a minute, despite its size. I think I ate a few seeds from its core, and found myself reinvigorated by the food. I even managed a smile.

I was running from pirates on a lush island with Peter Pan. And as the morning sun washed through the trees, glistening off fruit colorful as bulbs on a Christmas tree, even my experiences in Wonderland could not have prepared me for the beauty of it all.

And, of course, my medicine had probably worn off. This made me smile even more.

In short time a shadow fell over the forest. It wasn't from clouds or apple trees. In fact the forest grew much thinner. I looked up and saw branches bigger than trees. There was a dark brown trunk ahead, wide as a football field. My feet crunched over car-sized leaves and I slowed my pace, searching for where Peter might be going.

"You can't run anymore," Peter said.

"I can't?" I panted.

"No. You can't get to our village without flying." Peter tossed me the apple he'd picked.

I took a bite out of the fresh apple. "Oh. So is Tinkerbelle here? That sounds wonderful—where is she?"

"Excuse me?"

"That's how you fly, right? Pixie dust and a happy thought."

"Fairy dust. And yes," Peter said.

"So go get Tinkerbelle."

I took a big bite out of the apple.

Peter frowned, casting me a glare as he mulled over a thought.

Without another word, Peter put his arms around me. I might have shot him had he not pinned my arms to my sides. I flailed about and screamed, trying to head-butt him, but I froze the instant he rocketed upward.

I dropped the apple.

We rose through the tree, swooshing inches away from high-speed collision with branches the size of hillsides. In the time it took me to suck in a breath to scream, Peter stopped several hundred feet in the air.

When I opened my eyes and saw the island far below me, my first instinct was to cling to Peter's chest. When I realized he had stopped over a solid platform of wood, a flattened branch protruding from the immense tree trunk, I leapt out of Peter's arms and landed on the branch. It was fifty feet across, stable enough to easily stand on, with immense leaves all around.

"Do not do that again," I threatened, wiping down my dress with shaking hands.

"Oi Petah, wha'cha got 'ere?" asked a cockney-accented voice.

I turned to face the voice and raised my shotgun on instinct. "Stand back—stand back!"

"'old it there, dovey. No need for the rub, there is."

The boy was pudgy and short, though his voice sounded close to my age. He wore a frayed suit jacket with a stained shirt beneath and a bowler hat on his head. At his side was a massive brass revolver.

"I mean it!" I warned.

"Alice, drop the gun," Peter said.

I didn't hear Peter. I saw only what was before me. Something like an adobe village was carved into the side of the tree. There were dozens of caves with frayed cloth coverings, and a central seating area built around a fire pit. Before this was a wall of tree bark, with three boys aiming rifles at my head.

"You wouldn't want to shoot summun' who's not 'armin ya," the accented boy said. "I sure wouldn't. Now let's think this through an act a'friend, what say?"

"Greg, Gregg, Craig," Peter said to the boys on the wall. "Lower your guns."

The boys obeyed.

"See now, dovey? No need to throw a fuss when none's been made about you."

I scanned the tree a moment or two. I lowered the shotgun. Then I set it on the ground and stepped away from it, rubbing my shoulders with a sudden chill.

"You're lucky Jimmy's here," Peter said, holstering his pistol.

I hadn't realized he'd readied his weapon. He swooped down and picked up my shotgun, resting it on his shoulder.

"I'm sorry," I said. "I'm… a little jumpy."

"So long's you've kept from 'armin others it's no trouble at'all, dovey," Jimmy said with a smile. "What's the damage, Petah?"

"She's the one they were shooting at," Peter said.

"No wonda you're jumpy."

"I should have known better than to fly so close. That's what Hook does—shoot at the Lost Boys. You are the Lost Boys aren't you?" I asked.

"Pleased to make your acquaintance, it is," Jimmy said with a slight bow. "It's been a long time since we've 'ad a new Lost Boy, er, girl."

"I'm not a Lost Boy or a lost girl. I'm here because the Hatter sent me."

"Hatter?" Peter asked. "As in the Mad Hatter?"

"Yes, the Mad Hatter. He built that flying machine."

"Oh good, another crazy person infiltrating Neverland."

"I'm not crazy."

"You arrived on a flying machine built by the Mad Hatter and you're Alice of Wonderland. How is that not crazy?" Peter asked.

"Well, you live in a tree and fly with the help of fairy sparkles."

"Fairy dust."

"As if that's any better."

Peter stopped a moment. He looked at his clothes, the brass gun at his side, the picturesque island below, and his fortress of adolescent boys carved into the side of a mountainous tree.

"Guess we're both a little mad, then," Peter said.

"I guess," I agreed.

"Well come on then, mad girl. I'll show you around."

Peter walked me through the walls of bark and into the dwelling of the Lost Boys. It was still hard to believe, like a story come to life.

Out of the branch-built homes and carved-out trunk came dozens of dirty-faced boys. Greg, Gregg and Craig, each taller than the next, wearing a green, red and yellow shirt respectively, marched up and down the bark-walled entrance to the village as I passed.

There was a little dog sitting on his hind legs just inside the village. He barked when he saw me, and howled against his leash. As he barked he began to drift upwards, floating like a balloon on a string. When the little mutt noticed he was floating, his barking turned into whining and he paddled in mid-air to swim to the ground.

"He's scared of heights," shrugged the hairy boy holding the leash.

I smiled and pet the shuddering dog. The mutt wagged his tail.

"That's Jo and Monster," Peter said, pointing out the Lost Boys. "Over there is Derek."

Derek was a short boy with thick glasses, mixing leaves in a mortar and pestle. He positioned a makeshift Bunsen burner beneath a viscous liquid and frowned at the bubbling concoction. A long table set up at the far end of the tree village was covered in nuts and fruits, with more boys preparing skinned meats for cooking.

Peter named all the chefs and skinners. The well-muscled blacksmith with slicked-back hair was named Jonny. "That's Willy," Peter said, pointing out a twitching boy with daggers running up and down leather shoulder straps and belts. "He refuses to use guns. Not that we have that many—though we take as many as we can steal."

"Willy likes to walk with death," Willy declared, rubbing a dagger over a stone.

"And that's Jake."

Jake wore a bathrobe that at one time had been white. He wielded a rifle with a bayonet made out of a broken katana. Jake offered Peter a sage nod as he passed.

Despite all the activity and the mess, dirty clothes and leaves everywhere, the sounds seemed only to partially fill the vast tree village. Cloth coverings waved in the wind over empty dwellings.

Food covered only a portion of the table. An entire section of the village was overgrown with vines.

"This isn't exactly what it was like in the fairy tale," I noted.

"What was it like?" Peter asked.

"Happier?"

"Happy or not, we're the Lost Boys. And this is our home. Those who come to Neverland never grow up," Peter explained.

"That part's in the story."

"Really? What else is in it?"

I bit my lip, not sure how to explain. "The story is about Peter Pan and the Lost Boys. They never grow up, and play all day with mermaids and Indians. They were racially-insensitive versions of Native Americans, but it was a different time."

"And the story ends with… me fighting the crock'odial?"

"No, like I said, you feed Hook to the crocodile," I explained.

"That must be a fairy tale. Anything else?"

"That's really it."

"Then you're story's off on two things. For starters, Hook's still here. And for another, all the Indians and mermaids are dead," Peter said.

"Oh."

"So let me tell you about my story. It's called 'Alice's Adventures in Wonderland.' It's about a girl from the countryside in the sixties who goes to Wonderland. She gets in all sorts of trouble with a Cheshire Cat and Queen of Hearts, and wakes up and it's all a dream."

"How did you know about that?"

"Like I said, it was a story."

"Well I'm not from the sixties. I wasn't even born then," I said.

"Seventies then, I don't know. It was an older book when I was in London, but it was definitely published by 1870."

"What?" I laughed.

"1870. I left London in 1904. The book was at least thirty years old by the time I came to Neverland."

I sat down right there on the tree.

"You okay, Alice?" Peter asked, chuckling a bit. "It's still a little funny saying that. I mean, I'm talking to Alice of Wonderland. It's really neat."

"Are you from Earth?" I asked.

"What kind of question is that?"

"A legitimate one."

"Of course I'm from Earth. Tinkerbelle took me from London through this hole thing. Then we followed the stars to Neverland. It's been years since that happened. She always said Neverland was a different world. I thought she meant a sort of other continent, like America or something. It's safe to say it's not if you're here."

I stared at the enormous leaves, faced the distant shoreline and endless sky of Neverland. "Echoes," I said.

"What was that?"

"Echoes of Wonderland. And Neverland, I suppose. Maybe this is the past. Or a future that won't happen."

"Are you okay, Alice? You're talking nonsense," Peter said.

"It's something Tweedledee and Tweedledum said."

"Well that would explain it."

"The rabbit hole," I said, standing up with a smile on my face. "I understand what the White Rabbit meant about echoes. Even the Cheshire Cat said it when I was seven, it just didn't make sense 'til now."

"The rabbit hole? As in the hole you fell in that brought you to Wonderland?"

"Yes. The rabbit hole is a wormhole."

"Worms, rabbits, whatever," Peter said with a shrug.

"No, a wormhole is a tear in the universe. It's like a tunnel through distance and time. Tinkerbelle must have brought you through it too! Don't worry, we won't figure out black holes even exist until a few decades after 1904."

"So how do you know about them in 1870?"

"I'm not from then," I explained. "The wormhole must have opened in a different time. Look, I know about your story because an echo of it reached Earth and was written down as a fairy tale. I guess a similar echo reached whoever wrote my fairy tale."

"So the rabbit hole is real?"

"I'm having trouble enough dealing with it myself. I mean, you're Peter Pan," I said.

"And you're Alice!" said Peter Pan.

"And we're both fairy tales, or at least, fairy tales are echoes of what we did."

"I don't feel like a fairy tale."

"Neither do I." I frowned a moment. "Do you remember, in my fairy tale, anything about the Ace of Spades?"

"No."

"We must be in a different fairy tale then." I looked across the island, at the distant, glistening sea.

Peter stood beside me.

"So we're both from Earth, came here, and are living fairy tales," Peter said, trying to wrap his head around the idea.

"Looks like," I said, not sure if I believed it myself.

"What do characters do when they know they're in a fairy tale?"

"I have no idea. I guess they do what they need to do. Maybe an echo of this will go through the rabbit hole someday. Until then, I need to get back to that rabbit hole so I can get home. Peter, I need your help."

"For Alice of Wonderland, I could do a favor."

Peter led me to the center of the village. He pulled a carved wooden chair from beside the large fire pit, brushing aside crumbs. He leaned against the chair and let me sit.

"So, how do we get you back to Wonderland?" Peter asked.

"Well, for starters, they don't call it Wonderland anymore," I replied.

"What's it called now?"

"There is no name. Ace of Spades took over and refuses to call it Wonderland. He hasn't renamed it yet."

"Ooh, story time," said Greg as he and the other boys gathered around.

I wasn't sure how long the Lost Boys had been following Peter and I. I'd been so lost in our conversation I hadn't realized there were other people with us. Now that I realized I had an audience, I had to take a moment, and a deep breath, before I swallowed and continued.

"I arrived in Wonderland yesterday and found that Ace of Spades had removed all that was wonderful, and admittedly strange, about it," I explained. "He tried to kill me for refusing to rename it."

With each word I found myself speaking louder. My audience grew, and I spoke directly to attentive faces.

"The Mad Hatter rescued me," I continued. "And sent me here in his flying machine. He wants me to, um, wake the Sleeping Beauty."

The Lost Boys chuckled.

"That fairy tale real too?" Peter asked.

"I don't know. The Hatter just said I would find others who could help, and that I was to return to Wonderland with enough people to defeat Ace of Spades."

"Quite the fantastic story."

"I guess you could say that."

"So, Alice, you're not from Wonderland. Right?" Peter asked.

"No, I'm not."

"Then why do you care?"

"Excuse me?"

"Why do you care?"

"Because… because Wonderland is in danger," I answered. "The Hatter sent me here to get help. You have guns, you can fly. You can help."

"We're not exactly in a position to help."

"What's stopping you?"

"Hook."

"Hook," Jimmy said as the Lost Boys echoed the name.

Peter raised a hand and the Lost Boys quieted. "We've got our own troubles, Alice," he said. "As much as I'd love to help a fellow fairy tale, I can't leave Neverland."

"But the Hatter wouldn't have sent me here if you couldn't help," I said.

"He is mad." Peter shrugged. "You're not from Wonderland—it's not your fight."

"That doesn't matter."

"Where are you from?"

"Missouri."

"Why not call it Miseryland? That's the going rate on names these days. Wonderland, Neverland, not very original," Jimmy added.

"So go back to Missouri. Your story ended with you defeating the Queen of Hearts. Or you can stay with us. We always have a place for someone who knows how to use a shotgun," Peter said.

"I can't. I mean, I don't know how to get home," I said, suddenly realizing how trapped I was. "The rabbit hole, or, wormhole, is in Wonderland."

Peter was right, it wasn't my fight. It was the Hatter's, and those in Wonderland Ace was corrupting. But there was no way home outside of helping them.

I thought of the Mad Hatter, of his broken teapot he'd used as a weapon. He may have been mad, but he didn't deserve what fate awaited him. And now my fate was tied to his.

"How will I get home?" I whispered, shutting my mouth when I realized I'd said it out loud.

"Give me some fairy dust then," I said, clearing my throat. "Go get Tinkerbelle."

The Lost Boys laughed.

"What?" I said. "You can fly. I found my way here—I can just go backward and fly to Wonderland."

"Not an option," Peter said. "Tinkerbelle's gone."

"Well, go get her."

The Lost Boys stopped laughing.

"The first thing Hook did when he got here, after the crock'odial ripped off his hand," Peter explained, "was kidnap Tinkerbelle."

"'e's got 'er locked up in that ship of 'is," Jimmy added.

"Can't we rescue her?" I asked.

"Don't you think we've tried?" Peter asked, waving a hand at the vine-covered, unlit homes at the edge of the village.

I remembered the ship with the Gatling gun, the pirates with their rifles. This island was a lot more dangerous than the Neverland I'd read about.

I gulped, but thought of Wonderland. What was I more afraid of? Wonderland being destroyed? Or a murderous pirate? If I was really being honest with myself, I was most afraid of never making it back up the rabbit hole.

"If I can rescue Tinkerbelle," I began, "will you help me? Will you return with me to Wonderland and fight Ace of Spades?"

The Lost Boys laughed again. Peter didn't.

"If you can rescue Tinkerbelle," Peter said over the laugher, "we'll fight by your side. But not before."

When silence echoed his words, Peter glared at the Lost Boys.

"Tinkerbelle is the only reason we're here," Peter continued. "She taught us to fly—she brought us to Neverland. Don't forget that. Would you sit here and let her rot inside Hook's ship?"

The Lost Boys shook their heads and mumbled "no."

"Free Tinkerbelle, and we'll help you take back Wonderland," Peter said.

"Sounds good to me," I said and extended my hand.

"Hold on. We're not rushing into battle on your behalf. This is Hook we're dealing with. You have a plan?"

"Of course I do."

Of course I didn't. But a bluff would have to do for now. And hopefully I could make things up as I went.

Peter nodded, and shook my hand. His hand was warm. This was because he had spit in it.

"Welcome to the Lost Boys," Peter said.

This was still going to be difficult. But suddenly I was much less worried.

CHAPTER SEVEN

The first part of the plan, I told them, was to gather information. I couldn't make a good rescue plan with just a fly-over of where Tinkerbelle was being held. And my knowledge of Hook's ship from the Peter Pan fairy tale was completely useless.

There was a spot where Peter and the boys liked to spy on the pirates. Peter offered to carry me there. I didn't like being held like a bundled kid, and chose to hold him by his shoulders instead. This freed Peter's arms and turned me into a backpack instead of a child.

The wind stung my eyes as it rushed passed Peter's hair. He flew just above the trees, soaring down from his village to glide over the canopy.

I had my arms wrapped around his neck, doing my best not to choke him. Though he flew fast, I didn't feel like I was in any danger. He was sturdy and stable, cutting through the wind like a ship through water.

"Do you have to adjust for wind resistance?" I asked.

"What?" Peter replied as we descended through a valley.

High hills surrounded us on either side. The Lost Boys flew in formation around us, and our presence startled a grazing flock of antelopes.

"You don't move your arms like wings. And your feet don't make much of a tail."

"Greg wore a monkey tail for a while. It didn't help him fly. Fell off and landed on an Indian."

"Not that sort of tail, like a bird's tail. It's necessary to create lift and adjust altitude."

I was about to explain what little I knew about basic aerodynamics when Peter flew up and out of the valley. It was all I could do to hang on.

"What were you saying?" Peter asked.

"How are you moving?" I asked. "I always wondered how the magic works. You're like a rocket without the flames."

"Fairy dust and Neverland make an interesting combination. Why do you think we came here?"

"Fairy dust creates propulsion?"

"I haven't thought about how it works. I'm just happy it does."

"You really should try and discover how it works. You could modify or recreate it," I said.

"I already have it," Peter replied.

"What about your pistol? Do you just take it on faith that it works?"

"I know how a gun works."

"You can't just send bullets into the air with fairy dust?"

"Fairy dust needs a beating heart to work."

"Why's that?"

"Tinkerbelle says so."

"So what can be modified by fairy dust and what can't?" I asked.

"Just living things, not objects."

"But why?"

"That's for the fairies to decide. Just be happy they give us anything at all."

I grimaced at this thought. There had to be some logic behind Peter's flight. I kept looking at his feet to spot some sort of wake to indicate he had a method of propulsion.

Magic, it seemed, showed no sign of scientific reason. It was frustrating, yet made me joyful to know that something existed in this universe that was completely devoid of rational explanation.

As if Wonderland wasn't proof enough of that.

We soon reached a snaking river, dodging the spray where the water splashed over rocks and fallen logs. Peter flew low over the waterway 'til it widened. The sound of rushing water came from just past a turn, where the river fell in a sudden end.

We descended to the riverbank, and I hopped off Peter's back when I was close enough to the ground. The soil was moist. A lush smell like that of a plentiful garden came from all around, and I spotted a large cluster of berry bushes with only a handful of small trees.

"This way," Peter said as the Lost Boys, rifles shouldered, landed around us.

We pushed our way through the brush to the open air ahead. The ground tilted, and the soil felt loose. A few trees with exposed roots leaned over the eroded cliff edge. Here Peter pointed out a spot, hidden by rocks and trees, where we could stay hidden and look over the edge.

We were at one tip of a crescent-shaped beach. The cliff offered a tremendous view of the nearby waterfall, the rising mist making a rainbow where it struck the ocean below.

"You can see the ship from here," Peter said, pointing to the beach.

Even from this distance I could easily see the pirates' harbor. Wooden docks were built along green grass and golden sand, surrounded by high metal walls. Piles of timber and iron were littered everywhere. Fires blazed all along the water's edge, with men hammering away at anvils. A massive forge stood in the middle of the beach, pistons pounding red-hot iron and hissing steam.

At the center of all this activity was the black iron ship, its rivets and railings gilded brass. It was shaped like a huge fish, the brass linings making it look caged. Brass cannons protruded from its sides like blunted spikes surrounding two armored paddlewheels. Round turrets were locked forward at its bow while steam billowed from a smokestack just front of center. Pirates were busy polishing rails while a team manned the Gatling gun at the stern.

"They've got Tinkerbelle on that ship," Peter said.

"It's a weird ship," I admitted.

"You already saw how dangerous it is. So what's your plan for getting Tinkerbelle out?"

Well I'm stumped.

I refused to say that out loud, however. Instead I said, "What have you tried so far?"

The Lost Boys hunkered down behind the rocks and trees, frozen, their rifles at the ready. I heard Monster's faint whining as he hid in a blueberry bush.

"We've tried sneaking in, distracting them on another part of the island," Peter explained. "Derek once tried making a bomb. There were too many pirates and the bomb just bounced off the ship's armor. We tried a direct assault once. I won't be doing that again."

A steady stream of pirates came and went along the ship's gangplank. Some took raw materials of metal onboard. Some carried glowing raw materials off. A flurry of activity came from the mills and I soon saw what it was they were manufacturing.

"More guns," I said. "They're making more guns."

"And bigger ones," Peter nodded.

"I think you might want to just give up on Tinkerbelle," I said with a gulp.

"You said you had a plan."

"I do."

I didn't.

It's like a puzzle, Alice. A big, black, iron puzzle. The question is, how do we open it?

The beach was a fortress, pirates scurrying about like bees guarding honey.

"So we need a bear," I said, smiling.

"What do you need a bear for?" Peter asked. "To get the bees away from the honey."

"Hook killed all the bears in Neverland."

"It's a metaphor, not a real bear. More like a crocodile. Of course! The crocodile!" I laughed. "That's what happened in the story—that's what will work here!"

"Oi, quiet!" Jimmy said, pointing downward.

Peter shoved me against the rocks and placed a hand over my mouth so I wouldn't scream. I didn't appreciate that, but I reddened with the realization I had intended to.

Jimmy looked over the cliff and raised five fingers.

"Got it ready?" I heard a voice below.

"Just a minute," another replied.

"Stop dallying. Put it in—here we go."

I heard the sound of pistons and hissing. A cloud of steam rose through the rocks, along with the pounding of hammers. The pirates were operating a sort of jackhammer, mining into the side of the cliff.

I saw ripples in the waterfall as the jackhammer plunged into the rocks. It felt like an earthquake, and I suddenly found myself rattling across the ground. I reached for a stronger handhold and accidentally knocked over a stone that tumbled over the cliff's edge.

"What was that?" a pirate asked, the jackhammer stopping.

Peter glared at me.

"Up there—look!" another pirate shouted.

"Lost Boys! Lost Boys!"

Gunshots erupted and I couldn't keep myself from screaming, hugging the ground as the rocks exploded around me.

The Lost Boys returned fire, rifles aimed downward.

"Jimmy, take the Gregs to the river. We'll cover you," Peter said. He dashed into the air to fire his pistol, back to cover again an instant later.

It was all happening so fast I could hardly make sense of the movement and noise.

More gunfire came from the shore, and I saw activity on the ship. The turrets and Gatling gun were being turned in our direction as pirates assembled to battle stations. A small boat sped toward us, pirates on deck with rifles at the ready. The steam-powered speedboat spewed black smoke as its paddlewheel chewed through the water.

"Things are getting hot!" Jonny said.

Monster wailed and hid in Jo's hairy arms.

"Give some cover," Peter said, putting my father's shotgun into my hands.

I stared at the shotgun, hands trembling.

"Alice, we're pinned down," Peter said as he flew up and down.

And that's when I spotted the tree leaning over the edge of the cliff, a pile of rocks securing it to a tiny promontory.

I rolled away from Peter and slid to the tree. With one kick I removed the rocks. With another I kicked the tree loose. I didn't feel brave. I felt weak. I didn't want to use the gun, and the precariously positioned tree was the only other weapon in sight.

The tree fell over the eroded cliff in a shower of twigs and soil. It tumbled on top of the pirates, trapping them beneath branches and sap.

"Hah!" I cheered to the struggling pirates.

And that's when I saw him. Captain Hook, hair yellow as cornmeal. He wore a thick white mustache and a patchwork collection of clothes. Brass buttons shimmered on his multicolored jacket. His pants were a similar mishmash of color, and his boots were polished with silver buckles. He saw me. He stood on the fish-shaped ship's bow and pointed his brass hook just as the ground gave way beneath me.

The entire promontory disintegrated in a shower of rocks. I screamed and reached a hand out as I fell, finding hold in Peter's suddenly appearing hand. He grabbed me and pulled me into his arms.

A last volley from the Lost Boys sent the pirates in the approaching boat to cover, and Peter took to the sky. I looked down and saw the cliffs erupt in fire. The great guns of the fish-shaped ship were turning the cliffs into rubble.

We flew so fast I could barely breathe.

I kept my arms wrapped around Peter's waist as we soared over the treetops. With bullets whizzing over our heads, Peter and the boys dove through a narrow crevice. I felt the brush of granite against my elbows as Peter wove a snaking trail through the canyon. In a heartbeat we were through, and sailing over a plateau.

Trees ringed it, but the center was a flat clearing, with patches of black from what must have been a large fire. There was a mound in the middle of the clearing, and this was where Peter flew.

The Lost Boys formed a ring around the clearing, rifles at the ready, as Peter floated to the ground. He hovered there a moment, his eyes staring at mine, having saved my life twice in one day.

He dropped me on the ground.

"Oomph!" I said, landing on scorched grass.

"Are you happy?" Peter asked.

"What was that for?" I got to my feet and dusted myself off.

"Being a stupid girl and nearly getting us killed!"

Peter looked around as stragglers zoomed through the canyon and onto the burnt clearing. Peter made a count as Jimmy landed beside him.

"No cajooees, Petah. That was a tight one, that was, but we made it," Jimmy said.

"Casualties," Peter corrected.

"Is what I said. No cajooees."

"You have me to thank for that," I said, putting my fists on my hips, imitating Peter's go-to pose.

Peter made the same pose. He was much better at it.

"We have you to thank for starting it. Was that part of your plan, or were you just bumbling about?" Peter asked.

"I wasn't bumbling. I saved your life," I countered.

"And I saved yours twice."

"Oh, so we're keeping score are we?"

"I'm ahead by one. Serve to the girl with dirt on her dress." Peter made a motion like he was tossing an imaginary tennis ball.

I mimicked hitting it with an imaginary racket.

"That one went over the line," Peter said, looking at an imaginary tennis court.

"Ugh."

Despite the danger of what had happened, the boys seemed in a good mood. They were boys after all, and had survived a fight with an enemy and come out unscathed. They laughed like soldiers long overdue for a victory, even if it was a small one.

"I do have a plan, by the way. And I was just about to share it before Hook spotted us," I explained.

"And then you dropped a tree on them," Derek added.

"Yes, that."

"New weapon idea, Peter. Catapults of trees. Seems to be the only thing that works nowadays," Derek said with a smile.

The Lost Boys laughed at this suggestion.

"You get right on that, Derek," Peter said. He merely grinned while the Lost Boys laughed even louder.

"My plan isn't to drop trees on them," I said. "It's to drop the crocodile on them."

The Lost Boys stopped laughing.

"Come again?" Peter asked.

"I can't believe I didn't think of it in the first place. This is your fairy tale, Peter, and it ends with the crocodile eating Hook. So all we have to do is sick the croc on him."

"That's a fairy tale, Alice."

"So was my time in Wonderland, according to you. How did it end?"

"You woke up."

"After stomping around fifty feet tall in the Queen of Hearts' courtroom, right?"

"Yeah."

"That story is an echo of what happened," I explained. "Maybe the fairy tale of Peter Pan is an echo of this plan. Look, you brought that ticking clock out of your pocket and it scared the pirates to death. If you'd had time to use it back at the waterfall you'd have used it again—and it would have worked, right?"

"If the cliffs hadn't exploded, yes."

"So it's the one thing they're afraid of. That crocodile with the ticking clock in its belly can scare them to cover. It worked in the fairy tale, it worked with the clock, it can work here!"

"And then what?" Peter asked.

"Then you swoop in and rescue Tinkerbelle. Should be easy with all the pirates cowering in fear. Or with a crocodile eating them."

"I'm not sure you understand what you're suggesting."

"We can't capture the crock'odial," Jimmy exclaimed.

"It'd be suicide," agreed Jonny.

Monster whimpered.

"I didn't say we'd capture it," I countered. "We have it chase us. It's a little different than the fairy tale, sure, but we can fudge the details. Plus I don't remember Hook having a Gatling gun."

"That's it. She's a loony, this one. Let's pack it in and 'ope another girl comes crashin' on a doomed glider," Jimmy said.

The Lost Boys laughed and shook their heads.

"We have it chase us right up to Hook's ship," I continued.

The Lost Boys kept laughing.

"Don't tell me you boys can't outrun a wimpy old crocodile," I said, fists on hips.

The Lost Boys quieted.

"It's not a bad plan," Peter said, rubbing his stubble-laden chin. "But it's not a good plan, either."

"Oi Petah, that crock's mad. You can't trust it," Jimmy said.

"There's got to be a better way," added Jonny.

"We'll just wait the pirates out," said Craig.

"Wait them out," said Gregg.

"Wait," said Greg.

"Tiger Lily wanted to wait, too," Peter said, silencing all protest. "Look how that turned out."

Peter pointed to the mound at the center of the burnt clearing.

It was then that I noticed the other structures in the clearing. The burnt wood wasn't remains of trees, but charred tent posts. And the mound at the center wasn't a natural mound. It was marked with a hammered-in spear, a feathered headdress hanging from the haft.

"It's just a matter of time before Hook finds us too," Peter continued.

"You wouldn't have to fight them," I said. "You could just fly in and take Tinkerbelle without Hook noticing. They might just run away at the sight of the crocodile."

"I know I would," Jimmy said.

Monster whined in agreement.

"We're not going to take any risks. Everyone is going to fight," Peter said.

I hadn't noticed it, but Jimmy was holding my father's shotgun. Peter took it from the short lost boy and placed it in my hands.

"Everyone," Peter said.

"Thank you, Peter," I said, though my hands shook when I took the gun.

"Don't push it. You're sure this worked in my fairy tale?"

"Positive."

"Then arm up, Lost Boys. We're gonna rescue Tinkerbelle."

CHAPTER EIGHT

We flew from the burnt remains of the Indian village back to the Lost Boys' home. They assembled their arms with a steady concentration that seemed out of place for boys their age. These were not children playing at war. These were men barely into puberty who looked at a rifle the way a carpenter looked at a hammer. They were reluctant craftsmen preparing for work.

We shared a meal prepared in haste. Conversation was light.

It was Peter, once again, who found my gun for me, even when I tried to leave it behind.

"You won't last long if you don't know how to defend yourself," Peter said.

His hands were behind his back. I could see the butt of my father's shotgun behind him.

"I know how to get by," I replied.

Sparks flew where Jake sharpened his katana bayonet on a grindstone. Greg, Gregg and Craig loaded up with cross-belts of ammunition. Jonny admired the massive gun he carried. Jimmy did a check of each and every weapon, inspecting brass chambers for cracks and iron barrels for imperfections. Jo chased Monster to try and convince the animal it couldn't stay in the tree.

"Still," Peter said, "I thought the reason you kept leaving it behind was because it was so easy to lose, being bulky and all."

Peter took his hands from behind his back and revealed my father's shotgun. Only it was different. The barrel had been sawed off to the tip of its pump.

"I had Derek shorten it, make it more portable," Peter explained.

"Tell Derek I said thanks, but no thanks," I said, putting my hands behind my back. "We're using the crocodile as a distraction, remember?"

"Still. I'd hate to see, I mean… can't have any useless people in the group. Here, I'll show you."

Peter took my hand and placed it on the shotgun's action.

"Safety button on this is a little different than what I'm used to, but it's straight-forward enough," he explained. "Safety's here. Squeeze the trigger. You can load five shells so that's five shots before you need to reload. And remember, it'll kick like a mule and be a lot less accurate. But you can move it around more and have a wider shot."

Peter took my other hand and placed it on the pump. He stood behind me, showing me how to hold it.

"It's pump-action. You have to move the slider up and down after each shot. If you really get in trouble," he continued, "use the kick to help you pump. Make your motion back to an aiming position the same as your hand moving on the slider. And always—always find cover before you need to reload."

Peter took the gun out of my hands. He found a pocket in my trench coat of a jacket to place it in.

"Never hesitate," were Peter's final words of advice as he turned toward the boys. "All set?"

"Present and accounted for," Jimmy replied.

The Lost Boys assembled with their rifles shouldered. Some stood still as a seasoned soldier. Some did a last-minute check of their weapons. Some picked their nose. Monster tried to go back inside the tree, but leapt into Jo's arms in fear once he started to fly.

"Alright then."

Peter turned his head toward the sky. He motioned for me to hop onto his back. I did, and into the sky we went.

Twilight was settling over Neverland as we departed the tree village. A purple and pink sky dominated the horizon. Shafts of orange from the setting sun cast golden light on the glowing hills.

Peter dove through the massive tree's branches and zoomed once more over the treetops. He flew at a cautious pace, not wanting to stress the weapon-laden boys' flight.

"How long have you known where the crocodile lives?" I asked.

"We've always known," Peter replied through the wind.

"And you haven't gone after it?"

"Why would we? It's a monster."

"And Hook?"

"He'd never come close to that crock'odial. Ran away every time he saw it."

"I suppose that's what I'm counting on, isn't it?"

"I am, too."

Forest gave way to beach, and Peter dove across the surface of a blue-gold lagoon. Waters glistened and sand glowed. I saw clusters of red coral and a rainbow of fish. It was so breathtakingly beautiful I nearly sighed with delight, 'til I saw the skeleton lying on the beach.

I suppose I'd seen worse things than a skeleton in the last couple days. But it wasn't the bones that scared me. It was their shape. There was skull, arms, ribcage, and the bones of a fishtail attached at the sternum.

Peter landed in the sand not far from the skeleton.

"Mermaid," Peter said, tilting his head toward the bones. "Hook took them out first."

"Why would he kill a mermaid?" I asked as I stood on the beach.

"Why would he kidnap a fairy?"

"You have a question for every question I ask, don't you?"

"Neverland isn't about answers, Alice. It's not about endings. That's why it's got never at the front of it."

"Still. It can be annoying. It's supposed to be a magical place, a happy place."

"Like you said, we're fudging the details on the book." Peter drew his pistol. "Jimmy, Gregs, you're with us. Let's go."

Peter instructed the other Lost Boys to remain at the beach. They were to fan out in all directions once the crocodile began its chase. A Lost Boy would come in and distract the crocodile if it got too close, or divert its path if it veered away from Hook's ship.

The fortress harbor was perhaps two miles of beach distant. Each boy held rifle, pistol, or blunderbuss at the ready.

Peter approached a curved rock formation at the far end of the lagoon. It reminded me of a Roman archway, and led to a wave-echoing cavern. A spring-fed stream bubbled into the lagoon while gulls cackled from cracks in the ceiling. Shafts of light made misty pillars through the saltwater-eroded rock.

We splashed our way through the stream and into the cavern. There was a bend, the stream snaking its way through the stone. I thought we'd enter total darkness in a matter of moments, until we rounded another bend.

A single pillar of light lit the center of a dark chamber. I froze, listening to the stream as it diverted around a shallow mound of pebbles and seashells. Sitting on this mound was a nine foot tall, iron statue.

Peter put his hand on my shoulder to keep me still. The other boys hugged the wall.

"Is the crocodile in this room?" I asked.

Peter gave me the oddest look.

That's when I heard the ticking. *Tick-tock, tick-tock* in quick succession. Smoke and steam hissed out of the iron statue. I watched with eyes and mouth agape as the statue rose to its feet.

Gears cranked with effort to shift the statue's moving parts, and steam hissed with each groaning motion. Its limbs were big as cannons. Its arms moved like pistons on a train, turning at the joints to clench and unclench an iron fist.

At its center was a tremendous iron cylinder, brass rivets running up and down its sides like buttons on a great black suit. Its head resembled a medieval helm, rivets framing a narrow strip of thick glass.

I heard a deep intake of air like an inflating tire, and an outflow like the exhaust from a broken motor. The statue moved toward us, its body *tick tock*ing with every step.

Peter pulled me beside a boulder where Jimmy and the Gregs were already hiding. They held their weapons close, trying to swallow their fear.

"It's supposed to be a crocodile!" I said.

"It is. That's the crock'odial," Peter replied.

"That's not a crocodile—why do you call it a crocodile!"

"Because 'e's a crock o' dials, 'e is," Jimmy answered. "Look at all them dials and gears and whatnots on 'im. It's a crock!"

I took a peek at the creature. It did have a lot of dials, most of them on its back, along with a variety of pumps and gears.

"It's not a crocodile. It's an automaton," I said.

"I like crock'odial better," Jimmy replied.

"I wanted to call it a walking nightmare, but Jimmy kept calling it a crock'odial and the name just stuck," Peter explained.

The crock'odial, or automaton, took another step, and turned its back to us.

"Go away," I heard it say.

Its voice was like the gong of a massive church bell, resonant and metallic. Its words echoed through the cavern as the monster kneeled on the mound.

"Stick to the plan, boys. Alice, I think you'd better get back," Peter said.

"Oi, crock! Oi crock, look over 'ere!" Jimmy called, standing in the shallow spring. He drew his revolver and waved it like a bullfighter with a red flag.

"Crock!" shouted Greg.

"Hey, crock-crock!" shouted Gregg.

"Crockedy-crock! Hey, crocky!" shouted Craig.

The automaton shrank a bit as its arms wrapped around its body.

"Go, Alice!" Peter demanded.

"Crock!" Jimmy called, and threw a rock at the creature. It *clanged* against the automaton's iron shoulder.

More clangs came as the Gregs joined in throwing rocks.

"Crock! Crock, look over here!" shouted Greg.

"Crock! Get up! Get up and get over here!" Gregg demanded.

"Hey, rust bucket! Bet you can't catch me!" Craig challenged.

Jimmy started pounding a stone on the cavern walls and made so much noise I could barely hear the shouting. He continued to try and get the automaton's attention, or enrage it with more rocks.

The *tick-tock*ing as the creature stood drowned out the shouts and clangs of thrown rocks.

"Go Alice—now!" Peter shouted, grabbing me by the arm and trying to shove me out of the cavern.

The automaton took two quick steps toward us.

The Gregs screamed. They fled the cave like terrified bats. Jimmy flew as well, but kept hitting a rock against the cavern walls as he went.

"Alice, come on!" Peter said, hovering in the air. He grabbed my arm but I pulled loose.

The creature wasn't making a threatening motion. He was just stepping around the mound, putting the pile of seashells between him and the boys.

"Go away," the creature repeated.

"Alice, come on. Alice!" Peter insisted

"He's not chasing us," I replied.

"But he's about to—come on!"

I took a step out from behind the boulder. Smoke rose from where the automaton sat.

"Alice, if you don't," Peter began and grabbed me by the shoulder.

I twisted away. "Stop that! You're going to upset him."

"Upset him? It's a monster! Upsetting it is what we're here to do!"

"I've seen enough to know objects and creatures aren't always what they seem."

My feet made shallow splashes as I stepped through the spring. Seashells crackled with every step as I reached the mound.

Peter hovered beside me. His pistol was drawn and he remained close. But his eyes were wide and his finger was a too-quick breath away from shooting the smokestack in front of us.

My heart was pounding. I was glad Peter stayed close.

"Hello," I said. "Hello?" I peeked my head around the mound of seashells.

There, in the glow of the single shaft of light, sat the automaton. Its head was down, and it rocked itself back and forth on creaking hinges.

"I said go away," the walking nightmare repeated.

My hand shot up. Peter's hand was there. He took it, and I was glad he didn't fly away.

Peter kept his pistol trained on the automaton. His unflinching aim steeled my resolve. I did remove my hand from his, though.

"Are you... are you a person or a robot?" I asked.

It was a silly question. But my mind was still trying to understand how this creature functioned, or if it was a creature at all. It seemed all machine. But its voice was very much human.

"I'm neither," the automaton replied.

"That's not much of an answer."

"It's the right one."

"How can you be neither a person or a robot?" I asked.

"Do I look like a person?"

"A very… different person. But I've seen a grin without a cat and a baby that turned into a pig. There's room for all types of persons."

"Have you seen something like me?" the creature asked.

"I… no. That's why I'm asking. I'd like to know if you're an animal or a mineral, or something completely new."

"I'm neither and none."

"Alice, this isn't working," Peter insisted. "Let's go back to the tree and make a new plan."

"We're just talking," I said to Peter.

"What's your name?" I asked the automaton.

"I don't have one," the automaton replied. It turned its head to speak to the wall. "Names are for real boys. So I don't have a name."

"My name is Alice. This is Peter. Say hello, Peter."

Peter kept his pistol aimed at the crock'odial's dials.

"Peter says hello," I offered.

The creature didn't reply. He stood and turned around to face us, his gears *tick-tock*ing.

"I don't want to talk to you," he said.

The creature took a step toward us, shaking the ground and creating a wave of seashells.

This time I did take a step back. Peter put himself between the monster and I.

"That was rude!" I scolded.

I'm sure Peter would have grabbed me and flown away, and I probably would have let him, had the automaton not said, "I'm sorry."

"You scared me." I shrugged out of Peter's grasp and stepped closer to the iron creature.

"I want you to go away. I don't want to talk to you," said the automaton.

"And why is that?" I asked.

"Because."

"Now, now, there's no need to be rude again. I've seen creatures more frightening than you act with more respect. And I've done nothing to hurt you. Well, maybe Peter has. He and his friends did call you mean names. Apologize, Peter."

"What?" Peter asked.

"Apologize for insulting him," I insisted.

"No."

"Apologize to… I'm sorry, it's hard for Peter to apologize if we don't know your name."

"Pinocchio," the automaton replied.

My eyes bulged. "Pinocchio?"

"Yes."

"You can't be Pinocchio," I said.

"I know. I'm not real," Pinocchio replied.

"No, I mean, I know who you are. I've heard of you."

"You have?"

"You're in a fairy tale."

"Is it a good fairy tale?"

"Yes, yes it is. It ends with you becoming a real boy."

"A real boy?"

"But you're a puppet in the fairy tale. You're not a puppet are you?"

"No," Pinocchio answered.

"Curioser and curioser," I said, my mind racing with the fantasy before me.

Peter chuckled.

Peter's laughter snapped me back into the moment.

"Apologize to Pinocchio, Peter," I said.

"For what?" Peter asked.

"For calling him a crock'odial when his name is Pinocchio."

"I didn't know that was his name."

"That doesn't matter. I wouldn't want to be called crock'odial. My name is Alice."

"Sorry I didn't know what your name was, Pinocchio."

"See? Just a simple miscommunication," I said.

"Miscommunication that we have another fairy tale in Neverland?" Peter asked.

"The fairy tale we know must be an echo of this boy. If you knew he was Pinocchio, you might have become friends with him a long time ago."

"He ripped Hook's hand off. Didn't want to risk waiting around asking names and lose my hand too."

"It's not my name. It shouldn't be. Not anymore," said Pinocchio.

"There's no use talking here, Alice. He's not going to chase us. And listening to him pout isn't getting Tinkerbelle rescued any faster." Peter floated back toward the cavern entrance. He did not, however, lower his pistol. "Plus I don't remember Pinocchio and Alice ever joining forces."

"And I never heard of Alice joining Peter Pan, so we'll make this our own fairy tale," I said.

This time I held Peter still.

"He's not a fairy tale, he's a boy in an iron suit," Peter said.

"I wouldn't mind being in a fairy tale, so long as it ends with me becoming a real boy," Pinocchio intruded.

"Why don't you want to use your name, Pinocchio?" I asked.

"Because that's a real boy's name. And I'm not a real boy."

"You're a boy… inside there, right?"

Pinocchio inhaled through the expanding mechanisms deep inside the dials and gears. He exhaled through the valves and clanking switches.

"I'm inside here. But I'm not a real boy," Pinocchio said.

"What do you mean?" I asked.

"Do I look like a real boy?"

"You look like a boy in a costume. A very large, well-made costume. Like a big black knight or a walking tank."

"That's what a real boy looks like." Pinocchio pointed at Peter. "He and the others. I don't look like that."

"What? Peter? Look at those clothes. He looks like a cartoon soldier if you ask me."

"What's wrong with my clothes?" Peter asked.

"Oh shush, you look as ridiculous as the other Lost Boys," I said.

"I like my clothes. They're comfortable."

"I'm sure they are. And I'm sure Jake thinks his robe is comfortable and the Gregs think their rags are comfortable too. Point is, none of them look alike, Pinocchio. You're just wearing different clothes."

"If Peter takes his shirt off he won't die. If I take my clothes off, I will," Pinocchio replied with a burst of steam.

"I don't know," I said, grinning. "Let's prove it. Peter, take off your shirt."

"You're mad, Alice," Peter replied.

"I already knew that."

Pinocchio made a strange sound. It was like a marble clattering down a pipe.

"Was that laughter?" I asked.

"No," Pinocchio replied.

"I think you laughed. Peter, take off your shirt right now. Pinocchio thinks it's funny."

"Take off yours," Peter countered. He immediately turned a bright shade of red.

Pinocchio made the clattering, laughing sound again.

"There. You're a real boy after all. Real boys laugh," I said.

"I'm not a real boy," Pinocchio insisted. "If I were a real boy I wouldn't be here."

"And how's that?"

"Father says I have to stay here. Father says I have to stay in the suit. Father says if I don't I'll die. Real boys don't have to do that."

"Peter, can Tinkerbelle's fairy dust help with Pinocchio's problem?"

"Tinkerbelle fixes wounds every now and then, when we get hurt," Peter answered. "What's wrong with you?"

It was the first time Peter had addressed Pinocchio directly. I smiled.

"Everything. Nothing works. Only this," Pinocchio said, moving his great iron arm. "I'm not real under this. Just broken."

"I don't know if Tink can help," Peter said.

"But there's a chance," I insisted.

Peter shrugged.

"Pinocchio, did you rip Captain Hook's hand off?" I asked.

Pinocchio hung his head.

"Did you not do that?" I asked.

Pinocchio shook his head.

"So you did rip his hand off," I said.

Pinocchio's head creaked as he bobbed it up and down.

"Were you mad at him?" I asked.

"I didn't mean to," Pinocchio replied.

"Pinocchio, do you know Hook has been trying to hunt down and murder Peter and his friends?"

"He shouldn't do that."

"No, he shouldn't. He needs big boys like you to stand up to him."

"I didn't stand up to him. I got mad."

"We're all mad here," I said.

"I don't want to be mad," said Pinocchio.

"Still, I'd like to ask you a favor, Pinocchio."

"Alice, no," Peter said.

"Why not? It's the same plan. Except if Pinocchio willingly helps us we don't have to worry about getting ourselves hurt."

"I don't like you talking about me like that," Pinocchio said.

"Sorry. Peter's just nervous. He thought you were something you're not. Hook still thinks you're something you're not. And Hook has Tinkerbelle. Pinocchio, would you be willing to help us stop Captain Hook from hurting Peter and his friends, and in the process free Tinkerbelle?"

"Can she make me into a real boy?"

"Maybe. But she's not going to help anyone locked up in Hook's ship. What do you think, Peter? Is he a new Lost Boy?"

I could see the gears churning in Peter's mind. He bit his lip, and holstered his pistol.

"If you're a kid in Neverland, then you're a Lost Boy," Peter said. "And you're under my protection." Peter spat in his hand and extended it to Pinocchio.

Pinocchio didn't move.

"Are Lost Boys real boys?" Pinocchio asked.

"Lost Boys are just Lost Boys. And all you have to do to become one is shake Peter's hand," I said.

Pinocchio looked at Peter's hand. He looked at his own iron hand.

A flow of steam came out of Pinocchio's exhaust pipe and soaked his metal fingers. Peter didn't flinch a moment, and exchanged a spit-covered handshake with the iron boy.

"Welcome to the Lost Boys, Pinocchio," Peter Pan said. "Ready to have some fun?"

"Yeah," Pinocchio said.

"Good. Because I have an idea. It's nothing like your fairy tale, but I'm pretty sure it'll work."

CHAPTER NINE

The first thing the Lost Boys did when they saw Pinocchio was fly away.

I warned Pinocchio this would probably happen, since they were still under the impression that this was the plan.

"Plan's changed, boys, come down," Peter shouted.

We splashed our way out of the cavern and to the edge of the lagoon. Stars twinkled in the night sky and the crescent moon cast golden reflections on the glistening waters. The Lost Boys were nearly invisible in the dark, though I could just make out their shapes as they flew before the curtain of stars.

"Peter watch out!" shouted Derek.

"It's right behind you!" shouted Jonny.

The Lost Boys readied their guns and flew toward Peter to protect him from what they thought was a monster.

"Put your weapons down!" Peter commanded.

"He's not going to hurt you!" I added.

I put my arm around Pinocchio's massive iron hand, partially to comfort him and partially to ensure he didn't run away. I doubted I could have stopped him, but his ticking slowed down.

"Petah, ya crazy? The crock'odial's right there!" Jimmy said.

"He's not a crock'odial, he's a Lost Boy," Peter said. He looked at Pinocchio, and saw that I was holding his hand. There must have been a smidge of fear left in Peter, but seeing me standing so close to the iron boy appeared to strengthen his resolve. He rested a hand on Pinocchio's forearm. "Get down here already, Jimmy."

"What's going on, Peter? You get control of the thing?" Jonny asked.

"He's not a thing."

"His name is Pinocchio," I said.

"Like the fairy tale?" Jimmy asked.

"Yes."

"That's crazy, that is!"

"I've seen crazier. Believe me. Now, say hello, Pinocchio," I said.

The Lost Boys still hovered a distance away. They'd lowered their weapons, but weren't in a hurry to come any closer.

"Go on," I said.

"He... hello," Pinocchio said. His voice bellowed through the lagoon, sending some of the boys flying backwards.

"Pinocchio is going to help us rescue Tinkerbelle," Peter said.

Jimmy was the first Lost Boy to land beside us. He looked at Pinocchio with a cocked head. "You're a lost boy?" he asked.

"He is," Peter said.

"And you're a fairy tale?"

"Alice says you are too," Pinocchio replied.

"Am I now?" Jimmy looked at Pinocchio's iron body. He tapped on the broken child's round stomach, making a gong-like sound. "Heh. Neat." He *rat-a-tat-tat*ted against Pinocchio's side.

"Stop that, Jimmy," said Peter.

"Ya sound pretty solid, ya do. Might make quite the music when ya get 'it by bullets."

"I've been shot at before," Pinocchio said, sounding embarrassed. "It went like this." Pinocchio banged his fist against his chest, making a clanging sound like he was ringing the Liberty Bell.

The Lost Boys laughed. All at once they came closer, encircling Pinocchio to tap on his iron body.

"Are you really bulletproof?" Derek asked, poking at the dials on Pinocchio's back.

"Yes," Pinocchio replied.

"Cool! I wish I was bulletproof," said Greg.

"Are you under there?" Gregg asked, tapping on Pinocchio's helm.

"This is a fake body. I'm inside it," Pinocchio answered.

"Whoa! Can I wear it?" Craig asked. "Only for a bit—I'll give it back."

"I can't take it off."

"Why not?" asked Derek.

"Because it's keeping me alive."

"Too bad. It'd be fun to be bulletproof. Hey—are you really strong? You look really strong," said Craig.

"Go pick up that boulder!" said Greg.

"Why?" Pinocchio asked.

"Because it'd be awesome!"

"I don't want to."

"We're plannin' on attacking Hook, Pinoke. Might be good to take a look-see at what you can do," Jimmy said.

Pinocchio glanced at Peter and me. Peter shrugged.

"Can you pick up the boulder?" I asked.

Pinocchio walked toward the boulder that lay not far from the mermaid skeleton. Steam hissed out of his elbow joints as he put his arms around the massive rock. Pinocchio picked up the boulder like he was picking up a beach ball, then hurled it over our heads and into the lagoon. It made a tremendous splash and the Lost Boys cheered.

"Do it again!" Greg insisted.

"Let's find more stuff for him to break!" said Jonny.

"Hold it!" Peter said before the Lost Boys could search for other large objects to play with. "That's very impressive, Pinocchio."

Pinocchio turned away and shrank back on his heels.

"That's where you say thank you," Jimmy advised.

"Thank you," Pinocchio said.

"You're welcome," Peter replied. "The plan hasn't changed, boys. We're still going after Tinkerbelle. Except this time, we're working with the crock, er, Pinocchio. Sorry, still getting used to that name."

Pinocchio shrank back again.

"You gonna forgive 'im?" Jimmy asked.

"He said sorry," Pinocchio answered.

"So tell 'im all's well."

"That's okay, Peter. I forgive you."

"Good on ya, Pinoke."

"We're working with Pinocchio now," Peter continued.

"Yeah, and he can throw boulders at Hook!" Greg said.

"So Pinocchio is going to throw boulders at Hook while we watch?" Jonny asked.

"Even a boulder that size wouldn't puncture the armor on Hook's ship," Derek noted.

"Still, would be cool."

"Do I need to throw rocks at people?" Pinocchio asked.

"Only at Hook and the pirates," Peter answered. "And only if you have the chance. You're not going to just throw rocks at the ship—that wouldn't accomplish anything."

"Except being cool," Greg grumbled.

"Pinocchio will go after Hook, just like before. They're still afraid of him. And if they fire on him he'll be fine."

"I don't want to be shot at," Pinocchio said.

"You just got done saying bullets don't 'arm ya, Pinoke," Jimmy said.

"Yeah."

"Remember what we're going for. We're rescuing Tinkerbelle," Peter continued. "Pinocchio moves in, scares them to cover, we come around the other side and get Tinkerbelle out of there. If things get thick—and only if things get thick—we start shooting. I'll lead the attack on the ship. Pinocchio, I want you to draw their fire as much as you can. Alice, stay as far away as you can and we'll…"

"I want Alice to come with me."

"No, Pinocchio. Alice needs to stay out of the fight."

"Yeah, that's not happening," I said.

"There's not going to be any trees to drop on people, Alice."

I reddened a bit. Did I want to get into a gunfight? Definitely not. But Pinocchio was already shaking with worry. If I was going to rescue this fairy and get back to Wonderland, I needed to at least pretend I was brave.

"I have Pinocchio to throw trees," I said.

Peter glared at me.

I glared right back.

"I'll go with 'em," Jimmy offered.

Peter kept glaring at me.

"You need to keep the boys on the attack, Petah. And someone's gotta keep Pinoke on 'is toes," Jimmy continued.

Peter thought a moment, then nodded.

"My boots don't have toes," Pinocchio said.

"Well you let me know when you get off the flats o'your feet then."

"How will I do that?"

"Just give us a whistle." Jimmy let out a shrill whistle. "And I'll come bring you back upright, I will. You know 'ow to whistle don't ya?"

The gears on Pinocchio's body went *tick-tock* a moment. Steam burst out his backside and made a sound like the whistle of a freight train.

The Lost Boys burst into laughter.

"Alright. While we still have moonlight. Let's go, Lost Boys!" Peter said and took to the air.

Peter Pan led the formation of flying, armed boys across the night sky. Jimmy stayed behind with Pinocchio and me.

"What do we do?" Pinocchio asked.

"We go for a walk is what we do," Jimmy answered.

Before Pinocchio could take a *tick-tock*ing step, Peter Pan landed in front of us. He said nothing, but approached me. I froze as he grabbed me by the shoulders and reached into the pocket of my great coat. He took out the sawed-off shotgun and placed it in my hands.

He said nothing more, only paused a moment with his hand over mine, forcing me to grip the gun's action. Peter drew his pistol and rocketed back into the sky.

I watched him fly away. When he was out of sight, I put the gun back in my pocket.

"Hook's ship is this way, right?" I asked.

"That's the way," Jimmy replied.

"You're going to stay with me, right Alice? Right, Jimmy?" Pinocchio asked.

Jimmy drew his massive revolver. "Give us a whistle, Pinoke."

Pinocchio whistled his steaming whistle.

"There ya go then," Jimmy said with a nod. "Let's 'ave us a walk."

CHAPTER TEN

We walked along the beach with the whites of the shallow-breaking waves to guide our path. After a mile or so, Pinocchio asked why I kept my gun pocketed. I told him it was because I didn't want to use it and hoped he'd leave it at that. He kept asking, though, and I confessed I'd shot a man the previous day.

"It makes you scared?" Pinocchio asked.

"Yes," I answered.

"But how could you be scared?"

"What do you mean?"

"I don't believe you could be scared."

"I'm scared," I said.

"Oh." Pinocchio continued in silence for a few steps.

"It's okay to be scared. You just can't let it keep you from doing what you need to do," I said.

Pinocchio thought about this in silence for awhile.

"Why are you scared?" he finally asked.

"Lots of reasons," I replied.

"I'm scared that Tinkerbelle won't be able to make me a real boy."

"And I'm scared that I won't be able to go home."

"Why can't you go home?" Pinocchio asked.

"Because a man named Ace of Spades is hurting my friends," I answered.

"I wouldn't like it if my friends got hurt."

"I don't like it, either."

"So how are you going to stop him?"

"Peter agreed that once we rescue Tinkerbelle, he'll help me get back to Wonderland and fight Ace of Spades. I guess we both have a reason to be concerned over the results of this battle."

Pinocchio was silent again, his iron feet making ponds in the sand.

"You don't have to be scared, Alice," he finally said.

"Thank you," I replied.

"'specially with me around to look after the two a ya," Jimmy added. "'old up. Hook's ship is just 'round the bend."

We reached a cleft of rock at the tip of the crescent-shaped harbor. I spotted the lights of Hook's forges still burning, their smoke obscuring the stars.

"I'm scared," Pinocchio said.

"It's just a short walk now, it is," Jimmy said. "You stroll right up to them pirates and don't say nothin.' And if any of 'em gives you grief, just give us a whistle and Jimmy'll take care of 'em."

"I'll be here too, Pinocchio," I said.

Pinocchio nodded. He took two deep, clanking inhalations, and stepped around the bend.

Water splashed against Pinocchio's stomping, iron feet as he entered the sandy harbor. *Tick-tock*, his steps went, the sound echoing against the rocks.

Jimmy and I stayed behind and watched in silence.

There was a pirate standing watch from a tower set at the edge of the harbor. I could barely see his moonlit silhouette. He leaned against the tower walls with a rifle resting on his shoulder. At the sound of the *tick-tock, tick-tock,* the pirate jumped so high he banged his head on the little bell hanging from his tower. An instant later he was clanging the bell, shouting, "He's here! He's here!"

The pirate watched Pinocchio approach, stomp-stomping and *tick-tock*ing his way up the beach. I saw the pirate shoulder his rifle, the barrel shaking, before bells rang out all over the harbor. The pirate jumped out of the tower before Pinocchio could take another step. He hit the beach at a run, racing across the sand toward the iron wall that surrounded the wooden dock.

There was a flash of sparks, and I thought they were firing rockets at us. But these weren't weapons. The light came from bright magnesium, sparkling against polished steel mirrors. The pirates at the walls and ship turned these spotlights on Pinocchio and lit the beach.

Pinocchio staggered in the sparkling light, raising an iron arm to shield his eyes.

Jimmy and I saw this as an opportunity to move closer. We stayed in the shadows and ran to cover behind the vacated watchtower.

"You can do it, Pinocchio!" I said.

"Just need to go a little further, Pinoke," Jimmy encouraged. "Petah and the others are ready to go."

Exhaust flared from Pinocchio's steaming engines as he renewed his efforts. He walked toward the iron harbor walls as the pirates fled their posts. At the wall, Pinocchio stopped. He turned back to us.

"You gonna let a little wall stop you?" Jimmy asked.

Pinocchio turned back to the wall. His gears churned and clanked as he pulled his arm back like the cocked hammer of a gun. Pinocchio punched the wall and it flew into the harbor, crashing through the boardwalk to splash into the water.

The pirates screamed with fright to see their barricade destroyed so easily. One was on his hands and knees, backing away from the *tick-tock*ing monstrosity. In a panic, the pirate grabbed his rifle and fired.

Bullets sparked as they hit Pinocchio. Pinocchio stopped, shocked by the sound, but otherwise unharmed.

More pirates guarding the dock opened fire. Once the gunfire began, every man who saw Pinocchio rumble toward them blasted away with panicked futility.

Jimmy and I had gotten to the wall by then, and stayed out of sight. We were close enough that when Captain Hook came to the bow of his ironclad ship, we could see the hideous scorn on his face.

"Stop firing! You there, stop!" Captain Hook shouted.

Hook shouldered a gilded brass rifle and fired. The pirate he hit went down. Pinocchio stepped back.

There was little Hook could do to stop the gunfire. The pirates were more afraid of the *tick-tocking* Pinocchio than they were of Hook's indiscriminate executions. Those pinned against the walls fired as they tried to flee the harbor. Hook's ship was soon swarming with pirates, their bullets clanging off Pinocchio's body as they sought to reach the safety of the ironclad hull.

Pinocchio reached the edge of the harbor, docks with smaller boats between him and Hook's vessel. It was here that the pirates finally resorted to the Gatling gun.

Where before there had been a peppering of gunshots, now a river flowed. Sparks erupted all along Pinocchio's body as he tried to step through the whirlwind of bullets. He screamed, stumbling backward.

"He's not moving," I said.

"Give 'im a moment," Jimmy said.

"Tinkerbelle, Pinocchio! Remember Tinkerbelle!"

"Lost Boys! Lost Boys!" came a shout from the walls. "Lost Boys!"

I looked up to see muzzle flairs as Peter Pan and the Lost Boys dove out of the night sky. They flew like a formation of fighter planes and opened fire on the Gatling gun, soaring through the ship's rigging on a fast strike. The pirates were taken off-guard and had no time to return fire before the Lost Boys were once more a safe distance away, darting through the sky and firing on the walls and ship.

"Pan!" Hook roared. "Shoot Pan!" He tossed aside the bloodied Gatling gun crew and turned the massive weapon skyward.

Some of the pirates jumped overboard, fleeing for their lives. Some were emboldened, knowing how to face this familiar enemy.

"Keep going, Pinocchio!" Jimmy and I encouraged.

Now that only a few shots bounced off his iron skin, Pinocchio shook his dented head and resumed his *tick-tock*ing approach.

Hook now had firm command of his men, ducking and firing into the air to fight the buzzing Lost Boys. He ordered a new crew to take hold of the Gatling gun and directed the ship's lights skyward. The spotlights moved about the night sky like a city under an air raid.

Hook tossed blunderbusses to a four man team. They ran down the gangplank toward Pinocchio. One of them dropped his blunderbuss and jumped into the water, terrified. The other three stood firm and fired.

Instead of bullets, the blunderbusses fired nets, lead weights holding them down. The nets fell upon Pinocchio and entangled his body. He took a step, stumbling.

Bullets continued to spark against Pinocchio's iron skin, and now the brass cannons on the ironclad ship were firing. Explosions splashed across the harbor, and Pinocchio fell to his knees under a wave of water. And then I heard Pinocchio's train-like whistle over the echoing cannon fire.

"Stay 'ere, dovey," Jimmy said to me as he flew into the harbor.

I wanted to run after Jimmy, but I didn't know how I could help.

Jimmy opened fire with his massive revolver. He struck one of the blunderbuss-wielding pirates and then the next. He flew fast and close enough to pistol-whip the third, knocking the pirate into the water.

The Lost Boy dropped his weapon and drew a knife, cutting the nets tangling Pinocchio's legs.

"Give us a good tug, Pinoke," Jimmy said as he undid one of the nets.

"I'm trying," Pinocchio said.

The nets had gotten into his joints. Smoke billowed from the suit's exhaust as Pinocchio strained to escape.

With one last cut, Pinocchio was able to stand and snap the remaining nets.

In that moment there was a single gunshot, and Jimmy fell.

"Jimmy!" Pinocchio shouted and looked at the ironclad's deck.

Captain Hook stood looking down at Pinocchio, taking aim with his rifle to fire at Jimmy a second time.

Pinocchio stood between the gunshot and the downed lost boy. Hook fired, the bullet bouncing off Pinocchio's iron skin.

"Hook!" Pinocchio shouted and ran up the docks.

Four more pirates came with blunderbusses. The boy charged them, swiping the pirates into the water with an iron fist.

By this time I was so terrified for Jimmy that I ran to the boy's side. It was dark where he laid, the pirates' focus now on the charging Pinocchio.

"Jimmy," I said, kneeling at the boy's side.

"Tinkerbelle," Jimmy said. "Gotta get Tink, dovey."

The gangplank had been withdrawn, so Pinocchio ripped the dock apart. He swung it like a club, knocking back pirates at the black ship's rails, and turned the dock into an improvised gangplank. Pinocchio climbed over shattered wooden boards and leapt his way onto the ironclad.

"I'll get Tinkerbelle," I promised Jimmy. "Just stay put."

I ran after Pinocchio, watching the pirates flee the deck. The Gatling gun crew remained on the ship, however, firing into the sky. Hook remained as well. He stood alone, unflinching, as Pinocchio charged.

Just before he steam-rolled through the captain, Pinocchio stopped, inches from the brass-hooked man.

As I climbed the improvised gangplank I heard the boy say, "Hello, father."

"Pinocchio!" Hook shouted. "What have you done?"

"I need Tinkerbelle."

"Why do you think I took her in the first place?"

"I need her now. You shot Jimmy!"

"The Fairy with Turquoise Hair is for your use alone, boy."

"Where is she?"

Gunfire blasted into the sky as the Lost Boys fought the dug-in pirates.

"Stop shooting my friends!" Pinocchio shouted, raising a fist. He didn't strike Captain Hook, however, and Hook didn't flinch.

"What have they done to you, boy?" Hook asked.

"Captain Geppetto!" the Gatling gun crew shouted at Hook.

The pirates prepared to aim the massive weapon at Pinocchio, but the captain raised his brass hook to stop them. The crew understood the motion and returned to chasing after Lost Boys.

"They're my friends and I'm here to help them," Pinocchio insisted.

Captain Geppetto brought his hook down on a valve at Pinocchio's neck. Steam hissed out of a tube now dangling useless at Pinocchio's side. Pinocchio screamed and tried to step away, but Hook pulled out a pipe at Pinocchio's waist. The boy slumped to his knees, steam and oil leaking onto the ship's black deck.

"Everything I do is to protect you, son," Hook insisted.

"I don't want you to protect me—I want to save my friends!" Pinocchio said.

My hands shook with fury as I watched Pinocchio sink further onto the deck.

Pinocchio screamed in pain as Hook released another valve.

Without thinking, my hand went to the gun in my pocket.

"What corruption have they done to you, Pinocchio? No matter. All can be fixed," Geppetto said and raised his brass hook.

"Hey, Hook! How is a raven like a writing desk?" I said and fired my shotgun.

Hook fell to the deck.

"Captain Geppetto!" a Gatling gun crewman said and turned the massive weapon toward me.

I pumped my shotgun and fired at the Gatling gun. The crew went to cover behind their weapon and I fired again and again, using the recoil to aid my pumping of the shells, just like Peter taught me. When the gun clicked empty, I ducked behind Pinocchio.

I twisted shut the valves Hook had opened. I reattached the tube dangling at Pinocchio's side.

Pinocchio shot to his feet as I connected the final pipe. The innards of his engine burned red hot and sparks flew out of his exhaust.

The Gatling gun crew saw there was no more need to remain under cover, and rose to aim their great weapon. Pinocchio screamed the scream of an enraged child as the Gatling gun opened fire. The hailstorm of bullets didn't hurt him in the slightest, and he charged. With one swipe of his arm he sent the gun's crew flying into the harbor.

Once the danger was cleared, Pinocchio turned his attention to the rest of the ship. Beneath the iron armor were the cannons and dozens of pirates firing into the air.

Pinocchio cupped his hands and brought them down on the deck. He made a tremendous *clang*, and Pinocchio shuddered with the blow. It took one more solid punch, but Pinocchio broke through the hull.

I heard screams of pirates as the boy rampaged through the ship.

There was a crew of pirates still on the harbor walls. I saw Jake, his katana-tipped gun glistening with the searchlights' reflection, dive into the ocean for cover and come up again. Several other Lost Boys performed a similar maneuver, but couldn't shake the pirates.

I ignored the screams below deck and ran to the Gatling gun.

"Let's see. Horizontal adjuster, vertical position," I said, aiming the gun. "It looks like this loads it." I picked up the boxes of ammunition and stacked them on top of the vertical feeder. "And crank to fire."

I turned the crank and let loose with the Gatling gun. The pirates on the walls either fell to the barrage or quickly abandoned their positions.

It was hard operating the machine alone, but I managed to lock its aim and sweep its barrels across the harbor. The pirates had no cover from this direction, so they fled, fell or were picked off when they tried to return fire, the Lost Boys rallying.

I'd run out of ammunition in moments and returned to the wooden box to reload.

Peter Pan swept through the rigging. He hovered just above me, and raised his pistol to shoot into the mast, where a pirate fell from the crow's nest.

"You okay?" Peter asked.

"Yes," I replied. "Jimmy's hit. We need Tinkerbelle."

"She's probably below deck."

"Peter!" Derek said, sweeping to a hover beside Peter Pan. "Jake and Willy have the pirates in the harbor surrounded and surrendered. No shots from the ship."

"Mop up and make sure the pirates drop their weapons. We'll get Tinkerbelle," Peter commanded.

I heard a scream as a pirate flew out of the deck. He splashed into the water, swimming beside dozens of other pirates. They instantly surrendered to the Lost Boys flying above them.

A moment later, Pinocchio leapt out of the same hole and landed with a *clang* onto the deck. He held in his hands a glowing blue object.

I assumed it was an object, something like a neon light, or a crystal that reflected the moonlight.

"Tink!" Peter Pan said and flew to Pinocchio.

Pinocchio laid the object on the deck, where it staggered to its feet.

"Little boy Pan. You've grown up some," the fairy said.

CHAPTER ELEVEN

O nly then could I tell she was a fairy, as she unfurled her blue, butterfly-shaped wings. Her face looked like it belonged on a golden coin. She stood a head taller than Peter, and smiled down at him. Her turquoise hair moved like it was underwater, and her wings fluttered where she stood.

Every inch of her glowed blue. Her skin was the blue of a robin's egg, her eyes like blue lights on a Christmas tree.

"I only grew up a little. I had to," Peter insisted.

"Such a tragedy," said the Fairy with Turquoise Hair.

Greg and Gregg flew onto the deck with Jimmy held in a stretcher. A shirtless Craig flew behind them, his shirt used to make the stretcher.

"Awful big a' you to let me bloody your shirt, it is," Jimmy said as Greg and Gregg set him down before the fairy. "'ello, Tink."

Jimmy sucked in a breath of pain.

"Hello, Jimmy. You're hurt," said Tinkerbelle.

"Can you heal him?" Pinocchio asked, letting out an involuntary whistle.

More Lost Boys were brought to the fairy on makeshift gurneys.

"Your heart still beats, dear Jimmy," Tinkerbelle said with a smile.

"That it does, Tink," Jimmy said.

Tinkerbelle's wings cast a blue light on Jimmy's wound. The bullet hole was just above his chest, an inch from his heart. Blood soaked his body up and down. Jimmy was pale.

Tinkerbelle cupped her hand over the wound. The light from her body coalesced around her fingers and turned into a mound of glowing blue dust. She tilted her hand and let the fairy dust fall onto the wound.

The dust transformed into glowing blue skin. The bullet rose out of Jimmy's chest and plopped onto the deck. Dust turned to flesh and mended together. An instant later, the glow dimmed. Had he not been covered in blood, I wouldn't have been able to tell Jimmy had been shot.

Tinkerbelle did the same with the other Lost Boys. Some had broken bones, some gunshot wounds. Some had shrapnel all over their bodies.

"No losses, Peter," Derek said. "We flew fast and careful, just like you said."

"And the pirates?" Peter asked.

"Thirty captured. Twenty or so fled into the island. Eighteen lost, including Hook."

"I see that." Peter Pan looked at Captain Hook's ruined corpse. "Shotgun, it looks like."

Peter looked at me.

I looked right back, shotgun in hand.

"Can you heal him?" Pinocchio asked Tinkerbelle.

"His heart has stopped," Tinkerbelle answered. "I cannot help Captain Geppetto."

Pinocchio looked down at Hook. He knelt, hands reaching as if to pick up the body. I turned away, not wanting to see the mangled corpse fall apart. Pinocchio let it be.

"He truly did want the best for you, Pinocchio," said the fairy.

Pinocchio punched downward. I screamed a little, thinking he'd struck Hook's body. But Pinocchio had only struck Geppetto's hook, smashing it into a mound of brass.

"Hook was your father?" Peter asked.

"I heard the pirates call him Geppetto," I said. "But how can that be?"

"That was the name of Pinocchio's father in the fairy tale, right?"

"Yes, but, but it didn't end like this."

"We're fudging the details, remember?"

"The stories you've read in your world are not always true," Tinkerbelle explained. "In truth, Geppetto was a father who grieved so much for his dying son he would do anything to save him. Even if that meant killing those he saw as a danger."

"I'm sorry, Pinocchio," I said.

Pinocchio turned away from me. "My father's gone," he said.

I was certain he was crying, but it was impossible to see.

"Yes," Tinkerbelle answered.

"He was… he was…" Pinocchio stuttered. His voice was like a broken clock grinding its gears.

"He cared only about saving you, thus he was blind to the pain he inflicted on others. And the pain he inflicted on you." Tinkerbelle rested a glowing hand on Pinocchio's shoulder.

"Can you make me a real boy?" Pinocchio asked.

"What do you mean?"

"Heal me. Heal me like you did Jimmy and the others. My heart's still beating—you can heal me so I can take off this suit and be a real boy."

"My magic requires a happy thought, dear Pinocchio."

"It's true," Derek said.

"Pudding," Craig added.

"Christmas," Gregg said.

"A room full of sprinkles you can swim in," Greg said.

The Lost Boys looked at Greg.

"What? I can have any happy thought I want," Greg insisted.

"And a happy thought comes only from a beating heart," Tinkerbelle said. She laid her hand on Pinocchio's cylindrical, iron chest. "Your heart does not beat on its own."

"But it's beating. I can think happy thoughts—just let me!" Pinocchio pleaded.

"Can't you try?" I asked.

"There is iron between my magic and him," Tinkerbelle answered.

"So we can jury-rig the thing to keep his heart pumping. You don't need much time—we can open the suit and you can pour in the fairy dust."

"Magic does not work that way. Even if you could accomplish such a thing—and I would not dare risk it, you would need to fully detach him. He would last mere moments without the suit's mechanisms."

"That makes no sense," I said.

"Magic does not blend with technology. And my magic does not work beyond death. To blur the lines of either is a path I will not tread."

"But how will I become a real boy?" Pinocchio asked.

"Dear Pinocchio, you are a real boy. Underneath that iron suit, you are a real boy," Tinkerbelle said with a sage smile.

"But if I take off the suit, I'll die."

"That is what real boys do."

Pinocchio fell to his knees before Tinkerbelle, his collapsing body ringing against the iron deck.

"Come on, Tink, there's got to be something you can do," Peter said.

"I wish I could," Tinkerbelle said. "But I will tell you the same thing I told Geppetto, as he tortured me for a cure. Pinocchio's artificial condition is beyond the reach of magic. Geppetto refused to accept his child for who he was, even to the point of corrupting nature to change him."

Tears fell down my face. This wasn't how Pinocchio's fairy tale was supposed to end. This was all wrong! I didn't know if he'd throw me off the ship, but I didn't care. I wrapped my arms around Pinocchio's massive, iron body.

"You are a real boy," I said. "A real, brave boy."

Pinocchio shoved me away. He put his hand to a valve at his neck and stood erect. His hand trembled at the valve a moment, and I didn't know if he was going to hit us or make his engines explode.

The boy looked down at me.

"Alice, I'll help you fight Ace of Spades," Pinocchio said, taking his hand off the valve.

"You will?" I asked.

"But you have to promise me. After we've taken you home, help me take off the suit."

"Pinocchio..."

"Promise me!"

"I promise."

"No one ages in Neverland," Tinkerbelle noted. "This is a magic far greater than mine. I do not know how long you will survive outside its influence."

"This is my choice. I don't care if I rust or if Alice takes me apart," Pinocchio said. "I choose to help my friends. You are my friends aren't you?"

"Of course we are, Pinocchio," I said and hugged the boy.

"You're a Lost Boy. That makes you my friend to the end of time," Peter said.

And then all the Lost Boys were on him, Derek, Jonny, Willy, Jo and the Gregs. Even Monster flew at Pinocchio's face and licked his iron helmet.

"Chin up, Pinoke, this means you got what you wanted. You're a real boy!" Jimmy said. "Bit of a let-down, but be careful what you wish for and all. It's an irony, it is. Not exactly a fairy tale ending, but 'ope it doesn't dampen your spirits much."

"I feel better now," Pinocchio said. He stood proud, taller. Where before he had moved stiff and awkward, now he bent to a knee and pet Monster, his hand stroking the dog's fur.

It's amazing the look a person can have when they take control of their situation. Before, Pinocchio was a helpless, desperate child clinging to the hope of becoming real. Now he knew exactly who he was. Even if that meant death, at least he was making the choice for himself.

Still, I looked at the boy who was Pinocchio. He wasn't a puppet. His father was evil. And he would never become a real boy, not in the way he wanted at least. It was much, much worse than the fairy tale I knew.

"What troubles you, Alice of Wonderland?" Tinkerbelle asked.

I tried to smile, but had to turn away. "It's just… different than the fairy tale," I answered.

"What do you know of Pinocchio?"

I hesitated, not sure if Tinkerbelle would understand. "Where I'm from…"

"Earth. I have visited there."

"Really?"

"That is where I met Peter Pan. I brought him through the rabbit hole long ago, along with the rest of the Lost Boys. So many echoes travel through the rabbit hole, it is the one part of Wonderland where my magic still functions. And I allowed my curiosity to overcome me."

"London was awful, it was," Jimmy noted.

"When I traveled beyond London, I met Geppetto. He begged me to bring him and his son to Neverland, to save him. Out of compassion, I relented. Out of experience, I shall never do this again."

"I'm sorry. In the fairy tale, Geppetto builds a puppet named Pinocchio that comes to life. It ends with Pinocchio becoming a real boy, and they live happily ever after," I noted.

"The fairy tales you hear in your world are echoes of this one."

"So I've been told."

"In reality, Pinocchio is a sick boy in a mechanical suit, and in the fairy tale a puppet who gets eaten by a great fish. In reality, Alice is a girl from the twenty-first century United States, and in the fairy tale she is a young girl from Victorian England who learns about a Jabberwocky."

"Jabberwocky? I've never heard of a Jabberwocky," I said.

"You see? The stories are echoes, not truth. Though there is some truth in them," Tinkerbelle explained.

"I don't understand how all this works. I mean, a wormhole connecting two worlds together makes sense, I suppose. But how do the stories? How is magic real?"

"The universe is near-infinite, is it not?" Tinkerbelle asked.

"I guess."

"And in the infinitesimal vastness that is the universe, is it not probable there exists at least one place where magic is real?"

I lowered my head, embarrassed I had never considered this.

"Your world and ours are connected. We share similar languages, cultures, ideas. Echoes of both worlds leak into the other through the unstable, ever-moving rabbit hole," Tinkerbelle continued.

"So why do so few know about Wonderland, I mean, this planet?" I asked.

"Because the White Rabbit and I are the only ones to brave the journey. None wish to be trapped with the rabbit hole moving behind us. My magic, and the device the Mad Hatter created to help stabilize the rabbit hole, make it easier. But your world terrifies us, and we would rather it remain an echo, and you remain thinking us part of your imagination."

"But we could help each other. Work together!"

Tinkerbelle shook her head. "One day the rabbit hole may stabilize. One day it may disappear entirely. To cross over too much would mean the possibility of destruction for both worlds. These echoes should be treasured, because it is all we can be sure of in our communication between the two worlds."

"People should be able to see this," I said.

"They can see it. Some just choose not to," Tinkerbelle explained.

"I could make them. I could bring help from my world."

Tinkerbelle raised a hand in warning. "We will help you take back Wonderland, Alice. But I will not allow you to blur the lines between my world and yours. I have broken that barrier too many times already. I will not allow you to further that mistake."

"But… can I go home?"

"If you so choose. But once Wonderland and the rabbit hole are secure, I will ensure no traveler, intentional or otherwise, crosses the rabbit hole again. Henceforth, it shall be closed to all but echoes."

I looked to Peter. He frowned at me. My hand reached up, and I had to force it to my side. I wanted to feel some assurance, but wouldn't allow myself to reach for Peter's hand. He must have seen this, and patted my shoulder with a callused hand.

"You did your part, Alice. Now I'll do mine," Peter said. "If you want to go home, that's where I'll take you. I'll return to Wonderland with you and fight Ace of Spades."

"Ace's power grows stronger. You do not have the strength to face him," Tinkerbelle advised. "You must wake the Sleeping Beauty."

"That's what the Mad Hatter said. What is it? Is it the fairy tale?" I asked.

"You will discover that yourself."

"That's annoying. Why can't you just tell us?"

"You may not believe me. Suffice it to say, the Sleeping Beauty is not the tale you know."

"So, we're not going to Wonderland?" Peter asked.

"Is there another rabbit hole? Another way home?" I asked.

Tinkerbelle shook her head and said, "The Sleeping Beauty is Wonderland's greatest hope."

"Where will I find it?"

"I shall set a course for the Grimm Kingdom."

"You can't be serious," I said.

"What is the matter?" Tinkerbelle asked.

"Grimm. As in the Brothers Grimm?"

Tinkerbelle smiled. "The rabbit hole flows both ways, Alice. Even echoes of your world inspire this one. And if you are to face Ace of Spades, you must face your own disbelief. There is much yet for this world to teach you."

CHAPTER TWELVE

Water splashed against the ironclad. The ship rose and fell with the cresting of a wave. The armored paddlewheels on either side churned as they drove us forward, the spout-shaped smokestack sending a black cloud into the sky.

It turned out Captain Geppetto's ship was named the *Terrible Dogfish*. None of the Lost Boys thought this was a good name, and I agreed. But the name was spelt in riveted brass letters on the fish-shaped stern.

To save time, we renamed the ship the *Terrible Dog*fish *Monster*. Pinocchio punched a line through the brass letters for 'fish' and scratched the word 'Monster' into the iron. The Lost Boys thought this was a spectacular name, both because it was easily changed and everyone agreed that Monster was a terrible dog.

Monster took the insult in stride, and seemed happy to have a ship named after him.

It had taken most of the night to get the *Terrible Dog Monster* (or the *Terrible Dog*, for short) ready for sailing. First we had to decide what to do with the pirates. We had them bury those who'd fallen in the battle, and then asked what should be done with the rest.

Most insisted that they had not wanted to fight the Lost Boys, that they were just pirates and mercenaries hired by Captain Hook. They admitted their guilt, but no more the guilt of a common lawless man, and begged for mercy.

It was true that Hook had been the source of all the crime, and you couldn't really blame pirates for being pirates. So we agreed that if the remaining pirates who'd fled into the island joined them at the harbor, we would let them go.

The pirates agreed, and before the last grave had been dug, they were loaded onto the smaller steamboats and ready to depart. Where they went, I'll never know. Probably to whatever corner of the world Geppetto had found them. All we made sure of was that they would never return to Neverland, and that they toss their weapons into the sea. This done, they departed, unarmed but alive.

Pinocchio asked permission to find a spot for Geppetto, to bury him alone. I was convinced he went to his little cavern, beside the bones of the mermaids. It would make an honorable tomb, one I wasn't sure the pirate deserved. But none of us wanted to deny Pinocchio a resting place for his father.

After the pirates, and their captain, had been taken care of, everyone gathered around for a Lost Boy Feast.

I had never heard of a Lost Boy Feast. Craig said it was a time-honored tradition that went back centuries. Jimmy said they'd made it up on the spot. Still, I enjoyed the dancing around cook fires made from dismantled forges, sausages scrounged from the pirates' stores, cooked 'til they were dripping, and fruits of such variety I thought half of them must have been made with magic.

It was a thoroughly festive event, and we feasted and sang 'til we could no longer stand.

The next morning, we prepped the ship, loaded supplies, and set off. Pinocchio made this process much quicker, heaving massive loads of coal and ammunition onto the ship. Some of the coal was for his own use, and he made sure to keep his internal fuel well-stocked.

We had enjoyed our night of fun, but as the sun rose, all realized that we were sailing to war.

Sometime in the early afternoon, after we'd been sailing for several hours, I was standing on the ship's bow, feeling the wind in my hair and the salty spray on my face. The ship crested another wave and splashed forward.

There was normally no need for rigging on the steam-powered vessel, but the *Terrible Dog* had sails to ease the strain on the engine when wind could be harnessed. Such conditions existed today, and the sails bristled to full, adding speed to the churning paddlewheels.

I held onto the rigging just where it tied to the pointed bow. The ropes creaked as water sprayed from the rise and fall of the bow, making a slippery hand-hold.

The wooden planks laid on the iron deck were also slippery, which was why I lost my footing with a sudden tilt. My arms held onto the rigging and I laughed with the straining excitement. But there was no need for this thrill, as Peter had raced to my rescue, holding me up as he floated to the deck.

"The sea's getting choppy. You should go below," Peter insisted. He floated a few inches off the deck so the rolling ship wouldn't set him off balance.

"I'm fine right here, thank you," I insisted, mocking him with my hands on my hips.

Just then the ship plowed through a wave and sent a wall of water onto my head. I kept my balance, but was soaked. Peter dashed into the upper rigging to avoid the wave, and laughed at me.

"See?" I said, spitting out seawater. "Perfectly fine."

"You missed a spot," Peter said, pointing down at me.

"Where?"

The wind and waves had made a bowl of one of the foresails. Peter upended this canvas container onto my head and soaked me through again.

He laughed as he floated to the deck.

"Ha-ha," I said. "Now I know why they call you Peter Pan. They should call you Peter Bowl since you can find bowls of water so easy."

"That doesn't make sense," Peter said.

"I know. I was looking for a better comeback, but my access to seawater is more limited than yours."

"Try again."

"You'll just fly away if I try and get you."

"Consider it a challenge."

"Who's piloting the ship, anyway?"

"Derek has command," Peter said, pointing to the bridge.

The bridge was beneath the raised platform where the Gatling gun sat. Narrow windows, similar to those on Pinocchio's helmet, provided a view on all sides. Derek waved from behind the window.

"I need to keep him from fiddling with the engines," Peter added.

Derek steered the sheep like he'd been doing it for years, and I could feel we were moving faster than ever. He didn't try to avoid the waves, however, and our course became choppier. Even though he floated above the deck, Peter had to hold onto the rigging to keep from drifting away.

"Gregg and Craig are seasick. So is Jonny. Half the boys are tossing about like ping pong balls below deck," Peter said. "The only ones who seem to be enjoying themselves are you and Monster."

The dog barked up and down the ship's stern. He floated free of his leash with yelping excitement, biting at the splashing waves. His fear of heights must have gone away when he was bouncing over the ocean, though he made sure not to fly too high.

Jo was having a much worse time, leaning over the railing and spilling his guts. Between belches I heard him call Monster's name while waving an empty leash.

"If I didn't know better, I'd say Monster knows this is his ship," I said.

Monster barked and then I was sure he knew.

"Why are you just standing there?" Peter asked as another wave sprayed against my side. "Why not fly?"

"We're on a ship. It's what you're supposed to do on a ship," I said.

"Not if you can fly and avoid getting wet."

"Why would I not want to get wet?"

"You... wouldn't get wet?"

I pulled my chin up over a rope and held on as the *Terrible Dog* rose and fell, water licking my toes.

"But you'd miss out on all the fun," I said.

Peter continued to float up and away from the waves, rising and falling with the ship's motions.

It was possible we could have flown the entire way to the Grimm Kingdom. But Tinkerbelle wanted to make sure we had the right directions. The course wasn't like 'second star to the right and straight on 'til morning.' It needed maps and latitudes, all of which she charted into the ship's instruments. Plus Pinocchio couldn't fly, and he would be useful in the fight against Ace.

Tinkerbelle had to stay behind. She said her magic was tied to Neverland, and she wouldn't survive long outside its reach. Only the rabbit hole had a similar amount of power, with its constant flow of echoes. She promised she would come when the rabbit hole was secure, but not earlier. When she did, she vowed to make me the last person to journey between our two worlds.

Before we left, Tinkerbelle warned us that Ace was reaching beyond Wonderland. Other nations had tried to fight him, and were conquered. No safe place remained, and we needed to unite anyone who was still resisting with the Grimm Kingdom to have any chance against Ace.

This terrified me, but I had Peter and Pinocchio and the Lost Boys. That made me feel better.

The Fairy with Turquoise Hair wished us well, and claimed she'd watch over the island while Peter was gone. Peter insisted he'd return.

"You're just saying that because you're not very good at flying," Peter said.

"I am not. And I'm not that bad," I insisted.

"You're not that good either. You need practice. You remember how to do it? Think of your happy thought, and then…"

"I remember."

Peter had approached me late in the previous evening's festivities. The fires were going strong and the Lost Boys were dancing, though some were telling stories of their bravery in the battle against Hook.

"Alice," Peter began, "would you like to learn to fly?"

The feasting came to an abrupt halt and the Lost Boys stared at us. They smiled, some with food falling out of their mouths.

"I think I would like that very much," I said. After all, who doesn't wish they could fly? "It's the fairy dust, right?"

"It is a little more complicated than that," Tinkerbelle said, rising from her place beside the fire. Her blue wings glistened in the firelight.

Pinocchio had been dancing with Jimmy, but they stopped to watch. "Can I fly, too?" Pinocchio asked. He took a few *tick-tock*ing steps toward the fairy.

Jimmy tugged on Pinocchio's iron arm and shook his head.

"Can't I fly?" Pinocchio asked.

"Dear Pinocchio. I truly am sorry," Tinkerbelle said. "Were it in my power to grant even this little joy I would do it in a heartbeat. But the barrier to my magic is as it was before."

Pinocchio sat down.

"Chin up, Pinoke," Jimmy said. "You can leap heads and tails over all ones not flyin.' Toss boulders and walk through fire too. Why, I'd sprinkle myself in pixie dust to do 'alf the things you do, that I would."

"Thanks, Jimmy," Pinocchio said.

"You can try and sprinkle fairy dust on him at least," I offered.

Tinkerbelle shook her head.

"It's okay. I'll be happy just watching you fly," said Pinocchio.

"That's a good sport," Jimmy said. "'ow's about we become ground buddies you and I? I walk beside you and you aside me."

"Okay."

"And if we ever get in a spot, you just toss old Jimmy at who's ever comin' at us. We'd make a rocket of a pair, you and I, and we wouldn't get that without your special powers, no sir. Course I'd need a 'elmet like yours, I would."

Jimmy knocked on Pinocchio's iron helmet. The child laughed.

"Oh, but this will not do," Tinkerbelle said, examining my tattered Easter dress. "You will not want to fly downward while a lost boy stands below, Alice."

"Why not?" Jimmy asked.

I couldn't help but laugh.

"It gives me great joy to offer you something I am rarely able to provide, Alice of Wonderland," Tinkerbelle said and guided me to another part of the beach.

The unneeded loot and material from the ship had been piled next to the remains of the broken, iron walls. Barrels of wine, chains, crates full of silverware and the bones of exotic mammals killed on Neverland were stacked on top of one another, set aside until they could be disposed of. Piled with this loot was a round-top chest. Tinkerbelle smiled as she opened the chest, her shimmering blue wings casting a glow on the cloth inside.

Tinkerbelle removed a silk, red dress with a black bodice and lace sleeves. She held it in front of me.

"No, no, this will not do either," Tinkerbelle said.

I sighed with relief. That dress looked too tight.

"How about this?" Tinkerbelle asked, pressing a green riding dress against my shoulders.

The riding dress had a divided skirt and was beautiful, but I spotted an outfit in the chest that made me smile.

Blue pants with a white belt. A form-fitting blue top with white across the bodice. They were the same bright blue as my Easter dress, and had accenting white fringes. They were made of a light material, but sturdy, and reminded me of Peter's camouflage fatigues.

I held up the outfit and said, "This one."

"Practical, yet beautiful. Stunning, if worn on the correct person," Tinkerbelle said with approval.

"I don't need it to be pretty."

"True enough, Alice."

There were pockets in the pants where I could stow my shotgun shells. I found a white leather holster that attached to the back of the blue top and easily fit my sawed-off shotgun.

"I'm keeping my shoes, though. I like my purple shoes," I said.

"Of course." Tinkerbelle laughed.

I changed out of my Easter dress in an alcove set in the broken walls. When I returned to the feast, none of the Lost Boys seemed to notice my new appearance. None except Peter.

"Took ya long enough. You gonna fly or what?" Jimmy asked.

"I had to get ready," I challenged, brushing my blue pants smooth.

"Better for flying," Peter said, smiling as he saw me.

"Thanks."

The glow of the fire reflected off Peter's eyes as he scanned my new appearance up and down. There was more than just approval in his eyes.

"Are you ready, Alice?" Tinkerbelle asked, breaking my and Peter's gaze.

"I suppose," I answered.

I wondered if it was possible to be ready to fly. I wondered if it was possible to *not* be ready to fly. It seemed perfectly reasonable that every human being was born ready to fly. If anything, every second of life was anticipation for the moment you could learn.

"It's easy. And it doesn't hurt," Peter said.

I suppose my thoughts on the nature of flight made him assume I was concerned, but my focus was locked on Tinkerbelle, and I was eager to see the process through.

"All you have to do is think a happy thought," Tinkerbelle explained. She flapped her blue butterfly wings. The wings gave off puffs of sparkling dust, which she collected in the palm of her hand. "Just one wonderful thought."

I froze, my whole body warming with anticipation. I could feel my face redden as Tinkerbelle poured the fairy dust over me and said, "Think of a happy thought."

That had been the previous night.

The *Terrible Dog* continued its rolling course over the sea. I was soaked from the waves and my hair was billowing in the wind.

Peter looked down at me, and I looked up at him, as my feet rose from the glistening deck.

"Not so hard, is it?" Peter asked as I flew to his level. "You got your happy thought?"

"I think so," I replied.

"You think so?"

"Flying is… odd."

"You get used to it. Here, let me show you."

Peter took me by the hand and tugged me into the rigging. I wobbled, uncertain in the air, but allowed him to pull me along. All it took was holding onto that happy thought and I would stay airborne.

"Turns and dives come with practice," Peter said, continuing the lesson.

"I wish there was more science to it. Might be easier to learn if it made sense. I thought it had something to do with bending matter or something but…"

"Like Tink said, science and magic don't blend."

"I know. But I'd prefer if there was logic behind it."

"Don't think with logic. Think with your feelings. Feel your way through the air. Use your instincts and your happy thought to guide you. Think too hard and you'll fall out of the sky."

Peter let go and I hovered near the crow's nest. The ship splashed against a wave and shook, frightening me so much I grabbed hold of the mast. Peter steadied and encouraged me.

"Good, good," he said. "Now, let's try a dive. Watch."

Peter dove to the deck. He did a handstand and bounded back up.

"Showoff," I said.

"Now you try."

"Do I have to do a handstand?"

Peter laughed. "Just go down, touch the deck, and come back. I'll watch you."

I licked my lips. The deck was a long way down.

"Remember, let your emotions guide you," Peter said. "And keep hold of that happy thought."

I looked at Peter and nodded. Then I let go of the mast.

I screamed as I fell. It was falling, not flying, but I grabbed hold of my happy thought. I felt lighter, my mind in control of my emotions, and I urged my body to a slow descent. I reached the deck and touched it with my finger, thinking I would use the deck as a springboard, but chose instead to ascend on my ability alone.

The happy thought was what fueled my rise and fall. To descend meant I needed to relax my emotions, dampen the happy thought. To ascend required a burning intensity of emotions tossed onto the fire of my happy thought that split the air and overcame gravity.

I shot up and passed Peter like an out of control rocket, screaming and flying too fast. Peter was there to catch me, but I recovered, barely. My hands trembled as I gripped the mast.

"Not bad," Peter said as we descended together. "You probably fly better when you're not soaking wet, though. See why you should fly and not stand on the rocking boat?"

"I do," I said, my feet resting on the deck, my hand holding me steady against the rigging.

"Good."

Peter's feet were still just above the deck. That's why when the ship struck a massive wave, rising and diving into a valley-deep break in the sea, he merely flew to a safer height. I, however, tumbled across the rolling ship.

I let go of the rigging and flew upward, straight over the side.

"Alice!" Peter shouted as I hit the water.

Before Peter could dive in after me, I rose out of the waves with my arms cupping a bowl-full of water. I flew above Peter and dumped the water on his head.

"Hah!" I said, floating to the deck, laughing. "Wouldn't want you to miss out on the full ocean-going experience, Peter Pan. Or should I say, Peter Swam!"

Peter wiped the saltwater out of his eyes. "You're terrible at puns," he said.

"I know."

"But you're decent at flying."

I'm sure he or I were about to say something else, but just then Derek shouted from the bridge, "Land-ho!"

CHAPTER THIRTEEN

Grimm. That's what they called it. Tinkerbelle said its name came from an echo of my world, those fairy tale authors the brothers Grimm. Did that mean this was the echo that inspired their tales? Would I meet more fairy tales here? Which ones? I tried to hide my excitement, my fear, and dispel my disbelief as Tinkerbelle had instructed.

Tinkerbelle had advised us that the Grimm Kingdom was under naval lockdown. Bringing a warship like the *Terrible Dog* to the capital was not a good idea. So we avoided the river that led to the glistening city of Grimm, and landed at a remote beach.

"I want to go with you," Pinocchio said when Peter and I prepared to fly ashore.

"You'll swamp a lifeboat," Peter said. "And you're too heavy to fly."

Pinocchio nodded. Then he took a running leap off the bow. We weren't far from the beach, but it was still a considerable distance. Pinocchio's steam-spewing leap brought him only a few yards from the shore, where he landed in the shallows with a huge splash.

"I guess he's coming," I said. "It'll be good for protection."

"You're in charge while I'm gone, Jimmy," Peter said. "Fly over and check in with me on the hour. Stay sharp and hidden. We'll return when we've found our army, and our way to Wonderland."

"Count on me, Petah. Ship'll be right good when you get back," Jimmy said. He waved at Pinocchio. "You take care of 'em, Pinoke!"

Pinocchio waved at Jimmy and sounded off with a jovial whistle.

And so Pinocchio, Peter Pan, and I walked upon the sandy shores of the Grimm Kingdom. A forest grew at the edge of the beach, and beyond that a series of hills and low mountains rose skyward. Just beyond these, glistening in the sun, were the peaks of tall buildings. This was the city of Grimm, our destination.

"Can people fly in Grimm?" I asked as we entered the forest.

"Tinkerbelle says her magic is the only kind that lets people fly on their own, but she doesn't like to share it with everyone."

"That's too bad. Good for us, though. I'm just glad flying works outside Neverland."

"As long as you're on the same planet as Neverland, you can fly. So Tink says," Peter answered.

"Good reason to never leave this planet."

"My thoughts exactly. Tink also said Grimm has flying carpets, but the whole kingdom is on lockdown. Curfew, port inspections, laws against public indecency and a bunch of other stuff."

"The rulers must be very strict," I said.

"One ruler: Queen Charming," Peter said.

"That's odd."

"Are there any fairy tales about a Queen Charming?"

"Not that I recall. Do you know any?" I asked.

"None," Peter replied.

"Her name's kind of ironic if she's got the kingdom on lockdown."

"Let's hope she's charming when it comes to negotiating foreign policy. But we're coming as diplomats asking for war. Can't just fly through someone's window and say 'Hey, would you mind helping me invade Wonderland?'"

"It would get an answer quicker," I noted.

"And the answer would be no. That or we might get shot out of the sky before we made it past the walls. Best to go through proper channels. Tinkerbelle said we need to check with the Queen's Grand Seer to get an audience."

"And all the time the Hatter and the caterpillar are under Ace's rule."

"Rushing into things would only mean they'd never be saved."

I slapped at a low tree branch. "Time is not on our side."

"Is Ace so bad?" Pinocchio asked.

The question caught me off-guard. "Of course he is," I replied. "He's taking the wonder out of people."

"Oh. I don't know what that means."

"You weren't there when Tinkerbelle told the story," Peter said.

Pinocchio had been burying his father, and we were still cleaning up the debris from the battle, when I'd asked Tinkerbelle how Ace had come to power.

"I know not the full tale," Tinkerbelle had answered, standing on the ironclad with Peter and I beside her. "But I am told that Ace witnessed a child from another world, a child whose existence revolved around reason and logic, where magic did not exist, and where creatures aspired to nothing more than survival."

"That was me," I said.

"I suppose it was. Ace researched your world, and found it wholly different than his own. He obsessed with the perfection of it."

"Perfection?"

"Your world, from an outside perspective, operates under a sense of order."

"But people hurt each other. There's suffering," I countered.

"Suffering is immaterial. Sense is tantamount, to the mind of Ace of Spades," Tinkerbelle continued. "He lived in a world that made no sense, could not accept it, and sought to impose his own definition of sense. The first thing he did was remove his own wonder."

"How does that work?" Peter Pan had asked.

"The exact method, I do not know. But I am told it is a great awakening of knowledge. A life's worth of information compressed into the mind in moments."

"You lose your wonder by learning things? That doesn't make sense," I said.

"You lose your wonder, because when this information is so forcefully imparted, it creates its own rigidity. There is only the information provided. The ability to question, the mere thought that there exists knowledge outside of what is imparted, the ability to wonder, is destroyed. The mind cannot handle such forcefully-imposed data, and it has no choice but to surrender or be destroyed. Doubt, curiosity, questioning, these are lost in the wave of unbreakable logic."

"With his wonder gone," Tinkerbelle continued, "Ace solidified his belief. And with his position as a card, he executed the King of Hearts."

"How?" I asked.

"When you are surrounded by silliness, manipulation comes easily. Leadership in Wonderland was always a weak thing, with creatures that really did not need to be led. All Ace had to do was add rigidity to a system that already existed. He framed the King of Hearts for painting the Queen of Hearts' roses red. When she declared 'off with his head,' Ace simply complied."

I remembered that it was the King of Hearts who subdued the Queen's ridiculous sentences. I shuddered at the thought of the Queen of Hearts' rage being left unchecked.

"The Queen was always open to manipulation, and Ace married her to make himself King," Tinkerbelle continued. "He put the Cheshire Cat on trial, then, for crimes committed against the throne."

"I heard the Cheshire Cat was killed. How did that happen?" I asked.

"Ace cut off its head, just as he did the King of Hearts. He declared the Cheshire Cat a rebel, and all those who aligned themselves with the cat to be rebellious against Wonderland itself. Then, declaring all those who possessed magic like that of the Cheshire Cat criminals, he set the Queen loose."

"That wouldn't be good," Peter said.

"No. She declared everything she saw as worthy of execution. And Ace complied. But instead of killing, he offered pardon to those who elected to have their wonder removed. From there it was simply a matter of time. And when the Queen became more of a hindrance than a help, Ace removed her wonder as well."

"*And now he wants to take away the wonder from the rest of Wonderland,*" I said.

"*No, Alice,*" Tinkerbelle said. "*It has taken Ace years to manipulate and solidify the system of rule in Wonderland. It has taken as many years for him to send out his agents to the far corners of the world. He sees this world, not just Wonderland, as possessing a sickness. He wants to remove the wonder from this world, and his machinations are growing.*"

"So you see," I told Pinocchio, "Ace wants to change people. And he'll kill anyone who refuses to change."

"He's mad," Peter said.

"I wish. If he were mad, we might be able to find a weakness. But I think Ace is completely sure of what he's doing."

"But… what he's doing is evil. Right?" Pinocchio asked.

"Of course," I said.

"How can he be sure of something evil?"

"He's sure he's right," Peter answered. "If he kills people who disagree, no matter what he believes, he's wrong."

"Is that what evil means?" Pinocchio asked.

"There's lots of definitions of evil."

"But we're good. Right?"

"We're trying to be," I said.

Pinocchio's *tick-tock*ing, heavy steps heralded our way through the forest. Peter found a path that led to a gravel road. This made the going much easier, and with such a well-kept road I was certain it led to the city of Grimm.

Rays of light broke through the trees and lit the path with morning warmth, birds chirping through the calm.

"Besides it being a way home," Peter began, "what does Wonderland mean to you?"

"Excuse me?" I replied.

"It's called Wonderland. Doesn't that mean it's wonderful?" Pinocchio offered.

"At times."

"So why do you want to save it so badly?" Peter asked.

"Well, it's a nice place. Silly, but nice. And now it's anything but silly," I answered.

"Saving the silliness of a place is worth risking your life?"

"It's more than that. Ace of Spades is taking the wonder out of people, remember?"

"Again, worth risking your life?"

"You already agreed to help me, Peter," I said.

"I know. I'm not trying to back out. I just want to make sure you're squared away on this."

"What happens to Wonderland if the wonder is gone?" Pinocchio asked.

"It'd be... something else without it," I answered.

"And that something else is evil, right?"

"It's plainer. And it's being done against people's will."

"That's not good. I'd like to have a say in it if someone took something wonderful away from me."

"That's a good way of putting it, Pinocchio," I said.

"Put the wonder back in Wonderland. We should put that on a flag. Can we make a flag?" Pinocchio asked. "If we're going to make an army we should have a flag."

"I don't think Wonderland has a flag."

"We should make a flag."

Peter kept his eyes forward, not saying anything.

"Above all else, the rabbit hole is in Wonderland," I added. "And it's surrounded by Ace's soldiers and workers."

"All of this was a fairy tale two days ago. Now it's real," Peter noted. "How do you cope with that?"

Before I had a chance to answer, before I could question what had brought me this far, a black car exactly like a Model T Ford rumbled through the forest and onto the road. It stopped in front of us, blocking our path. I didn't see a driver, but once the car stopped, a little head poked out of the driver's side window.

There sat a dwarf in a fedora, aiming what looked like a Thompson machinegun at us.

Peter's first instinct was to grab me and fly. We rocketed into the air just before the dwarf opened fire.

I heard bullets erupting against Pinocchio's iron body. The armored boy charged the car and punched it hard, sending it screeching across the gravel road.

Five more dwarves with pistols and shotguns drawn stepped out of the forest. They surrounded Pinocchio on all sides and opened fire.

"You okay?" Peter asked, letting me fly on my own.

"Yes," I replied. We'd both drawn our weapons.

"Crash course on flying and fighting. The key is to never stop and never slow down."

My heart sank and I wavered a little. The dwarves were too busy with Pinocchio to notice us. The iron boy had picked up the Model T and raised it above his head to throw at the ambushing dwarves.

"Don't worry about hitting anything," Peter advised. "Just never slow down! Ready?"

I nodded and looked down at the dwarves. Just before Peter and I dove into a strafe, just before Pinocchio threw the car, a woman stepped out from the forest and shouted in a voice that sounded like a song, "Stop! Stop this now!"

The dwarves lowered their guns. I grabbed Peter to stop him.

"Who are you?" the woman asked.

Pinocchio hesitated.

"Go on," the woman said.

"Alice? Peter?" Pinocchio shouted.

"Alice Peter is your name? That's a strange name."

"His name is Pinocchio," I called down.

The woman looked up at me. She wore a tight-fitting, sleeveless dress cut with a variety of patterns in the bodice and skirt. Her dress was short enough to expose a garter belt that held a silver flask against her leg. Her ebony black hair was tucked into a bun. Her lips were blood red, and her face was white as the driven snow.

"That's an even stranger name," said the white-faced woman.

Before the dwarves could shoulder their guns again, the woman whistled. It was like the sound of a songbird, and the dwarves lowered their weapons.

"Care to join us down here?" the woman asked.

"Have your men put down their weapons," Peter commanded, not lowering his.

"We're not men, we're dwarves!" shouted one of the dwarves.

"Yeah! And who are you to order us around?" another yelled.

"You tell this metal behemoth to put me down!" cried the dwarf inside the Model T. He banged on the door and yelled at Pinocchio, who still had the car over his head.

"Dwarves, please. Let's welcome these wonderful guests. You aren't from around here are you?" the woman asked.

"No," I replied.

"Then come down. We'll be nice and hospitable."

Peter lowered his gun, but he didn't put it away. I did the same, and we lowered ourselves to the ground in front of the woman.

"That's better. What's your name?" the woman asked.

"I'm Alice," I replied.

"Peter," Peter said.

"I'm called Snow White," Snow White said. "How do you do."

"Snow White!?" Peter and I exclaimed.

"Heard of me?"

Peter and I exchanged a glance.

"We have," I said.

"What were you doing here?" Peter challenged.

"Well aren't you a spunky one. I should ask you the same question," said Snow White.

"We were on our way to Grimm," I said.

"No fun to be had there."

The dwarves laughed. The dwarf in the car laughed too, then he said, "Hey! I'm still up here!"

"Oh, sorry," Pinocchio said.

Since the road was crowded with dwarves, there was no safe place to put down the car. So Pinocchio tilted the car on its side and shook the dwarf free. The dwarf fell to the gravel and brushed himself off.

"Thanks," the dwarf said.

The dwarves all looked alike from their shoes to their collars. They wore little pinstripe suits with white shirts and black ties. Each had a well-groomed, long beard tucked into their jacket

The only thing that distinguished them from one another was their hats, each a different size and style. One wore a beret, another a bowler, a fez, a top hat, and one had a cowboy hat that was really out of place. The dwarf who was shaken from the car picked up his fallen fedora and returned it to his hairy head.

"Why did you ambush us? Were you trying to rob us?" Peter asked.

"We're here for a robbery, that's for sure. But it wasn't you I was looking for," Snow White replied.

"Not the fairy tale Snow White at all, are you?"

"Excuse me?"

I was about to ask who the robbery was for when gunfire echoed farther up the road.

A seventh dwarf ran through the forest, his hand bracing a trilby hat to keep it on his head. "He's coming!" the dwarf shouted.

A speeding car came around the corner before any of us could react. Its driver leaned out the window blazing a Tommy gun. All of us dove for cover into the woods at the sight of the gunman. But as the car roared past I could see that the gunman wasn't a man at all.

"Hah-hah!" the driver shouted, gun ripping through the road. "Run-run, as fast as you can. You can't catch me I'm the Gingerbread—uh-oh."

Pinocchio had been holding the dwarves' Model T above his head this whole time. This led to a win-win solution where he could not only stop holding it, but stop the new vehicle as well. He threw the Model T at the speeding car.

The cars crashed together with shattered glass and dented steel. The force of the impact drove the new car sideways and crushed it against a tree.

Snow White peeked out from behind a bush. "Nice toss, lug nut," she said.

"Sorry I broke your car," Pinocchio said.

The dwarves swarmed the car with guns drawn, but Peter was the first to reach this new threat. He hovered over the car, pistol holding the driver still.

"Don't move," Peter threatened as the dwarves pulled open the dented door.

Crumbs fell out of the driver's seat as the dwarves yanked out what looked like a walking, talking cookie.

"You can't catch me, you can't catch me!" the talking cookie kept repeating.

He looked just like one of the gingerbread men my grandmother made at Christmas. His hair was white frosting, his eyes red cinnamon drops. A lit cigar dangled from his red frosting lips, and he fiddled with his suit's cufflinks once the dwarves set him on his feet.

I laughed at the sight of him. The echo of this creature had been very wrong.

"You boys are in for a big trouble, see," the child-sized cookie threatened, still a little woozy from his crash. "You can't catch me, see. No one catches the Gingerbread Man."

"We just did," Snow White said, glaring down at the cookie man.

"Does this whole thing seem weird to anyone else?" Peter asked, holstering his pistol.

"You're a flying boy who's friends with a child automaton and a blue fairy," I pointed out.

"Yeah, but talking cookies is… odd. Even for me."

"And what's it to you, greenie?" the Gingerbread Man asked.

The dwarves who weren't holding the Gingerbread Man rifled through the ruined car. One popped out of the back with a pair of clear bottles. "It's the shipment alright," he said.

"Good looking, too," another dwarf said, hopping out of the car with a case of the bottles.

"That's my goods! Lay your hands off my goods—I'll murder ya!" the Gingerbread Man threatened.

"They're our goods now," Snow White said. "Get the cases out of the car and let's get going. Tie this one to his steering wheel. Make sure he can't chew himself loose."

"Look, missy, this is Red Riding's hood, see. She don't take kindly to no broad filching her shipment."

"I'm not some broad." Snow White took the cigar out of the Gingerbread Man's mouth and stamped it out. "I'm Snow White."

"You're Snow White?" the Gingerbread Man asked.

"That's my name."

"Doll, you're in for a heap a' trouble when Red Riding finds out about this. She's gonna bring the wolves, see."

"Make sure to tell her when she comes looking for you. If you don't get eaten by squirrels first," said Snow White.

"Ah come on, doll, don't do me like that."

"Shut him up already."

Two dwarves tied and gagged the Gingerbread Man as the others continued to unload the shipment of bottles. Snow White smiled at Peter, Pinocchio and I as she crossed her arms.

"Well," Snow White said, "that could have gone better. Could have gone worse, but we got over that little rough spot, didn't we?"

"Sorry I wrecked your robbery," Pinocchio apologized.

"That's okay, lug nut. You can make up for it by carrying some cases. Look like you can take quite a load."

Another dwarf, the one with the trilby hat, drove a truck that had been hidden in the woods. He parked beside the wrecked cars and the dwarves began loading it with the stolen crates. Pinocchio, eager to help, took armfuls of cases and put them in the truck.

"Hold up, Pinocchio," Peter said. "I'm all for an ambush if it's against the right people, er, cookies."

Snow White smiled at Peter, then at me. "He yours?" she asked.

"Excuse me?" I asked.

"He's cute. You guys seem pretty clutch in a tussle. Why don't you join me back at our place and we can tell you all about our lovely little kingdom?" Snow White hopped into the bed of the truck and tapped on its side, encouraging us to join.

"We're headed to Grimm."

"It's on the way. Plus you owe me for wrecking my ambush. And I owe you for saving it. Let's have a drink and call it even."

I looked around at the well-armed dwarves. They moved about like ants at work, unloading and loading the crates. It was nothing like the seven dwarves, Snow White, or Gingerbread Man I'd heard of in fairy tales. And if this Red Riding the Gingerbread Man spoke of was who I thought she was, Grimm was turning out to be a very strange place.

Even though it was hard to pretend they weren't cartoon creatures from fairy tales, the dwarves were quite capable, handling their weapons with experienced aim. It would be useful to have them in a fight. I'd never recruited an army before, or even imagined anything like invading Wonderland, but if I could turn these creatures into allies it would be worth trying. I could definitely use all the help I could get.

Peter seemed to have the same thought, and hovered to the truck's roof. I joined him.

"Seven dwarves," Peter said to me.

"I know. Weird right?" I replied.

"I'm going to have to throw out everything I learned in my nursery."

"That would be a tragedy."

"That flying thing is a neat trick. You'll have to teach it to me sometime," Snow White said, hopping into the truck. "Alright boys, let's get gone before the watch comes looking in on the racket."

"I'm sorry, I've met Ms White, but I don't think we've been properly introduced," I said to the dwarf with the fedora.

"Hiya, toots," the dwarf with the fedora said, tilting his hat.

"No, what's your name?"

"Don't got a name."

"What?"

"Don't got a name. Don't need one."

"But how do you know who's talking to you?"

"Easy. Hey!"

"What?" shouted the dwarf with the fez, as if his name had been called.

"You're ugly!"

"He's ugly too."

"Hey!" shouted the dwarf with the bowler.

"Shut your traps and help him," called the dwarf with the top hat.

"I don't need help," said the dwarf with the cowboy hat, making sure the crates were tied down.

"Yes, you do," said the dwarf with the trilby hat.

"Shut up!" said the dwarf with the beret.

"I'm just explaining to Alice," said the dwarf with the fedora.

"They didn't have a need for names before I came along," Snow White explained. "I've tried like mad to get them to take names. But they don't want them. And they get along just fine without."

The dwarves finished loading the truck and hopped aboard. I decided right then and there that even if they didn't want names, I would name them after their hats. It made no sense not to have a name. How would you know who you were?

The second the dwarves finished loading, we were off, rumbling down the gravel road. The truck was weighed down with cases full of clanking bottles, allowing Pinocchio to easily keep pace.

"Nice scenery, isn't it?" Snow White asked.

"It's very pretty," I said.

Snow White whistled a lighthearted tune, the sound echoing through the forest. She raised her arm as if to add emphasis to the whistled song, and out from the trees came a flutter of birds. A pair of mockingbirds were the first to land on her shoulder, along with a blue jay and a cardinal that rested on her head. The birds sang in tune with Snow White's whistling, and the dwarves applauded as they listened.

"That's a neat trick," I said.

"I'm guessing what the Gingerbread Man was doing was against the law," Peter said.

"How astute of you," Snow White said as she nuzzled the cardinal.

"And obviously what you're doing is illegal too. The question is, which of you is the more honorable criminal?"

"Don't I look honorable?"

"You look like a Christmas card," I noted.

"See? I'm an honorable Christmas card. What about you? Too much of a goodie two-shoes to like the looks of a criminal?"

"You don't know me that well," Peter said.

"Ooh, I'd like to learn more. So what brings you to our little Grimm kingdom?" Snow White asked.

Peter tilted his head at me.

"We're looking for an audience with the queen," I said.

Snow White frowned. "Not a good idea."

"Why not?"

"The queen isn't exactly in the best mood."

"Not been in a good mood for years," the dwarf with the bowler added.

"Nine inches of beard since she's cracked a smile," said Top Hat.

"She hired a jester last month and glared at him so much he hanged himself," said Beret.

"That's awful," I said.

"Yeah, should have beaten him to death. Would have made a better punch-line," said Cowboy Hat.

The dwarves cackled with laughter.

Snow White laughed a little. "Truth is, the queen hasn't been in a good mood since her daughter was murdered," she said.

"I'm sorry to hear that," I said.

"So am I. Sorry she's taking it out on the people. Happened long before I was around, though. So why do you need to talk to her?"

"Well, is there an army in Grimm?"

"Of course there is."

"I need to ask her to help me return to Wonderland and stop Ace of Spades," I said.

"And you need the Grimm Army for that?" Snow White asked.

"I need something."

"Little miss Alice, Grimm's got plenty of its own problems. Best look elsewhere before you start making new ones."

The truck turned off the gravel road and onto a narrow, dirt path. It was just wide enough for the truck, with tight curves that forced the rumbling vehicle to slow. At the end of this winding path was a massive tree trunk.

A flower-lined, stone path led to a red door at the tree trunk's front. Windows were carved into its sides and copper chimneys poked out of the top, billowing smoke.

There was a smaller tree near this trunk that also had a door. The tree was ancient and gnarled, and had a chimney of its own. I wondered if I was missing something by not living in a tree. It seemed to be a common preference.

There must be a whole industry of people who sell trees that can be lived in, I imagined. *Traveling salesmen with acorns guaranteed to grow into a four bedroom, two-and-a-half bath Dutch colonial. Of course there would be no way to guarantee it, not just as an acorn. There'd have to be regulators or something, wouldn't there?*

There was a second, larger door at the side of the trunk. Several Model Ts and another truck were parked outside. Cowboy Hat hopped out and opened the trunk's door, which was just big enough for the truck to drive inside. The sound of us clanking through silenced my thoughts on tree-based realtor regulations.

An astounding smell of sweet and sour assaulted my nose. I sneezed at the shock of it. The side of the hollowed-out trunk where the garage door opened was a warehouse of sorts, shelves running to the ceiling filled with more crates and more clear and brown bottles. On the other side of the trunk were half a dozen copper pots twice as tall as me.

I'd never seen one outside of a book before, so it took me a moment before I recognized the copper pots as stills.

"You're making moonshine!" I declared.

Before the truck had come to a stop, the dwarves began unloading the crates. They placed the stolen moonshine alongside the existing contents of the warehouse. Those who weren't unloading or cataloging the heist went to work on the stills, checking the dripping contents or stoking the fires.

"What's moonshine?" Snow White asked as she hopped out of the truck.

The birds fluttered off Snow White's arm and returned to the forest as the dwarves shut the door.

Pinocchio, Peter and I walked beside Snow White as she went to a table and chairs set at the center of the building. There were glasses, papers, maps and dirty plates strewn about the table. Snow White went to work cleaning the plates and organizing the papers as she spoke.

"It's illegal alcohol," I answered.

"Oh. Then that's exactly what we're making," Snow White said with a smile.

"Moonshine's a good name for it," said Fedora.

"Why not sunshine?" asked Beret.

"Can't drink sunshine," said Cowboy Hat.

"Can't drink moonshine either," said Bowler.

"Moon don't shine—it glows," said Trilby Hat.

"So should we call it moonglow?" asked Top Hat.

"Moonglow it is!" declared Fez.

"Alcohol is illegal?" Peter asked, examining the open bottles on the table.

"It's not illegal, Peter. Moonshine…" I began.

"Moonglow!" interrupted the dwarves.

"Moon… glow, or moonshine is just alcohol made illegally. You have to get licenses and pay taxes on it to make it legal," I said, proud of myself for knowing this.

"No, it's illegal," Snow White said.

"Oh."

"Wasn't always. Queen Charming made gambling, booze, smoking, synthetic music, and anything declared immoral by the Grand Seer of Grimm to be illegal. That's why there's good money selling those things."

Pinocchio picked up one of the bottles on the desk. He turned it over in his hands, examining the clear liquid inside. "I don't get it," he said.

"You'll understand when you're older, sweetie. Or a bit rustier—how old exactly are you under there?"

"I was eight, last I checked."

"Well you don't sound much older, so none for you. Unless it's for cleaning oil off your gears—then by all means."

"How good is the money you make on moonglow?" Peter asked.

"Honey, we make gobs on the stuff. That's why so many want in on the business. You met our esteemed competitor just now. Seems Miss Red Riding is eager to expand."

"But why is it illegal?" I asked.

I'd never tried alcohol, though I'd been offered several times in school. I had no need for another chemical that modified my behavior. But despite all the obvious drawbacks to alcohol in society, making it illegal seemed a bit extreme.

And what's wrong with synthetic music?

"Queen's a bore," said Fez.

"I heard she eats nothing but crackers for food," said Trilby Hat.

"Can't call it crackers though. Might make one crack up," said Cowboy Hat.

"Right, so she calls it ers," said Bowler.

"Most boring food ever," said Beret.

"You can't really blame the queen, that's not fair," Snow White said. "She's just overreacting. Bit harsh, but at least there's some reason with her."

"Good beer would wash down those crackers nicely. Mouth's probably dry without," said Fedora.

"That's a lack of reason right there," noted Top Hat.

"You forget the girl?" Snow White asked.

The dwarves were silent.

"The girl?" I asked.

"The queen's daughter. Murdered, like I said. Husband dies, then her daughter. Blamed it on injustice and lawlessness. So the queen made the laws so harsh even more people became lawless. Not the best of plans, but good intentions make opportunities for those with bad ones." Snow White rubbed a lacquered fingernail across her silver flask.

I started to doubt if there was any opportunity here. And I didn't exactly have time to wait for whatever fairy tale prince was supposed to save Snow White, if this fairy tale even got that part right.

Peter must have been thinking the same thing, because he looked at me and said, "Tink must have known about this. She knew what she was doing sending us here."

Before Snow White could answer this, there was a knock at the door.

In half a heartbeat the dwarves were armed, Tommy guns and rifles and shotguns and a big Browning Automatic Rifle shouldered.

"Weren't you watchin?" Fedora scolded.

"I was," replied Cowboy Hat.

"Not well enough," Snow White said, drawing a .45 caliber semi-automatic pistol from a holster hidden beneath her skirt.

"Just here to talk, Ms White," came a muffled voice from the door.

"No wonder you didn't see him coming. Put your guns down and let him in."

I hadn't realized how easy it'd become for me to draw and ready my shotgun. I wasn't sure if it made me uneasy or confident, but I put it back in my white leather holster as everyone else lowered their weapons.

The door opened to reveal an older man with a pointed, red goatee. He was tall, with incredibly wide shoulders. He wore a camouflage green cloak draped thickly over his body. On his head he wore a turkey feather-adorned, green cap and had a crossbow slung on his back.

"Robin," Snow White said, embracing the man. "It's been too long."

"Hello, White," the man named Robin said. "Got the shipment?"

"Where's John?"

"John got nabbed Tuesday."

"That's awful! What about the other merries?"

"You know we don't like that term," Robin said.

"I'm sorry, it's just such a fun word to say. You forgive me, don't you, Robin?" Snow White asked.

"Sure thing, doll."

"You know I don't like being called doll."

"Course I do. Now be a doll and get the shipment."

Snow White snapped her fingers and the dwarves went to work loading crates onto one of the Model Ts outside.

"Robin? Merries?" I whispered to Peter.

"He doesn't look like, well, like what I'd expect," Peter replied.

"Disappointed?"

"Kinda."

"Why are you taking this one yourself, Robin?" Snow White asked.

"Need to take a closer interest in things. Too easy to slip up," Robin answered.

"It's getting more dangerous all the time."

Robin looked at Peter and me. "New recruits?"

"Just passing through," Peter answered on our behalf.

"You're not a prince are you?" I asked.

Robin raised an eyebrow and said, "Not that I know of."

"That's what I thought."

"That a walking still?"

"My name's Pinocchio," Pinocchio replied.

"Cute. So. You're taking kids and… iron men in," Robin said and un-slung his crossbow. He set it loudly on the table, rattling maps and almost knocking over a bottle of moonglow. "You change your mind?"

"I have not. You heard yourself, they're just passing through," Snow White answered.

"They look ready for a fight, you ask me. All of us are. If you'd just confront the queen and…"

"Not today. You just keep slinging that good stuff." Snow White held out her hand. Robin handed over a leather pouch full of jingling coins. "And keep coming back for more."

Robin sighed and put his crossbow back over his shoulder. "You know we're ready if you change your mind. All of us are," he said.

"I do. You be careful now, Robin. You and the merries."

"Sure thing, doll."

With a nod to me and the slightest of bows to Snow White, Robin left.

"Sorry about that," Snow White said. "That was old Robin. He handles some of my distribution territory. He used to run the 'hood around these parts. I filled the gap when the queen took him and half his band apart."

"That's… too bad," I said, not sure if I should be sympathetic.

Snow White shrugged. "He's looked out for me my whole life. Least I can do is return the favor."

"What was that business with the crossbow?" Peter asked.

"Nothing," Snow White replied.

"Looked like a pledge of loyalty."

"A pledge to foolishness is all."

"You've got men. You've got a network, so you said. These dwarves look good in a fight. Alice, I didn't think so at first, but it looks like you've got part of your army right here."

"Hardly. Robin wants me to incite a rebellion. Invasion is not on the priority list. And becoming a martyr isn't, either," Snow White said.

"Would enough people follow your rebellion?" I asked.

"Don't think about it too hard, cutie. I don't. Look, you seem like a nice girl, boy, lug nut. I have half a mind to help you."

"Good. We'll need to get all of your people together. If you need weapons we have some on our ship…"

"Not that," Snow White laughed. "I'm helping you because I might get something out of it. No battles or heroics, capisce?"

"What does *capisce* mean?" Pinocchio asked.

"It means okay," Peter said. "Okay. So you won't help Alice take back Wonderland. How can you help us?"

"By getting you that army," Snow White explained. "You can't just walk up and get an audience with Queen Charming. No one sees the queen without the say-so of the Grand Seer, and the Grand Seer only grants audiences to those he likes, or those who have valuable information."

Snow White took a piece of paper, one that already had ledgers of shipments on one side. On the other side she wrote a list of names.

"You give this to the Seer, and then Queen Charming. Say you'll give away my whole distribution network in exchange for her army," said Snow White.

"Why would she do that?" I asked.

"She's been chasing me for years. And apparently I'm a bit of a revolutionary threat. You use that to your advantage. Bluff her Charming heart out."

"You starting a revolution is a bluff?" Peter asked, doubtful.

"This whole list is a bluff. I'm not actually giving you my people—these are names I made up for the dwarves when I was seven."

"We hated them," Fez noted.

"I also put John and Robin's names on there. But she knows those already."

"What if she thinks there's more to the list?" Peter asked.

"You must have left the rest of the list in a safe location. How clever of you. Anyway, you can pledge money and resources and whatever you get after you take your Wonderland back to come and root me out."

"And you get out of this, what?"

"If the army's out of Grimm, it's less resources chasing me. Gives me a little breathing room to take on Red Riding and the rest of her hood. By the time you get back, I'll be solid enough even the queen will have to leave me alone."

"What if the queen thinks I'm making the list up?" I asked.

I looked at the names on the list. They were names like "Mophead Tom" and "Hank the Nose-Picker," names I likely would have chosen for the dwarves myself if given the chance.

"You'll need something to show you stole it from me." Snow White pulled a tiny comb from her ebony hair, undoing her bun. She presented it to me. "Well go on, take it—it's not poisoned."

I took the comb. It was silver, sharp.

"Show her the list, show her the comb. You'll get an audience at least," Snow White said. "I hope you get your army. Then come back when you're queen of Wonderland and we can have a nice chat. Maybe actually have that drink. You too, lug nut."

"Any chance we can talk you into coming with us instead?" I offered. "I'm sure we can find a place for you in Wonderland."

"I doubt that."

"But they have talking hamsters and playing cards for soldiers. There has to be a place for moonshiners…"

"Moonglowers!" shouted the dwarves.

"And dwarves with no names."

"Sounds like a neat place, toots. Hope you get it back—really I do," Snow White said with a sigh. "But I gotta look after my people. And you gotta look after yours. So let's get you on your way."

CHAPTER FOURTEEN

The truck was strong enough to carry Pinocchio, now that it was unloaded. Peter and I didn't need the truck, but Snow White confirmed that flying into Grimm would be a bad idea.

Thick forest made a tunnel out of the road leaving Snow White's 'hood. Branches like gnarled hands reached out to scrape the truck's sides.

Snow White regaled us with stories of her outrunning authorities on these roads, transporting various illicit goods. Most of the time it was moonglow, but she'd move anything that needed smuggling. Tobacco, art, music discs, even a pallet of ice cream that required some high-speed transport to get it to its destination before it could melt.

"It's the getting into Grimm that's the hard part," Snow White explained as the forest rose.

The trees soon gave way to foothills of mountains, and finally the winding road of the mountain itself.

The road rose like a tightly-turning staircase. With Snow White behind the wheel, we capped the mountain in no time. The only thing that kept me from being terrified of careening off the mountain was the knowledge that I could fly. I'm sure if Pinocchio didn't have such a powerful suit, he'd be equally disturbed by the way the tires dragged off cliff edges in hairpin turns. Knowing we were safe even if we fell off the mountain, we sat back and enjoyed the ride.

Once we crested the snow-dusted mountain's peak, we finally saw the city of Grimm.

It was a circular city, with a high wall, made of polished, white marble. A river bisected the city and ran in rivulets throughout the streets. Seven bridges of ornate lacework metal criss-crossed the river, each painted a different color of the rainbow. Outside the walls, the river spilled through various gates to form a thick moat that circled the entire city.

The buildings rose from low, white-painted houses to broad-stoned structures. Each layer of buildings met a different colored bridge and ended at the center, where four skyscrapers dominated the skyline.

The four skyscrapers glimmered like crystals in the noon-day sun, tall enough to rival the buildings of New York, but too marvelous to exist in the real world. Each was a different shape, one resembling a rocket, one an obelisk, one a sword and one a spiral. Each was covered in clear glass so crystalline the buildings seemed natural growths, like stalagmites from the land of the titans.

The four skyscrapers formed a square, at the center of which stood a magnificent castle made entirely of precious stone. I had to blink, because I thought it was too impossible to be real. But there it stood. Its sides were black, blue, pink and green marble accented with copper edging. It had four towers that mirrored the four skyscrapers, though they were made of marble and capped by actual crystal points. At the center of the castle's front-facing wall was a stained glass window that had so many colors, so many shapes, it seemed a glowing eruption of unshaped beauty.

The thing that made me rub my eyes wasn't the castle itself, though. It was that it appeared to be floating. I blinked and saw this was not entirely the case, as four stout posts, enormous in their own right, tied the castle to the four skyscrapers. This effectively made the skyscrapers stakes holding the castle aloft. An arched walkway made entirely of glass led from the ground to the gold and silver castle gates.

"Amazing," I said.

"Give it a second," Snow White advised.

I wondered what more this city could offer, when a rainbow erupted from the far side of the city. It arched over the tops of the skyscrapers like a rocket, landing to complete the rainbow on the opposite side of the wall. The rainbow flashed and was gone.

"The brothers Grimm never wrote anything like this," I said.

"There's something you don't see every day," Peter said, whistling.

"Actually you do. The rainbow powers most things in Grimm. Light bulbs, cars, flying carpets, robots," Snow White explained.

"We were told about the flying carpets. Didn't believe them at first."

"Flying *without* one is unbelievable. The guards might shoot you down just for the insanity of seeing someone flying without a carpet."

I frowned at this. The city of Grimm looked so magical.

If I lived there, I wouldn't be surprised at anything. Of course if I lived in a fantasy, it would be reality that would be hard to understand. Or would reality feel like a fantasy?

My mind wondered over the difference between reality and fantasy, dreams and thoughts of Wonderland, as we descended the mountain.

I spied ships coming up and down the river. They stopped at the docks inside the city to unload vast quantities of goods, but not before passing through a steady line of warships.

Some warships weaved about the water, but others hovered over the land. They were stainless steel and shaped like something between a blimp and a commercial aircraft. They had glowing engines that put off no exhaust, and patrolled all along the walls and river.

Beasts of vehicles sat at the gates with soldiers manning their turrets. They were like tanks, but had crystalline exteriors. They monitored the steady flow of people and vehicles entering and exiting the city. There was a similar flow on the walls, this time with mounted guns watching people entering and exiting the city on flying carpets.

As Snow White had said, the real trick would be getting into Grimm undetected.

Snow White drove the truck past a brick farmhouse about a half mile from the main gates. Three pigs sat on the farmhouse porch. One was chewing a piece of straw, another whittling a stick, another repairing their brick mailbox. Each waved at Snow White as she passed. They pointed her toward a road behind their house with a salute.

An orchard of cherry trees hid the road. It ended at a large crack in the city walls just big enough to fit the truck through. The moat was low here, making a ford all the way to the crack. The crack opened up to an under-populated part of the city; the perfect smuggling location.

"This is where we part ways," Snow White said, stopping the truck. "The shield that protects the city only keeps high-speed things from getting inside. You can walk right through it. Doesn't keep high-speed things from getting out, though. Could be useful in a pinch."

"Are they worried about being attacked?" I asked.

"Queen's always worrying about attacks these days. Now, I gotta go. Need to get back to the dwarves before they try and make fireworks again."

Peter, Pinocchio and I hopped out of the truck.

"Remember, you don't have the papers or ID to be wandering around Grimm," Snow White advised. "Go straight to the castle. Get Mrs. Charming to take you and her goons out of here. Then come find me when you're queen."

"I'm not trying to be queen of Wonderland. I just want to stop Ace from destroying it," I explained.

"Might as well become queen while you're at it." Snow White winked and put the truck in gear.

"Wait, before you go, do you know what the Sleeping Beauty is?" I asked.

"Never heard of it. Good luck though." Snow White blew a kiss and drove away.

"You don't have to become queen if you don't want, Alice," Peter said.

"Were you a queen, um, king of Neverland, Peter?" Pinocchio asked as we traveled across the fjord.

"Some said I was. I never did."

"I don't think I want to be queen. I'd rather give Wonderland back to those who lost it," I said, floating over the moat to keep my purple shoes dry.

"That is a very queenly thing to do."

We entered the city without too much attention. Pinocchio stood out, but he wasn't the most exotic thing by far. Besides the flying carpets, there were floating signals, lighting up red, yellow and green at crosswalks. Shops sold crystals that glowed, hummed with music, or could be shaped like clay. A stall sold elephants that were a foot tall, mice big enough to ride, and scrolls advertised as spells. Pinocchio wasn't even the only automaton. One shoved past me as it rolled on a gyroscopic orb to sweep the streets.

I was hungry, and suggested we stop for lunch. There weren't as many fruits as there were in Neverland, but we found a stall that sold sandwiches. They were surprisingly stale, with colorful cheese that was too hard.

Peter had a few gold coins he'd taken from the *Terrible Dog*'s holds and used these to pay for our lunch. When he asked for the best way to make it to the castle, the shopkeeper just laughed at him.

There were more automatons at every corner. Some were street sweepers like the first. Others just rolled around, red crystal eyes glaring at everyone. Posts stood at every street corner with a glowing red crystal atop them. A uniformed guard stood beneath each of these posts, dressed in white with a rainbow sash and golden badge. The badges would have looked pretty if they weren't displayed next to black assault rifles and narrowed gazes.

No one talked to each other, and the market seemed too big for the amount of shoppers. Shoppers simply went straight to the stalls, bought their goods, and hurried away. Some kept their heads low, others their eyes fixed straight ahead. No one even stopped to say hello.

No children were visible in the streets, though there were lots of fountains and squares where children could play.

After we passed stalls selling more curiosities, we asked another shopkeeper about the castle. No one was allowed to enter the castle, we learned, not unless they were dragged there by the guards. It was suggested—more than once—that we inquire at the guardhouse set at the base of the glass walkway. That, or get arrested.

Getting arrested, it was said, was easy. Just insult the queen near one of the red crystals.

While the population was thin around the markets, it was near deserted at the city's center. People went in and out of the four skyscrapers, but made purposeful strides away from the glass arch leading to the castle. It was here that a gray gatehouse blocked passage.

The gatehouse was the only concrete building I'd seen, a bit of gray in an otherwise colorful city. The gatehouse was stark and sturdy and bristling with turrets. Guards glared at all who passed, and I felt my legs begin to shake nervously as we approached.

"Just think, Alice," Peter said, putting an arm around my shoulder, "they've got lots of soldiers. Better for taking Wonderland, right?"

"I suppose," I said, feeling braver.

I thought about the Hatter then, and swallowed my nerves.

"Halt," commanded a guard with two rainbow sashes and a

badge shaped like the sun. He stood before the guardhouse, his finger braced against the trigger guard of his assault rifle. "Come no further."

"We seek an audience with Queen Charming," I said to the guard.

"Go away. You don't need to see the queen."

I swallowed my fear and remembered what Snow White had said. It helped that Peter was close. "I have information on the criminal Snow White."

This caused a stir of whispers amongst the guards.

"What sort of information?" the guard with two sashes asked.

"Information the Grand Seer would find valuable," Peter added. He nudged me and I held out the folded piece of paper.

The guards must have thought I was reaching for a weapon, because their guns were instantly trained on me. Had I not faced the dangers I'd already seen, this might have frightened me into flying away. With Peter and Pinocchio at my side, my hand only wavered a bit.

"Don't be foolish," I said. "This is valuable information that could destroy Snow White."

"What is it?" the guard asked.

"A list of her distributors, names of everyone in her network."

The guards whispered vigorously at that. The guard with the double sash ran inside the gatehouse. He was gone maybe half a minute before the door opened.

"The Seer will see you at the courtyard," said the guard with two sashes.

The three of us stepped forward.

"Not you," the guard said to Pinocchio. "No mechs allowed in the castle."

"But I'm not a mech," Pinocchio insisted.

"They don't know the difference," Peter said.

"Besides, we need you to watch the door for us. Just in case anything goes wrong," I said, tugging at Pinocchio's arm.

"Will you whistle?" Pinocchio asked.

"That's right. If I give a whistle, you come running."

"Okay."

The guards also confiscated our weapons, or at least tried to. I gave my shotgun to Pinocchio for safe-keeping. Even after they patted him down, the guards didn't find Peter's pistol. It was all I could do not to stare at him, wondering where he'd hidden his weapon, as we were ushered through the gates.

I'd climbed lots of staircases, some grand and some plain. I'd been in tall buildings where the floor was thick glass, making it seem like you were standing on air. Approaching the castle was something like that. It would have felt like flying slowly upward, had I not become recently familiar with that sensation.

Climbing the glass arch made me think we were walking upward on air, which gave me the urge to start flying. I could see Peter struggling with this as well. I surprised myself that in such a fantastical setting my only thought was how long it was taking. We could have just flown there in a fraction of the time.

The castle's gold and silver-inlaid doors opened to us and the guards stopped. A new pair of guards, these wearing platinum badges, replaced them. We were in a sort of courtyard inside the castle. Shimmering pillars of colorful marble held up a ceiling painted with dancing mice and carriages that looked like pumpkins. The new guards gave us a second pat-down. I obviously had no weapon, and they discovered none on Peter.

"So who is this Seer?" Peter asked, still in the midst of a pat-down.

The guards didn't reply.

"When will we see the queen?" I asked.

"You have a list? A list of Snow White's distributors?" came a new voice.

A slamming door heralded his approach, along with the *pat-pat*ting of his pointed shoes as he raced across the marble floor. He was short and squat, and he half waddled, half ran to us from the other side of the courtyard.

"Grand Seer, we will announce the guests when…" one of the guards said, his voice that of an old sergeant.

"Enough of that. Where's the list—show me the list!" the Grand Seer demanded.

The Grand Seer sounded like he was talking through his strawberry-shaped nose, and he wheezed from his short run. His clothes reminded me of a painting I once saw of Napoleon, save that his leggings were puffed and covered in gold thread and purple silk. Golden tassels waved from his shoulders as he wobbled with anticipation.

"Alice has it," Peter said.

"Give it to me." The Seer adjusted his diamond-studded, four-pointed hat. Aside from his clothes and his goblin-like shape, the Seer's most striking feature was a pair of glistening eyeglasses. They were thick as bottles and set in silver frames. The glasses hid his eyes with a mirror sheen, and I saw my reflection in them when he looked at me.

"We are here to present it to the queen," I insisted.

"That's nice—now show me the list!" the Seer demanded.

"Is the queen here?"

"No one sees the queen without my permission. And my permission won't come without that list—now give it here!"

I wanted to tell the short man how I felt about his manners. But I thought that since I was in such a rich place, and since the guards were behind us, I should be respectful.

"Here," I said.

I showed the Seer the piece of paper, which he took before I'd fully taken it out of my pocket.

The Seer held the list so close to his face his glasses were practically touching the paper. "Okay—take them away," he said.

"Excuse me?" I asked.

The platinum-badged guard already had a hand on my shoulder. Peter ducked away from the other, who growled at the boy's resistance.

"You're no longer needed. Now go," the Seer said with a dismissive wave of his hand.

"But that's not the whole list!" I said.

"Hold it. What?"

The guard stopped me at the door.

"The list isn't complete," I said.

The Seer's reflective glasses almost pierced the list as he scanned it again.

"There are too few, too few names for this to be all," said the Seer. "Who else is in Snow White's network—tell me now!"

"We'll only tell the queen."

"Tell me!"

"How many times does she have to tell you we're here to see the queen? Go get the queen already," Peter insisted.

"You will cut your tongue, boy. Or better yet, I'll cut it out. To the dungeons unless you tell me the rest of the names!"

"You can't do that," I said.

"I can, and I will. Unless I get those names."

"Listen, you disgusting little man. I need to see the queen and…"

"To the dungeon!" the Seer shouted.

"I'll whistle! I'll whistle if you don't take us to the queen."

"Who cares if you whistle?"

"I got these two, Alice. Save Pinocchio for the rest," Peter said, putting a hand to his hidden pistol.

The other guard locked his arms around mine. The Seer was still shouting, "I want those names now!" when the inner doors burst open.

"What is the disturbance causing tremors in my domain?" asked the figure who strode through the doors.

Her words echoed through the courtyard like they were projected through a loudspeaker. It was the voice of authority, someone used to being heard over crowds.

The guards bowed at the sound of her voice. The one holding my arms forced me down as well.

The woman's footsteps were like gavels on the marble floor. She took two steps and stopped.

"Bow before the queen," the guard holding Peter insisted.

Peter stayed standing.

"It's all right, Sergeant Whitebird. Sergeant Hazeltree, get that girl up," the queen said.

The guard behind me lifted me to my feet.

"We have a list," I said.

"No need to bother yourself with this matter, my queen," the Grand Seer said, rising from his knees. "It is well in hand."

"Is torture a part of the welcoming committee?" Peter asked.

"Well in hand."

"We must speak with you," I insisted.

"If it was deemed worthy for you to see to it with such enthusiasm, Grand Seer, then it must needs be dealt with directly," said the queen.

Queen Charming wore flowing garments of a rich, dark purple. The dress fit her snug about the waist and arms. She wore no jewelry or ornamentation of any kind, save a diamond-set, platinum tiara. The crown reflected a rainbow of colors as she moved.

"Is that not true?" asked the queen.

"A fair judgment, my queen," the Seer said with a hint of a bow.

"Then see them in."

Without waiting for the Seer's say-so, the two sergeants shoved us forward.

We followed the queen through a den decorated with a frescoed ceiling and gold-framed paintings. Purple-cushioned chairs and sofas lined the walls, making me think this was some kind of waiting area. There was a painting of a rat in a suit, a pair of mice wearing ornate saddles, and two lizards in livery. I recognized the images as scenes from fairy tales, wondering if they had really happened, or if these were just fantasies even here.

The sergeants opened a door and led us to the throne room. I expected a grandness equal to the majesty of the castle's exterior. But no gilding covered the throne room. The floor was white marble, the pillars shimmering stone, each a different color of the rainbow. Flags with a rainbow and sunburst hung from the far end, obviously Grimm's national flag, where an arched stained glass window depicted a winged lady drawing a rainbow with a saintly hand.

More flags I didn't recognize hung from the walls. I assumed they were of different nations, as they varied so widely. One had a giant standing before a tiny man armed with a stone. Another was a tower with a long strand of hair blowing from a window. Another was the Ace of Spades.

The only other person in the throne room was a servant. He wore plain clothes, and worked with the shaking motions of someone who wanted to leave as soon as possible. He stood upon a ladder and plucked a flag from the wall. The flag was a white lightning bolt striking from a mountain-top temple in a field of sky blue.

The servant took down the flag, folded his ladder, and hurried out of the throne room, leaving nothing but an empty slot beside the rest of the flags.

I wondered what nation this flag represented, and why its flag was removed, as I spotted several other empty sockets on the wall.

The queen ignored the flag's removal and sat upon a glass throne. The throne was curved at the back, with four shoes carved into its posts. Once she was in her place of authority, the queen waved us forward.

The Seer scampered to the queen's side as we approached. More guards moved into this room, and an itching at my back told me even more eyes were upon us.

"Speak your piece," the queen commanded.

"They have a list of Snow White's distributors. But they won't share the complete list," the Seer said, showing the queen the document.

"Does he speak the truth?"

"Your majesty," I said, trying to remember how to curtsey, no doubt failing at it.

"Speak truly, not buttered in compliments."

"Sorry. Um. We gave you that list, but I came here to have an audience with you."

"Treachery!" the Seer shouted. "To the dungeon with her!"

The queen held up a hand. "Is the portioned list accurate, Grand Seer?" she asked.

"Some of these names I know," the Seer admitted.

"Then she's earned the opportunity to speak. If she speaks with treachery, you may do with her as you please. Is that not fair?"

"Fair, my queen."

"Then, as has been instructed, speak truly."

"Your…" I said, preparing to begin again with compliments and curtsies. Instead, I took a breath and thought of my friends in Wonderland. "My name is Alice. And I need your help to save Wonderland."

The Seer looked about to say something, but the queen silenced him once more.

"Speak the whole of your plea," the queen instructed.

The truth, and the pain I felt for the loss of those wonderfully silly creatures, made the plea come easy.

"Wonderland has been taken over by a horrible man. He's the Ace of Spades. He killed the Cheshire Cat, is arresting anyone who acts out of his order, and worst of all he's taking the wonder out of creatures. He refuses to even call it Wonderland anymore. I need an army. We have a small one, a group of boys led by Peter Pan."

Peter nodded in support.

"Peter has lent his Lost Boys, his soldiers, to fight Ace of Spades," I continued. "But we aren't enough. We need more soldiers. Will you help me take back Wonderland?" I licked my lips, wondering what to add as punctuation. "Please?"

The queen stared at me a moment or two, her eyes revealing no emotion. "You wish me to wake the Sleeping Beauty?" she asked.

"I... yes." I remembered the Mad Hatter's advice. Had I found this Sleeping Beauty at last, whatever it was?

"To rally the armies of Grimm. To invade Wonderland?" Queen Charming asked.

"To save Wonderland," I said.

"To color an invasion with a just cause doesn't make it any less an invasion."

"Then yes."

"We're willing to invade Wonderland with Alice," Peter said, striking his fists-on-hip pose. It made him look stunning and in command, but it had no visible effect upon the queen.

"What are you to Wonderland?" the queen asked.

"I've never been there. But I gave Alice my word."

"And you, Alice of Wonderland. What are you to Wonderland? Are you its rightful ruler in exile? Are you a wealthy lady seeking to recover confiscated lands? Or has your lover been taken from you and you seek his release?"

"No," I replied.

"I thought not."

The queen looked to Peter, then back to me.

"Wonderland is a special place. I don't want Ace to destroy it," I said.

"We all want many things, child," said the queen. "I want my kingdom to prosper with justice and peace. Do you think I have soldiers to spare for your cause?"

"I don't need the whole army."

"And do you think it fair that I send soldiers to save your Wonderland while Grimm falls to lawlessness?"

I bit my lip.

"What do you think, Grand Seer? Is that fair?" the queen asked, her reflection showing in the Seer's thick spectacles.

"Not fair at all, my queen," the Seer grinned.

"Please," I said, fighting back tears. "My friends are being killed.

That or they're losing who they are."

The queen held up a hand and silenced me. "Do you have the remainder of this list, as you claimed?" she asked.

"I…"

"I said speak only truth. So if you can't answer that truly, speak this truly. How did you come about this first list?"

"We met Snow White."

"And you know where she is? Who her associates are?"

I bit my lip.

"Grand Seer," the queen said, "who is the greater threat to the Kingdom of Grimm? Wonderland? Or Snow White?"

"Snow White, beyond the mountains with the seven dwarves, is a thousand times greater threat than Wonderland," the Seer answered.

"You see? First a dragon kills my husband, then bandits murder my daughter. Has this kingdom not had enough sorrow? Explain to me why I should devote resources to Wonderland, when Snow White and her rebellious ilk stand waiting to destroy what remains of our Grimm joy."

"I'm… sorry about your family," I said.

The queen didn't reply. Her face was ice.

"But Snow White isn't a rebel," I pleaded.

"She's no threat to you," Peter added. "She's just trying to live her life. If you'd lay off with your police everywhere then she…"

"Peter."

I put a hand on the boy's arm. I was worried he'd start floating with anger if I didn't hold him down.

"She is a threat. And she will be dealt with. I have received emissaries from this Ace of Spades," said the queen.

"He is no threat to us, queen," the Seer advised.

"For now. If he becomes one, I must shore up my defenses and secure our homeland. Do you see the flags of the nations in this world?"

The queen motioned toward the flags hanging over the throne room.

"They are the alliances Grimm has made in its long history," the queen explained. "Word has come to me that many are joining Ace, submitting to his rule willingly. Many more are allying with him."

"That can't be true," I said. "Why would they want their wonder taken away?"

"It is not for me to say. Each of these kingdoms must face their threats on their own. We must each look to ourselves. They have their concerns, I have Snow White."

"Can't you ask for their help?" I asked.

"I've sent messengers. The other nations have declined to assist Grimm in its struggle. Even the Sleeping Beauty may not be able to call them out of their isolation, and that is only meant to be used as a last resort."

The queen paused, thinking a moment. Then she shook away the thought and stared at me with cold eyes.

"I will not submit to outside control, from Ace or from Snow White," the queen said with a scowl.

"Let me talk to them," I said. "Maybe they don't know who Ace is. If the whole world is in danger of having its wonder taken away then we need to fight back. Together!"

"The other nations are free to do as they wish, but I will not risk an invasion that could stretch our resources thin, or lead to a defeat that would put us under the thumb of the Ace of Spades."

"Then you know how horrible he is," I said.

"Peter Pan, you said you owe this girl a promise. What is it she did to earn your promise?"

"She killed Captain Hook and saved Tinkerbelle," Peter answered, glaring at Queen Charming as he offered this vague answer.

"Then you did not make your promise without receiving a deed in kind," said the queen.

"Sure."

"I say this is a good time for the apple, Queen," said the Seer.

The queen sighed and said, "I suppose."

The Grand Seer grinned and left the room. Peter and I exchanged a look. We both recalled what the apple was in the fairy tale of Snow White and the Seven Dwarves. It meant death.

"What deed do you wish, queen?" I asked, trying to cool my nerves.

"A deed that has been a long time in coming. Compromise has reached its limits, and thus I am willing to take extreme measures," said the queen.

The Grand Seer returned, bearing a small, wooden crate.

"Alice of Wonderland," the queen continued, "I do agree that Ace of Spades is not a force to be taken lightly. Nor is he a desirable element in Grimm. Destroy Snow White. Eliminate her and all those lawbreakers who remain loyal to her. Once that is done, you will have your soldiers."

The queen looked into the reflective lenses of the Grand Seer's spectacles and asked, "Am I not fair in my judgment, Grand Seer?"

"You, my queen, are fairest of all," the Grand Seer replied.

"But... how will we do that?" I asked.

The Grand Seer laid the crate at my feet and opened it, revealing a round, red object. It looked like a metal apple, wires sticking out its sides. This was not the poison apple of the echo I'd read. It was much worse.

"Bring this to her. Detonate it, and destroy Snow White," the queen said, her face ice once more. "And I shall offer what support I can."

"You want us to kill Snow White?" Peter Pan asked. "Forget it."

"Peter, don't be rude," I said.

"Excuse me?"

"There's no army between here and the end of the world that can face Ace of Spades," said the Grand Seer, his fingers stuck through his belt. "You can go ask the Olympians, but they just joined with Ace. We're all you've got."

"You haven't seen my boys," Peter said.

"We need your support," I conceded, holding Peter on the ground. "But there has to be another way."

"There is no other way. Snow White must be destroyed. Or Wonderland will fall. It makes no difference to me which one you choose to execute," the queen said.

"Are you really that cold?"

"I am that pragmatic."

"Don't think your need to save Wonderland is more important than Grimm's need for security," the Seer said. "We have enough trouble with our supposed allies as it is."

"How does it work?" I asked.

"What?" Peter exclaimed.

"You arm the apple by pulling on the stem," the Seer said. He mimed the motion before the wired apple, but didn't perform the action. "Then you'll have five minutes before it detonates. I'd get far away if I were you."

"Go ahead and pull that trigger and blow…"

"Thank you, Peter. I'll do it," I said, shushing the boy.

"Alice, you can't be serious," Peter said.

"We'll talk about this, Peter."

"I'll talk, sure. Outside. Without the bomb."

I didn't know whether the queen was trustworthy or not. I didn't know if I had many options. But one thing I knew was I needed help. So I stuck out my hand.

"I'll do it. I'll stop Snow White, if you help stop Ace," I said.

"Done," the queen said, and shook my hand, sealing the deal.

"Get moving now. Lots to do, lots to do," the Grand Seer said, grinning from ear to ear. He left the throne room by a side door without waiting to be dismissed.

"I'm not carrying that thing," Peter said.

"Thank you, your highness," I said.

"I suggest you heed the Seer's advice. If you are indeed seeing your friends perish in Wonderland, you'd best hurry," the queen remarked.

"Sure."

I bent to pick up the bomb, but Peter shoved me aside and scooped it up. He walked to the door without waiting for me.

I held back whatever insult I was going to say, not wanting to look even more foolish in front of the queen, and followed Peter.

When we reached the door, the queen called out, "Alice. Come back safely. Someone in this world deserves a happily ever after."

I paused, not sure how to respond.

"Okay," I said.

It was a silly thing to say to a queen, but it was also a silly thing for a queen to say.

CHAPTER FIFTEEN

We were silent until we reached the bottom of the glass archway. Pinocchio was waiting for us. The metal boy practically bounced off his gear-clad feet when he saw us.

"So how'd it go?" Pinocchio asked. "What was the queen like? Is she going to help us?"

Peter ignored him and walked ahead.

"What's in Peter's box?" Pinocchio asked me.

"A bomb," I replied.

"A what?"

"Don't talk about it in public," Peter called back.

"We need to talk about it somewhere," I said.

"How about over the ocean? I'll drop the bomb there and we can have a nice chat."

"How about just somewhere further out of sight."

I glanced around, still feeling the guards' eyes on me. I kept my mouth shut and walked toward the market. Peter occasionally asked where we were going, and if I intended to use the bomb. I kept telling him to shut up. Pinocchio was wise enough to stay quiet.

It wasn't until we got to the crack in the wall that I felt

comfortable speaking. I told Peter we should stop in an empty alley near the crack. Peter set the bomb down and put his fists on his hips, waiting for an explanation.

"We're not going to blow her up," I said.

"That's a relief," Peter said. "I'm glad I didn't have to drop this thing on your head to knock some sense into you. I'll just fly it back to the castle."

"We have to blow someone up?" Pinocchio asked.

"We're not returning it either," I said.

"These guys are bad news, Alice," Peter said. "You don't need their help."

"Yes, I do."

"Well you don't need to do stupid things to get their help."

"Stupid things?"

"Killing people. It's not good and it's not you."

"I killed Captain Hook, Peter."

Peter bit his lip.

"Sorry, Pinocchio," I said, hating myself for losing my temper. "Peter, don't think I won't do what it takes to get Wonderland back."

"Why do you care about it so much?" Peter asked.

"It's Wonderland."

"Yeah, I get that. But you don't have to go back there."

"Let's not bring this up again."

"Let's. It's a valid thing to bring up before you flat out murder someone," Peter said.

"We're not murdering anyone. We're faking a murder."

Pinocchio raised his hand.

"Yes, Pinocchio," I said.

"Who are we maybe killing or not killing so you can get back something you want or don't want and where is that and, um, stuff?" Pinocchio asked.

"Valid question," Peter said.

"Was it? Good. I wasn't sure."

"The queen ordered us to bring this bomb to Snow White's home and detonate it, killing Snow White. But we're not going to do that. We're going to bring it to Snow White, tell her about the plan, have her to go into hiding, bomb her home with no one inside, and tell the queen Snow White's dead," I explained.

"A fake out," Peter said. "Not a bad idea."

"I can be clever when I want to be."

"Save that you'll need proof she's dead."

"We'll get another token from her, like the comb she gave me. I'm sure Snow White will go along with it," I said. "After all, she'll get what she wants. The queen's army will leave. Snow White will lose her house, but it's a stump—she can grow another one. She'll just have to stay hidden until we get to Wonderland, so the soldiers aren't called back."

"If you can convince Snow White to go along with it," Peter noted.

"Stop being so pessimistic. I don't like solving problems by killing people."

"Yet you want to kill Ace."

"I didn't say that. I want to stop him."

"Fair enough."

"And I'll need your sunny disposition to win over Snow White to this plan," I said.

Peter picked up the bomb and said, "So long as we're not killing kids to help terrible grownups, I'll help."

"That's a very grownup way to think, Peter."

"Shut up."

"Plus, Snow White is hardly a kid. Neither are you."

"Shut up."

I didn't push the issue, and was just happy Peter was onboard. I had come up with the plan as a visceral reaction. The deception seemed obvious, at least to someone who didn't like the idea of murdering her enemies. I just hoped the queen and the Seer wouldn't have the same thought, and wouldn't see through the trick.

Plan in place, the three of us walked through the crack in the city wall. I expected to do nothing more than exit the city and be on our way, with Pinocchio *tick-tock*ing beside us. But we had to stop, for Robin stood in the middle of the shallow moat, crossbow at his side.

"So you're not just passing through," said Robin.

"And you're not delivering a shipment," said Peter.

"That's Robin, isn't it?" Pinocchio asked. "I remember because of the crossbow. Not a very good weapon if you ask me."

Robin raised an empty hand.

A crossbow bolt twanged as it stuck into the side of the walls. Robin's crossbow was still at his side.

"Say hello to the Merry Men," Robin said, pointing to the trees a hundred yards back.

I saw no Merry Men.

Peter nodded at the trees and said, "Hello."

"They want to know why you were inside Charming Castle, and what the Seer offered you," Robin said with the calm assurance of someone who's got his enemy cornered.

Pinocchio raised his fists, ready to charge Robin, as Peter put a hand to his pistol.

"Robin, put the weapons down. We're not going to hurt anyone," I said.

"No, you're not," Robin said.

Peter rose off the ground.

"Boys—boys! Calm down, we're on the same side here," I said.

"No one goes in and out of that castle who's not an ally of the Seer," Robin said. "Now, tell me…"

"We're going to fake Snow White's death so the queen will send her soldiers to Wonderland," I yelled back at him. "Happy? Now tell your crossbowmen to put down their weapons."

"Wonderland?"

"Yes."

Robin's eyes widened a moment. Whatever shock he had melted

away as he considered my words. "Not a bad plan," he said. "It could work."

"See? I'm not going to hurt anybody," I said.

"Not unless they move first," Peter threatened.

"Shut up, Peter."

Robin nodded. "So," he said. "Deceive the queen. You go with the army to save Wonderland. Snow White is safe. I can get behind that."

"How did you know we'd seen the queen?"

"I go by many names. One of them is Huntsman. Another is Robin of Hearts. I always keep a card up my sleeve."

Robin tilted his chin toward us, where a crystal-eyed automaton emerged from behind an alley.

"He who is prudent and lies in wait for an enemy who is not, will be victorious. The Mad Hatter said that," Robin quoted.

"That's a good quote," Peter said. Then he crowed.

It was a strange sound, and completely unexpected. A few seconds later, before I could ask Peter if he'd gone mad, out from the trees flew half a dozen Lost Boys, with Jimmy in the center. They each had a tied-up crossbowman in their grasp, and set them and their weapons down in front of us.

"Always have air support. I said that," Peter quoted.

Robin laughed. He tilted his hat to Peter and shook the man's hand.

"Were they there the whole time?" I asked.

"Remember when I told Jimmy to check in on the hour?" Peter asked.

"Yes, but I never saw them."

"Doesn't mean they weren't there."

"You could have told me."

Peter laughed. "Lost Boys, Merry Men. Merry Men, Lost Boys," Peter said, introducing the groups to each other.

"Pleased to make your acquaintance, boys," Jimmy added. "Not every day you meet folk 'eroes."

The Merry Men seemed a little agitated after having been tied up, but calmed down once they were formally introduced.

"Alright, that's just about enough rooster strutting for now," I said.

"Yes. Let's see this bomb," Robin said.

"You got ya'self a bomb, Petah?" Jimmy asked.

"I'll explain in a minute," Peter replied.

Robin examined the crate with the apple inside. He took off the lid and looked down, cringing.

"Gentlemen, and lady," Robin said, "are you aware that this bomb is armed?"

"No, the Seer said we have to pull the stem to start the five minute countdown," I said.

"I've handled lots of bombs, stopped a few just like this. This bomb is armed."

"Alice, let's get back," Peter insisted.

"Hold on," I said. "That can't be true. The Seer said we…"

Before I could fully protest, Robin removed the bomb's faceplate. There was a digital clock at its front. I supposed this would activate once we pulled the stem, but it was currently ticking down the seconds. There was a little less than an hour left on the timer.

"It seems the Seer had no intention of you surviving long enough to reach Snow White," said Robin.

"But… but…" I mumbled.

"I told you he was bad news," Peter said. "Let's get out of here."

Robin held up a hand as he knelt beside the bomb and said, "No need to rush."

"I don't like being near a ticking bomb," Pinocchio said.

"That's a rightly good perspective ta have there, Pinoke, that it is," Jimmy echoed. "I second that sent'ment."

"You said you intend to invade Wonderland?" Robin asked as he tapped a dagger against one of the bomb's wires.

"Yes," I replied.

"And the Seer gave you this bomb?" Robin put the blade against a different wire.

"Yes. Do you know what you're doing?"

"I don't like this." Robin tugged a wire out of the apple-shaped bomb. The clock stopped.

I breathed a sigh of relief. So did everyone else.

"Maybe he activated it by accident?" I asked.

"Not likely."

"I say we ask Mr. Big Glasses why he wants us dead," Peter said, drawing his pistol.

"Agreed. We need information," said Robin.

"We?" I asked.

"Someone wants you dead, Alice. I want to know why," Robin explained.

"Jimmy, take the boys back to the ship. Make sure everything's in order," Peter ordered.

"No. Check on Snow White," Robin countered.

"Alright. On the way, bring the Merry Men to Snow White. Pinocchio, you go with them. I have a feeling Alice and I need to be subtle about this."

"Why would the Seer want me dead? I'm just Alice!" I pleaded.

"Alice of Wonderland, readying an invasion army."

"Well… yeah."

I gritted my teeth, angry for not seeing through such a deception. I'd tried to deceive the Seer, and he'd played me right back.

"Where will we find him? Maybe we can expose his tricks and get the queen to support us," I suggested.

"One thing at a time," said Peter.

"Agreed," said Robin. "We'll find the Seer in his office. It's on the top floor of the northwest tower. I'll have my automaton deactivate the security and open the elevators."

"Why not just open the windows?"

"…that would work."

"How can your automaton do that?" I asked.

"I've been stealing things for quite some time, Alice. I've gotten pretty good at it."

"Let's go," said Peter.

The Lost Boys and Merry Men, along with Pinocchio, set off toward Snow White while we ran back to the skyscrapers. We didn't want to draw suspicion from the guards and automatons, however, so we had to zigzag between buildings. Robin knew his way around, keeping his head hooded to avoid being recognized as he leapt between dark alleys.

In short time, we made it to the base of the skyscraper. Its glass edifice shimmered in the late-afternoon sun. People in business suits and ties went in and out of the building. They didn't look up or down, only straight ahead, and kept their eyes away from the numerous police officers.

"Top floor," Robin said, his back against the skyscraper.

We stood just out of sight of a police officer watching the door. Robin reached into the thick folds of his cloak and drew a rolled-up carpet. I couldn't believe he had space for such an item. He must have been much skinnier beneath that cloak than its folds implied.

Robin unfurled the carpet with a snap. It floated a foot above the ground.

"I could just carry you," I offered.

"I prefer this way," said Robin.

"You sure they won't know we're coming?" Peter asked.

"My automaton has turned these alarms off before."

The automaton wasn't in sight, but no doubt had accessed whatever mechanisms powered the building's security. Sure enough, the windows on the top floor, high above our heads, slid open.

"Here we go," Robin said. The instant he sat upon his floating carpet it shot skyward.

Peter drew his pistol and looked at me. "Watch yourself," he said. He disappeared a moment later, blasting off like a rocket.

I drew my shotgun and followed, my ascent nowhere near fast as Peter's. I hugged the building's glass surface, catching my reflection in the windows as I flew.

I saw myself for the first time in days. I didn't recognize my own reflection, flying with a gun in my hands, racing toward someone who wanted to kill me. I didn't recognize the reflection of the city I saw either. It was strange, alien. It excited me, I hated to admit, and I looked up with a smile toward what mystery I might find in that top floor.

By the time I reached the open windows, Peter was already inside the corner office. He trained his gun on the Grand Seer, who braced himself against a massive shelf of leather-bound tomes. Robin, beside Peter, leapt off his carpet, crossbow in hand.

"What is the meaning of this!?" the Seer asked. He had a large, folded parchment in his hands that he held to his chest, as if it could offer some protection.

"I expected a greater deception from you, Seer," Robin said.

"You! What are you doing here, Knave?"

"These two have a question."

The Grand Seer's office was massive. Broad windows offered a wide view of the surrounding countryside, with the city spanning below. The interior was slate and steel, polished and tiled from floor to ceiling. There was a granite statue—a twisted shape I couldn't recognize—on a pedestal by the windows. A map of Grimm dominated the non-windowed wall. Several more parchment scrolls, imprinted with colorful wax seals, lay strewn about the office.

The Seer's desk was glass and steel, with a fanned-out deck of cards face-down on the surface. The Seer kept looking at the desk like it contained something he wanted. He stopped, however, when Robin took the bomb from beneath his cloak and set it on top of the cards.

The Grand Seer jumped back, trying to pass through the bookshelf.

"Why did you try to kill me?" I asked, no longer afraid to aim my gun.

"Get that thing out of here!" the Seer yelped, dropping his rolled-up parchment.

"Calm down, you despicable man, it's not armed." I opened the crate and showed him the apple's frozen timer. "Now, explain yourself."

The Seer scowled a moment. He readjusted his silk hat and dusted off his ornate sleeves. "I have my reasons."

"That's not an answer," I said.

"You best start talking, Seer," Robin warned.

"And you best leave," the Seer challenged. "Or give yourself up. Might be better for you. Go ahead and sit down. I'll make sure you're only beaten to near death."

"No one's coming to your rescue. We're going to have a nice chat, just the four of us."

"You still haven't answered Alice's question," Peter said.

"And you still need to put that gun down," the Seer replied.

Peter's hand didn't waver.

"I'll answer this way," the Seer began, "why would anyone want dear little Alice dead?"

"I don't think you need an answer, Alice. I'll just shoot him and we'll go fetch Snow White. Back to plan A," said Peter.

"You don't want to do that!" The Seer put his hands up.

"I could do that," Robin said.

"Crossbow is quieter than a gun," Peter admitted.

"No!" the Seer said. "You'll never save her that way."

Robin tilted his head. "What game are you playing, Seer?" he asked.

"So many questions. But you don't realize the questions themselves are the answer. Who would want Alice of Wonderland dead? What game would I play to send you with a bomb to Snow White?"

Robin lowered his crossbow and grabbed the Seer by the collar. The Seer's silk shirt ripped as Robin held his feet off the ground.

"What have you done?" Robin asked.

"Two birds with one stone," said the Seer. "Two deeds with one…"

"What have you done with Snow White!?"

"I have done nothing."

"If you harm her…"

"Why would I want to harm her? She is too much a danger to destroy. The queen is ever-so worried about the instability little Snow White represents. She might lose her throne to the woman. You and I, Knave, know how very real that threat is."

"So why kill me?" I asked.

"Has it really taken you so long to figure out?" asked the Seer.

"Ace."

"Word has spread."

The Seer picked up the parchment and unfurled it on the desk. Peter made sure the Seer didn't make any more sudden motions, but the Seer was able to flatten the scroll so we could read it.

"See for yourself. Ace is conquering," said the Seer.

Red words were written on the parchment. They were formal, like the words on some kind of ancient treaty. The parchment read, *You must help us. You must come to our aid or Olympus will fall. Hercules fights on, but there is little hope without the Grimm Army. You must wake the Sleeping Beauty!—Mercury.*

"Mercury… Hercules?" I said, unable to believe what I saw.

"I thought the queen said the Olympians chose to join Ace," Peter noted.

"The Olympians fell while they were still punching each other over petty squabbles," said the Seer.

I saw a parchment near the misshapen statue. I unfurled it and read, *None remain. All frozen. Hope fading. Send help.* The words were written in a dull brown. The seal was a black raven.

"Yes, Loki has been hard at work. Good thing that old Jack of Clubs got his wonder taken out of him—he's much more devious in Valhalla than he ever was in Wonderland," said the Seer.

I read another scroll, this one in eloquent script, *We must flee these lands. I await your word, but cannot hold out for long. We pray the Sleeping Beauty be awoken soon.—Arthur, King, First of His Name.*

Then I read another scroll that cried out in rough handwriting, *Nuts to the enemy. We won't let them take us alive. Remember us!—David Crocket.*

I picked up more parchments. They were all pleas for help. Some were in gold, some in black. Some used flowery language, some simple. All begged that Grimm wake the Sleeping Beauty and save them from the Ace of Spades. None of them, it seemed, had any idea the rest were under attack.

I recognized the seals from the flags in the throne room. There was a golden cup, a longhorn skeleton, and a dozen others.

"Grimm is the last remaining," said the Seer. "Its shield has kept Ace out. But not for long. And when all that I've done comes together, it will be good to have our benefactor in what once was Wonderland as an ally, don't you think, Alice?"

"Not if I kill you, Jester," said Robin. "I don't care about the other nations. I can stop you, and make sure Snow White is safe."

"My dear fool of a Knave, you must know you're too late."

Robin's eyes went wide. He dropped the Seer and grabbed the bomb. He leapt onto his magic carpet and flew out the window fast enough he knocked the tomes off the Seer's bookshelf. I noticed the deck of cards, however, was not disturbed.

"Best join him if you want to save Snow White," grinned the Seer. "But one moment further, dear Alice. Ace still offers his partnership. And I offer you mine. You can have Grimm, you can have what was Wonderland."

"Where is Snow White?" I asked.

"Go after the Knave—you'll see. It's unlikely you'll find her, but…"

"Then tell me." I leveled my shotgun with a heavy slap of its barrel against my palm.

"It's rude to interrupt others when they're making an offer that can save your life." The Seer rubbed his hands together. His gloves didn't match; the right was white velvet, the left orange silk.

"This world, and Wonderland with it, is the property of the Ace of Spades," the Seer said. "Look around you. You read the cries for help. Olympus, Valhalla, Marduk, the Two-Land Kingdoms, even Merlin and the Frontiers have fallen. All is lost. And what is Wonderland to you, dear Alice, that you would fight such hopelessness?"

"How is a raven like a writing desk? How's that for a question?" I asked, shoving the barrel of my gun beneath the Seer's chin.

There was so much written on those scrolls I couldn't believe them. I couldn't believe that this world could be so big, and that so many echoes I'd read about lived here. Most of all, I couldn't believe that Ace could be responsible for destroying them all.

"Such a violent response must hint at indecision," said the Seer. "Look at you. Poor Alice. Having to team up with killers. You're not from Wonderland—it never asked you to help it. Perhaps Wonderland is better off without you. Alice certainly is better off without Wonderland."

"Shut up," I said.

"If I might make a proposition," said the Seer.

The Seer slid away from my gun and backed around his desk. Peter still had his gun trained on the man. The Seer seemed to acknowledge this as he clapped his gloved hands together, extending them toward me in a pleading gesture.

"You don't have to fight, Alice. You can go home," the Seer explained. "What is Wonderland to you but death, now? Even when you first went there you nearly got your head cut off."

"What Ace is doing is wrong," I countered.

"Ace extended you friendship. Wonderland before him made you grow or shrink without control. Wonderland was no friend to you—you must remember."

"But he's hurting people."

"And you're fighting a war," the Seer countered. "If morality is what you fight for, look at the weapon you're holding against an unarmed man."

I lowered my shotgun.

"How many have you killed? And you claim a moral high ground," the Seer said with a mournful shake of the head. "Only take my hand, Alice."

The Seer unraveled his gloved hands, extending his right to me.

"Take my hand," the Seer said. "And we will journey back to Wonderland. Ace will welcome you and allow you to leave freely through the rabbit hole. All the death will be gone. Take my hand, and this will be nothing but another dream."

Tears welled in my eyes. The world around me was massive. I stood on a glistening, high building overlooking miles of country that wanted nothing to do with me. There was no hope. There was no army, just papers from echoes begging for help from a queen who ignored them. Everywhere I looked I saw proof of Ace's power.

How could I help those Ace had hurt if even Hercules couldn't stop him? And those I'd tried to help? Had I actually done them any good? Or did I unknowingly help Ace? Did they really need me? Did Wonderland really need me?

And what about me?

Why did I want to save Wonderland in the first place? What use would it be if the fight killed me? Did it really matter if Ace took over this world if, after all, it was nothing but echoes and dreams? What was Wonderland to me?

"How is a raven like a writing desk?" Peter asked.

"What?" I replied.

Peter lowered his gun and looked at me. "Before you go. What you just said to the Seer, I heard you say it to Hook too. How *is* a raven like a writing desk? I'd like to know."

Before I could answer, I saw the Seer through my tear-blurred vision. He reached for a space beneath his deck of cards. There must have been a hidden slot in the glass desk, because he drew a blue-chrome pistol from beneath the cards.

The Seer turned to Peter.

I raised my shotgun and pulled the trigger.

The glass desk shattered.

The Seer fell against his tomes and collapsed to the ground, the bloodied deck of cards raining around him. It was only then that I realized the cards were all jokers.

Peter looked at me, eyes wide.

I wiped a tear from my cheek.

"That makes us even," I said.

"You stupid girl!" sputtered the Seer.

Peter had his gun on the man in an instant, kicking the blue-chrome pistol across the floor. The Seer was shredded, sputtering as blood soaked his immaculate clothes.

"You stupid Alice! Why did you do that?" the Seer coughed.

"Snow White," Peter said. "Where is she?"

"Forget that. Alice, you can still take my hand." The Seer raised his blood-stained glove with cringing effort. "Ace can heal me—he has the power. We can take you home. You can still end it."

"Can he be helped?" I asked.

Peter shook his head.

"Ace can! Ace can heal me—he can heal you! You can be whole, whole and at home," the Seer pleaded.

Alarms went off. The gunshot must have attracted security.

"It's mine," I answered. "That's what Wonderland means to me, Seer. I'm Alice of Wonderland, and I don't care if the whole world is against me. I don't care if my parents and Mrs. Friend and all *my* world are against me. I've finally found something I believe in. And I'm not going to have it taken from me."

I tilted my head toward the window. Peter stood by my side.

"You stupid girl," the Seer said. "Do you know what you're doing? You can't defeat Ace! You can't leave me! Don't you know who I am? I'm Rumpelstiltskin!"

I looked back at Rumpelstiltskin and said, "Who cares?"

Rumpelstiltskin's gloved hand fell, his head lolling to the side.

"Let's go," Peter said, taking my hand.

CHAPTER SIXTEEN

Wc leapt out the window with a kick against the wall to speed our way. My happy thought burned in my mind and I rocketed over Grimm. All speed was needed, both to reach Snow White quickly, and to avoid being targeted by the city's vigilant air-to-air cannon.

Peter and I were out of Grimm in an instant. I knew the danger, so I closed my eyes and let my happy thought lead me. Peter held my hand, more experienced at rapid flight, and followed the road back to Snow White's.

I soon discovered that a road wasn't necessary. When I felt Peter slow, I opened my eyes. A pillar of black smoke billowed before us, rising from the center of the forest. Peter slowed to a hover, and made sure I saw what he did.

Peter drew his pistol. I drew my shotgun. Peter held my hand a moment longer, then let go.

"Keep your eyes open," he cautioned and flew toward the smoke.

I was ready to fight. I was ready to stand up and save the girl who was in over her head against powerful forces wanting to do nothing but use or misguide her. What I wasn't ready for, though, was the carnage in front of me.

Charred trees crackled around what had once been the moonglow stump. The stump itself was collapsed and blackened. Cars lay on their sides, burnt-out wrecks amidst the fallen trees.

I landed beside a charcoal-black shape. It had no fingers. It had no hair, and its body was near flat. I couldn't help but laugh, a grim chuckle amidst the darkness, because it looked just like a cookie that had been left in the oven too long.

The Gingerbread Man was running no longer.

All around me lay more blackened bodies. These had skin and bone, though they weren't human. Their vicious, blackened teeth told me these had been wolves. The smell of them made me cough, though I didn't dare cover my nose. I needed both hands on my gun.

"Alice," Peter said, motioning me toward the ruined stump.

With a *tick-tock*, Pinocchio rose from the rubble, bits of ceiling falling off him. Lost Boys, Merry Men, and the seven dwarves huddled in a chamber beneath his protective body.

"Is it gone?" Pinocchio asked.

"Is what gone?" I asked.

"The dragon."

"Jimmy, what happened?" Peter asked as the Lost Boys flew above the fires.

"They took Snow White!" said Fedora.

"It took Snow White!" said Bowler.

"Snow White's gone!" said Fez.

"Get her!" said Top Hat.

Cowboy Hat was about to speak before Peter silenced him with a, "Shut up! Jimmy?"

"It's as Pinoke says, Petah," Jimmy answered, wiping the soot from his shoulders. "We was just crossing into the trees when we seen it swooping down from the skies."

"Fire came out its mouth thick as a river," said one of the Merry Men.

"The place was in ashes when we got 'ere. Barely 'ad time to open a volley. Bullets bounced off its hide like pebbles, they did."

"Anyone hurt?" Peter asked.

"Pinoke saw the dwarves, grabbed us and took off into the stump. Saved us, 'e did," Jimmy explained.

"Where's Robin?" I asked.

"Didn't see 'im."

"I didn't save everyone," Pinocchio said, sifting through the rubble. He picked up half a wall, his arms *click-clank*ing as he searched.

"Who are all these?" I asked, referring to the bodies surrounding the stump.

"Red Riding's hoods," answered Cowboy Hat, looking happy to speak.

Trilby Hat pointed his rifle at the trees like they were going to attack him. "She brought the wolves!" he said.

"We would have won, too," said Beret.

"Maybe," said Fedora.

"Maybe," said Bowler. "Dragon means it's a tie."

"Why would the dragon attack two different gangs?" I asked.

"Because that's what the Seer wanted," said Robin, above us. He was on his magic carpet, and dove through the burnt-out clearing to stand beside me. "Two birds with one stone. He kills off the gangs, but keeps Snow White alive. The threat still exists, but in name only."

"Here she is!" said Pinocchio, holding up what used to be the stump's door.

There beneath the smoldering flames lay a woman wearing a thick red cloak.

Jimmy was at Pinocchio's side in a moment. He checked the girl's pulse. He shook his head.

"Good riddance," said Cowboy Hat.

"She brought the dragon on us," said Top Hat.

"No," said Robin. "That was the Seer. He sent the dragon. He took Snow White. You men all right?"

The Merry Men nodded, sounding off that they were fine, thanks to the iron boy.

"The dwarves would be dead too if Pinocchio hadn't been here. The dragon was gone by the time I arrived," Robin explained.

"Then let's go after it," I said. "We can still save her!"

"Bad idea, that is," countered Jimmy. "We need more firepower than what little we got 'ere."

"Little?" countered Trilby Hat.

"Yeah! We can get Snow White," said Bowler.

"Save Snow White!" shouted Beret.

"A dragon. We're talking about a dragon 'ere," said Jimmy. "Logical thing would be to say pox to it a'tirely."

"We have to get Snow White!" countered Fedora.

"We're not going to let a dragon stop us," challenged Fez.

"Did you see that thing? It was a monster, it was," said Jimmy. "I'll not see the likes of us burnt to a crisp just to save a merry young girl. No offense intended, gents."

"None taken," answered one of the Merry Men. The rest of his fellows kept quiet, looking about the smoldering ruins, cringing at the wolf corpses.

"If the Seer sent the dragon, can you ask him to make it bring Snow White back?" asked Pinocchio.

"The Seer would never relent," answered Robin.

"How much control does the Seer have over the dragon?" I asked, biting my lip.

"It obeys his orders. So far as I've seen."

"So say, hypothetically, the Seer was dead?"

"We shot and killed the Seer," Peter explained.

"You what!" shouted Robin.

Robin had shouted at Peter, not me. I reddened with embarrassment and a little joy that Peter shared the blame.

"I shot him, Robin. It's my fault," I explained.

"Do you realize what you've done! Do you realize why I didn't kill him ages ago?!" Robin scolded.

"You threatened to kill him."

"It was a bluff. He has a dragon up his sleeve—that's quite the card to carry! And now it's loose."

"There's nothing left here, Alice," said Peter. "The deal we had with the queen and the Seer is sunk. Forget the Sleeping Beauty, we need to find another kingdom. Regroup. Maybe the Seer was wrong, maybe one of the kingdoms is still standing."

"But what about Snow White?" I asked.

"The queen wanted us to kill her. Saving her won't help you stop Ace. We've already risked enough in this kingdom as it is."

"You don't understand," Robin insisted. "If you want the Sleeping Beauty, Snow White is exactly who you need."

"I'm done making deals with people in this kingdom, thanks," said Peter.

"I'm not from this kingdom."

"Do you think we should tell the queen Snow White is dead?" I asked. "That was our original plan. The Seer can't exactly say we're lying. We could say we were the ones who burnt her home, not the dragon."

"Hah!" said Trilby Hat, crossing his arms. "Like you could blow up our house."

"We could say Pinocchio did it."

"That might work," noted Top Hat.

"You shot the Seer in his office. Nothing you do or say will fix that in the queen's mind," Robin explained. "She'll be more isolated than ever now, convinced the entire world is out to get her. The only way to prove the Seer was working against her, the only way to win her support, is to kill that dragon, and bring her Snow White."

"And how is that better than killing Snow White?" I replied.

"Because she's the queen's daughter."

"What?" I cried.

"Explain yourself," Peter said, pistol at the ready.

"Put that gun away, boy—there are lives at stake!"

"That's why you should explain," I said, raising my shotgun.

I expected a standoff of sorts, the Merry Men leveling weapons against dwarves and Lost Boys. The Lost Boys did draw their weapons, but the dwarves had dropped theirs in shock, and the Merry Men were still looking for an excuse to slip away.

"The queen's daughter has been dead for years," said Fedora.

Robin found himself alone, and lowered his head. "I was ordered to kill her," he explained. "A deal. To save my life."

"You're the huntsman! From Snow White—you're from her fairy tale!" I exclaimed, remembering characters from the echo I knew.

"Not entirely."

Robin took his cloak in his hands. I thought he might be reaching for a weapon, but he tore the cloth away. The massive cloak came off in a heap, revealing a six foot playing card with arms and feet. Robin spread his hands in surrender, and I knew exactly who he was. *How had I not seen it before?*

"The Knave of Hearts!" I cried.

"I remember you too, Alice of Wonderland, though you've grown since we last met," Robin, the Knave of Hearts, answered. "I remember us being held at the same trial. I remember you growing fifty feet tall and running away with the Cheshire Cat and the White Rabbit on your shoulders. The Queen of Hearts sentenced us both to death. Where you escaped, I was forced to make a deal."

"He's a playing card?" Peter asked.

"So was the Seer, only he had the wonder taken out of him."

"Did the Queen of Hearts pardon you?" I asked.

"No," said Robin of Hearts. "I was sent to the chopping block. Ace came to me while the Queen of Hearts was distracted with her silly game. He said that if I left Wonderland and killed the princess of Grimm, he would let me live. He's done deals like this all over this world. Loki, Rumpelstiltskin, Eris: all playing cards with the wonder taken out of them."

"But why didn't you try and escape? Try and fight him?"

"I'm not as brave as you, Alice."

I reddened. I didn't feel very brave.

"You didn't kill Snow White, obviously," I said. "That was brave."

"Another cowardice. I wanted to save my life, so I couldn't resist Ace. But I couldn't harm this little girl. So I hid her in the forest, and claimed she'd been killed. All to save my own paper-thin skin."

"Why didn't you just tell the queen? She could protect you."

"Not from Ace. And not from Rumpelstiltskin. He knew I disobeyed Ace's orders. Ace used the Seer to keep Grimm in fear, keep the queen from waking the Sleeping Beauty and uniting the nations against him. I could do nothing but protect my own head, and pray Rumpelstiltskin kept my secret."

"Rumpelstiltskin is dead. He was a jerk, in this world and in the fairy tale. And I'm going to stop Ace."

"Not without an army you're not," said Robin. "You can still wake the Sleeping Beauty."

"I don't even know what that is," I said.

"A powerful magic. Any who pledged loyalty on the Sleeping Beauty will be summoned by the one who wakes her. Wherever they are, whatever danger they're in, they'll be transported. This is the only way to unite those few remaining who stand against Ace."

"And the queen has it," said Peter.

"Join me, Alice," said Robin. "All of you. If we present Queen Cinderella Charming with her rescued daughter, you'll have your army. Cinderella will wake the Sleeping Beauty, but only when her daughter is saved."

My eyes went wide. I was surrounded by Fairy tales. But they had no magic, only the smell of smoke and ruin from the fire and danger around me.

I looked at my friends. I saw the fear in their eyes. They'd faced the dragon already. But devastating as that was, I knew what Ace would do if he succeeded in taking control. I'd seen the factories and jails of what was once Wonderland. Against that, a dragon couldn't compare.

And despite the fact that worlds were against me, this one and my own, I was willing to make a stand.

"Alright, Robin," I said.

"You used to call me the Knave of Hearts," said Robin.

"I prefer Robin."

We shook on the agreement.

"Great," said Peter, holstering his pistol. "Now all we have to do is slay a dragon."

"How hard could it be?" I asked.

CHAPTER SEVENTEEN

We loaded the *Terrible Dog* with all the weapons that could be salvaged. Lost Boys, Merry Men, seven dwarves, Pinocchio, Robin of Hearts, Peter Pan and I readied the fish-shaped ironclad fast as we could. Despite the danger, my heart soared with the knowledge of my companions' true identities.

The dragon inhabited a ruined castle built on a rocky island. It had once been a strategic location for Grimm. Queen Charming's husband died trying to restore the island, so Robin had said.

Not a promising omen.

It was dark by the time the island came into sight. We spotted it only by the castle's last remaining tower, lit with the glow of a small flame.

"The dragon?" Peter asked of the flame.

"Who knows," Robin answered.

"Best to sneak in on it quick."

"If that falls apart, Snow White's good as dead."

"It's the least risky to my boys. We fly in, grab the girl and go."

"The dragon will come after us. We need to kill it," said Robin.

"So we lure it to a place we can kill it," said Peter.

"How do we kill it?" I asked.

Robin was silent. His eyes were fixed on the lonely tower.

"Does it have any weaknesses?" I asked. "If a king couldn't kill it with modern weapons, we need to know more about it."

"We've got enough weapons," said Robin.

Peter looked doubtful, and cast a worried glance my direction.

"You both have the right idea. We need to kill it, but we need to sneak inside first," I explained. "Robin, you and Jimmy lead a team to the castle gates. I'm assuming it's empty except for the dragon?"

"So the stories go," Robin answered.

"Then let's hope stories from stories are true. Lie in wait with all the firepower you've got. Peter and I will go inside and see if we can find a weakness."

"We'll go with you, Alice," Pinocchio insisted.

"Peter and I will be enough. We need to be silent. Plus you've got the biggest punch of anyone here."

"We'll see about that," countered Cowboy Hat, brandishing his BAR machinegun.

"It's a good plan," Peter said. "But you're leaving out the ship. There's more firepower here than anywhere else."

"Fighting on the ship is suicide with a dragon," Robin countered.

"Didn't say we'd do that. We go with Alice's plan. But once Alice and I clear the castle, we blast it with a broadside. I'll send up a flare to signal we're clear." Peter showed me a flare gun he had hidden in his pocket. "If we can take the castle down on top of the dragon, great. If not, you and Pinocchio will be ready to strike at its back."

Peter smacked his fist into his palm to illustrate the plan.

"And if the dragon attacks the ship?" Robin asked.

"The Lost Boys can fly away. They know how to look after their own skins. But the point here is to kill the dragon in the first volley, or blow the walls down so Pinocchio can rip its head off."

"Alright," Robin agreed.

"Just one thing. If this goes south, we bug out," Peter added, looking at me. "You hear me? We fly away. We pick up everyone and we get out. This girl isn't worth dying over."

"That's where you're wrong, Peter Pan."

"It won't come to that," I insisted. "Stay sharp. Stay out of sight and quiet. Focus on the dragon's weak spot. And don't engage until we find out what that weak spot is."

Peter took me by the arm and whispered in my ear, "And what if Snow White's already dead?"

I shivered at the thought and ignored the question. "Get ready."

The seven dwarves ensured their Tommy guns, shotguns, pistols, and BAR's were locked and loaded. The Merry Men readied rifles, submachine guns, and what looked like modern-day assault rifles they'd no doubt stolen from Grimm authorities.

The Lost Boys readied their rifles and pistols as they had before battling Captain Hook. Derek was placed in charge of the *Terrible Dog*, and showed Pinocchio something he'd come up with.

"The cannons and deck guns we already retrofitted from Hook's equipment," Derek explained, walking with Pinocchio to the stern. "But you need a bit more firepower out there. And this will give it to you." He smiled where the ship's Gatling gun sat.

Derek had removed the bolts holding down the terrible weapon. Two curved arms were welded onto its top, along with a massive ammunition box.

"Try it on," Derek said to Pinocchio.

"Excuse me?" Pinocchio asked.

"With this, you'll be a walking artillery piece. Just slip it on—there." Derek guided Pinocchio under the curved bars, turning them into shoulder straps. "And I'll just—there!"

With the ammunition belt attached and the crank armed, Pinocchio stood ready with his portable Gatling cannon.

"You'll need someone to make sure the feed doesn't get tangled," Derek advised.

"I'll guide your aim," Jimmy volunteered, standing beside Pinocchio. "Looking good, Pinoke."

"Thanks," Pinocchio said, testing the machine's weight. He wielded it with more ease than the dwarves did their Tommy guns.

The castle came further into view, and with the help of the crescent moon and twinkling stars I was able to see the dark island. It was tiny as islands go, probably no more than half a mile across. A high cliff dominated the island's center, and aside from a cluster of trees this was the extent of the landscape. The cliff rose a hundred feet above the ocean, waves crashing against razor-sharp rocks at its base. The castle had been built upon this cliff, with a high ring of walls on the landward side, seawalls hanging over the water.

What surprised and confused me was the castle's erratic construction. While the castle in Grimm was built along straight lines, this building was nothing but hyperbolic or elliptical angles. Towers bulged and turned. The walls of massive stone blocks twisted in a way I didn't think possible. Looking at it too long made my eyes hurt, so I turned away.

A natural harbor led the approach to the castle gates. Derek guided the ship into the harbor, with all but a tiny crew of Lost Boys leaping off.

Robin led Pinocchio, the Merry Men, the dwarves and Lost Boys. Robin armed himself with nothing but his crossbow and the apple bomb. He tucked this under his cloak, concealing it against his playing card skin.

The instant Pinocchio and the assault team were off, Derek and the remaining Lost Boys took the *Terrible Dog* back to sea.

With both groups approaching their positions, Peter and I flew toward the dark castle.

"Don't suppose we can grab her and bolt?" Peter suggested.

"The dragon came after Snow White in the middle of the woods. He'll track her down again," I said.

"And when Grimm's city guns blow it out of the sky?"

"I don't want to lure something that deadly to a city. Don't forget, the king himself attacked the dragon and failed. Guns may not be the answer."

"So what hope do we have?"

"You have me," I said.

"Wonderful."

Thorns grew thick all over the castle. Its stone was warped where it was visible, twisted and broken. Holes dotted the walls, damage from explosions, I guessed.

Peter and I hugged the churning water, breakers splashing around us. We flew against the seawalls and stopped when we reached the top. Peter looked over the side of the wall. He motioned for me to follow and we hopped inside.

The twisted seawalls gave way to a wide courtyard. I spotted the large, wooden castle gates on the far side. Closer to us stood the keep, thorns hugging its stone edifice. The stones created more erratic lines and hyperbolic surfaces, with not a single right angle or straight edge.

Robin had given us flashlights and a lock picking kit, the tools of a good thief. There was no need for the lock pick, however, as the fortress's entrance was demolished. We kept our flashlights low as Peter and I hovered over the entrance.

A grand staircase dominated the castle foyer. It was irregular in shape, the railings widening and narrowing in unnatural waves. What once had been a lush red carpet decorating the stairs and floor was now covered in soot and shattered stone.

The ceiling looked like a deformed sphere, ornate pillars holding it aloft. Some of the pillars lay on their side, felled like trees before an unstoppable force. Where the pillars had collapsed, so had the ceiling, leaving scattered ruins all around.

Peter and I stayed silent, sticking close to the ceiling. I listened to my heartbeat as I tried to see or hear the dragon. There was only the distant crashing of waves against the cliffs.

Finding no sign of the dragon, I took a closer look around. Here, amidst the crumbled towers and shattered pieces of stained glass, lay dozens of bodies.

They wore armor from head to toe. I flew down to one that lay sprawled on the staircase. His thick boots were melted into the stones. He wore a vest of scaled plastic armor, like the Kevlar vests American Special Forces use. Instead of the stars and stripes, however, his burnt uniform bore the rainbow with a sunburst flag of Grimm. Only a metal bowl remained of his helmet. The rest had melted around his ruined face.

Some soldiers were crushed. Others were in pieces. But there was something common to all of them.

"They were running away," Peter said.

I ignored this revelation, and continued up the stairs.

We traveled down a wide, ornate hallway, empty torch sconces the only remaining decoration. My flashlight cast shadows all about the carved stonework. I blinked and thought the passage was turning, but we were walking straight. Ash lay in wind-blown piles on either side of the hallway. Perhaps they'd once been tapestries, or beautiful paintings.

"It's a good thing I'm already mad," I said, shaking my head for the curious way the hall was designed. "Or this building would make me so."

"I'm trying not to look too close," Peter admitted.

We passed through a passageway and arrived at a great hall. The ceiling was high and angled to a point, with two rows of round pillars spaced erratically throughout the oval-shaped room. It must have been a banquet hall once; pieces of blackened wood were all that remained of the feasting tables. Cobwebs littered the floor, concealing broken plates and candelabras beneath a thick layer of gray.

Darkness seemed to absorb the flashlight's glow, turning it into a small dot on the wall. Every once in a while the dot of light would fall on a skeleton. The bodies were covered in cobwebs as well, a shallow grave for those who'd fallen.

A sudden rumble made me turn off the light. It was guttural sound, and it echoed from the other side of a barred door. When it rose it sucked dust-clouded air through cracks in the doorframe. When it fell it seemed the air was pressing against the walls like an inflating balloon.

"I think the dragon's snoring," I said.

Peter flew to the doorway. He put his hand against the wood, hissed, and pulled his hand back.

"Hot," Peter whispered. "Must be on the other side."

We were running out of space and time. The best way to find a weakness would be to examine the dragon's body. If we found it sleeping, this would be much easier. But I didn't want to go near the thing.

The ceiling had caved in on the far side of the hall, allowing the moon to form a hazy spotlight. From this, I caught a faint glow.

"What's that? Hold on, Peter," I said, stopping him at the door. "Come see."

I flew to the moonlight. There lay an utterly crushed body. It was armored like the others had been, layers of futuristic materials forming protection stronger than steel. Strong, but not powerful enough to stop a dragon's assault.

The armor was gold. It had likely been shimmering once, but its sheen had faded. While others bore printed flags, this man's chest plate was platinum, a golden sunburst and rainbow hammered into the metal.

"Must be King Charming," I whispered.

Peter nodded, examining the body.

The caved-in ceiling told the tale of this fallen knight. He had been crushed from above, burnt, and mauled.

There was only one part of him still intact. In his still-clenched hand the king held a sword. It glowed in the moonlight.

"The other bodies have guns, or explosives," I noted. "Why does the king have a sword?"

"Maybe the others had swords too. Dragons are hoarders," Peter noted.

"Then why leave the king's?"

I touched the sword like it was a hot stove, afraid it held some strange power. The sword was nothing more than cold metal to my touch, though, so I gently twisted it out of the king's hand.

The sword didn't seem anything more than a normal sword, save for the strange letters carved into the fuller.

When I pulled the sword free, I discovered something else in the king's skeletal palm. It was a piece of brown, leathery parchment.

"Hold this," I said, handing Peter the sword. I reached for the parchment.

"What do the engravings mean?" Peter asked.

"Maybe they have something to do with what's written here."

I read the parchment aloud, stuttering at the strange words, "'Beware the Jb'rwock, my son! The jaws that bite, the claws that catch! Beware the Shub bird, and shun the frumious Ngyr-Korath. Take the vorpal sword in hand, your blow shall shake the sea, for Jb'rwock is death, but 'neath the earth he may yet be.'"

"So the sword can kill the dragon?" Peter asked.

"I suppose that's what the king thought."

I looked at the parchment. It was torn, no doubt taken from a much larger book. "If that's the end of the poem," I said.

"Maybe these markings mean something?" Peter asked, trying to read the sword's engravings. "Ph'nglui mglaw'nafh… what?"

"Let me see. R'lyeh wgah'nagl ftagn."

"Sounds like gibberish to me."

"They could be magic words. Jimmy said bullets bounced off the dragon's skin. This might be a magic sword, Peter, the vorpal sword from the poem. Maybe it's enchanted to kill the dragon," I suggested.

"Called a Jb'rwock," said Peter.

"Exactly."

"Sounds good to me."

We heard the dragon's rumbling snore echo once more through the castle.

"Come on," Peter said. "The others are probably in position by now. Let's sneak in, grab Snow White, and kill the dragon in its sleep."

"Not kill the dragon first?" I asked.

"I want to make sure Snow White's still alive."

"She is, Peter."

"Look."

Peter pointed through the hole in the ceiling. Just beyond it lay the dark, twisted tower we'd seen from the sea. It was the only lit tower, and taller than the others.

"That's gotta be where she is," Peter said. "The room where the dragon's sleeping is right below it." Peter pointed to the doorway. "We grab Snow White, and sneak in on the dragon through the tower's back door."

"I doubt the Jb'rwock is expecting someone to come up behind it," I said.

"Exactly. Let's make sure it never wakes up."

"Okay."

Peter rose through the ceiling. I followed, and we glided silently over the masonry to the tower. We couldn't fly too close, since the thorny vines grew thicker and thicker all the way to the window.

I looked through the thorn bushes to see what lay inside the tower. The only furniture was a thickly-padded bed and a small table with a lantern. Through the flickering lantern light I spotted Snow White. She lay upon a thin layer of threshes, hands clasped over her chest.

"Psst," I whispered.

Snow White didn't move.

The Jb'rwock's snores rumbled up the tower's spiral staircase.

I took a shotgun shell out of my pocket and tossed it at Snow White. It bounced off her fingers and rolled across the threshes.

Snow White shot up, back to the wall. She grabbed the lantern like it was a cudgel and prepared to strike whatever had touched her.

"Shh!" I warned. "Snow White. We're here to rescue you."

Snow White turned to the window. She glared at us. "Of course it's you," she said.

Peter struck the thorns with the vorpal sword. They split like they were nothing more than string. Peter examined the blade, impressed, as we flew inside.

"Did you summon that beast?" Snow White accused.

"What? No," I said.

"Shh," Peter cautioned. He checked the room with his pistol drawn, hovering down the staircase to ensure there was no danger. He tossed me the dropped shotgun shell and I put it back in my pocket.

"The Grand Seer controls the dragon. Or did," I explained.

"Why would the Grand Seer have a dragon kidnap me? Are the dwarves okay?" Snow White asked.

"Short answer, the dwarves are fine, Red Riding's dead, you're the queen's daughter, the Seer kidnapped you to extort the queen, Alice shot the Seer, we're fetching you to get your mom's support," Peter explained.

Snow White raised an eyebrow. She turned to me.

I shrugged.

Snow White's eyes bulged.

"I would have given a more sympathetic explanation, but yes," I said.

"That's… not possible. The queen's been trying to kill me for years," Snow White replied.

"We don't really have time or need for talk. There's a dragon downstairs I'd like to keep from waking up," Peter said, brandishing the vorpal sword. "Alice, take Snow White clear. I want you far away in case I don't kill it."

I was about to explain to Peter that his sense of heroics was unnecessary and a bit irritating after all we'd been through, but Snow White said, "I can't leave the tower."

"It's okay. Alice will fly you out," Peter explained.

"No, I mean, if I take a step outside the tower, the dragon grabs me and throws me back in here. It's like he knows where I am."

"You tried going out the window?"

"I'm not the kind of person who just sits in a tower waiting for a couple flying kids with delusions of grandeur to come rescue me."

"Beggars can't be choosers, Princess."

Snow White was about to say something, but I jumped in and asked, "Why weren't you resting on the bed?"

"Because that dragon can take his bed and shove it," Snow White answered. "So if you've got guns—let's kill this thing and get going."

"Stay here," Peter said.

"Not likely," I replied.

"Give me a gun," Snow White insisted.

"You won't need one, hopefully," Peter said, showing the engraved sword. "Magic sword. Only thing that can kill it, so we've read."

"Guess that's why the dragon didn't flinch when I hit it with a rock." Snow White's fingers twitched, so she picked up the lantern, balancing it to use as a weapon of last resort.

"Stay quiet."

Peter gave me a hesitant look. I responded by hefting my shotgun. Peter nodded.

We descended the staircase as quietly as we could. Hovering made this easy, and Snow White moved with the dexterity of someone who'd spent her life sneaking around.

Darkness converged upon the last stair. An arched, open doorway led to a room of utter black. There was no way of knowing anything existed on the other side. It felt like a doorway to an endless pit, darkness and madness in the center of the world.

The Jb'rwock's rumbling snores banished these thoughts, and I knew what danger lay in that room. Peter led the way, sword before him, and stepped into the darkness. I followed, the barrel of my shotgun suddenly cold.

Snow White stopped at the door's threshold, unable to move from the tower. She lifted the lantern. Light rose to the domed ceiling like water seeping through oil. Through the darkness I could see the drum-shaped room, and mounds of gold reflecting the dim light.

Treasures I could never dream of lay scattered in piles of wealth. Gold coins, gold bars, uncut diamonds and inset gemstones of a hundred colors. The most spectacular crowns that would have made the wearer look king of the world sat amongst platinum discs. It was off these mirror-like discs that the lantern's glow reflected the beast himself.

It looked like a he, though the rainbow-refracted light showed little more than silver scales and a horned head. His viper-fanged teeth were too large for his skull. Antenna like an ant's twitched on the ground. His wings were tucked against his thick hide, and his tail was so long it wrapped around the room beneath piles of gold. A greenish color shone at the edges of his scales, oozing like a dark slime, though my eyes would lose sight of it every time I looked directly at him. His arms and legs were curled beneath his body, with one claw, big as a car, clutching the stone floor.

Peter held the vorpal sword ready to strike as I tried to move. My terror-filled paralysis was temporary, but my heart pounded in fear as I shook my senses to focus.

With his feet hovering over stacks of gems, Peter rose to where the Jb'rwock's thin neck met its horned skull. The horns were like a demon's, pointed and turned back to offer protection against what I hoped was a weak point.

With the light glinting off the dragon's silver and green scales, Peter Pan hefted the vorpal sword. His strike bore down on the Jb'rwock's neck with a *crack-oom* loud as thunder.

Peter flew back, the sword ricocheting off the beast's hide.

Smoke rose in the air, and I heard incoherent words whispered through the thunder that died echoing against the walls.

The Jb'rwock's eyes opened. They burned the same green color as the slime seeping through its scales. It was an impossible color, the dragon's eyes glowing and stinking like the air of an open grave.

Peter lost no time and struck once more at the beast's neck. The dragon reared in pain from the thunderous blow. But even as the deafened echoes fell, the Jb'rwock showed no sign of damage. Not a scale had been disturbed, and the beast roared with fury.

It wasn't out of bravery, though I wish I could say I was brave, but terror that I fired my weapon. I pulled the trigger fast as I could. But the blasts did nothing, and the dragon lunged at Peter.

Peter was able to slip past the Jb'rwock. He held his pistol in one hand and the vorpal sword in the other, striking and firing in hopes of finding a weak spot.

"Alice! Take Snow White and get out of here!" Peter shouted as he deflected the Jb'rwock's swiping claw.

The beast roared as Peter delivered a thunderous blow beneath its head. This did no more damage than before, and the dragon whipped its tail against Peter's side, sending him tumbling to the ground.

"Peter!" I shouted, diving through the avalanche of gold coins to stand between him and the beast.

I fired my shotgun. Snow White picked up a gilded sword from the hoard of treasure and swung it at the creature, but it was no more effective than my bullets

The Jb'rwock reared its head and took in a breath as my gun clicked empty.

The massive inhalation stank of rotting flesh and methane, but in that brief moment of silence I heard a *tick-tock, tick-tock, tick-tock* racing toward us.

The treasure room doors exploded inward. There stood Pinocchio, Gatling gun braced.

"Get away from her you beast!" Pinocchio shouted and turned the crank.

The Gatling gun erupted into the dragon's open mouth. In sudden pain, the Jb'rwock fell back, his exhalation blossoming into the domed ceiling. He raised his claws and stood on his feet, striking all directions as he backed away from Pinocchio's onslaught.

Through the light of the dragon's flame, I spotted something on the ground. The Jb'rwock removed its massive clawed foot from where it had dug into the stone, revealing a tan-colored book, its pages remarkably similar to the one I'd found on King Charming.

"Come on, Alice, we've gotta get out of here!" Peter said, adding his pistol to Pinocchio's blasts. "Grab Snow White and let's bolt!"

"Not yet," I said, reloading my gun.

I tried to move around the dragon's hideous claws, but it struck at the ground, throwing me and a wave of coins skyward. I recovered in mid-air, flying to dodge the dragon's snapping jaws. Peter's well-timed swing with the vorpal sword and another round from the Gatling gun caught the dragon's attention.

"Alice, now!" Peter shouted.

"You grab Snow White—I'll grab the book."

Peter glared.

"Trust me!" I shouted.

"Pinocchio! Get Snow White!" Peter ordered.

In an instant, Peter was zipping across the dragon's spine, pecking it like a horsefly with sword strikes. The dragon roared fire into the ceiling once more.

Pinocchio lunged across the room and picked up the shrieking Snow White. At the same time I darted to the ground and fired a shotgun blast point-blank into the Jb'rwock's toes. The dragon roared and leapt away, exposing the book.

The book's cover was leather, thick, and bore the words "Necronomicon" in jagged scratches.

I picked up the book just before the Jb'rwock's mighty claw dug a crater in the floor.

Pinocchio opened fire once more, Snow White holding onto his neck. With this, and another strike from the vorpal sword, the dragon backed away. And yet there was still no sign of damage on the creature, his flame lighting the room and revealing his terrible, unhurt form.

Peter drew his flare gun and fired through a tiny crack in the ceiling, a burst of red light glowing against his face as he shouted, "Run!"

The walls shook an instant after the flare went up. Thunder rang against the drum-shaped room and a chunk of wall collapsed inward.

We didn't run but flew, racing through the door with Pinocchio's *tick-tock*ing bounds leading the charge. The dragon chased us and burst through the doorway just as the walls erupted with cannon fire.

We flew through the columned hall with the castle raining down around us. The mighty pillars fell, and I saw one crash atop the Jb'rwock's head. We dodged crumbling pieces of enormous masonry as we flew over the grand staircase to exit the twisted castle.

A cloud of dust burst around us as Peter and I flew to a stop outside the castle walls. Pinocchio set Snow White down and we watched the castle collapse from a safe distance.

I spotted the *Terrible Dog* to my right, just off the shoreline, flashes from its turrets heralding the booms as shot after shot exploded against the castle.

The foundations of the seaward cliff gave way and a good portion of the castle crashed into the waves. The tower that had imprisoned Snow White toppled like a tree.

The cannons continued to fire, though they simply churned up debris. They stopped moments after the last of the seawalls collapsed into the ocean.

Moonlight turned the cloud of dust hanging over the rubble into a silvery mist.

Snow White was the first to exhale.

"Well," she said. "Glad that's over. Who's up for a drink?"

"This will make for quite the story," Peter said with a smile. "Nothing like the fairy tales, though."

I frowned. Something in the poem had been nagging at my thoughts the instant Peter's strike with the vorpal sword failed to kill the Jb'rwock.

"Underneath he may yet be," I read from the torn paper.

When I opened the book, the Necronomicon, I flipped through the thick pages to find the one from which the poem had been torn.

There, I found the poem's second page, and read aloud, "Say these words and say them well, the elder ones they grumber: R'leah calls—the burbling spell, to make the Jb'rwock slumber."

Before I could say another word, I heard a rumble from the pile of debris. The mist glowed a fiery green. Stone crumbled over the side of the cliff and splashed into the sea. With a mighty roar the Jb'rwock rose from the ground and blotted out the moon in its dreadful flight. It raged with fire and fury and set the island aflame.

"I thought you said the sword would kill it!" Snow White accused.

"Not helping, Princess," Peter said, raising the blade.

"It will kill it, we just have to use it right," I said.

"How?"

"I don't know."

The dragon roared and found us by the broken castle gates. So did the rest of the landing party. Robin, the seven dwarves, Merry Men, and Lost Boys joined us with guns drawn.

"Pinocchio. Get the dragon's attention. Give us all the time you can. Snow White, get to cover," I said.

"Not likely," Snow White said.

Fedora tossed Snow White her .45 caliber pistol. "Get going," said the dwarf.

"We got this," said Top Hat.

"Bring it, dragon!" shouted Cowboy Hat.

"We who are about to kill," said Trilby Hat.

"Moon you!" called Fez.

"Snow White and the seven dwarves," said Beret.

"Eat your heart out!" cried Bowler.

The dragon roared and flew down to meet us. Pinocchio and the rest opened fire.

Peter and I took to the sky while the Jb'rwock smashed into the ground. He came up with gunfire blasting away at his side. His tail slashed and his teeth *snicker-snash*ed and he struck against his foes. Pinocchio blasted away with his Gatling gun 'til the dragon turned its head toward him and exhaled fire into the iron boy's face.

Pinocchio reached through the flames and grabbed the Jb'rwock by the tooth, pulling it down and punching its skull.

"Yog-Sothoth the gate is known, Yog-Sothoth the gate is you, Yog-Sothoth the gate comes down, Yog-Sothoth the doors of blue," I read on the poem's next page as the Jb'rwock struck Pinocchio. It bit down on the iron boy and threw him into the air. I didn't see where Pinocchio landed, but I saw the beast's eyes turn toward me.

The dragon turned away when the *Terrible Dog*'s cannon struck its side. Explosions lit up the Jb'rwock's scales and sent him roaring into the sky.

"In nethermost caverns of fathom he lies, cursed be the realm where dead thoughts live, out of corruption and horrid life rise, rise from the path that I now give," I continued to read.

The dragon rose to attack, growling as it dodged cannon fire. It roared, its burning eyes flaring with rage as it dove atop of the *Terrible Dog*. Masts cracked and fell in furious strikes of the beast's flicking tail. The Jb'rwock tore into the iron hull and rose when the cannons chased it back into the air. The ferocious creature hovered over the ironclad and bathed it in flame.

"The wind gibbers with his coming voice," I continued as the wind howled. "The sunken seal engraved below." The waves rose. "Azathoth release your choice, and come to claim your lost fellow."

The Necronomicon grew hot in my hands, and the words on its pages glowed.

The dragon spotted us and once more prepared to attack. Peter and I dodged a barrage of flame and flew across the sky. I was barely able to hold onto the Necronomicon and maintain focus on its maddening pages.

My mouth opened to read the next words, and in the process my altitude floundered. I couldn't maintain focus on the spell and my happy thought at once. Peter had to slow to collect me, and in that instant left us exposed to the dragon's attack.

The Jb'rwock did not, however, burn us to cinders. When it inhaled, it turned away, a crossbow bolt stuck in its tongue. The dragon's flaming eyes looked to the distant dock. There stood Robin, the Knave of Hearts, the huntsman, adding a second bolt to his crossbow.

The dragon roared and charged the playing card with flame already spewing out its mouth. Robin stood unwavering and fired once more, landing his bolt in a gash across the beast's eye. It was a shot beyond perfect, and sent the Jb'rwock stumbling in pain. Instead of burning Robin away, he merely collided with him, crashing into the docks.

"The words, Peter. The spell needs the Jb'rwock to fly over the ocean," I said, barely maintaining my focus on the spell. I glanced at the pages, my mind swimming with the words. "I need the sword. And I need him to chase me."

Peter held me aloft. He put the vorpal sword in my hand.

"Keep reading," Peter said, and we dove toward the dragon.

"Vorpal sword across the waves strike I," I called into the wind. The words on the Necronomicon glowed a sickly black.

Peter set my feet on the docks beside the thrashing Jb'rwock. He fired his pistol, darting here and there to turn the dragon's attention away from Robin.

"Cut the gate between the sky!" I shouted and ran between the Jb'rwock's legs.

I swung the vorpal sword against the dragon's hide. It was nothing more than a weak lunge, since I was carrying the

Necronomicon in one arm and the sword in the other. But the sparking strike did the trick.

The Jb'rwock roared and faced me. I braced the burning Necronomicon and jetted across the ocean. Low and fast I flew, the Jb'rwock racing behind me. The ocean became a sheet of black glass beneath me, flattening with the spell's dark power.

I heard the Jb'rwock inhale even as the words crossed my tongue.

"That is not dead which can eternal lie. And with strange aeons even death may die," I said

As the book commanded, I swung the vorpal sword across the flattened water while shouting the final words, "Cthulhu fhtagn!"

Two doors fell inward where the sword cut, and out from this portal of utter blackness came a creature of such maddening size I fell out of the sky at the mere sight of it. Its skin was green, its mouth a series of tentacles, its wings too small for its body and beating a storm as it rose from beneath the world.

The mountain-tall creature grabbed the Jb'rwock in its green claw just before the dragon doused me in flame. The Jb'rwock roared in panic and pain, as the green monstrosity sank beneath the waves with the dragon in hand.

Was I mad before I saw this horror? Perhaps it was my madness that saved what little sanity I had left. All thoughts went to nothing in that gaping portal to oblivion.

The dark hole to madness seemed a solid thing, pulling me like the Jb'rwock to its black embrace. But something took my hand. It pulled me away from the horror. It tugged me out of madness. It took me into the air and kept going 'til I was far above the water, looking down through the clouds as the great gate sealed itself once more.

The Jb'rwock was gone forever, along with the green elder thing that had collected it.

"Alice. Alice!" the voice above me said.

I turned toward it.

"Alice, are you okay?" asked the boy. He held me, my shoulders heavy under his arms.

I blinked, eyes glossed over with the image of that green nightmare stuck in my mind.

The next sensation I felt was strange. Not as strange as the green horror. Not as strange as the Jb'rwock. It was a different kind of strange. With rising awareness, I felt lips pressed against mine.

The madness left me. The fury departed. All that remained in my mind was him, was my happy thought, and I found myself flying over the clouds.

"Peter," I said, my wits returned.

Peter smiled, his green eyes glowing in the fading moonlight. "You owe me one," he said.

I wrapped my arms around his neck and kissed him. We spun through the sky as the sun broke over the horizon.

Still braced in each other's arms, he said to me, "I guess we'll call it even."

CHAPTER EIGHTEEN

Grimm glistened before us. Its rainbow-tinted shield glowed in the afternoon sun. Half a dozen ships of war, three on each side, escorted our limping ironclad up the river.

It had taken most of the morning to recover from the battle with the Jb'rwock. Burns and other injuries to the dwarves, Lost Boys and Merry Men were the first things to address. Some of these were severe, and required medical attention Snow White was thankfully skilled enough to provide.

Pinocchio had not suffered seriously from his injuries. The Jb'rwock had been unable to penetrate his iron body, and he walked away with only a few dents.

The same could not be said of the *Terrible Dog*. Its masts were destroyed, its main deck in ruins. Only its iron hide had saved its crew from death.

While repairs were being made to the men and the ship, those who could be spared went to work searching what was left of the castle. Only the abundance of treasure we'd recovered, along with the golden-armored body of the fallen King Charming, allowed us to approach Grimm in the first place.

Upon seeing our wounded vessel, the hyper-vigilant Grimm fleet demanded we state our business or be destroyed.

It's amazing how quickly someone can become your friend when you show them a fist full of rubies and say you're going to give them to the queen. A boarding party that inspected our claims of treasure soon welcomed us to Grimm, and they guided our ship to the harbor.

Despite our offers of friendship and treasure, the Grimm officers arrested us the instant they saw Snow White. The only thing that kept them from killing us then and there was the recovered body of their beloved king.

Onlookers from the city of Grimm flocked the stone-lined riverside to watch the strange vessel go by. Word had spread that this ship had recovered a true treasure: the body of King Charming.

Even with a gun at my back and my hands in cuffs, I still managed to smile and wave.

The crowd grew thicker and thicker as we reached the docks. As requested, ambulances met us and our wounded were taken care of.

Our captors ignored our claims that Snow White was the queen's daughter, but I insisted we be taken directly to the queen. The fact that we had so bravely destroyed the beast which had killed their king, and recovered his body was the only thing that convinced the authorities to agree to this request. The fact that I was wanted on high crimes of murder and espionage meant they kept us chained and guarded.

Our police escort soon became a parade as onlookers cheered our entrance. Some recognized Snow White. I thought they might be cheering for her arrest, but no. They were cheering her presence, shouting encouragement for her cause. Automatons and shield-wielding police were unable to shepherd the populace, and the crowd threatened to become a mob. This encouraged the police to bring us to the castle with all haste, and in short time we arrived at the throne room.

Queen Cinderella Charming was there waiting for us. She rose from her throne the second we entered and stormed across the white marble floor.

"How dare you betray the trust I laid in you, Alice of Wonderland!" Cinderella scolded. "And you, Snow White, you shall pay for the crimes you have committed in my kingdom."

The elite guards Hazeltree and Whitebird took command of our chains and brought Snow White and myself to our knees. Peter was in bonds as well, and glared at the two guards. Robin stood behind him, not bothering to hide his playing card body.

Cinderella placed a hand beneath Snow White's chin and examined her with a cold criticism. "Such a pretty thing," she said. "A pity you chose crime."

"Your highness, there is something you must know," I began.

"I charged you with a simple task. You may have brought me Snow White, but you betrayed me nonetheless. What possessed you to murder the Grand Seer?"

"I stopped his plan, and saved your daughter."

Cinderella laughed. "Fairytales won't save you from the dungeons, little Alice. Confess now and I might show you leniency."

"Dear queen," Robin began, "Alice speaks the truth. The Grand Seer was manipulating you. Under the authority and approval of Ace of Spades of Wonderland, he has undermined your rule for years."

"Preposterous," said the queen.

"Do you recall my face, dear queen?"

"I certainly would recall a walking playing card."

"No. My face."

Cinderella glared at Robin. "You're the huntsman who brought news of my daughter's murder."

"Indeed. I was tasked with carrying out the murder of the infant Princess Charming by Ace of Spades himself."

"What!"

"You recall my face, Cinderella. Do you recall her face?" Robin asked.

Cinderella glared at Snow White. Snow White looked at the queen, her red lips quivering with worry. As the two women's eyes met, tears welled in the queen's. Her stiffness melted like ice in the sun, and Cinderella's eyes went wide.

"My child?" the queen whispered.

Cinderella ran her fingers through Snow White's raven-black hair, her hands touching the girl's face and arms as if she were an illusion that might disappear any moment.

"My child!" Cinderella said and embraced Snow White with tears running down her face. "Where have you been, my princess?"

"I…" Snow White was lost for words. She held back tears as best she could, struggling with the realization that the woman who'd been her enemy was her mother.

"Whitebird, Hazeltree, remove these cuffs this instant. We have heroes in our midst. Dear child, dear child, how did I not know it was you?" Cinderella asked.

"That was my doing," Robin confessed. "Ace of Spades agreed to pardon my crimes in Wonderland if I killed your daughter. I couldn't do it. But I couldn't reveal she was alive. That would be my head."

Cinderella bit her lip. She shook away a sudden thought and embraced Robin. "You saved my daughter twice then. Thank you."

"The Grand Seer knew. He controlled the dragon. He wanted to keep Snow White alive as a danger, so he could control you," I explained.

"And the dragon?" the queen asked.

"Gone."

Cinderella held her daughter. "Dear child, what horrors you've been through. Can you ever forgive me?"

Snow White was still struggling against tears. "I… don't remember anything about being your daughter," she said. "I don't even know my real name."

"Do you know who you are?"

"I'm Snow White."

"Now you're Snow White Charming. And now you're here. You're my daughter, my long-lost, beloved daughter, who has survived all trials I unwittingly put her through. I know you, Snow White. My eyes are clear. For the first time since I lost you, my eyes are clear."

"You're... going to help my friends? You're going to help the people?" Snow White asked.

"Of course," said the queen.

Snow White nodded. She extended a hand like she was going to shake hands with the queen. She bit her lip, withdrew her hand, and threw her arms around her mother.

Snow White let out a breath so deep it sounded like she'd been holding it for years. "Mom," she said and let the tears flow.

They embraced for some time. Watching them cry together, their mutual hate washing away, brought a pain to my heart I didn't fully understand. I hadn't realized I was still on my knees until the queen urged me to my feet.

"Alice of Wonderland. You set about the events that brought us together. You befriended my daughter, even before either of us knew this sad truth," Cinderella said.

"I was, just... just doing what I could," I mumbled.

"You brought me my husband and my daughter. Both I thought were dead. I can now grieve for the one and rejoice for the other."

"Alice is pretty amazing," Peter said, giving me a wink of encouragement.

"Indeed," agreed the queen.

Cinderella looked beyond me to the flags hanging from the throne room's walls. There were even more empty pegs than before, and only a few colorful flags remained.

"What madness has blinded me that I would not see this manipulation? Ace of Spades must be stopped, before his evil infects Grimm's allies," the queen said.

"Queen Cinderella," I said. "We found messages in the Seer's office."

"Olympus didn't join Ace. It fell," Robin explained. "It fell to

Ace's manipulation and violence."

"What?" Cinderella asked. "Why was I not informed? Why was I not..." The queen understood the answer to her own question. "While despair took my wits, this world has lost its way. Arthur, Crocket, Thor, are they still fighting? Do any of our allies remain?"

"Other cards were working in secret in those lands too. The Seer said every nation from the Frontiers to the Two-Land Kingdoms is under Ace's control."

"The messages said there were still people fighting," I said. "They thought they were alone, that only Grimm could help them."

"They are not alone," Cinderella said. "Not anymore."

"They were waiting for you to wake the Sleeping Beauty. What is it?"

Cinderella smiled. "I will show you. Even though the world had already fallen, you pressed on, dear Alice. Know that your efforts were not in vain. You asked for support in your efforts to retake Wonderland. You asked for soldiers, you shall have an army. Hazeltree, the rose."

Sergeant Hazeltree made a slight bow and left the throne room.

"Today we rejoice," Cinderella continued. "My daughter who was dead is alive. My fear of monsters is destroyed. Let there be singing in the streets and feasting to be remembered. Tomorrow, we march on Wonderland."

Hazeltree returned bearing a golden box. He presented it to the queen. Inside was a crystal rose.

"This is what you have been seeking, Alice. Anyone who pledges loyalty, each nation these flags represent, is bound to that oath. They are brought together through a magic second only to the rabbit hole in power. It is time we wake the Sleeping Beauty. It is time we unite the heroes of our world," Cinderella said and snapped the rose where the bulb met the stem.

The rose flashed and glowed a brilliant red. With a low hum, a holographic projection of a woman stood atop the crystal. She was nude, the hair on her head wrapping around her body like Lady Godiva. The tiny hologram looked at Cinderella.

"So that's what the Sleeping Beauty is," I whispered, finding it much more fascinating than the fairy tale.

"Summon those who have made the oaths," Cinderella spoke to the hologram. "Travel to all kingdoms and nations, and let them know that they are not alone. Alice is leading an army to take back Wonderland. We assemble at the beanstalk at first light on the morrow."

The hologram nodded and flew off the rose, taking to the sky like a campfire spark.

"Twelve hours," the queen said. "That is how long it will take. Half a day to fetch heroes from across the world."

"Not bad," Peter said.

"What do we do till then?" I asked.

"We celebrate like it's the last night we have on this world," said Cinderella.

I had never been in a triumph before. I didn't really know what one was. Cinderella had to explain it to me. Why I was at the seat of honor made very little sense.

I suppose a triumph was like a parade, only with a military victory as its inspiration. Peter and I were placed in a golden chariot that hovered over the streets. The soldiers of Grimm marched at the head of the parade in formation. Crystalline tanks, mobile artillery and armored personnel carriers, along with magic carpet-riding shock troops led the way. They escorted the jewel-encrusted coffin of King Charming, which sat on a cloth-of-gold magic carpet.

The Merry Men marched behind the soldiers. The band of thieves waved at the cheering crowd, saying hello to friends and breaking formation to kiss their wives and children.

Next came the seven dwarves, who marched with enough pride they seemed ten feet tall.

Then came the Lost Boys. Jimmy led the group. They didn't seem to enjoy the attention all that much, but gobbled up the candies and sweets that were thrown to them, blushing at the girls blowing kisses. Pinocchio walked beside Jimmy. He waved his iron hands, and though he walked with a hunched shyness, he soon stood tall. Those who learned his name cheered it, and streamers were thrown over his metal body.

A platinum-laced, hovering chariot held Queen Cinderella with Princess Snow White at her side. The queen was dressed in her finest gown, though Snow White refused to change from her form-fitting dress. She did, however, concede to wearing the platinum and diamond tiara of a Princess of Grimm. She wore the crown with a smile, and held her mother's hand without ever letting go.

Robin marched at their side. He wasn't in the best of spirits, ignoring the cheers of the crowd. But every now and then he'd look up at the queen and princess, and he'd smile.

Peter and I were at the rear, where we received the lion share of the cheers. The crowd called "Alice and Peter!"

I blushed, and waved, and kept my hand clasped in Peter's.

The celebration paused just long enough to bury King Charming. The royal tomb looked like a solid piece of crystal. It was thick and multi-faceted, cut and glowing like a diamond. Each edge refracted the sunlight, casting endless rainbows throughout the chamber. The sunburst and rainbow flags of Grimm covered the tomb, and were lowered to half-mast as the king's coffin was silently slid into the vault.

Cinderella and Snow White entered the tomb alone, allowed a moment's silence to bid farewell.

"Do you know the story of how they met, the king and queen?" Robin asked me.

"Yes," I replied, "it's a fairy tale where I'm from."

"It's a fairy tale here too. He was a prince then. Gallant Prince Charming and beautiful Cinderella. They met at a ball, while she was a servant who somehow made a beautiful gown. But nothing was more beautiful than her heart, and the prince fell in love. He searched the kingdom for her after the ball, ignoring all precedent so he could marry a commoner."

"I'm glad that part stayed the same."

"Are there other fairy tales here you've met?"

"Many. Some are the same. Some are different. I like the ones that are the same."

"I like the ones that are real," said Robin.

"Yes, I suppose those are the best fairy tales," I said with a smile. "Was he a good king, Charming?"

"You see the cheers and smiles in the crowd?"

I looked around. There were tears in many eyes, appropriate for a funeral. They were both tears of joy and tears of hope. Smiles and good cheer had come to Grimm like rain to a parched land.

"They knew King Charming. And they knew the queen, before I brought her to despair," Robin continued.

"You've made up for that, Robin," I said.

"What's done is done. But look how they cheer. They cheer because Snow White is the king and queen they once loved brought back to life. And they cheer you, because you brought her to them."

"I don't understand why everyone's celebrating. We're probably going to have a battle tomorrow."

"That's exactly why they're celebrating," Peter said. "They have something worth fighting for."

Peter squeezed my hand a little tighter.

A platform had been set up near the tomb. Sergeants Hazeltree and Whitebird, in their medal-encrusted finest, stood near Robin, Pinocchio, Peter and myself.

I had given Cinderella the vorpal sword. It was the king's, and I guessed they'd want to bury him with it. Burying kings with their swords seemed the right thing to do. But when Cinderella emerged from the tomb, a black veil over her face, Snow White followed her bearing the vorpal sword and its platinum sheath on the king's cloth-of-gold magic carpet.

The queen removed her veil and stepped onto the platform. Snow White joined her.

The crowd grew silent.

"Alice of Wonderland," the queen said, beckoning me to step toward her. "You have saved the kingdom of Grimm from assassination, insurrection, and invasion. What's more, you have saved my daughter."

The queen's voice echoed across the city. People leaned out of skyscraper windows, children sat on their fathers' shoulders, thousands edged forward to cheer the queen's words.

Cinderella raised her hand and the crowd grew silent once more. "For these great deeds, what do you ask in return?" she asked.

I bit my lip. It would have been nice if someone told me there was going to be a big ceremony. I didn't know what to say.

Looking for help, I turned to Peter. He mouthed my answer.

"Wonderland," I replied.

"Then Wonderland you shall have."

Cinderella turned to Snow White, who stepped forward with the vorpal sword. Cinderella took the sword and held it over me.

"I name you General of the armies of Grimm, and Commander of the Heroes of this world," the queen announced. "From the Two-Land Kingdoms to the Frontiers, the Sleeping Beauty is collecting those bound by their oaths. Our forces are yours to command. And the Sword of Many Words is yours to bear."

I took the vorpal sword. All I could think to say in reply was, "Thank you."

I could feel the hush of the crowd. I could feel their eyes upon me, waiting for something. It felt like the most natural thing in the world, so I raised the vorpal sword high above my head. It caught the light and shimmered over the crowd. And all of Grimm cheered.

The next thing I felt was Hazeltree and Whitebird strapping a golden set of armor around my body and cinching the vorpal sword's sheath around my waist. The armor was scaled, the same Kevlar-like protection I'd found on King Charming, and fitted to my size. The sheath was light, beautiful, and made me feel ten feet tall with the sword strapped to my side.

Peter was offered a set of his own, but he refused. He wasn't used to armor, and didn't want to restrict his flight.

Robin, however, took his offered armor and wore the sunburst and rainbow with pride. For Pinocchio, they couldn't offer any more protection than what he already had, but pinned a sunburst and rainbow flag to his back so that it became a cape.

"People of Grimm!" Cinderella called when the ceremony was complete.

Hazeltree and Whitebird had brought the queen a set of armor as well. She shimmered in her platinum breastplate. Snow White wore a silver and gold imitation that looked no less protective.

While Snow White kept her semi-automatic pistol, she also accepted a short saber attached to her side. Cinderella bore another, larger version of this weapon and raised it above the assembling troops.

"Gather your weapons and harness your courage!" the queen said. "The great feast is laid before us. Eat hearty and love well. Tomorrow, Alice takes back Wonderland!"

The cheer that followed shook the buildings, and the shield over the city erupted with light.

Cinderella was good as her word, and the celebration was indeed great. We had a variety of foods I'd never dreamed could exist. There was wild boar as big as a car roasted on a spit, aged meats brought from smokehouses all across the country, countless types of fish and shellfish, pheasant and quail and bacon-wrapped Brussels sprouts and black walnuts mixed with wild rice and peppers and grilled asparagus.

We ate like we would never eat again. All the while, soldiers checked their weapons. Tank crews inspected their vehicles. Volunteers arrived to claim arms.

Fear created a mighty appetite. Every bite was savored. Every kiss from a loved one savored more. Each laugh from a friend was magnified with the joyful terror that this one would be by your side when there was killing and dying.

It was during the fireside tales of Grimm's past, the royal banquet hall erupting with laughter at the comedies and shedding tears at the tragedies that I snuck away.

Peter was waiting for me at the roof of the tallest skyscraper. He didn't say anything when I landed. He approached, silent and quick, and wrapped me in his arms.

We shared a kiss, and he held me tight.

"I'm afraid," I confessed to Peter after we'd been on the roof for some time.

"You should be," Peter said.

"Promise you won't let anything happen."

"I can't promise that."

"Then promise you won't let me give up."

"Why would I need to promise that? You've gotten this far."

"With you."

"With yourself. I'm only here to help, Alice. It's you who will win this. I'll do the best I can. But you're the leader of this army. You're the one who made all this happen. You saved Tinkerbelle, rescued Snow White, and kept us alive."

"You helped," I said.

Peter nodded. "Helped. But you led."

"Do you remember when you asked me if I could just go back to Wonderland and leave through the rabbit hole?"

"You are a little bunny aren't you," Peter laughed.

I elbowed him in the shoulder. "I'm serious. You remember?"

"Yes."

"It's still an option. But having you here beside me, I don't want to go."

"Can you stay in Wonderland?"

"I don't know," I said.

"Don't hit me for asking this, but why do you want Wonderland if you can't have it?" Peter asked.

"How is a raven like a writing desk?"

"You never told me what that means."

"I haven't the slightest idea."

CHAPTER NINETEEN

The armies of Grimm marched out of the city.

We rode in tanks, armored vehicles, magic carpets and civilian transports who'd volunteered to join the fight.

The rising sun heralded our journey through the city walls, and we soon emerged outside the rainbow-tinted city shield.

Peter held my hand as we flew beside the marching soldiers.

About a mile outside the city we came upon a wide field with row crops of corn and soybeans. Cattle grazed along the well-kept farmhouse grounds. Just to the side of the farmhouse was a beanstalk thick as the Empire State building, and likely ten times as tall.

A rainbow-tinted block of clouds concealed the beanstalk until we were up close. Whether these were technologically or naturally created, I couldn't tell. As we approached, I spotted what looked like a man hanging from the enormous plant.

"Beanstalk," Peter said, nudging me with a smile.

"So is that Jack?" I asked.

Though the beanstalk would dwarf any creature that stood beside it, the man hanging from its vines seemed large, and fitting for the vegetation's size. The giant spotted our convoy and leapt from the beanstalk. It shook the earth when it landed, and I realized it wasn't a man or a beast.

Blinking lights on its head told me this was a giant of a robot. The robot's pistons and joints squealed as its head lowered. A slot like the cockpit of a fighter jet opened behind the robot's eyes, and out slid a man wearing a green jumpsuit.

Cinderella smiled as the man approached, and shook his hand. "Jack the giant slayer," the queen said.

The man in the jumpsuit bowed. "Your majesty," he said. "And you must be the fabled Alice."

Jack took my hand and kissed it.

"Charmed," he said.

I pulled my hand away, and said, "A simple handshake is fine."

"Very well then, put 'er there. Like what you see?" Jack shook my hand and pointed to the giant robot.

"It's impressive."

"Not just that." Jack motioned beyond the robot, to the army that lay encamped beneath the beanstalk.

They rose to greet us. There were steel-clad knights beneath a golden cup banner, a man armed with a great axe who was half as tall as Jack's robot riding a blue ox big as a house, revolver-wielding miscreants led by a coonskin-capped warrior, spitting and heckling as they fired their pistols in celebration of our arrival.

There was a company of bronze-shielded soldiers marching under a golden fleece, a diminutive woman in fleur-de-lis embroidered armor with a flamethrower strapped to her back, two knights with golden haloes about their heads bearing lances with their tips carved in the shape of dragons.

A golden-crowned, marble-skinned warrior, statue-like in his regality, waved a curved sword in greeting. Beside him was another regal figure who held a leashed minotaur, a man armed with a thick table leg wearing armor that looked like it was made entirely out of tables, and a lion skin-draped man with curly black hair whose thick muscles glowed as he gripped a massive club. He rode a winged, sky-blue horse that whinnied with anticipation as she flew her rider beside the giant robot.

They greeted Cinderella, but they were staring at me. When I saw them, I raised the vorpal sword.

"We fought Ace alone. We thought there was no one who could unite us. Now, we come at the call of the Sleeping Beauty re-awakened," Jack said.

"So few," Cinderella said. "Where are the heroes of the Two-Land Kingdoms? Where are those from Valhalla?"

Jack shook his head. "I don't know. Maybe they're still fighting. Maybe the Sleeping Beauty is still fetching them."

"Is it enough to stop Ace?" I asked.

"It's all we have," said Cinderella.

"From what I've heard, you're not the type to worry about odds, Alice," said Jack.

I tried not to blush.

"We must press on. The beanstalk will lead us to Wonderland, Alice," Cinderella said. "What are your orders?"

This was no longer a fairy tale. These were not characters in stories, though their legends shone in my gleeful mind. Hercules, King Arthur, Davey Crocket, Odysseus, and more. They were all here. I had no trouble believing what was in front of me as I looked into the eyes of the heroes assembled under my command, sure of the task that lay before us.

"To the beanstalk," I commanded, finding the ceremony silly, and yet wholly enjoyable.

"Right then," Jack the giant slayer said and hopped back inside his robot. "We'll clear the path."

"Colonels to your regiments, captains to your companies. Stay in formation and march in good order," Cinderella commanded. "Onward."

The beanstalk had a wide, winding path. It reminded me of the ascending road in a parking garage. Though it was vegetation, the beanstalk was stable and large enough for three tanks to drive side by side at full speed.

Up the beanstalk the army went, with the fliers rising alongside. Everyone had something to ride: truck, tank, flying or normal horse, magic carpet or motorcycle. The troops needed to keep their strength, and vehicles both magical and mechanical ascended the beanstalk at good speed.

Peter Pan and I, flying with the Lost Boys, were the only ones who lacked a mount. But we didn't need one. We flew beside the magic carpets and Hercules on his flying blue horse, up and up the never-ending beanstalk.

I knew the names of the warriors in my army. I knew their legends. But they were only echoes before. Now they were marching in front of me. This was my story now, and I focused only on what each could contribute, not the stories that earned them a place in my army.

Up and up the beanstalk we went, until we reached a ceiling of clouds.

We had passed drifting rainclouds in our climb, sporadic gusts of puffy mist. They turned to fog in the disappointing way clouds do when they transform from far-off fantasy to up-close reality. This ceiling of clouds, however, was different.

The clouds looked solid, and stretched endlessly over the horizon. Jack was the first to reach the ceiling, and passed through without pause, disappearing onto the other side.

I held Peter's hand as we followed, flying through the cloud ceiling.

It was like breaking the surface of the ocean. I took a deep breath, and marveled at what lay before me.

The ceiling of clouds now became an unbroken plain of white. It was still morning, yet the night sky twinkled all around. The heavens themselves opened before us with a canopy of stars shining like a black sea covered in jewels. There was no moon, no sun, only stars and a colorful array of stellar bodies.

A galaxy entirely different than the Milky Way shone with a billion stars, while distant galaxies made dust clouds of extraterrestrial green, red, yellow and blue in a million hues. Just as I caught my breath for the wonder of it all, a snaking green aurora borealis flickered across the sky.

Peter Pan held me close and kissed me. It seemed the most appropriate thing to do.

"Plenty of time for that after our labors are done," laughed Hercules as his flying horse danced across the clouds. "Come. I do not wish to delay Olympus' vengeance any further."

I thought I should warn the army at first. We were standing on clouds, not something you could drive on. But Jack the giant slayer stepped his robot onto the surface of the clouds without concern. He walked as if he were walking on the earth, and continued forward in an unbroken stride.

Knowing I could fly made me brave the clouds. I stood upon them, holding my happy thought just in case I fell through.

The clouds were solid beneath me. I hopped to test their strength and stayed firmly planted.

There comes a point in a child's life when they encounter their first cloud. It's not uncommon in human history, though modern technology has made it easier. Early peoples, I'm sure, climbed the mountains and hills in search of clouds. Perhaps they thought, as I did as a child, that you could sit upon the clouds, that you could hold them in your hand and toss them like weightless snow.

Whether it was climbing up to meet them, or flying through them in an airplane, children quickly discovered the tragic truth about clouds. They're not solid things. They're barely visible. Clouds almost disappear when you get up close.

But these clouds, these were the clouds of dreams. These were what you dreamt about as a child while pondering what it would be like to fly up and sit upon the cottony landscape so far out of reach. I could pass through them at will, and stand upon them when I chose.

Even though I'd been able to fly for several days now, the sensation of walking upon these dreamy clouds brought elation to my heart. I danced over the clouds as shooting stars dazzled overhead.

"What kind of dancing is that?" Peter asked.

"The kind you dance on clouds," I answered.

"I don't think there's a dance for that."

"It's this kind."

"Did you learn it somewhere?"

"Nope. Made it up," I said.

"Then how do you know it's for dancing on clouds?" Peter asked.

"Because there should be a dance for it."

"Alright then."

Peter twirled me about. We kept the dance short, however. Hercules was right. The army needed to move on.

Crystalline tanks, horses, and Paul Bunyan's big blue ox rode over the clouds and drove beneath the stars. I rejoined the center, where Snow White and Cinderella were riding in their platinum armored car. Pinocchio took a moment to step out of the truck he was riding in to walk upon the clouds. If I could have seen through his iron helmet, I'm sure I would have seen him smiling ear to ear.

He was still, despite it all, a child.

It took the rest of the morning to travel across the clouds. At noon, we stopped to eat a modest meal. The soldiers of Grimm unwrapped pre-packaged food that self-heated when opened. Davey Crocket's ruffians chewed on salted meat and hard biscuits. King Arthur's knights and the bronze-shielded warriors marching with Odysseus ate thick bread with honey and a helping of smoked meat.

I knew the stories of every hero before me, and tried not to think of them fighting. The idea that they would die in battle at my command was... difficult to bear.

As I walked amongst the army, I caught sight of the lady with the flamethrower and the fleur-de-lis armor. She saluted, and smiled, as I passed.

There were a few heroes I didn't recognize, like the ones with the dragon-shaped lances or the Russian-accented man with the table leg. But I was pretty sure the lady with the flamethrower was Joan of Arc, or at least this world's version of her. Seeing her smile, confident of my leadership, filled me with hope.

Here was a hero who had done what I was doing, a mirror who existed on both sides of the rabbit hole. I fed off her hope, and believed in myself.

I just hoped my story didn't end like Joan's, burnt at the stake for heresy.

"Won't be long now," Cinderella said to me as I joined her by the other Grimm soldiers.

"Nervous?" Snow White asked.

"A little," I replied.

"Me too."

"I have no doubt of your bravery, Alice," Cinderella said. "When the time comes, you will be able to face this."

"Because of the people you've brought," I said.

"Not just that. Because of who you are. That is why we're here. Because you brought us together."

"I want to thank you, Alice," Snow White said. "In case I don't get the chance later. Thank you for all you've done."

"I wouldn't thank me," I said. "I just wanted to save Wonderland, and couldn't kill someone innocent to do it."

"Precisely, Alice," Cinderella replied. "You didn't get what you want by hurting others. You chose to do what was right, and could sense right from wrong in both Wonderland and Grimm. By judging good actions from evil actions, you saved my daughter, and won us to your cause. Whether you appreciate it or not, you act for the good in all things. We who fight by your side must do no less."

"Thank you."

"It's been a kick in the pants, Alice," Snow White said and gave me a sisterly hug.

"Indeed," said Queen Cinderella as she hugged me as well. "Now get something to eat. There is much left to be done."

Peter and I sat beside Robin and helped ourselves to a Grimm meal.

"Are you okay with what we're about to do?" I asked Robin.

"Of course," Robin answered.

"We're going to be fighting Ace of Spades. There will be other playing cards fighting."

"They're not playing cards anymore."

"No. But they used to be. They were your brothers in arms, weren't they?"

"I've found something more valuable to protect." Robin looked at Snow White, who ate with her mother. Then he smiled at me. "You'll have to fight the cards too. Are you comfortable with that?"

"It's what we have to do," I said.

Robin nodded. "Necessity drives survival. We just have to make sure we don't lose who we are in the battle."

"I'll remember that."

"I know you will." Robin nodded, and looked at Peter. "Watch out for her."

"Count on it," Peter said, and shook hands with the playing card.

"And the Merry Men will watch out for you," Robin said.

Robin motioned with his crossbow to the thieves-turned-soldiers around him. They raised their weapons in salute. I tipped my sword to them.

"You're getting good at that," Peter said as we departed the Merry Men.

"At what?" I asked.

"Saluting. Leading. Maybe they'll put a crown on you too. Your mother's not a queen somewhere is she?"

I laughed. "Hardly." It was the first time I'd thought of my mother in a while. I put the thought away and focused on the sword in my hand.

Not far from the queen's elite guards were the three Model T's the seven dwarves drove. They readied their guns, oiling and loading, and chided one another with encouraging insults about who had the best aim.

"You boys ready?" I asked.

"Won't know what hit 'em," answered Fedora.

"What'll hit 'em is this," said Trilby Hat, brandishing his BAR machinegun.

"I'll hit 'em with this first," said Top Hat with his Tommy gun.

"You'll hit nothing before I do," said Beret with his Springfield long rifle.

"Don't need to hit nothing, just gotta get there first," said Fez with his pair of .45 semi-automatic pistols.

"Don't even need to aim," said Bowler with his shotgun.

"Don't need to choose," laughed Cowboy Hat, armed with a BAR in one hand, Tommy gun in the other, pistols at his side, shotgun and Springfield on his back and a chain of ammunition strapped across his shoulders. He was a miniature madman of guns and bullets and held an unlit cigar between his teeth.

"I'm glad you're on our side," I said.

"We'll get that Ace."

"Get him good."

"Good and dead."

"That's what it means to get him."

"And then Alice gets Wonderland."

"We're with you Alice."

"For Alice!"

The seven dwarves hefted their variety of weapons, and I saluted them with my sword.

Just beyond the dwarves sat the Lost Boys. It turned out there was a small piece of chocolate in every pre-packaged Grimm meal. Some of the soldiers didn't like chocolate. This amazed the boys, who spent a good portion of their rest time negotiating for the sweets.

Greg, Gregg and Craig investigated their haul with glee, while Jake honed his katana-tipped gun, Willy sharpened his daggers, and

Derek fiddled with an automaton he'd turned into an armored exoskeleton. Jonny had his weapons at his side, while Jo was focused on consoling an absolutely terrified Monster. The dog could not be convinced walking on the clouds was not the worst thing ever.

"You boys know what we're up against, right?" Peter asked his companions.

"It's much bigger than Captain Hook," Gregg answered.

"Don't know if it's bigger than a dragon," added Greg.

"It is," said Craig.

"Okay."

"It's bigger than a dragon. But we've got a bigger army," Peter added. "You all know what you're supposed to do?"

"All stratagems have been devised and distributed," answered Derek.

"Good." Peter pet Monster when the dog whimpered. "Don't worry, Monster. We'll be on the ground soon. You'll need your courage. You can help Alice, can't you, Monster?"

The dog looked up at me. He whimpered a bit, so I scratched him behind his ears. This calmed him, and he relaxed in Jo's arms.

"Good dog," I said.

The Lost Boys finished their sweets, while nearby Pinocchio was sharing his meal with Jimmy.

"'Tain't right they forget to give you a full meal. Why I oughta give them a whipping I oughta," Jimmy said as he ate his chocolate.

"I don't need it," Pinocchio answered. "I get my nutrients…"

"It's the principle, Pinoke."

"You just want my chocolate."

"Reason enough to not deprive ya of one!"

"Hi, Pinocchio. Hi, Jimmy," I said to the two boys.

"Alice, tell them to get us another meal, wouldya?" Jimmy insisted.

"I don't need it. Really," Pinocchio said.

"Suit yaself, Pinoke."

"You two okay?" Peter asked.

"Aside from the need for another bit 'o chocolate, we're right as rain. We just got done loading Pinoke's Gatling gun. Right piece of machinery, that is." Jimmy patted Pinocchio's immense weapon.

"Good."

"Alice, tell me about Wonderland," Pinocchio said.

"It's a beautiful place," I replied with a smile. "At least it was. Before Ace."

"Tell me what it was like before Ace."

I had to think about it. "It was like Easter morning. Everything was green, and colorful. Flowers were budding with spring sunshine, and there were little treasures hidden everywhere. Except the flowers would sing and the treasures might be animals that would say very silly things. It was beautiful, and a little dangerous. But not so much you didn't find it, well, wonderful."

"I hope you get to see it again," said Pinocchio.

"You'll see it too."

Pinocchio shook his head. "I'm doing this for you, Alice, remember? I'm doing this to become a real boy."

"Tut-tut with that nonsense, Pinoke. Why with all we've found on this adventure, there's no doubt we'll find someone who can make ya whole. Right Petah?" Jimmy asked.

Peter didn't respond.

Pinocchio rose to his feet with a *tick-tock* of gears. He hefted the Gatling gun onto his shoulders.

"What was it you like to say, Alice?" Pinocchio asked.

"How is a raven like a writing desk?" I proposed.

Pinocchio primed the action in his gun. "Let's get moving."

The army set off once more across the clouds. It was maybe an hour later when Jack called a halt.

The enormous robot stood at attention where the clouds suddenly ended. It reminded me of a cliff's edge. The stars met the sky and the world below lay dark and terrible. Peter and I flew to the edge and looked down. A thick layer of black clouds, ones you probably couldn't walk on, hid the ground from view.

"Wonderland should be below us," Jack the giant slayer announced.

"Then here the battle will commence," Cinderella said. "Drop the seeds."

"Last ones I got."

Jack tossed a handful of seeds over the side of the clouds. They fell through the sky and landed out of sight. Moments later, a beanstalk big as the one we'd climbed in Grimm shot up like a rocket. It broke the clouds and stopped a hundred feet over our heads, green leaves and peapods decorating the vines.

"All flyers, form a landing zone for the ground troops," Cinderella ordered. "We will join you with all haste."

"Understood," I said and drew my weapons, my shotgun and the vorpal sword. I took one last embrace in Peter's arms, one last kiss, and shouted to the troops. "To Wonderland!"

CHAPTER TWENTY

I jumped off the cloud.

Freefalling long as I could, I clung to my happy thought and leveled out a short distance from the ground.

Wonderland had changed.

My feet touched the ground with a little puff of ash. I knelt to caress what had once been grass and flowers and colorful fields. Ashen dirt was all I found. Lightning crackled in a shadowy sky. It was early afternoon, yet black twilight covered the land. An unnatural glow, like the reflection of fire through fog, was all that allowed me to see.

The valley I stood in was bare. Not a thing grew in the ashy soil, and all around was empty and dark. Low hills lay in front of me, black as the valley they looked down upon. Beyond the hills, a pillar of smoke rose into the air.

The smoke wasn't just blackness, it was the absence of light. As it seeped into the sky it absorbed what illumination there might be, and muffled the lightning striking the oil-thick cloud.

"Wonderland," I said, at a loss for words.

This was not the place I'd spent my childhood. This was not where I'd run over walls while fifty feet tall with the White Rabbit and the Cheshire Cat on my shoulders.

I almost thought we'd made a mistake, made a wrong turn in the clouds. But this was Wonderland. I knew it in the heartbreak I felt for the barren wasteland all around me. And I knew it in the black spade banner over the company of troops standing on the hill.

It was a small group, perhaps a dozen soldiers. They froze in shock when they spotted the beanstalk.

I looked up at magic carpets and Lost Boys descending. Peter was just above me, and had also spotted the spade-marked soldiers.

"Willy, Jake, take them out. Scout ahead," Peter commanded, pointing to the hills.

The small company of enemy soldiers turned on their heels and fled. The Lost Boys flew after them. A couple flying carpets joined the pursuit, but I ordered no more to follow.

"That's enough to take care of them," I shouted. "We don't want to be drawn away from the beanstalk."

"Tight circles around the stalk," Peter added.

"I don't know if they have flying machines or not."

"Did they before?"

"Nothing looked like this before. There's no telling what Ace has."

"Keep your eyes peeled! Nothing gets through 'til the army's on the ground!"

Peter joined the others flying in protective formation around the beanstalk. Hercules and his mount landed where the beanstalk met the ground, standing vigil and vowing to slaughter anything that approached.

Long minutes passed as lightning crackled and thunder rumbled. The ashen hills revealed nothing but shadows.

I spotted a gaping hole in the clouds, over the opposite hill and beyond the pillar of smoke. The hole shimmered, blinking on and off like a fluorescent light struggling to stay on.

"The rabbit hole," I said.

A thought struck my mind, to fly through the rabbit hole, leave before the battle took place. I banished this cowardice from my heart the moment it arose, turning my attention to the smoke and ruin I'd come to challenge.

Pinocchio was the first off the beanstalk, arriving in the seven dwarves' speeding Model T. I'm certain it wasn't designed to move that quickly, but the dwarves didn't seem to care. They hopped out and readied their weapons. Pinocchio *tick-tocked* as he approached, and readied his Gatling gun.

"Where's Ace?" Pinocchio asked.

"I'm not sure," I replied.

"What about this Mad Hatter?" Peter asked, hovering above us. "He helped you escape, right?"

I had told the commanders about my recent encounter with Wonderland. I'd thought it might be useful tactical information. None of what I'd shared existed anymore.

"It's possible he's still leading a resistance," I proposed.

"And it's possible nothing's left alive," Peter said.

Jack the giant slayer arrived next, with Robin in an armored car close behind. His Merry Men followed in armored vehicles of their own.

Robin heralded the approach of Queen Cinderella's platinum armored car. Snow White sat beside her in the gilded passenger seat, with Hazeltree driving and Whitebird manning a .50 caliber machinegun mounted on top.

"Alice! Report!" Cinderella called, leaning out the window as her car slid to a halt.

"A small group was on the hill. Scouts went after them. No sign of anyone else," I replied.

"Where is everything?" Snow White asked, popping her head out of the car's high-caliber gun mount.

"Patience, Snow White," her mother advised, exiting the vehicle to survey the surroundings.

Snow White joined her, gun in hand. "I don't like this."

"Nor do I. Make all haste to get the remainder of our forces in formation, Hazeltree."

The elite guard passed the radio call up the beanstalk.

As the seconds ticked by, our lines spread. Tanks, armored personnel carriers, trucks by the dozens hit the dirt and fanned out, taking what cover they could find. Artillery dug in, infantry readied arms, and soon the horses came galloping down the beanstalk.

Our army was nearly assembled when we heard the first report of a gun. I looked up and saw a plume of smoke, a magic carpet plummeting out of the sky. It landed with a burst of flames on the summit of the hills.

"They're coming! They're coming!" shouted Jake as he flew, pulling Willy away from the hills.

"Who's coming?" Peter Pan asked, rising to meet them.

"Everyone!"

Lightning cracked and illuminated the silvery rise of bayonets across the horizon. They crested the hill and came into sight, marching under the banner of a black spade.

Their armor was a pixilated black and white that turned them into a blurry specter when looked upon. Dark visors concealed their faces. Their guns were shouldered as they marched to a halt. Tanks in the same pixilated camouflage came behind, taking position alongside mobile artillery.

The black and white army stopped. I couldn't see where they began or ended on either side of the long hill. In their center, hobbling on a cane, was the silhouetted image of a man in a high top hat.

Without waiting a moment longer, I shouted to the troops at my command, "Open fire!"

Cannons roared. Artillery thundered. Tanks blasted. All along the line rifles erupted with hot lead.

Even as I gave the order, echoed through the line by company commanders, the guns along the hill burst to life.

Dark shapes flew above us. I looked up to see black and white, metal versions of the wood and cloth aircraft I'd flown to Neverland.

They strafed our lines with machinegun fire. Magic carpet-riding Grimm soldiers and flying Lost Boys rose to engage.

Our full army had reached the lines by then. The dug-in Grimm soldiers were in front, best-equipped to handle the gunfire blasting down from the hill. But even their futuristic armor couldn't withstand the death raining down upon them.

"We're outnumbered!" Robin said.

"Good!" rumbled Hercules. "The greater glory for us."

"Where is Ace of Spades?" Cinderella asked.

"I don't see him," I said.

I scanned the battlefield. Jack the giant slayer offered cover for the troops and blasted rockets from the fingertips of his colossal robot. All along our lines explosions ripped into the soldiers, blasting craters and blowing troops into the air. I felt ashy dirt rain upon my face as a shell landed close by.

Three crystalline Grimm tanks dug trenches in the dirt between our lines. The black and white tanks roared down to meet them and exchanged fire. One of ours ramped across a mound and fired at high speed. A second later the multi-colored tank burst into flames, the steel pyre grinding to a halt.

Machineguns and rockets zipped overhead, aircraft crashing and exploding as screaming magic carpet riders fell out of the sky.

Despite all the firepower before us, a strong portion of the blasts were directed at the beanstalk. Peapods exploded, vines tore apart, and fires grew along the vegetation high into the air.

"They mean to trap us," Cinderella said.

"Then let's make them regret it," Snow White threatened.

"We can't take this for long!" Jack advised through his robot's static-laden speakers.

"Is that Ace of Spades?" Cinderella asked me, pointing to the man with the tall hat.

The man with the tall hat rode upon a tank at the center of the black and white lines, directing artillery fire with his cane.

"No," I replied.

I didn't recognize anything about this Wonderland. But I knew where Ace would be. He was the source of all that had happened, and if he wasn't here, he could only be one place.

"There!" I said, pointing to the pillar of black smoke. "His tower is there."

"Then that is where you go," said Queen Cinderella.

"Cut the head off the snake, Alice," Snow White encouraged.

"Take your men down the center. We'll lead a charge to draw their fire and allow you to break through."

"Who knows, might just blow them away on our own." Snow White smiled at her mother.

"Defeat Ace and his army will fall apart," said the queen. "We'll hold them off as long as we can."

In situations like these, heroes are probably supposed to disagree, to make some sort of plea that these souls not make such a sacrifice on my behalf. But I'm not a hero. I'm Alice. And with the guns raging and our men pinned down, there was no time to argue.

"Until we meet again, Alice of Wonderland," Cinderella said.

"Knock 'em dead for me," Snow White added and shook my hand.

"Arthur! Have your knights charge along the right flank," Cinderella ordered.

"May God be with us!" called King Arthur, raising his golden cup banner. The knights with the dragon-tipped lances joined in formation as their horses reared with anticipation.

"Odysseus! Have your men charge the left."

"Onward to eternity!" shouted the commander to his three hundred bronze-shielded warriors marching beneath a golden fleece. The chained minotaur roared beside them.

"Crocket! Sweep in behind and give us cover fire."

"Live free or die!" Crocket shouted as he readied his ruffians.

"Think that beast can move, Bunyan?" asked Hercules as he readied his own steed, its wings twitching in anticipation.

"Ah reck'n, it can, Herc," replied the axe-wielding giant as his blue ox stomped the ground.

"For Wonderland?" Peter asked.

"How about, how is a raven like a writing desk?" I replied.

"Not the best in the world—but I'll take it."

"Charge!"

Horses galloped, tanks churned, magic carpets zipped and Jack the giant slayer stomped as men lunged forward up and down the line.

The army of heroes advanced with terrible speed, Jack's robot shielding us from gunfire as he staggered with direct hits from artillery. Though we raced forward fast as we could, it was the flying blue horse and the giant blue ox who reached the enemy first. It was impossible to know who won the race, but it didn't matter. The blue ox roared with fury equal to Paul Bunyan's axe-swinging might. Beside him, Hercules lifted an enemy tank and threw it down the line.

The lances of a hundred knights slammed into the black and white soldiers. Javelins flew through the air to herald the approach of the three hundred bronze-shielded warriors as they thrust their spears with methodical expertise. Thrust-shield-step, thrust-shield-step, they advanced and cut through the enemy.

Behind them came the ruffians with their six-shooters blazing. Davey Crocket rode atop a tank and fired his rifle, picking off soldiers without wavering. Joan of Arc charged with her flamethrower and set half the hill ablaze. Fighting side by side with the bronze-shields was the marble man and the man with the table armor, swinging their weapons and calling challenges to all-comers.

The charge's success was short-lived. The black and white soldiers withdrew a step, and poured into the gaps in the right and left flanks. But this was part of our strategy, because it left the center open.

"Now!" I shouted.

Pinocchio led the charge with his Gatling gun roaring. The seven dwarves rode in their Model T's, firing Tommy guns out the windows. The Merry Men rode magic carpets beside Robin the huntsman and hugged the ground for speed.

Snow White and Cinderella took to the field. The queen made a mighty target and twirled her shimmering sword to draw as much attention as she could. This further cleared the center, and allowed Peter Pan, myself, and the Lost Boys, including a barking Monster, to take to the sky.

We flew in formation above the battlefield, and scattered when three flying machines opened fire directly ahead of us. The Lost Boys barrel-rolled away from the gunfire and chased after one, while Peter shot his pistol at the second. I drove straight at the third, catching light with the vorpal sword to blind the pilot.

The pilot turned the aircraft's nose upward and I gave chase. I got within arm's length and blasted the cockpit glass with my shotgun. The pilot wore a black jumpsuit with an oxygen mask hiding his face. I set my feet on the side of the aircraft and pulled him loose, tossing him out.

I grabbed the stick and maneuvered the aircraft. Its flight controls were familiar, and I was able to turn it into a dive. Just beside me I saw Peter shoot down the second aircraft, and the Lost Boys downing the third.

Directly below me were the black and white lines. The man with the cane continued to guide artillery fire. I caught a glimpse of the beanstalk engulfed in flames, and Jack the giant slayer catching a blast that blew away one of the robot's arms.

The man with the cane, he had to be the Mad Hatter. He'd designed this flying machine. He'd invented weapons of maddening variety. Ace must have taken the wonder out of him, and forced him to make this black and white army.

I swallowed my remorse and prayed I was wrong.

At the last second the corrupted Mad Hatter saw me and leapt away. I jumped clear of the nose-diving aircraft. The aircraft struck a tank and exploded, cutting a hole in the lines that let Pinocchio blast his way clear. The dwarves, the Merry Men, the Lost Boys, Peter Pan and I broke through and chased after the Hatter.

"Nice move," Peter said when he caught up to me.

I was about to thank him, or perhaps make a snarky reply, but a loud *snap* caught my ear.

"Look out!" I shouted.

The beanstalk teetered a moment. Then it collapsed like a great tree, the fire roaring as the beanstalk fell. It crashed against the black hills and threw up a mountain of ashen dirt.

The beanstalk's burning hulk cut us off from the rest of the Grimm army. The last I saw of them was Jack the giant slayer's robot taking another explosive shot to the chest, falling beside his beanstalk.

"Come on, Alice!" Peter insisted.

CHAPTER TWENTY-ONE

T he collapsing beanstalk had given the Hatter time to get away, and we chased him toward the pillar of black smoke.

As we got closer, we saw smokestacks rising from the ground like black fingers. They enveloped the plateau on which Ace's tower stood. There was no remnant of the town that had surrounded it, but the walls and the towers, these I remembered.

I'd been there when I was fifty feet tall and laughing at the silliness around me. I'd been there just a few days ago when I was scared and thought I could outsmart Ace. Now I stood, terrified, in a burnt plain with what was left of my army.

The Hatter reached the fortress's black gate and disappeared inside.

I shouted to the Lost Boys, dwarves, Merry Men and Pinocchio, "That's it! We have to get in there!"

Even as I made the announcement the ground erupted around me. We were perhaps a hundred yards from the fortress when the gun emplacements lining the walls roared to life. Artillery pieces, machineguns, and multi-barreled anti-aircraft guns spewed lead.

We took what cover we could as the Lost Boys scrambled to get around the guns. They couldn't land a clear shot, and the walls were too high for the dwarves or Merry Men to find a target.

Pinocchio, Peter, Jimmy and I huddled behind the ruined foundation of what used to be a country house. My heart broke at the thought that it could have been the White Rabbit's.

"Can we go around?" Peter asked.

"There's guns all 'round, there is," Jimmy answered, bullets whizzing over his head. "And anti-air's too thick. No 'ope of punchin' in from above."

Spinning barrels of anti-aircraft guns were crowded into a tower just inside the outer wall. This tower alone kept the Lost Boys from approaching, as the guards fed endless streams of death into the sky.

"Standing here shooting into the walls isn't doing anything!" Peter said.

"Come on and let's take them!" I shouted, standing up to make a charge.

The second I rose from cover the guns blasted at me. If Peter hadn't dragged me back to the ground, I'd have been cut in half.

"Charging that wall will kill you!" Peter shouted.

I shook myself out of Peter's arms and chanced a look behind us. Black and white tanks turned from the battle with the Grimm soldiers and blazed a trail our direction. They were out of range, but barely.

"We don't have time," I said.

"Stay put. I'll handle this," Pinocchio said.

"No, Pinoke," Jimmy said. "You can't…"

"Jimmy, if I whistle, don't come."

Pinocchio charged the walls with his gears *tick-tock*ing in a steam-blowing frenzy. He cranked his Gatling gun as he ran, pinning the soldiers against the walls as he closed the distance. Gunfire *tink-tank*ed off his iron body. An artillery shell exploded nearby, raining dirt and shrapnel around him. Another shell blasted closer and forced Pinocchio to step to the side.

A third artillery shell struck Pinocchio fully in chest. It knocked him backward.

The hit left a broken cavity in the boy's iron body, his pale leg showing through the crack. Pinocchio blasted away with his Gatling gun and took another direct hit, firing until the gun jammed. As he reached the walls, Pinocchio hurled the Gatling gun at an artillery emplacement, destroying both weapons.

I shouted for Pinocchio to come back, but the guns deafened my cries. Peter had to hold Jimmy down to keep him from flying into the sea of bullets.

The armored boy reached the fortress's black gates and pounded them. His fists rang out like the clanging of a bell as he swung again and again. Artillery struck him, and Pinocchio fell against the gates, more of his metal skin ripped away.

Pinocchio raised his great arms against a crack in the gate and took hold. Even from this distance I could hear the roaring whistle of steam escaping his body as Pinocchio hefted the gates off the walls and they crumbled. Stone and iron collapsed around Pinocchio as the guns fell silent.

Pinocchio hurled the gates at the tower of anti-aircraft guns. Stone shattered with the impact, and the tower collapsed, crushing the guns and freeing the skies. Pinocchio fell to his knees once the burden was gone.

With most of the guns on the outer wall destroyed, the Merry Men, Lost Boys and dwarves charged forward. The remaining guards were chased back to the secondary walls, and our troops manned what guns were left.

I raced to Pinocchio's side and reached him just as the iron boy collapsed on his back.

Gunfire faded into background noise as I leaned close.

"Pinocchio!" I said, not bothering to ask if he was okay.

The front of the boy's armor was completely gone.

He lay on his back, his shriveled, pale body exposed to the smoke-filled air. Frayed wires were all that connected him to the iron suit. He wheezed through his half-attached breathing apparatus, choking on leaking pipes and hissing tubes.

"Pinocchio, can you hear me?" I asked.

He gagged on the mask, so I took it off.

For the first time, I was able to see Pinocchio. He was a tiny boy, thin, wrinkled, pale. His bright blue eyes were wide and he choked on the ashen air.

"Am I…" Pinocchio said, his voice pure as a silver bell, "am I a real boy?"

I took his hand in mine. "You always were."

"Good."

Pinocchio gagged, struggling for breath. His grip on my hand went still.

"Come on Alice," Peter said, grabbing me by the shoulder.

I couldn't move.

"Come on!" Peter insisted, hoisting me to my feet. "We've got to move!"

"Move your crew forward. My men will man the guns and watch your back," Robin said as we pressed through the gates. He shook my hand beside the ruined anti-aircraft tower. "Tell Ace the Knave of Hearts sends his regards."

"I will," I said, wiping away tears as I focused on what still needed to be done.

I took one last look at Pinocchio, and followed Peter inside the fortress.

There we met the remnants of the wall guards, along with more gun emplacements and well-defended troops. We found excellent cover along the rubble of the outer wall, but couldn't land good shots against the defenders.

"We don't have time to draw this out," I insisted.

"Hey, guess what I still have!" said Fedora.

"Is it a block of cheddar?" asked Bowler.

"Why would you bring cheese to a battle?" asked Top Hat.

"Why would you not?" asked Fez.

Fedora took the apple bomb out of his pocket.

"Now that would go great with cheese," said Trilby Hat.

"We'll cover you," said Beret.

"And give you time to cut the cheese!" said Cowboy Hat as he opened fire with his BAR and Tommy gun. The two guns were powerful by themselves, but unwieldy and inaccurate when fired at the same time. Still, it created a spectacular sight, and the stream of hot lead sent the guards to cover.

The dwarves blasted away at the walls as Fedora ran. He reattached the wires Robin had removed and re-armed the apple bomb, then set the timer to a few seconds. He placed the bomb by the walls and ran away laughing.

"Everybody down!" Peter shouted as the bomb detonated.

The inner wall collapsed in a plume of dust, and its defenders fell or jumped to avoid being crushed by falling stone. The dwarves and Lost Boys charged forward, blasting away at those who'd escaped the explosion and taking charge of the gun emplacements that were still usable.

"Go on! We've got you covered!" shouted the seven dwarves.

Lost Boys, Peter Pan and I gave a silent nod of thanks as we ran into the black smoke.

It was here that I recalled not actually seeing Ace's tower. I'd met him on a golf course. His palatial fortress had been obscured by mist when I'd first seen it. Now, I could plainly see the dark tower that dominated the plateau.

It was cylindrical. Completely solid from top to bottom, and glistening with a smooth, black polish. Once we passed through the obscuring mist, I spotted two soldiers standing vigil at the tower's base.

The twin soldiers were covered in thick-plated armor. They had bulbous bodies and tiny, round heads. They looked at us with cold, uncaring eyes and shouldered rocket launchers at our approach.

Monster barked at them. The twin soldiers leapt back in shock, momentarily frightened of the yipping creature. Then they glared, readjusting their aim to obliterate the dog.

"Good thing we cleared those AA guns," Peter said and whistled, pointing at the guards.

Lost Boys dropped out of the sky and picked up the soldiers. Monster's distraction had bought just enough time for the twins to be caught completely off-guard. The twins let out a squeal of fright as they were flown away from the tower and deposited safely off the battlefield.

"I think that was Tweedledee and Tweedledum," I said.

"They didn't seem very pleasant," Peter said.

"They never were, really. They're worse now that the wonder's been taken out of them. I guess it's too much to hope there's at least one creature who has their wonder left."

"It's never too much to hope," said the White Rabbit as he hopped out from behind the black tower.

Peter leveled his pistol.

"Stop, Peter, I know him," I said.

"Please don't shoot!" the rabbit quivered. "It's not my fault!"

"What's not your fault?"

"What Ace has done. I never wanted it—no one did. He wasn't supposed to do this. He was supposed to see you and stop."

"How did you survive all this time?" I asked.

"I suppose I was useful. I suppose these abominations are my fault. I brought the knowledge through the rabbit hole."

"Where is Ace of Spades?"

"I only wanted to stop him—that's why you're here. Forgive me, but I was too afraid."

"Tell me how to find him."

"He's in the tower," the rabbit said, pointing up. "The doors are barred and the way is guarded. But there's a window near the top.

You can break through the glass. He won't expect it."

"You're clever to have lasted this long without Ace brainwashing you," Peter said.

"I'm cleverer than you might think. I brought Alice here, didn't I?"

"Thank you for bringing me, White Rabbit," I said.

"Just stop Ace."

"Jimmy, Greg, Gregg, Craig, guard the tower," Peter said.

Peter held out his hand. I took it.

"One last push," Peter said.

We held tight and took to the air. My happy thought flew us along the shimmering black tower 'til we reached the top. There we found a round window that looked upon the battle raging in the distant field.

Peter blasted the window with his pistol and flew into the tower amidst a shower of glass.

We entered a round room with pillars lining the walls. Behind the pillars were the leather jacketed elite guards Ten of Spades, Jack of Spades, Queen of Spades, and King of Spades, along with half a dozen more spade-marked soldiers. Peter shot Jack the moment we flew through the window, and then began exchanging fire with King and Queen.

I was right behind him, shotgun firing again and again as I strafed from one side of the room to the next, knocking out Ten before he could duck for cover. The other men were caught completely off guard and fell, only King and Queen able to reach protection in time. Peter drew King out with his flying maneuvers, finally landing a shot as he spun around a pillar. Queen ducked, but must have forgotten I was in the room, because she found cover not ten feet from where I stood.

My shotgun roared.

A shell clattered to the black marble floor.

I held the vorpal sword in my left hand, the sawed-off shotgun in my right. Peter hovered beside me, and we stared down the shimmering onyx throne where Ace of Spades sat.

"Alice," said Ace of Spades, "what have you done?"

"Call off your troops, Ace." I commanded.

Peter and I had our weapons leveled against the tyrant. He looked no different from the last time I'd seen him. His black suit was still immaculate. His eyes were still that chalky blue. And he still regarded me with a cold calculation, sizing me up and finding me wanting.

Ace rose. Shallow steps led from his pedestal of a throne. He descended the steps, and I spotted two figures come out of hiding on either side of him. One was the Queen of Hearts, weeping into her hands. The other was the Mad Hatter.

The Hatter was pale. His suit, formerly a mishmash of colors, was a plain tuxedo with a new-looking top hat. He leaned against a thick cane, a blank expression on his face.

"I said call off your troops," I repeated.

"Do you realize the cost of your actions?" Ace asked.

"You'd best listen to her," Peter threatened.

"I gave you a chance to cooperate willingly. I gave you a chance to name this world."

"It has a name," I said.

"And what has that name caused? I offered you serenity and prosperity and you've delivered suffering and death!"

"Call off your troops."

"You still have no idea what you're doing," Ace said. "What's your plan here, Alice? Hmm? You plan on staying in Wonderland? You plan on indulging in a madness that will lead you nowhere?"

"That's not your decision."

"It's mine! This is my world now—not yours—it never was yours!"

"Call off your troops," I repeated.

Ace laughed. "I should have suspected you'd be leading an attack into madness, in support only of madness. What was that maddening phrase you always used, Hatter? How is a raven like a writing desk? Absolute stupidity."

My focus was so rage-filled with holding Ace of Spades at

gunpoint that it was too late for me to realize that the Mad Hatter's cane wasn't a cane at all. Peter didn't see it either.

Before I could shout, "No!" the Hatter fired his cane-gun at Peter Pan. The shot came a split second before mine, and I killed the thing that had once been the Mad Hatter.

I dropped my gun and screamed, "Peter!"

I cried and dove to his side.

Peter lay bleeding on the black marble floor, clutching his stomach and heaving with pain.

"Peter! Oh no, Peter, hold on!" I pleaded, applying pressure to the wound.

Peter Pan struggled for breath, gasping as he said, "Kill him." He tried to raise his pistol but his hand shook, and the gun fell from his fingers.

The Queen of Hearts fled the room in terror, the door slamming behind her as she let out a mournful scream.

I expected Ace to laugh. I thought it was the appropriate thing for a villain to do. Even as the tears streamed down my face and I couldn't look away from Peter's bleeding body, I felt the coming of triumphant laughter from my enemy.

Instead, all I heard was the soft clacking of polished shoes, as Ace of Spades returned to his throne.

"You no longer need them," Ace said. "These limitations. These maddening distractions. What point is there to them? What is it you're trying to achieve?"

I wailed through blinding tears, keeping pressure on Peter's wound.

"I was once mad as the lot of them," Ace continued. "Then I saw you, how you bested the Queen of Hearts without even trying. You came when I was a card, and I saw that I could be much more. I demanded the White Rabbit tell me more about your world, and through that knowledge I learned how to become human, how to do as I wished without limitations. I am the cure to your madness, Alice, just as you were the inspiration to cure mine. I am the cure to Wonderland. Even now I offer you a chance."

Ace reached into his deep-black jacket pocket. I flinched, covering Peter as I was sure Ace was going to shoot us both. Instead, Ace displayed an orange plastic bottle of blue pills. He shook the pills, a dim crackle amidst the distant gunfire.

"Remember these?" Ace asked. "I'm told they were for your mania, to help you separate reality from fantasy. Here is your way out of all this."

I glared at him through my tears.

"Take the pills," Ace continued. "And you can imagine all this was a dream. My one inability is to imagine a name that can last for this realm. This is the only good you can provide a world you've left suffering. Here is your cure. Give me the name for this fantasy. Then go home."

"A cure? Why would you want a cure?" came a voice that echoed through the pillars.

Ace paused, searching for the source of the echoing words.

"We're all mad here. And we quite like it that way," said the voice as it coalesced in the center of the room. There, hanging above my head, was a toothy grin.

"No," said Ace of Spades.

The grin grew into the shape of a cat's head, never wavering in its glee.

"You think us mad for acting free. What fun is there in black and white?" asked the cat.

The cat's head rolled about in mid-air, and finally became a full cat that clung to the ceiling upside down.

"If acting outside a set list of things to do is what you call mad, then we're all mad here. And mad we happily be," said the Cheshire Cat.

"I killed you!" shouted Ace of Spades.

"Answer me this, Ace of Spades." The cat hopped to the ground, his grin never wavering. "How do you kill a memory?"

"I cut off your head!"

"That's not the way at all. Try again."

"Cheshire Cat," I whispered, my voice low in disbelief.

"I'll answer for you. The way you kill a memory is to simply forget it. You have not forgotten me," said the Cheshire Cat.

"No. No I killed you once—I can kill you again!" Ace of Spades shouted.

Ace drew a chrome and black pistol and fired at the Cheshire Cat. The cat's body disappeared, leaving only a grin. Bullets ricocheted against the marble floor as Ace kept firing until his gun clicked empty.

"Remember, Alice? Do you remember me?" asked the invisible cat.

"I do," I replied.

"Do you remember how it was in Wonderland?"

"I do."

"Never forget it." The grin flew into the air, and landed on the vorpal sword. "Never forget who you are. Never forget Wonderland, and it can never be taken from you."

The cat's grin disappeared inside the vorpal sword and the engravings took on a new life. Instead of static letters of gibberish, the sword lit up with word after word. I read paragraphs, chapters, whole manuscripts flooding along the speaking blade. As I stood, the sword spoke my actions.

Alice hefted the Sword of Many Words and looked upon the Ace of Spades. Ace of Spades raised his hands to offer one last plea, saying, "Why would you give up reason for madness?"

Alice replied, "How is a raven like a writing desk?" and plunged her sword into Ace's chest.

The bottle of pills fell from Ace's hands, scattering across the marble floor.

I let go of the vorpal sword and stopped reading it, running to Peter's bleeding side.

"Peter, Peter say something," I said.

"You're pretty when you're angry," Peter replied.

I laughed. "Peter, you're going to be okay. We're going to get you to Tinkerbelle and she's going to make you better. Just hold on."

"Glad you stuck with Wonderland. Better name."

"Peter."

Peter gasped, blood spraying from his mouth.

"Hold on," I said, hefting his body in my arms.

My armor pinched my sides, preventing me from getting a good grip on Peter's body, so I tore it off. I still had on the clothes Tinkerbelle had given me, and Peter's blood soaked into the cloth when I tried to pick him up again.

The movement caused Peter to cry out in pain, and I nearly dropped him in my hurry.

As I set the screaming Peter Pan back on the floor, the door at the far end of the room burst open. The White Rabbit slammed the door shut behind him, gunfire echoing in the staircase he'd just escaped.

"Is he dead?" the White Rabbit asked.

"He's still alive," I said, not looking away from Peter.

"Not him. Ace! Is he dead?"

I tilted my head to the dead body sitting on the throne. The White Rabbit bounded over and reached inside Ace's pocket. He found a little black spade, an object about the size of a cell phone.

The White Rabbit pressed a button at the center of the spade and said, "All units! Ace of Spades is dead. Abandon your posts and lay down your weapons at once."

"Rabbit, you have to help me!" I insisted.

The rabbit paused a moment, listening. The sounds of battle out the broken window stopped. Gunfire, explosions, all faded to the wind as an eerie silence descended upon Wonderland.

Then came the sound of cheering.

"Rabbit!" I shouted.

The White Rabbit shook a smile off his face and bounded to my side. I lay over Peter, applying pressure to his wound as he groaned in pain, color draining from his face.

"You have to help me," I insisted.

"I don't know how to treat a gunshot," the White Rabbit answered.

"Please!"

"I'm sorry, Alice."

"'sokay," Peter said, wincing. He reached for my hand, his grip weak and slippery with blood.

"We won!" I heard Jimmy call as he, Greg, Gregg and Craig flew through the window. Jimmy carried Robin while Greg held a squirming Fedora. "A great victory for the…"

Jimmy stopped when he saw Peter bleeding on the ground. "Petah! Petah—you okay?" he asked.

"He needs Tinkerbelle," I said. "He needs to be healed."

"We'd 'ave to fly 'til morning."

"We can fly faster!"

"'fraid that's not how Nevaland works, dovey."

"Robin, get a medic! He won't make it to Neverland!"

Robin stood over Peter, shaking his head. "There's not a doctor in Wonderland who could heal a wound like that," he said.

"Nor Grimm," Fedora said, removing his hat and holding it over his heart, a tear in his eye.

"I'm sorry, Alice."

"No! There has to be a magic! There has to be a way to heal him. Cheshire Cat! Where are you—come and help us!"

"The Cheshire Cat can't heal him, nothing in Wonderland can. Ace never asked me to bring doctors, only guns," the White Rabbit said, trying to console me with a pat on the hand. "I'd suggest you say goodbye while he's still here."

"Alice…" Peter tried to say.

"It's just a gunshot to the stomach!" I said. "There have to be doctors, magicians besides Tinkerbelle who can heal him!"

"There's no one. And no time. Goodbye, Peter," Robin said.

The Lost Boys all bowed their heads, tears in their eyes as they wished Peter farewell.

"No. No!" I shouted. Tears streaked through the grime on my face as I looked at the faces around me, searching for help. "This isn't how a fairy tale is supposed to end!"

"You're not in a fairy tale, Alice. If there was a magic that could heal Peter, we'd use it on the Hatter too," the White Rabbit said. "We'd fix all that went wrong when we started moving through the rabbit hole."

The rabbit hole. I turned my eyes to the window, the dark clouds separating. In the distance, I spotted a small gap in the light, a dark hole in the sky. It flickered open and shut, colorful and dark, nothing but echoes bridging the gap.

"We have to go through the rabbit hole, get Peter to a hospital. It's the only way to save him," I said.

"What?" the White Rabbit asked.

"There's no doctor in Wonderland who can save him, but there are doctors in my world who can. White Rabbit, your watch controls where the hole opens, right?"

"It's a delicate magic. But yes."

I picked up the White Rabbit by his little suit collar and placed him on Peter's chest. The rabbit yelped in protest, but I held him close.

"Hold still," I said, hefting Peter with a great exertion that was more desperation than strength. I paused a moment, Peter in my arms, and said, "Goodbye," to those around me. Then I flew.

The wind blasted against my face as I rocketed over the battlefield. Cheering Grimm soldiers waved at my passage. I flew over the fallen heroes, the charred remains of the beanstalk, until I reached the shell of the concrete city where I'd first entered Wonderland. It seemed like an eternity since I'd fallen through the rabbit hole, even though it had only been a few days.

I cried every time Peter screamed, pain convulsing his body. Tears ran more fully down my face when he stopped screaming, and I shouted, "Hold on Peter!" as we reached the rabbit hole.

"Alice, wait!" the White Rabbit said, grabbing my hair to maintain balance.

"Have the rabbit hole open inside a hospital," I told him.

"I can do that—but there's no telling if you'll be able to come back!"

"I don't care."

"Don't give up on Wonderland, Alice." The White Rabbit wiped a tear from his eye with a white-furred paw.

"I won't. I'll never stop believing in Wonderland."

The White Rabbit nodded. He held up his silver pocket watch, turned the dials, and shut the lid. Whatever magic that little watch contained made a sound that reverberated against the walls of the rabbit hole. The hole vibrated, then froze, a chasm of utter black above me.

"You'd better hurry," the White Rabbit insisted.

"Thank you," I said, and flew.

When I reached the rabbit hole's entrance, gravity seemed to give way. There was no longer a force pulling me down. It was like flying through water, the current stronger than any headwind barring my path.

"Farewell, Alice," the White Rabbit said as he hopped into the air. He floated down to the safety of Wonderland as I flew into the rabbit hole.

My vision narrowed as all I saw was the empty blackness of the rabbit hole's sides. I didn't know if the sides were infinite, or if I could reach out and touch them. Distance became an intangible concept as my vision blurred and my mind twisted to comprehend the shape of the universe around me.

In the blink of an eye there was color again.

I found myself in a room so bright it was near blinding. When I blinked my vision clear, I saw that I was in front of a tall mirror in a hospital examination room, hovering a few inches off the tiled floor.

In half a heartbeat, I felt gravity command its pull on my body and my feet slammed to the ground.

"Help!" I shouted, unable to maintain my balance and falling to the floor with Peter in my arms.

Peter groaned in pain. He was weak, pale.

"Help!" I cried again.

The room had a weight scale and a rectangular bed. It reminded me of the rooms where I'd gotten physicals, or had childhood checkups to receive booster shots. The mirror had a movable ruler with a flat tip that could check a person's height. It looked like a regular mirror, but there was a light breeze blowing through, and the sound of distant cheering.

"Help!" I shouted again, and this time a nurse entered.

The nurse looked annoyed, the dark lines of a long shift on her aged face, but she sprang to life at the sight of so much blood on the floor.

"Doctor!" the nurse shouted and ran into the hallway.

"Please help him—you have to help him!" I insisted.

A team of doctors ran in, shocked beyond words at my appearance, but setting quickly about caring for Peter.

Moments later, more doctors entered with a stretcher. They gave me various assurances, mainly trying to keep me away, before wheeling Peter out. They wouldn't let me follow, and the nurse escorted me out of the room.

As I left the examination room, I turned back to the mirror. It was just a normal mirror, and no sound or breeze came out of it. All I saw in the looking glass was my bloody reflection.

CHAPTER TWENTY-TWO

The coffee in the waiting room tasted terrible.

I was on my third cup, sleep a laughably distant concept.

The waiting room was like most hospital waiting rooms, long rows of uncomfortably-cushioned chairs and flickering fluorescent lights. I walked across the tiled floor, worried by how people kept looking at the stains on my pants and formerly blue and white top. No matter how many times I tried to visit the bathroom to wash off the blood, I couldn't get completely clean.

I had already told my story half a dozen times. First to the doctors, then to the police.

"He's been shot. I found him like this and took him here," was all I said.

The idea of by whom and where, I couldn't answer. I told them I didn't know who shot him. I told them I found him like that. The police said they'd be in touch, and that I should call my parents.

It'd been hours. The clock on the waiting room wall said it was two a.m. When I first heard the clock ticking, I started to cry.

While pacing the waiting room, I realized I was driving myself mad with thoughts of Peter in the operating room, how he was, if he would die on the operating table, me unable to say goodbye. I wiped my tears and decided to find a magazine or something to pass the time.

There was a small bookshelf at the other side of the waiting room, meant for children or families that had to stew in similar worry. They were picture books, outdoor magazines, all cheery and happy. I smiled at the copy of "Grimm's Fairy Tales," then froze upon reading the pink and blue cover of a book I'd never seen before.

My hands shook, touching the paperback with a mixture of fright and painful curiosity.

"Alice!" I heard my mother's voice.

I tucked the book into my pocket and turned to face my mother as she stormed through the hospital doors.

"Hello, mother," I said.

"What have you done?" my mother asked as she crossed her arms and looked down at me, demanding an answer. "In a single evening you disappear, you get involved with some gangster violence? And what are you wearing?"

My father was with her, wearing his suit, his hair parted. He wrapped his arms around me the moment he entered the waiting room, unconcerned that he might get blood on his clothes.

"Are you okay?" my father asked.

"I'm fine," I replied.

"You're fine. What madness have you gotten into?" my mother scolded. "Alice, I can't believe what you've done, you…"

"I'm not taking my medication anymore."

"What?"

"The pills. I'm not taking them."

"How absurd. After an incident like this we'll need the doctors to increase your prescription!"

"I don't need them," I said.

"Are you still having trouble?" my father asked.

"You don't know the difference between the real world and fantasy," my mother challenged.

"Actually, mother, tonight has shown me exactly what's true and what's fantasy," I said, fists on my hips just like Peter Pan. "And I don't care if you believe me or not."

"Excuse me? Alice?" I heard a doctor say as he entered the waiting room, armed with a clipboard and a frown.

I practically charged the doctor, asking him, "Is he okay?"

"Your friend, Mr…"

"Peter Pan."

My mother's eyes widened with righteous indignation.

"That's what I thought you'd say," said the doctor. "Mr. Pan is going to be fine. He's had a rough bit of surgery, but we were able to remove the bullet. He's recovering in the ICU. Strange bullet, it was. Not like anything I'd ever seen."

"Can I see him?" I asked.

"Yes. He's asked that only you see him."

"You can't possibly be encouraging her like this! Peter Pan getting shot!" my mother said, stomping over to the doctor to demand answers. "This is more of her madness."

"I thought it was crazy too. But then we found this in his room's mailbox. Apparently it arrived this morning, and, well, it's addressed to you, Alice."

The doctor handed me a box. It was covered in brown shipping paper, along with stamps and the hospital's address. It had already been opened, and inside was an American passport, driver's license, social security card and birth certificate for a 'Peter Pan.' According to the documents, he was born two months before me in New London, Connecticut.

Along with the identification, and insurance card, was a letter. A rabbit's paw was imprinted in the letter's red wax seal. I held the letter in my hands, smiling ear to ear as I broke the seal and read it out loud.

"Hello, Alice," I read. "I'm sure by now you've had an encouraging time and were able to revive Mr. Pan with no undue difficulty. Included in this package you'll find his documents. While we couldn't help his condition, there are other things we are more capable of doing, and I hope these make up for our shortcomings. You should know that our fairy friend has forbidden any further travel between our worlds. This doesn't mean I can't bend the rules a little. Perhaps one day we will meet again. Perhaps not. Until then, I hope this bit of magic between you and I means we can still call each other friend. Oh, and don't worry about any trouble with the authorities. I've seen to it. All is well here, and all give greetings. Give our regards to Peter. I remain your humble friend. —W.R."

My parents were speechless.

"The police just called," the doctor said. "They also got a package. It was a cane-gun. Some curiosity shop owner taped a confession that it was his, and that Peter accidentally shot himself. The police say there's no charges, so long as Peter, um, Mr. Pan says it was an accident too."

"Can I see him now?" I asked the doctor.

"Um, yeah."

I didn't wait another second and rushed through the doors into the Intensive Care Unit. There Peter was, in the second room on the right, all the way at the end of the hall. He lay on a bed surrounded by blinking machines. Even wearing a hospital gown, and with an IV attached to his arm, he was beautiful.

He smiled when he saw me.

I felt like I could fly as I rushed to his side.

"Oh Peter!" I said, flinging my arms around him.

Peter grunted in joyful pain, refusing to let me go as he embraced me from the bed.

"I'm so sorry, Peter," I said.

"For what?" he asked.

"I've taken you away from Neverland. You'll grow up now."

"I'm going to grow up because of you. I'm alive because of you. How's that a problem?"

"I feel awful though."

"Don't be. I've been avoiding our world for so long, I guess I was afraid of it. So long as you're here…" Peter put his hand in mine. "What do I have to be afraid of?"

Peter pulled me close and kissed me.

"Look!" I said, showing Peter the book.

"I've seen it before," he said.

"I haven't!"

I smiled as I turned the pages. "*Alice's Adventures in Wonderland,*" I said, reading the book's title.

"It was real, wasn't it, Peter?" I asked.

Peter nodded and said, "Never thought I'd be in a fairy tale. Never thought I'd be shot in one either."

"Did this book exist before? I don't know how that's possible."

"After all you've seen, you really think anything is impossible?"

"Time is relative," I said, recalling the words of Tweedledee and Tweedledum. "Maybe this is the past, or a future that won't happen."

Peter stroked my hair and smiled. "Maybe you should read your book, and decide for yourself what's real and what's not."

I thought of all the horrible things I'd done in Wonderland. I thought of all the amazing things. I mourned for the bad, and rejoiced for the good. What greater reality could there be?

"You know what happens at the end of fairy tales, right?" Peter asked with a laugh.

"And they all lived happily ever after," I said, closing the book. "Will we?"

"Sure."

EPILOGUE

There was a lot of work to do. A lot of life to live. **But** Peter and I would face reality together. And the White Rabbit's regular letters always made us smile.

I learned shortly after, in another of the rabbit's letters, what happened in Wonderland. With Ace of Spades dead, his soldiers surrendered. Snow White and Cinderella returned to Grimm with their victorious army. They restored freedom and peace. They ended the overbearing laws and ensured justice was done to true criminals, creating a golden age in the kingdom.

The soldiers of my army dispersed, heroes returning to the lands they called home and the Sleeping Beauty gone back to rest. There was a week's celebration in Grimm, and the armies shared stories about which company, giant robot, or force of arm had won the greatest glory. Nobody questioned the verdict that it was Pinocchio.

The Merry Men weren't terribly happy about the return of law and order to Grimm, at least not at first. They got over their worry once they received their handsome rewards and pardons, returning to their families.

Robin, Knave of Hearts, was instrumental to Wonderland's reconstruction. As the only playing card who hadn't had the wonder taken out of him, he was effectively the highest ranking creature in Wonderland. He oversaw the return of wonder, and along with the White Rabbit and the Cheshire Cat, helped the people regain what they'd lost under Ace's rule.

The seven dwarves rebuilt their stump home. Moonglow making was enjoyable for them, and they soon discovered that doing it legally was much more profitable. Their craft was sold all over the kingdom, with Queen Cinderella and Princess Snow White frequently throwing festivals where the dwarves could provide food and drink. The dwarves used their newfound wealth for the only purpose they deemed worthy. They bought new hats.

The Lost Boys returned to Neverland. Jimmy was placed in charge. They wished their leader had been able to join them, but they wished a lot of people had survived who didn't. In the end, they got their Neverland back, and were overjoyed with that victory.

Pinocchio was buried in the cavern beside his father. It was a sad event, but quickly gave way to joy. The Lost Boys knew Pinocchio wanted to be a real boy, but these real boys thought him the greatest of heroes, imitating him as best they could. They even created iron suits of their own. The White Rabbit says they use them to go deep sea diving, and to pester the mermaids that returned to the island. The Lost Boys resumed their life of never-ending childhood, playing games all day in their island paradise.

The Cheshire Cat returned shortly after I left, though he came and went as he pleased. He was part of what brought the wonder back to Wonderland, and remained a useful, if not terribly reliable, advisor to the Knave of Hearts. He insisted the Mad Hatter be given a hero's funeral. A statue was built in his honor. It's a giant tea pot. Everyone felt he'd like that best.

Wonderland soon began to resemble what it once had been. It wasn't the same. It never could be again. That Wonderland was gone forever, but what Wonderland became was something just as wonderful.

The beauty of Wonderland is it doesn't have to be anything. It just is. And as long as Wonderland is remembered, it will always have that wonderfully mad quality to it.

Peter Pan and I went on to live in the world that wasn't Wonderland. We thought of it often, but we had a happily ever after to live. And that was the most maddening reality I could ever have imagined.

ABOUT THE AUTHOR

While visiting Cambridge during my time studying abroad, I tried to sneak into C. S. Lewis's old apartment. I wanted to stand where the old master stood. I wanted to glean bits of imagination that no-doubt still clung to those walls. A locked door barred my path, and I fled to the safety of the campus pub.

It has been my goal to live a life that is notable as the life of that master of writing. I've climbed the slopes of Machu Picchu, swam in Loch Ness, smuggled ice cream into China, and made moonshine in my hometown. I studied writing and business in school, and gave up a position in my family's Black Walnut company to chase my dream. Life, if you make it so, can be an adventure.

Despite all my adventures, there is no greater journey than that which can be found in a book. It was cartoons that got me into writing, works meant for children that as an adult fascinated me with their joyful outlook. It was the old masters, Lewis, Tolkien, Hemmingway, Vonnegut, who challenged me to live an adventure of a life, and then write even greater adventures in books.

Perhaps one day I'll make it into that old Cambridge apartment. Perhaps one day I'll be invited.

THANK YOU
FOR READING

Please visit http://curiosityquills.com/reader-survey
to share your reading experience with the author of
this book!

Escape from Witchwood Hollow, by Jordan Elizabeth

Everyone in Arnn—a small farming town with more legends than residents—knows the story of Witchwood Hollow: if you venture into the whispering forest, the witch will trap your soul among the trees. After losing her parents in a horrific terrorist attack on the Twin Towers, fifteen-year-old Honoria and her younger brother escape New York City to Arnn. In the lure of that perpetual darkness, Honoria finds hope, when she should be afraid. Perhaps the witch can reunite her with her lost parents...

Night of Pan, by Gail Strickland

Fifteen-year-old Thaleia is haunted by visions: roofs dripping blood, Athens burning. She tries to convince her best friend and all the villagers that she's not crazy. The gods do speak to her. And the gods have plans for this girl. When Xerxes' army of a million Persians marches straight to the mountain village Delphi to claim the Temple of Apollo's treasures and sacred power, Thaleia's gift may be her people's last line of defense. Her destiny may be to save Greece... but is one girl strong enough to stop an entire army?

Please Don't Tell my Parents I'm a Supervillain, by Richard Roberts

Penelope Akk wants to be a superhero. She's got superhero parents. She's got the ultimate mad science power, filling her life with crazy gadgets even she doesn't understand. She has two super-powered best friends. In middle school, the line between good and evil looks clear. In real life, nothing is that clear. All it takes is one hero's sidekick picking a fight, and Penny and her friends are labeled supervillains. In the process, Penny learns a hard lesson about villainy: She's good at it.

Homunculus and the Cat, by Nathan Croft

In a world where every culture's mythology is real, Medusa's sisters want revenge on Poseidon, Troy is under siege again, and the Yakuza want their homunculi (mythological artificial humans) back. Near Atlantis' Chinatown, a kitten and her human campaign for homunculi rights. Against them are Japanese death gods, an underworld cult, and a fat Atlantean bureaucrat. The main character dies (more than once) and a few underworlds' way of death is threatened. Also with giant armored battle squids.

A Curse of Ash & Iron, by Christine Norris

Benjamin Grimm knows the theater is much like real life. In 1876 Philadelphia, people play their parts, hiding behind the illusion of their lives, and never revealing their secrets. When he reunites with his childhood friend Eleanor Banneker, he discovers she has been under a spell for the past 7 years, being forced to live as a servant in her own home. Even if he doesn't believe in 'real' magic, he can't abandon her. But time is running short. If they do not find a way to break the spell before midnight on New Year's Eve, then Ellie will be bound forever.

Sweet Dreams are Made of Teeth, by Richard Roberts

How does a nightmare hunt? He tracks your dreams into the Light, and chases them into the Dark. How does a nightmare love? With passion and obsession and lust and amazement. How does a nightmare grow up? With pain and grief and doubt and kindness and learning and dedication and courage. First Fang hunted, now he loves, and soon he'll have to grow up.